## About the Author

**Samantha Hastings** met her husband in a turkey-sandwich line. They live in Salt Lake City, Utah, where she spends most of her time reading, having tea parties and chasing her kids. She has degrees from Brigham Young University, University of North Texas and University of Reading (UK). She's the author of *The Last Word*, *The Invention of Sophie Carter*, *A Royal Christmas Quandary*, *The Girl with the Golden Eyes*, *Jane Austen Trivia*, *The Duchess Contract*, *Secret of the Sonnets* and *A Novel Disguise*. She also writes cosy murder mysteries under Samantha Larsen. Learn more at her website: SamanthaHastings.com or connect with Samantha on social media: X: @HastingSamantha, Instagram: @SamanthaHastings Author, Facebook: SamanthaHastingsAuthor

GW00372727

# Regency Whispers

# Regency Whispers:

# Inconvenient Temptation

SAMANTHA HASTINGS

**MILLS & BOON**

First Published in Great Britain 2024
By Mills & Boon, an imprint of HarperCollins*Publishers* Ltd,
1 London Bridge Street, London, SE1 9GF

www.harpercollins.co.uk

HarperCollins*Publishers*
Macken House, 39/40 Mayor Street Upper,
Dublin 1, D01 C9W8, Ireland

ISBN: 978-0-263-34494-3

# THE MARQUESS AND
# THE RUNAWAY LADY

To Violet

# Chapter One

*England, 1810*

Louisa didn't expect gifts on her twenty-first birthday. Her aunt and uncle had never given her a present in the ten and a half years she had been their ward. If she ever complained about her threadbare dresses, or the lack of fire in her room, Aunt Rockingham would explain that it was all *her* fault.

Lady Louisa Bracken was the only child of the Fourth and deceased Earl of Rockingham. His younger brother, Alfred, had become the Fifth Earl of Rockingham and had brought with him his wife and four sons. She had been left in their care, and her mother's fortune, which Louisa was to inherit, had been entrusted to three trustees. A yearly stipend was paid to her uncle for Louisa's upkeep.

Aunt Rockingham protested that this allowance barely kept her niece in gloves, and would rage for days at a time at Louisa's selfish father, who hadn't trusted his only brother to care for the financial interests of his niece. Strangely enough, Aunt Rockingham herself dressed in

the finest of silks and muslins. And had a pair of gloves dyed to match every gown. She also never missed a London season, claiming that she must be there for Uncle Rockingham to take his seat in Parliament.

Every time Louisa begged to go her aunt claimed that there simply wasn't enough money for such an expensive endeavour.

Pulling on her stocking, Louisa felt her big toe go straight through. With a humourless laugh, she thought that she had to be the poorest heiress in all of England. She didn't even have a maid to help her dress. And the maids had finer clothing than she did. Louisa had never once seen a darn in a servant's stocking, or a tear in their clothing.

She took out the needle that she always kept stuck in the hem of her skirt and deftly repaired the new hole in her stocking.

It was all going to change today. Louisa was finally one-and-twenty years of age and she could now take possession of her fortune. Buttoning up her gown, she determined she would no longer be under her aunt's thumb. With her inheritance she would go to London, be presented to the Queen—as her mother had been—and find a suitable match of her own.

She wouldn't even miss her home, Greystone Hall. She had loved it as a child, but in the last few years it had begun to feel like a prison. Her aunt would only let her attend church, never the local assemblies. Not that it mattered... Louisa didn't know how to dance. Her aunt had insisted that she could not afford to employ a governess for Louisa, let alone a dancing master. She'd dismissed Louisa's former governess the day after her father's funeral.

Pulling on boots that were too small and pinched, Louisa sighed. What sort of match would she make when she didn't even know how to behave like a young lady?

Louisa found her aunt in the newly refurbished blue drawing room, writing letters at her desk. Her aunt was a formidable woman of middling years. She had a distinguished face with a black mole on the side of her cheek. Today, she was wearing a lovely day gown of jaconet, with a necklace of three strands of pearls. Her cap did not fully hide her greying black hair.

How long Louisa had wished to please this woman! To change her behaviour and earn her aunt's elusive approval. But it didn't matter how agreeable, effacing or obedient she was, Aunt Rockingham did not love her. Nor even like her. There must be something wrong with her, thought Louisa, that not even her closest relatives could abide her.

'Hello, Aunt,' Louisa began, feeling the blood rushing to her face. 'I was hoping to talk to you today.'

Her aunt's countenance tightened into an expression of annoyance. 'I am very busy writing letters at this moment. Perhaps I will be able to find time for you later this morning.'

'Today I am of age,' Louisa continued, clutching the sides of her gown with both hands to steel her courage. 'Now that I am possessed of my inheritance I wish to go to London. Immediately.'

Her aunt snorted, shaking her head. 'Oh, you silly girl. You couldn't possibly go to London without me. Poor Barnabas has lost a fortune, due to unscrupulous card sharps, so there's no money for you to go. Besides, a young lady of birth must have a chaperone to attend parties, and I find that I am much too weary this year to

take you. You will simply have to wait until next year. Or perhaps the year after.'

Louisa's shoulders drooped, but she was not going to give up yet. 'I am sure one of my trustees has a wife who could be my chaperone and present me to the Queen.'

'But they are not your guardians.'

'I am one-and-twenty, ma'am. I do not need a guardian any longer.'

Aunt Rockingham set down her pen. Her mouth pinched into a fine line. 'I agree that you are quite old enough to make your own choices. But your late father's will does not allow you to touch your inheritance until you are five-and-twenty years old or married to someone with your guardian's approval.'

*Four more years?*

Louisa's stomach dropped in dismay. She could have lain on the floor and thrown a tantrum like a small child—kicking and screaming. She could not endure being locked up in her own home for four more years, with an aunt who didn't like her and an uncle who ignored her very existence.

'But I am already old to be a debutante. Most young ladies are presented at court when they are seventeen. I fear I am losing all my chances.'

'I hadn't wanted to mention this to you,' her aunt said, frowning. 'But you are an ill-favoured, extremely freckled young woman. It would be highly unlikely, even if I did take you to London, for you to find a suitable husband. It would be a waste of time and money.'

Touching her hot cheeks, Louisa felt her heart drop as she wondered if her aunt's words could be true. Her hair was like the red of leaves in autumn. Her eyes the same

green as moss. But her face and arms *were* covered in freckles. Tiny reddish-brown blemishes.

Glancing down, she knew that she was tall and skinny. At least compared to her aunt. What if she was ugly? Was her unprepossessing appearance the reason why her aunt could never feel affection for her?

Louisa gulped, trying to hold in the tears that threatened to spill down her cheeks. 'Then I am to stay home for another four years?'

'Let me be frank with you, Louisa,' her aunt said, giving her niece a withering stare. 'I had hoped that Barnabas could be brought up to scratch before now. But he insists that he is too young to marry yet, and there are his debts that must be repaid. So you'll have to wait another year or two. Then you will be married. After the ceremony you will be presented to the Queen of England as Barnabas's wife.'

Barnabas was her eldest cousin and heir to the earldom. He was a stocky and sullen young man who was several inches shorter than her. Like his mother, he had a distinguished black mole on his face, but it was on his chin. His only notable accomplishments so far were being sent down from both Eton and Oxford. Barnabas ate too much. Drank too much. Gambled too much. If the maids were to be believed—and Louisa thought they were—he had a lascivious eye and wandering hands. He was five years her senior and the last man in the world she would ever want to marry. Her entire body shivered in revulsion from just thinking of it. She could not be his wife.

Louisa shook her head slowly, her heart sinking further. 'I don't blame my cousin for not wishing to marry me. I don't want to marry him either.'

'Of course Barnabas wishes to marry you,' her aunt said in a scolding tone. 'He simply isn't ready to do so yet.'

'But Aunt—'

'Louisa!' she said, in a high shrill voice. 'I am done with discussing the matter. You had best go and see if Mrs Barker has any mending for you to do. I can't have you underneath my feet all day. You've already wasted half of my morning, and I have important correspondence to write.'

Shoulders slumped, Louisa left the parlour and went to the kitchens to find the housekeeper. When she opened the door, she saw the entire staff were lined up They all began to wish her a happy birthday and the cook, Mrs Hatch, held out a small cake that was decorated with a delicate white swan on top.

Louisa couldn't help but smile as tears fell down her cheeks. Mrs Barker and the rest of the staff had not forgotten her birthday. They loved her even if she was ugly.

'Thank you! Oh, thank you!' Louisa said, accepting the cake from the cook. 'I have never seen a more beautifully decorated cake. I am the luckiest young lady in the world! Come, we must all have a piece of it together.'

'We can't eat with you, my lady,' the butler, Mr Meadows, insisted. 'It wouldn't be proper.'

She sniffed and wiped at her eyes. 'Oh, please do join me. Or I shall have to eat this marvellous cake by myself, and that would be such a sad thing on my birthday.'

Mrs Hatch had a merry red face and she cut the cake into perfectly even slices and gave Louisa the first one. Louisa took a bite and it was like tasting heaven—sweet, buttery and light. Her aunt rarely let her partake of any-

thing sweet. She insisted that it was to preserve Louisa's figure.

She took another bite of cake, but this time it tasted like ash. She forced herself to swallow it and then played with her fork, unable to eat any more.

'Am I truly ugly?' she blurted out.

Mrs Hatch dropped the knife she was holding and it clattered on the table top. 'Why would ye ask such a thing, my lady?'

'Of course not,' Mrs Barker said, patting Louisa's shoulder with her bony hand. She was an extremely slender elderly woman, with fine features and soft white hair. 'You're a beauty, just like your mother was.'

Louisa could feel a blush coming on. Her red hair and light complexion were unfortunately prone to blushes.

She glanced down at the slice of cake on her plate. 'My aunt said that I was ill-favoured and would not be able to find a suitable husband. She insists that I marry my cousin Barnabas. Only he doesn't want to marry me yet…so I have to wait a few more years.'

'Don't marry that lecher, my lady!' said Lily, a pretty blonde maid a year or two younger than Louisa. She squeezed Louisa's wrist. 'He ain't worthy of you.'

'The old witch just wants your fortune for her son,' said Goodman. He was a bald, gruff elderly man who had been head groom under her father, but now was relegated to a lowlier position in the stables.

Louisa clutched at her throat. It felt as hot as her face. She had no family who loved her or would help her.

'I don't want to marry Barnabas. He's a dreadful person. Only, I don't know what to do. Or who to ask for help. I don't even know the names of my trustees. My mother's only brother is a vicar in Somerset, but I've

never been in contact with their family... And look at me. No one would believe I was a lady or an heiress.'

'Right,' said Mrs Barker, pointing a bony finger at her. 'First things first. You'll need a new dress. There's a bit of material left from the curtains in the blue parlour.'

'I can sew it. But I'll need new boots,' Louisa added. Her toes were starting to feel numb in her too-tight ones.

'Mine have grown too small, if you don't mind having second-hand,' Lily offered. 'Mrs Barker has already purchased a new pair for me.'

Louisa patted the maid's hand. 'I would be most grateful.'

Mrs Hatch touched the end of Louisa's nose. 'And I've trimmed a straw bonnet that would look very fetching on ye.'

'Lady Rockingham has so many pairs of gloves she wouldn't notice if one went astray,' offered Miss Talley. She was her aunt's lady's maid, and a handsome middle-aged woman with a trim figure and lovely auburn hair.

Goodman cleared his throat. 'I could take the gig and drive you to your uncle's vicarage in Somerset, my lady. I'm not allowed to drive the carriage any more... Me not being fancy enough for the Countess.'

Hope filled Louisa's chest for the first time in years, but she didn't want to hurt these servants who had been kinder to her than her family...who had loved her when no one else did.

'But won't you all get into trouble?'

'For what?' the butler said in his snobbish tones. Meadows was more polished than a duke, and looked like one with his dark hair and aquiline nose.

He gazed haughtily down that same aristocratic nose

now, as he added, 'I don't know what you are talking about. I will certainly never say I saw Lady Louisa leave.'

'And neither did I,' Mrs Hatch said with a merry wink. 'And you can take this month's leftover housekeeping money.'

Louisa listened as one by one they all vowed to claim no knowledge of her plans or whereabouts. Wiping happy tears from her eyes, she thanked them with all her heart. Maybe she wasn't completely ugly and unlovable…

## Chapter Two

Lord Simon Anthony Peregrine Stringham, the Marquess of Cheswick, known to his family as 'Wick', was head of the family whilst his parents, the Duke and Duchess of Hampford, were travelling in Africa to return animals to the wild. They would be gone for about a year, and he'd been tasked to keep an eye on his five younger siblings.

It was enough to put a fellow into a permanent cold sweat.

Wick had been forced to leave his best friend the Duke of Sunderland's shooting party early, for he feared the mayhem that his family would cause during his absence. Or, worse, that scarlet fever would strike again, as it had the last time his parents had gone to Africa, nearly ten years ago. His youngest sister Becca had only been three years old at the time.

After travelling to London, he had at least reassured himself of his brother's health and wellness. Lord Matthew Stringham was living in bachelor's rooms and working with their maternal grandfather, Mr Stubbs. Like their grandfather, Matthew had a head for legal af-

fairs and was busy building his own fortune in business. He'd laughed at his elder brother's concern.

Wick had also checked on his married sister Mantheria, the Duchess of Glastonbury, and her three-year-old son, Andrew. He'd taken them on a drive around the park in his phaeton and then to Gunter's for ices, carefully cementing his position as favourite uncle.

His two middle sisters, Lady Frederica and Lady Helen, were safely at a school in Bath run by the eminently respectable Miss Victoria Cluess. And his youngest sister, Lady Rebecca—Becca—hadn't liked the school, so he had hired her a governess—Miss Young, a niece of the Reverend Robertson, the vicar from the village near the castle.

He hadn't actually met the woman, but she'd come highly recommended. He'd written for her to take up the position at Hampford Castle immediately. Becca was a darling, and his favourite sister, but left to her own devices she could be quite a handful…and she was unfortunately fond of making rodents her pets.

Lifting his whip, he snapped it above his greys' heads. The horses immediately increased their pace. As if they, too, knew how close they were to being home.

Now all he had to do was check on the Hampford estate and the new governess and all his worries for his family would be put to rest.

Wrinkling his nose, Wick manoeuvred his horses through the south gate of Hampford Castle. To the average viewer the old place was large, dark and forbidding. But to Wick this stone pile with its many towers and parapets was home.

Handing his reins to a groom, Wick jumped out of the phaeton in time to be caught in a tight embrace. His little

sister Becca's head barely reached his shoulders, but at the moment she was pushing it most painfully into his stomach. He gently took her arms and pushed her away from him, so that he might see her face.

Becca had the same brown hair as he did, but instead of brown eyes she had bright blue ones that sparkled with mischief. Today, however, her eyes were full of tears. There was a new line of freckles on her nose, and her dress and apron were covered in mud—not an unusual occurrence.

'What's the matter, Becca, my heart?'

She sniffed and rubbed a dirty finger under her nose, smudging dirt on her face. 'Wick, it wasn't my fault. Truly!'

'What wasn't your fault, love?'

Becca blinked and grabbed the end of her untidy plait. She fingered it as her eyes focused on his feet. 'Miss Young has left.'

It took Wick a moment or two to remember who the blazes Miss Young was—the governess who had come so highly recommended by the vicar and his wife.

A trickle of worry ran down his neck like a bead of sweat. 'What happened? What did you do?'

His littlest sister took in a deep breath. 'Mademoiselle Jaune wouldn't stop calling her a tasty tart.'

Wick was torn between a desire to yell in frustration and another to laugh.

Their yellow macaw with a missing claw was known for her bawdy language. Papa had purchased her from a one-eyed man in a rookery. He had been keeping her in a small, dirty cage. His father had tried to free the bird, but Mademoiselle Jaune had always come back to the castle. Papa had explained that some animals, particu-

larly those born in captivity, became too domesticated ever to go back in the wild. They did not know how to hunt or how to take care of themselves.

'She left because of the bird?'

Becca bit her lower lip and looked even younger than her thirteen years. 'Miss Young said that either she or the bird had to go. Then Frederica said that we infinitely preferred Mademoiselle Jaune's company to hers. Miss Young left in a huff on foot over an hour ago. She didn't even take her things with her.'

'Wait a minute,' Wick said, holding up a hand and trying to take it all in. A frisson of fear was crawling down his spine and his left eye had started to twitch. 'What is Frederica doing home? She's supposed to be at school. The summer holidays aren't for another two months.'

Two more *glorious* months of relative peace and quiet.

Becca's honest little face went red. 'Well, Helen and Frederica being sent home from finishing school *is* my fault.'

A dozen curses ran through his mind and he had to grind his teeth together to keep them from coming out in front of his sister.

He shook his head. 'How could it be your fault, Becca? You weren't there.'

She sniffed and her chin quivered. 'I told Frederica the name of the girl who had bullied me at school and called me stupid…and Frederica cut off all her hair while she was sleeping. So the headmistress sent her home.'

Wick was torn between pride and disapproval. He'd been more angry than fire when Becca had written to him asking to come home because of a girl who had mercilessly teased and excluded her. He had removed Becca from Bath, but there hadn't been much else he could do

to make it better. Now, he couldn't help but feel a tiny bit satisfied that the nasty girl had got her due.

'And what did Helen do to get sent home from school?'

'Nothing much.'

'Becca…' He said her name this time without the usual added endearment. His left eye was twitching again.

His little sister grabbed the end of her plait again—a nervous habit. 'Helen put a snake in the bed of every girl my age who had not befriended me. They weren't poisonous, though! Just simple grass snakes.'

Wick could only close his eyes and moan. How long had his sisters planned their revenge that they'd been able to find enough snakes?

'So now I have all three of you home and no governess?'

Becca nodded and his two other sisters popped out from behind the main double doors of the castle. Frederica looked smug, but Helen gave him a tremulous smile.

Frederica, his second to eldest sister, could usually slither her way out of trouble—but not this time. She had been blessed with the same brown hair and buxom figure as their mother; at nearly seventeen, she should have known better than to participate in schoolgirl pranks.

Helen was younger by two years and did not look like either sister. She was small and slight, almost waif-like. Her hair was flaxen-yellow and her blue eyes seemed to take up most of her face. Helen was a naturalist, like their father, with an unfortunate affinity to snakes.

Taking off his hat, Wick raked one hand through his hair. He could have used an entire dictionary of curses. Twice. 'I cannot believe you two! This is beyond anything you've ever done before.'

'We are really sorry to have upset you, Wick,' Helen

said, holding her clasped hands together beseechingly. 'Truly.'

'But you aren't sorry for what you've done?'

Frederica snorted, folding her arms across her chest. 'Of course not. Those little beasts deserved everything that they got and more.'

Wick swallowed; his throat felt dry and scratchy. 'Mama will be furious. You two are supposed to be at school, preparing for your debuts, not behaving like hoydens. This little stunt might have ruined your chances of ever finding a suitable match and harmed Becca's.'

Becca was practically chewing off her lower lip. Helen sniffed, and one theatrical tear fell from her eye and slid down her cheek. She could cry on command—a useful talent that she'd used to weasel her way out of trouble more than once. Frederica merely snorted again, and gave him a glare very similar to their mother's stare.

'We're *Stringhams*, Wick,' Frederica said, unimpressed by his threats. 'We could parade down the street in our small clothes and every blasted peer would still beg to marry us.'

'We might get even *more* offers!' Helen said with a high giggle.

Before he knew it, all three of his little sisters were laughing. Wick experienced a full-body shiver. His sisters were wild and stubborn enough to do anything. And he'd learned from the last time he'd been in charge that he could not do it alone.

He had to get that governess back *now*.

He wouldn't fail his family this time.

# Chapter Three

Louisa sewed through the night to finish the dress. It was a simple high-necked gown with a small puff at the top of long sleeves that tightened at her wrists. Miss Talley, her aunt's lady's maid, had pilfered not only a pair of white gloves, but stockings without holes. They felt amazingly soft on Louisa's feet.

Mrs Hatch put the new bonnet on Louisa's head and tied the ribbons. The cook must have spent hours adding the artificial flowers and ribbons, but instead of keeping it for herself, she was giving it to Louisa. A few tears escaped Louisa's eyes as she hugged Mrs Hatch and thanked her. Mrs Hatch squeezed her back tightly. She had always given the best embraces. Ever since Louisa was little the cook had chased her around the kitchen and when she'd caught her kissed the top of Louisa's head.

Mrs Hatch had always made her feel safe and loved. Unlike her aunt, who had continually reminded her niece that she was an unwanted encumbrance.

Lily brought her the old boots, which fitted much better than Louisa's own and were much nicer and newly polished. The only thing that Louisa was missing was a

spencer or a shawl, but that did not matter. She was in a new dress, hat, gloves, stockings, and even boots. The leftover housekeeping coins jiggled against each other in her pocket.

Then Mrs Barker came up behind her and wrapped a beautiful lace shawl around her shoulders. 'I tatted it myself. I always planned to give it to you on your wedding day, but needs must.'

Delicately fingering the lace, Louisa thought that the shawl was the loveliest piece of clothing she had ever seen. Not even Aunt Rockingham had anything so fine. Oh, the hours it must have taken Mrs Barker to make it!

Tears filled Louisa's eyes as she hugged the bony woman for the first time. She wasn't soft and cuddly, like Mrs Hatch, but she returned the hug.

'I will take great care of it,' Louisa promised her. 'And when I marry I shall wear it around my shoulders. I promise you.'

'We'd best hurry, my lady,' said Goodman in his usual gruff voice. 'Daylight is coming and it would be best for us to be out of sight.'

Swallowing her emotions, Louisa shook hands with him and thanked everyone again, before following Goodman out into the cold and wet dawn. He had already hooked the old gig to a pair of horses. They weren't the flashy ones that her uncle drove his curricle with, but strong, reliable work horses from the farm. She accepted his hand up into the carriage and sat beside him.

He flicked the reins. 'Giddy up.'

The Greystone Hall estate's circumference was over ten miles. Louisa had not been off it in over a decade. Still, she wanted to memorise every detail. Each tree. The paths. The valley. Because she never intended to

come back. She planned to have a London season and marry a man she loved, just as her mother had. Even as a child she had known that her parents loved each other. And they had loved her dearly. That knowledge had often been the only thing that had helped Louisa through all her monotonous days stuck at Greystone Hall.

Yawning, Louisa found it harder and harder to keep her eyes open. Her late-night sewing was catching up with her, and the jolts and bumps of the carriage were gentle. She fought to keep her eyelids open, but eventually the struggle was too great.

When Louisa woke up, a few hours later, her neck was sore from sleeping while sitting, and her stomach growled with hunger. She moved her hand to her nape and rubbed it gently.

'Almost there, my lady,' Goodman said, pointing to a lonely house further down the road, nestled by a church.

She picked up her small bag from the floor and clutched it to her stomach. What if her uncle refused to help her? What if he sent her back to Aunt Rockingham? Her aunt was shrewd enough to put a watch on her to make sure that she never escaped again. She did not like to be crossed. This was Louisa's only chance for freedom. She prayed that she hadn't made a foolish choice.

Goodman stopped the gig on the road, a few dozen yards away from the vicarage in Frome. ''Tis best if I leave you here.'

Holding his hand, she stepped out of the carriage. Her knees were shaky. 'Thank you, Goodman. I appreciate your assistance more than I can say.'

He touched his hat to her and then clicked his tongue. The horses moved forward and she watched him turn the vehicle on the small pike road and return in the same di-

rection he had come. The poor man had a long carriage ride in front of him.

Taking a deep breath, Louisa forced her quaking limbs to walk down the gravel drive. She paused as she reached the house. Should she go to the front door or the back? She wanted her aunt and uncle's first impression of her to be the best possible. Glancing down, she saw her new blue dress was covered in dust from the drive. Even her lovely new shawl would need to be soaked in vinegar and washed. She hardly looked like the respectable daughter of an earl. She'd best go to the servants' entrance.

Louisa knocked sharply on the door.

A middle-aged woman with white hair pulled severely back, wearing a white cap and apron, answered it. 'What can I help you with, miss?'

Louisa jumped, felt her mouth dry. 'I am here to see the Reverend Laybourne.'

The woman shook her head and harrumphed. 'He's not here, miss.'

Lowering her chin, Louisa felt her confidence receding. 'When will he be back?'

'Never. He was promoted to Canon of Sherborne and now he and his family live in a fine house there. The new man, Reverend Nance, kept me on as housekeeper. But he ain't married so it wouldn't be proper for you to stay.'

Her heart sank in her chest. 'How far is the town of Sherborne from here?'

The woman scratched her arm. 'Thirty miles, I'd say.'

Louisa felt dizzy and her limbs tingled with fatigue. She kneaded her chest with the heel of her hand, trying to soothe the pain there. Such a distance was unfathomable, but what choice did she have?

'Which way?'

The housekeeper stepped out of the vicarage and Louisa trudged behind her. The woman pointed down the path. 'Just head south through the town and continue down the road. You can't miss it. But first come in my kitchen for a cup of tea and something to eat, miss. Can't have you setting off on an empty stomach.'

'Thank you.'

Louisa was grateful for the meal as she walked and walked until she thought that her feet had more blisters than skin. She feared that by the time she reached her uncle's house that she would give her relatives a bad first impression. She was dusty, sweaty, and her once tidy hair blown about.

She dimly recalled her Uncle Laybourne from her mother's funeral. He'd seemed solemn and had not spoken a word to her. His wife had wrapped her thin arms around Louisa and promised to invite her for a visit to meet all her cousins. Louisa had longed to go home with her. But she had not realised how serious her aunt's perpetual cough was until she'd died not long after, of consumption. Her uncle had remarried, but his new wife had never attempted to make contact with Louisa.

What if they rejected her, like Uncle and Aunt Rockingham?

What if she wasn't good enough for them either?

She swallowed; her throat was parched and her stomach continued to make loud noises of hunger. Wiping off her brow, she gazed further down the road and saw a lone rider coming towards her. The hairs on her arms stood up and her pulse quickened. She was all alone. No family. No friends.

Could he mean her harm?

## Chapter Four

There was nothing for it. He would have to find the erstwhile governess and offer her more money. His sisters needed constant supervision and he was not able to give it to them whilst he took care of the affairs of the estate.

Wick heaved a sigh filled with exhaustion and frustration. He pointed his finger at his three youngest sisters. 'Don't get into any mischief while I'm gone.'

'We won't,' Helen assured him with her most charming smile.

It set him on his guard. His usually sweet sister was like the snakes she carried around; you never knew when she was going to strike with her strongest venom.

'Don't count on it!' Frederica said.

At least she was always honest.

'Where are you going, Wick?' Becca asked, taking his hand and pulling on it. 'You have only just got home.'

'To find your blasted governess. No thanks to any of *you*,' he said gruffly.

Wick called for the groom to harness a horse to the curricle. His greys were already spent from the drive to Hampford. Shoving on his hat, he climbed up into the

driver's seat. He was dusty, tired and abominably thirsty, but there was nothing else to be done.

'Which way did she go, Becca?'

His little sister hesitantly pointed to the north gate—a direction he usually avoided. It was the opposite way from the village and the vicarage where Miss Young's aunt and uncle lived. The foolish governess had headed in the wrong direction.

Wick flicked the reins to urge his horse forward. The north gate was not used as often as the south. Both still had the wrought-iron pulleys of another age, but the gates were rarely closed in these modern days. The only time he remembered them being shut had been when Papa had lost control of his emu and contained it by closing the iron gates.

Wick only wished that he could have kept the governess in the same way.

His heartbeat was irregular as he passed Animal Island, the animal sanctuary where his father kept those creatures too domesticated to be freed. The island was close to the family crypt, where those they'd loved were buried. The grief had not lessened over time. If anything, it had become more keen and painful.

Wick felt an overall feeling of weakness, but it was growing dark now. He had to find Miss Young and make sure that she was safe.

He drove for another five miles, his headache increasing with each furlong.

Where could the blasted woman be? She clearly had no sense of direction or she would have long before realised that the village was in the opposite direction and much closer to the castle. She should have been at her uncle's vicarage long before now.

Wick had nearly given up hope of locating the governess when he saw a woman trudging down the road. She was coming his way. He rocked back and forth in his seat in relief. Perhaps the governess had finally realised that she was heading in the wrong direction. Or that it had been foolish to walk away without her belongings.

Urging the horse on, he sped towards her. The woman wore a blue dress that was liberally covered in dirt from the knees down. She clutched a small bag in her hands as if it possessed her entire fortune. Mayhap the woman wasn't as careless as Becca had said, and hadn't left all her money and belongings at the castle.

As he got closer to her the woman looked up at him. He'd been expecting a plain governess with sensible hair, a no-nonsense stern mouth, and hands like cricket bats. The young woman before him had none of those things. She was tall and slender, but with gentle curves. Her hair was a riot of red curls, completely untamed. Her pale skin was covered in hundreds of sweet freckles. Wick had the most unaccountable thought that it would be lovely to kiss every single one.

The young woman smiled at him, but it was fearful. Her expression was like his little sister Becca's when she was in trouble.

Wick felt the hardening in his stomach lessen. The poor woman was already scared—he didn't need to bite her head off. Though he dearly wished to.

'It would appear that you are in need of a lift, miss.'

She tipped her head up to look at him. Her eyes were a bright green that sparkled like emeralds in her face. There was a freckle just above her lips—that was the one he'd kiss first. If he kissed any of them. Which he wouldn't. Because she was the governess, and such things

weren't done. And, frankly, he'd never been tempted to kiss his own governess. Miss Nix hadn't inspired affection or physical admiration. She'd been an old battle-axe, who had retired after Mantheria's debut four years before.

'I should not wish to put you out, sir,' the lady said in a soft tone, and well-spoken accent. It was no wonder that his sisters had ridden roughshod over her. They were wild animals compared to this gentle woman.

Wick held out his gloved hand to her. 'You can sit by me.'

The young woman looked down at her feet. Her shoulders were tight. Presumably with embarrassment.

'There is no need to be missish,' he said, a little of his frustration coming out in his tone. 'It's already dusk and you don't want to be alone on the road.'

'Where are you going to take me?'

'Hampford Castle, of course.'

'But I don't want to go there.'

Wick huffed, gritting his teeth. 'It's too late to go anywhere else. And I promise that my sisters will be on their best behaviour. We can discuss where you want to go tomorrow. I will send you anywhere you wish to go in a blasted carriage.'

If he couldn't convince her to stay. At least until he could find a suitable replacement. It was clear that this shy miss was too young, too pretty and too sweet to be anyone's governess. Certainly not wild hellions like his sisters.

He offered his hand again and this time she took it. Wick pulled her up beside him. They were too close, their bodies lined up next to each other. Her wild curls were in his face and she smelled of vanilla. It was his favourite scent. Breathing her in once more, Wick resolved to be

as impersonal as possible. He scooted over on the seat so that they were no longer touching and urged the horse into a brisk trot. He forced himself not to think of her lovely shape, or of the fact that she was sitting next to him.

The young woman said not a word. Which was good—for Wick had no idea how to speak to a governess. Particularly a recalcitrant one who was attracting him against his will.

His mouth was dry when they finally reached the north gate. The courtyard was full of lanterns and torches. He drove to where a groom stood waiting to take care of the curricle and horse.

'Time to get down, miss,' he said, jumping out of the vehicle.

Without waiting for her to respond, he lifted her down. Her soft form rubbed against him and he felt another wave of desire for the woman. He released his hold on her waist as if she was a hot potato, burning his hand. The heir to a dukedom did not court a governess, and Wick had no intention of paying his addresses to any woman. No matter her rank. He was perfectly happy to remain a bachelor and he already had enough responsibilities.

Wick strode towards the house.

Glancing over his shoulder, he saw that the young woman was still standing where he had put her. 'Why aren't you coming?'

She pointed at herself with her thumb. 'Me?'

'Yes, you,' he said impatiently, beckoning her with his hand. 'Come. I'll put you in the capable hands of the housekeeper and you can get dressed for dinner. I'm dashed thirsty and starving.'

The governess took a few shaky steps towards him. 'I am to eat with you?'

'And my sisters, of course,' he said, taking off his hat and running his hand through his sweaty hair. 'Unless you'd prefer to eat alone? Then a tray will be sent to your room.'

'I should like to eat with your sisters,' she said, taking the last few steps until she was at his side.

Blast it! Did a marquess offer his arm to a governess? He was too tired to care. He squashed his hat back on his head and grabbed her hand, pulling her into the house where Mrs May, the housekeeper, stood waiting. She was a thin, middle-aged woman, with dark hair and eyes, a hooked nose, and a smile that could melt butter. Except she wasn't smiling now and her gaze was dull and flat.

'Please show her to the governess's room and give her any assistance she needs to dress for dinner,' Wick said, dropping the young woman's hand. He'd liked holding it all too well. 'I should like to eat dinner in no more than a half an hour. Please ensure that my sisters join me.'

'Yes, my lord,' Mrs May said with a sharp curtsy.

Wick felt a pain in the back of his throat. He shouldn't have been so curt with the housekeeper. She'd been his ally since he was a boy in small coats.

Striding to his father's study, he pulled out the best whisky and poured himself a glass, knocking it back with one large swallow. How quickly he'd lost control of his sisters. He dared not leave them unattended again. The alcohol burned out the dryness and pain in his throat. He wanted a second glass, but he didn't dare before dinner and on an empty stomach. He couldn't afford to be incapacitated with his sisters at home. Who knew what trouble they would concoct?

Wick found his valet in his room, already laying out his dinner clothes. He was only too happy to change out

of his dusty riding coat. Giving himself a sponge bath, he wiped away the grime of his trip from London and his second outing to find the governess. His valet handed him his clothes, lastly his dark green double-breasted tailcoat of superfine with gilt brass buttons. Then he arranged his hair in the style of the Brutus and Wick went down to the breakfast room.

The family rarely used the formal dining room for dinner, unless they had company. It could hold over fifty people. It was also farther from the kitchens, which caused the food to be a bit cold. He passed the large painting of Charles II on a horse that took up an entire wall. The dead King with his long black locks leered down at him and did nothing to improve Wick's mood.

His sisters entered the room together. They all looked cleaner and in the best of spirits. There was no mud to be found on their faces or skirts, but Helen's four-foot-long pet African snake was draped around her neck and shoulders like a wrap.

'No reptiles at the table,' he snapped.

'No one is here but us,' Helen protested, patting her snake as most people might stroke a dog. 'Besides, Theodosia is family.'

Wick would be boiled in his own pudding before he ate his supper with a snake named Theodosia. 'Your governess is back and I don't want you to scare her away again with your reptile friends.'

'Go on, Helen,' Frederica said with a wave of her hand. 'Your snake deserves somewhere warmer...like Wick's bed.'

'If I find that blasted snake in my bed, I'll throw it in the fire,' he said, massaging the back of his neck. His patience was long gone.

Helen covered her mouth with her hand. 'You wouldn't!'

'I would.'

Becca placed a hand on Helen's arm, near the snake's tail. 'He won't. Wick wouldn't harm a fly. Let alone a lovely creature like Theodosia.'

Helen gave her brother a withering stare and left the room with a sniff.

The door opened again shortly after, and it wasn't his sister, but the pretty governess. The cream dress she wore was clean, but it seemed to have been made for another woman. It was six inches too short and showed her lovely ankles. The bodice seemed to hang on her slim frame, showing the gentle swell of flesh at the top of her chest. He felt his body tighten again.

The governess's wild curls had been mostly tamed into a bun at the back of her head, but a few tendrils escaped from it. Both of his hands itched to touch her hair, to pull out the pins that contained it. He had to resist the animal attraction that he felt for her. It was improper. Unseemly. And dashed inconvenient.

Shaking his head to clear it, he pointed to his sister. 'Frederica, apologise to the governess.'

His sister blinked, and then glanced from the young woman to Wick and back again. It wasn't like Frederica to be silent on any occasion. Her mouth hung open.

'Wick,' Becca said, tugging on the sleeve of his coat. 'You've brought home the wrong governess.'

His mind had difficulty processing her words. He pointed stupidly at the redheaded young woman. 'This isn't Miss Young?'

The not-governess's cheeks flushed a pretty pink. 'I am not.'

'She is not,' his sisters said, at the same time as the unknown lady.

Wick gulped. Could this day get any worse? 'Then who the devil *are* you?'

The young woman shook her head and a few more red curls escaped. His hands twitched.

'I am afraid I cannot tell you,' she said.

Wick groaned and brought a fist to his forehead. 'There is no need to play coy, miss. Tell us your name and we will see that you are taken home safely.'

Her green eyes watched him mournfully. 'I would tell you my name if I could…only I can't. Because I do not wish to go home.'

The young woman spoke and acted like a lady, but why had she been all alone on the road? Could she have run away from home? Did she live in a vicarage? A manor? His teeth clenched. The last thing he needed was another wild young woman on his hands. He already had three. He had no intention of taking on more responsibility.

Frederica clapped her hands together. 'Ooh! A lady travelling incognito. I *knew* coming home from school would not be dull.'

'It will be dull as soon as we return this young woman to her home,' Wick threatened. 'Now, no more games, miss. What is your name? And where is your home?'

She looked at him with luminous green eyes. They were filled with unshed tears. 'Please, sir. I cannot tell you.'

He raked his hands through his hair and took a deep breath, trying to rein in his impatience and failing. 'Cannot or will not, miss?'

The young woman pulled her shawl up around her

shoulders. It appeared to very fine—like something his mother would have worn. Perhaps she wasn't from the middle class, but the upper one. But if that were the case surely he would know of her family?

She shook her head resolutely, but her chin quivered. 'I have worked too hard to escape. I will not go back home. I should be grateful to spend the night here, but I will not tell you my name.'

Wick sighed. A string of the foulest curses went through his mind. He had mistaken a runaway for his governess. If he wasn't careful he'd end up in hot water. He needed to find out who she was and return her home as quickly as possible. In the meantime, Mrs May would have to be chaperone. He didn't want to put himself in a compromising position and be forced to marry her if she was indeed a lady.

'Does she look like anyone you know?' Becca asked her sister, in a loud whisper that everyone in the room could hear.

'I'm afraid not,' Frederica said loudly, not even attempting to be discreet. She turned back to look at the not-governess. 'Your hair is entirely gorgeous, and I am sure that if I had ever seen this particular shade before I would remember. I'm Frederica, by the way. If you want to be formal and tedious my name is Lady Frederica Stringham. And this is Lady Rebecca. But we all call her Becca.'

The young woman bowed her head. She certainly had good manners, whatever her real name and situation. 'It is an honour to make your acquaintance.'

Becca took the young woman's hand—a sign of her approval. 'And that's our eldest brother, Wick. His real name is Simon, but no one calls him that because his

courtesy title is the Marquess of Cheswick—one of our father's other titles. Our brother Matthew is in London. As is our elder sister Mantheria… What would you like us to call you if you can't tell us your name?'

Wick had to bite his lower lip to keep himself from saying something caustic. Trust his sisters to take the young runaway into the bosom of the family like a stray animal…

# *Chapter Five*

Louisa opened her mouth stupidly. She didn't know what to say. Nor could she believe her luck. She had somehow landed in a castle with a handsome marquess and his two little sisters.

She only had her male cousins to compare him with, but this man named Wick was nothing at all like them. His clothing fitted his frame as if it had been sewn onto his skin. Louisa longed to run her hands over the seams of his sleeves and the darts on the back of his coat. The garments showed that Wick was a muscular man. Not at all like Barnabas. Even his knee breeches were snug on his frame, and showed his calves and what was above them to be perfectly toned.

But it was his face that caused her to feel wobbly in the knees. His brown hair was thick and curly and exactly the same shade as his eyes, as if they had been embroidered with the same thread. He had a square jaw, with lips that were not too small, nor too large for his face. She found herself looking at his mouth again, blushing.

'You're not Miss Young,' a voice said from behind her.

Turning, she realised that there were three sisters. The

third sister did not at all look like the others, who were brown-haired, sturdy and powerful-looking. This one was a slight young woman with the palest blonde hair Louisa had ever seen. She could tell that even though Lady Becca was younger, she was already taller than this sister.

'She can't tell us her name,' Lady Frederica said, grinning like a cat with a bowl of cream. 'Isn't that the most delicious mystery? She could be a lost princess. Or hiding from pirates or vagabonds. And Wick is positively boiling.'

'There is definitely something nefarious going on,' said the handsome Marquess named Wick, his lovely kissable lips tightening into a straight line.

Did he think that she had tricked him on purpose? That she was trying to catch his title by compromising him? The very thought made Louisa blush all over. What a scrape she was in.

'I know what we will call her!' the youngest sister shouted. 'We can call her Miss Nemo—because *nemo* means *no one* in Latin.'

Louisa attempted a smile, her heart beating rapidly. 'That would be perfect. You must be a very clever young lady to know Latin.'

Lady Becca grinned up at her, looking part little girl and part young woman. On the cusp of changing.

'Oh, I say we keep Miss Nemo,' Lady Helen said, taking a seat beside Louisa. 'I already like her so much better than Miss Young.'

Louisa's heart and spirits lifted. She would love to stay with such a charming family—even for only a little while.

The Marquess cleared his throat. 'You can't just take

a young woman in like a stray cat. She must be returned to her home.'

'Anyone would be preferrable to Miss Young,' Lady Frederica added, ignoring her brother and picking up her napkin.

Louisa heart fell back down in her chest. It would be too much to hope that these young ladies and their handsome elder brother would *like* an uneducated and unprepossessing young woman like herself. They would respect her, but only if they knew she was a titled lady with a fortune. Aunt Rockingham had been right.

Lord Cheswick hit his fist on the table. 'Be that as it may, I have to find your cursed governess. She is my responsibility. I can't have her toiling alone down the wrong road. Blast! I'll have to go out again and find her.'

He strode to the door, as if to leave, but the eldest sister said, 'There's no need for you to be a hero, Wick. I'm sure the horrendous Miss Young is happily drinking tea at the vicarage now, and telling all sorts of unflattering stories about us to her cousins.'

Lord Cheswick shook his head. 'The vicarage is south. Becca said that she went north.'

The littlest sister buried her head in Frederica's shoulder. Obviously not wanting to face her furious brother. 'I lied.'

The Marquess came towards them both and knelt down by his standing sisters. 'Becca, my heart, why did you lie to me?'

Lady Becca said something, but it was mumbled. Louisa couldn't quite hear her.

'I can't understand you,' said the Marquess.

Becca released Lady Frederica and turned to face her brother. Her round face was completely red. 'Miss Young

said I was slow in the head and that she would have more success trying to tutor a cow. I didn't want you to bring her back, so I told you to go in the wrong direction on purpose. I'm sorry that I lied to you, Wick.'

Louisa thought that she had seen the Marquess angry before, but the expression on his face now was positively murderous. His hands were clenched again into tight fists. She watched him get to his feet, breathing heavily.

'Frederica, take Miss Nemo up to your rooms and find her a suitable gown. Then have a maid pack Miss Young's things. A groom will take them to the vicarage this very night. That *woman* will never enter our home again, and if she asks for a letter of recommendation I will write such a blistering reply that not even the devil will hire her.'

Lady Becca all but jumped into her brother's arms.

His face softened. 'Come, Becca. Let's get your former governess's wages and send them with her trunk. Once she is paid, we will never have anything to do with her again.'

'If you'll come with me, Miss Nemo?' Lady Frederica said, walking to the door.

Nodding, she followed the young woman out of the room. They were quiet until they reached a bedchamber at the top of the stairs. It was an opulently furnished room, with a grand four-poster bed with scarlet hangings. One wall held a large tapestry and the floor was carpeted. A fire burned in the hearth. Such luxury Louisa had never experienced.

'I hope you don't mind if I act as your lady's maid?'

Louisa found herself blushing again. Even though she was the daughter of an earl. 'Oh, I couldn't allow that, Lady Frederica.'

The young woman began to unbutton the back of the too-large gown. 'We're only formal when there's company. Not to say that we don't consider *you* company... Do you think you could stay on and be our governess? I agree with Helen. I already like you better than Miss Young.'

Louisa stepped out of the dress. 'You—you don't even know who I am.'

Lady Frederica shrugged. 'Becca likes you. That's enough for us.'

'And the Marquess?'

'Wick?' Lady Frederica laughed. 'You'll soon see that Becca's got the big lump wrapped around her little finger.'

Louisa watched the bold young woman take a beautiful emerald silk gown trimmed with golden string out of her bureau. She couldn't help but gasp when she saw it. Not even Aunt Rockingham had a dress so fine. Instinctively, she put her arms up, and Frederica pulled the dress over her head. Like Miss Young's, the dress was a little too large in the bodice. Lady Frederica, although several years Louisa's junior, was already very well endowed.

'And your parents?' Louisa asked. 'Won't they mind?'

She laughed. 'They're in Africa, freeing captive animals back into the wild. By the time they might mind I dare say we will have solved the mystery of your identity and helped you find your rightful place in the world.'

Louisa went still and let her arms hang loosely at her sides. 'Are your parents really in Africa?'

The younger woman laughed again. 'If you are an adventuress, you're also a fantastic actress. Don't you know who we are?'

Louisa could only shake her head, not trusting her tongue to speak.

'My parents are the Duke and Duchess of Hampford,' Lady Frederica said. 'My father is a famous naturalist, who doesn't believe in taking animals from their natural habitats, and my mother owns a world-renowned perfume house on Bond Street in London.'

Louisa knew that her mouth was hanging open. But she couldn't quite believe her luck. She had somehow, by the help of Providence, landed in a loving family like the one she'd always dreamed of. But no doubt such fashionable people would know Aunt and Uncle Rockingham. She briefly considered asking them for a ride to her Uncle Laybourne's home, but thought better of it. If the Marquess knew her true identity, he might try to return her to Greystone Hall and she could not bear it.

She yelped as Frederica stuck her with a pin.

'Sorry! But now you don't look as if you're wearing your older sister's gown.'

Louisa turned and gazed into the full-length mirror. Somehow, with a few pins, Lady Frederica had tucked and pulled the bodice so that it appeared to have been made for her. 'It's beautiful.'

'Come!' Lady Frederica said, laughing. 'But don't eat too much at dinner or you'll get poked.'

Louisa followed her back down the stairs, wondering if she was somehow in a beautiful dream.

## Chapter Six

Wick woke up with a pounding hangover. He didn't recall drinking that much the night before, but he'd been dashed thirsty, and so angry that he hadn't been able to see straight. Perhaps it was for the best that he had never met Miss Young. He still wanted to wring her neck. How could a woman who was supposed to be a teacher and a mentor treat a pupil with such callousness? Especially one so winsome as Becca?

He knew that Becca struggled with reading, writing and arithmetic. For her, the numbers and letters didn't stay in their right places. But it didn't mean that she was stupid. Becca had a great memory. Once someone told her something, it was there to stay. Like the Latin word for *no one*. He'd told her that over five years ago, and she had popped out with it as if it were yesterday.

No. His Becca was not stupid. She simply learned differently from most girls, and any governess worth her salt should have realised it.

Unbidden and unwanted, the image of Miss Nemo in that emerald gown the night before filled his mind. She had looked magnificent. He had almost believed his sis-

ter's opinion that the young woman must be a missing princess. He had never seen a more vibrant and beautiful woman in his life. His hands had twitched throughout the entire meal. He'd wanted so badly to touch her again. To feel her slender body against his. To kiss her senseless.

He shook his head to clear away the image. For all he knew she might be already married. They didn't know her name, her family, or where she was from. Her manners suggested that she was well born, but perhaps she'd been a servant in a grand house. Or the base-born daughter of an aristocrat. He'd always been glad that his own father wasn't like that. Papa didn't have a mistress, and nor was he unfaithful to his wife. A smile grew on Wick's lips. Not that Mama would have stood for it. She'd probably have poisoned Papa if he'd tried.

His parents weren't at all alike, but there was a deep and abiding love between them. A love that they freely shared with their children. Growing up, Wick had always wanted to find a similar match for himself—but that had been before he had buried two of his siblings in the cold family crypt. Before he'd learned that love wasn't always enough.

Rubbing his eyes, he caught a whiff of vanilla from his soap. Again Miss Nemo's face and shy smile filled his mind. She had smelled like a vanilla cake that he would like to bite into. Or simply lick.

What was she doing this morning? Did she want to be his sisters' governess? Did he want her to stay? It would be dangerous for him to keep her in the castle. He'd never felt such an overwhelming attraction before. Not to the *ton* debutantes he'd flirted and danced with. Nor to the pretty barmaids he'd kissed. He didn't trust himself to

be near her without touching her. The pull towards her was simply too great.

No. She would have to go. He would give her some money and send her anywhere she wanted in the carriage. As long as it was away from him.

He pulled the cord for a servant. The butler came into the room. He was a portly fellow with a distinctly snobbish air and never a hair out of place. Wick had always respected Mr Harper, and secretly attempted to copy his dignified manners.

The butler bowed. 'You called, my lord?'

'Harper, I should like to speak to my sisters.'

'I am afraid the young ladies have already gone.'

Fear gripped his chest. He wanted to see Miss Nemo again. At least once. He had to touch her hand as he bowed over it.

*'Gone?'*

'Gone to see the new baby camel leopard, my lord,' the butler intoned. 'Mrs May has accompanied them to act as chaperone.'

Wick bowed his head in relief and said a prayer of thanks for the housekeeper. His little sisters were going to be the death of him.

'That will be all, Harper.'

'Very good, my lord.'

Yawning, Wick returned to the estate's books. Unlike his father, he had a natural flair for estate management—one he'd inherited from his mother and maternal grandfather. Ever since he'd graduated from Oxford he'd been handling the estate. The Duke, frankly, was not interested, and his mother, who had previously overseen the estate's finances, was already busier than she needed to be with her perfume company.

He'd also found that whilst Mama was excellent with numbers, she was less focused on the needs of their tenants. She wasn't unfeeling—she was simply a businesswoman. Wick, however, liked to spend time with the farmers and learn their methods. He planned to farm the home fields next year. He would also replace the roofs on all the cottages instead of taking the less expensive option of continuing to patch them.

After completing his work on the books, Wick had the less pleasant job of riding over to Animal Island to find his sisters.

He should stop at the family crypt and pay his respects. He hadn't visited it in nearly a year. He liked to suppose that if he didn't go there, maybe his little brother Charles and his little sister Elizabeth would still be alive. He liked to imagine that they were away at school. He tried not to remember that they had died when *he* was in charge…whilst his parents were in Africa.

Wick had been only sixteen years old at the time—too young for the responsibility of watching over his younger siblings. Matthew had been fourteen and Charles only twelve when they had brought home scarlet fever from school and all five of their younger sisters had caught it. But none so badly as Elizabeth, Mantheria's identical twin.

They'd been ten years old at the time, and Elizabeth had been slim and frail even before she had contracted the disease. Papa had called her his Little Songbird. She'd never walked when she could skip, nor talked when she could sing. Elizabeth must have made up hundreds of songs for she'd rarely sung the same song twice.

After she'd died, none of his sisters had ever sung again.

He had been powerless to help those he'd loved the most. He had failed his little siblings and his parents. It had been the hardest time of his life.

Now, after riding to the edge of the cemetery, he tried to force himself to get off his horse and go into the family crypt. But his body wouldn't move.

He was a coward.

Turning his horse, Wick rode through a field of sheep and across the bridge that connected Animal Island to the land.

'Lord Cheswick,' said Mr Merrell, doffing his hat. 'Good to see ye.'

Swinging out of the saddle, Wick held out his hand to the brawny man. 'And you, sir. Everything appears to be in excellent order.'

Merrell laughed heartily. 'Ye haven't even seen the animals yet, my lord. How would ye know?'

Wick wrinkled his nose. 'My sense of smell tells me all I need to know.'

The head animal keeper barked another loud laugh. 'Too right. Ye never cared much for any of the creatures. Not like wee Charles. Now, he would've made a right fine naturalist. Poor Sadie still misses him.'

'We all do,' Wick said quietly.

Sadie was an Indian elephant that the Marchioness of Hastings had sent to Charles who, at the age of seven, had already been a budding naturalist. Before she'd gone to India, the Marchioness had asked Charles what he would like as a pet.

'Oh, nothing smaller than an elephant,' he had said.

Little had Charles or his parents expected a beautiful female of the species to be delivered to their home several months later.

Papa had been remorseful, wishing that his son's ill-timed remark had not resulted in the captivity of such a majestic creature. Wick had been too young to understand his father's moral objections to keeping an elephant as a pet. He'd loved Sadie from the first time he saw her. Almost as much as Charles.

Wick had even helped his father build Sadie a large house on Animal Island. It was well ventilated, with every particular arranged for Sadie's comfort. Nor was she kept in a paddock. She was free to roam all around Animal Island as far as the iron gate before the bridge. But Sadie preferred her house, which Charles had taught her to clean herself. The clever elephant would take up a bucket of fresh water from the river and then, using a broom or scrubbing brush, begin to wash her home.

Merrell cleared his throat, recalling Wick from his memories.

'Is there anything you need, or something you would like to bring to my attention?' Wick asked.

'Naught, my lord. All is as it should be. Your sisters are in the camel leopard enclosure.'

*'Inside?'*

The horror that Wick felt must have shown on his face, for Merrell clapped him hard on the back. 'Don't worry, my lord. Them's gentle creatures who wouldn't hurt a fly.'

'I assume you mean the camel leopards? For I can assure you that my sisters most certainly are anything but gentle.'

Merrell laughed again, but Wick had not been joking. He tipped his hat to the head keeper and tied his horse to the bridge. He'd learned at an early age that horses did not get along with the creatures on the island.

Crossing the bridge, he unlocked the fence on the other side and stepped onto the river island.

He saw the llama, which stood by the elks. The kangaroo bounded towards him but didn't kick. His luminous eyes seemed to say he remembered Wick. Next, he passed the emus and ostriches—impressive flightless birds. They were rather mean creatures, though, so they had to be kept apart from the cockatoo, peacocks and the gold and silver pheasants. Then came the paddocks for the Neapolitan pig, the coatimundi, the different varieties of goats and the Indian bull.

He saw the elephant's house ahead of him, but he didn't have it in him to go there either. It reminded him too much of Charles. Turning to the left, he went to the camel leopard enclosure. There were two long-necked creatures there, that were nearly eighteen feet high. Between them was a baby which was six feet tall and had been nearly four stones at birth. It swayed on its thin legs.

Frederica, Helen and Becca were stroking the baby calf. Dear Mrs May was next to them, as fearless as his sisters. Miss Nemo stood near the gate of the enclosure, her face pale. She was wearing the same dress he'd found her in the day before, except it was no longer dusty from travel. Mrs May must have had a maid tidy it up.

Wick opened the gate. 'Good morning, miss.'

He tipped his hat to Miss Nemo. A beautiful flush formed in her freckled cheeks and she gave him a glittering smile. Heat spread throughout his body. The woman was too fetching for her own good, and her temperament even sweeter.

'Good morning, my lord,' she said, in a low, sultry voice.

Wick swallowed down his desire.

She had to go.

*Immediately.*

'I will have a carriage take you wherever you wish to go, and provide enough money for you to start again elsewhere. But it is time for you to leave, Miss Nemo.'

The young woman lowered her head. 'I understand, my lord. I will go immediately. I have an uncle who might help me.'

'His name?'

She sniffed. 'I would like to retain my anonymity. Your driver may drop me off in the city of Sherborne. I can make my way from there.'

He saw that her hands were shaking and felt a pang of guilt. But he was not like his parents. He did not take in strays. His only responsibility was to ensure she was returned to her family.

'Oh, stuff it, Wick,' Frederica said, walking up to them and taking Miss Nemo's arm. 'She's staying with us until we solve the mystery of who she is and why she has run away.'

Helen took Miss Nemo's other arm. 'And we need a governess anyway.'

Since both of Miss Nemo's arms had already been taken, Becca leaned on his. 'Please, oh, please, Wick. Miss Nemo will make an excellent governess. She has already taught me so many things on our walk here, and she has promised to show me how to do an embroidery stitch called a French knot.'

Breathing heavily, Mrs May reached them. Both her hands rested on her slender hips. 'My lord, stitching is hardly as important as arithmetic or literature, but it *is* part of a female's education. I don't think it would hurt for the young woman to stay a little longer. It might

even encourage your sisters to try new things. And I will watch them all very carefully.'

It seemed Miss Nemo had somehow bewitched his housekeeper—a typically stern, but loving woman.

However, someone to distract his sisters and keep them out of trouble until he found a new governess was not a bad thing. Obviously she couldn't stay with them indefinitely. But what harm could a few more days do? Besides, he might be able to discover her true identity and therefore make sure she safely arrived with her relatives, instead of leaving her alone in the town square.

'That sounds very promising,' he said, 'but I shall need to give Miss Nemo a proper interview.'

Becca stood on her tiptoes and kissed Wick on the cheek. Then she whirled around. 'Come, Miss Nemo. You can show us that French embroidery knot that you promised to teach us.'

Still holding Miss Nemo's arms, his sisters began to walk away, without a look at him. Miss Nemo's emerald eyes glanced back at him, softening his hard heart. She appeared so young. So vulnerable. He could hardly throw her to the wolves yet. But she couldn't stay with his sisters for long. With him…

'Wick isn't normally this bad,' Frederica said loftily, loudly enough for him to hear. 'But he's taken his position as temporary head of the family a little too seriously.'

'He's been worse than a rattlesnake without its rattle,' Helen added.

'Wick means well,' Becca put in. 'But he's a man. Mother says they are all a bit stupid. It's in their nature. They cannot help themselves.'

A wiser man would have retired from the lists, but Wick wasn't about to let his headstrong sisters win. He

offered Mrs May the support of his arm and they trailed behind them. He meant to interview Miss Nemo to find out who she truly was. And he would do it even if his three sisters pestered him the entire time.

# Chapter Seven

Louisa felt dazed as the Stringham sisters led her to their mother's favourite parlour. It was not even midday and she'd already had the best day of her life. She'd been warmly welcomed into the family and taken to see the most extraordinary baby calf that was taller than all of them! The camel leopard's two parents had towered above them with long necks and made not a sound. Louisa had felt safest near the fence, but she'd enjoyed every minute of it.

Even when Lord Cheswick had come. He clearly disapproved of her presence, but he allowed his sisters a great deal of freedom. More than Louisa had ever known.

Now, Lord Cheswick and Mrs May followed them into the room and watched as Louisa tried to teach the Stringham sisters the complicated French knot, but when Louisa realised that the young ladies couldn't even thread a needle, she had to start on basic stitches. She taught the girls how to do a backstitch and a running stitch. They were the two easiest.

Lady Helen shrugged, pulling her needle through. 'I've never been any good at my stitches. All I ever do is prick myself and bleed on the material.'

Louisa smiled and showed her how to always point the needle away from herself. Her housekeeper at Greystone Hall, Mrs Barker, did not approve of bleeding on material, and had made sure that Louisa never did. Once all three girls were doing a running stitch, she turned to glance at Mrs May and the handsome Marquess on the other side of the room.

He beckoned her with one hand. Lowering her head, she moved towards him.

'Will you not sit down? I have some questions about your qualifications for being a governess to my sisters.'

Louisa took a seat on the sofa next to Mrs May and the woman briefly patted her hand before folding her arms. Louisa was grateful for the encouragement.

Touching her hot cheeks, Louisa opened her mouth to say, 'Sewing and embroidery are my only talents, my lord.'

Lord Cheswick cleared his throat. 'Do you sew your own clothing, Miss Nemo?'

'I have sewn my wardrobe for the last ten years.'

'And before that?' Mrs May asked.

She felt more blood rush to her face and internally cursed her fair complexion. 'No. There was no need to make my own clothes when my father was alive.'

'I knew she was an orphan!' Lady Frederica shouted from the other side of the room.

Lord Cheswick scoffed. 'How?'

'All the heroines in novels are,' his sister answered smugly.

The Marquess turned his attention back to Louisa. 'Do you like to read novels, Miss Nemo?'

Louisa shrugged and ducked her head, embarrassed by his scrutiny and afraid that the Stringhams would no

longer like her when they knew how ignorant she was. 'I have never had the opportunity. My aunt is not a great reader, and the only books at the hall are of a scientific or mathematical nature.'

Lord Cheswick's lips twitched. 'Our first clue to your true identity.'

Startled, Louisa jumped in her seat. 'What do you mean?'

'You said that you lived in a hall, which means that you grew up in an aristocratic household,' he said, tapping his fingers on his knees. 'There are probably only five or six such homes within a day's journey of Hampford. I will send a groom to each one with a description of you.'

Louisa's hands flew to her face. 'Oh, no, please! I do not wish to go back to my aunt.'

'I bet her aunt is wicked,' Lady Helen added from across the room, stabbing her needle through the counterpoint.

Louisa swallowed in surprise and coughed. 'How— how do you know that?'

'Why else would you run away from home?' Lady Frederica said, glancing up from her stitching. 'Your aunt is clearly a horrid woman who has made your life a misery. Why else would your shift be little more than strings? Mrs May was shocked by the state of it.'

As she slid down in her chair, Louisa's thoughts were muddied. She was embarrassed that they'd seen and spoken of her poor clothing. Perhaps even more embarrassed that she had not received a proper education or upbringing underneath her aunt. She was unfit to join fine society.

'Stick to your sewing and stop making up stories

about Miss Nemo,' Lord Cheswick said, holding up a hand. 'This is supposed to be a proper interview. We need real information, not guesses.'

Ignoring him, Lady Helen set down her embroidery on the table. 'And your aunt must be jealous of your beauty, or she would have had someone teach your maid how to arrange your hair attractively.'

Self-consciously, Louisa touched her hair. The wild red curls had already escaped her attempt at a chignon. She remembered her aunt's words: *'You are an ill-favoured, extremely freckled young woman.'* Did Lord Cheswick think she was ugly? Such a handsome man with a title had probably met all the most beautiful London debutantes. Stealing a glance at him, she saw that he watched her closely.

Lady Becca plonked her feet on the table in front of her. 'Don't listen to them, Miss Nemo. I think your hair is positively beautiful. I've never seen a shade like it before. It's like the pelt of a fox.'

Louisa felt herself flush as red as a fox at the young girl's compliment. She stole another glance and saw that Lord Cheswick's tawny eyes were still on her.

'It is,' Lady Helen said, brandishing a needle like a sword at her little sister. 'Which is why with a little bit of skill it could be perfect.'

'Now, now…' Lord Cheswick said, holding up both hands. 'Either be quiet during the interview or leave the room.'

Lady Frederica stuck her tongue out at her brother but didn't say anything.

Mrs May cleared her throat. 'Now, where were we, my lord?'

Lord Cheswick cleared his throat. 'Miss Nemo, did you attend school or have a governess?'

Louisa flushed under their open scrutiny and her palms felt sweaty. 'I had a governess until I was ten, but when my father died she was dismissed.'

Mrs May wore a sympathetic look and shook her head, but Lord Cheswick's expression was unreadable as he asked, 'Then your formal education ended at the age of ten?'

Louisa brought a hand to her forehead, feeling rather faint. 'Yes, my lord. I had already learned to read, but I do not play any musical instruments. Our housekeeper taught me arithmetic, sewing, embroidery, and how to run a household. But I have never been taught to speak French or Italian, nor deportment or how to dance. I am afraid that I am a poor candidate to be anyone's governess.'

She took a hitching breath, shame covering her like a shawl. She could no longer meet the handsome man's gaze. She was not worthy of being his little sisters' friend let alone their governess. They would probably despise her now for her ignorance, just like Aunt Rockingham.

Louisa felt a slender hand on her shoulder and glanced up to see Lady Helen. 'Don't worry, Miss Nemo. I cannot play a musical instrument either. The only one of my sisters who does is Frederica. The rest of us are abysmal at the pianoforte, and Papa says that our harp-playing sounds like a rhinoceros in mating season.'

'I thought that was your attempts at the violin?' Lady Becca said, cupping her hands as she called out from the opposite side of the room.

Lady Helen scowled at her little sister. 'You're wrong. He compared my violin music to a hissing hyena.'

Louisa's heart lifted a little and Lord Cheswick laughed—a low, attractive sound.

'And your flute-playing to a dying dodo bird.'

Louisa felt her lips twitch upwards almost into a smile as the other four in the room broke out into raucous laughter. Even Mrs May chortled. They did not seem to think less of her for not being an accomplished musician.

'You know more than I do, Miss Nemo,' Lady Becca said, walking closer to them and fidgeting with her hands. 'I cannot read very well. The words won't stay still. They dance about on the page.'

Her brother grunted, sitting up in his chair. 'Don't let Becca disparage herself. She's one of the cleverest people I know. Never forgets a thing you tell her.'

Louisa saw his little sister turn pink with pleasure from the compliment. She couldn't help but be impressed that Lord Cheswick had stood up for his sister, despite her educational shortcomings. Aunt Rockingham would never have done the same for her.

'And we can teach you deportment and how to dance,' Lady Frederica said, coming over to join the conversation. 'If there's one thing all Stringhams do well, it's dancing.'

'Wick, it would be such fun to be the teacher instead of the student,' Lady Becca suggested shyly.

Uncertain, Louisa swallowed. Her stomach felt tense. Could she accept so much from them? Should she? Would Lord Cheswick let her?

The handsome young Marquess was already in her thoughts more than was proper. She'd stayed up late the night before, wondering how his lips would feel against hers. But she was being unpardonably foolish. Lord Cheswick was wealthy, educated, handsome and titled.

The bride he selected would be both beautiful and accomplished. And Louisa was neither. She didn't even know how to dance. Yet, stitch by stich, he seemed to have woven his way into her mind, no matter how hard she tried to not think about him. Or how badly she longed to earn his approbation.

Louisa's gaze flickered from the young girl to her elder brother. She could tell from his tender expression that he would not refuse her anything. Her opinion of him rose even higher, if that were possible.

'Very well, Becca, my heart,' he said. 'You can teach Miss Nemo to dance and she can stay until we find her proper family.'

Lady Helen's eyes widened. 'But not the wicked aunt?'

Lord Cheswick sighed, noddingly slowly. 'Not the wicked aunt.'

Exhaling, Louisa couldn't hide her relief. The Stringhams were not going to send her back to Aunt Rockingham.

## Chapter Eight

Lord Cheswick made Cousin Barnabas and his younger brothers seem even more ordinary. His tall, muscular frame radiated strength and virility. He was patient and kind. Especially with his three sisters, who seemed to live to plague him. Louisa couldn't imagine teasing any of her aunt's sons. Nor speaking as freely as the Stringham sisters did. It would seem that in their home—*castle!*—the daughters were treated the same way as the sons.

She wished that she had grown up with such a large and loving family.

She wished that she had known Wick sooner.

Lady Frederica had lent her another gown, and a maid helped her into it and added several pins. Louisa desperately needed new clothing, which would require money from her inheritance. She needed to find her Uncle Laybourne and ask for his help, but she feared that he would send her back to Aunt Rockingham's care. He had seemed stern and cold at her father's funeral, but perhaps he'd only been mourning as she had.

Lady Helen and Lady Becca were waiting for her out-

side the door. They each took one of her hands and led her down the stairs to the breakfast room, where it seemed the family dined informally. They passed the butler.

'Harper,' Lady Becca said, 'this is our new friend.'

The butler bowed deeply to Louisa. 'My lady.'

Louisa curtsied in return, and jumped when Lady Helen squealed.

'Miss Nemo is a real lady, Becca. I told you. Now all we have to do is discover your first name.'

Louisa swallowed; her throat felt painfully dry. 'Lady Helen, I don't mean to be taciturn…'

'Do you admit that you are a lady?'

Louisa felt her face go red. She had never been a good liar. 'I never said I wasn't a lady.'

Lady Helen shook her head, smiling widely. 'I meant do you bear the title *Lady* because you are the daughter of a peer? Or do you deny it?'

She swallowed again, and then opened her mouth. 'Yes, I am Lady Lou—' She broke off in confusion. She had nearly given them her entire name.

Nudging her sister with her elbow, Lady Helen grinned in apparent victory. 'Becca, her name starts with *Lou*.'

Lady Becca squeezed Louisa's hand tightly. 'Let me see… There's Louella, Lucetta, Lucille, Lucretia, Louise, Louisa… It's got to be one of those.'

Louisa had involuntarily gasped when the young girl said her name.

Lady Becca beamed up at her. 'I guessed it! You're Lady Louisa.'

There was no point in trying to lie. Louisa's face was hot and no doubt she looked extremely guilty.

'Lady Louisa is much better than Miss Nemo,' Lady Helen said, grabbing both Louisa's and Becca's free

hands so they made a circle. 'But now that you are our social equal, and not our governess, we really must insist that you simply call us by our names. Saying "Lady" all the time is a trifle tedious and extremely pretentious.'

'Yes,' Becca agreed, wrinkling her nose at her sister. 'Although you love it when people you dislike have to call you Lady Helen.'

Her sister gave a dignified sniff and chose to ignore her.

Harper opened the door to the breakfast room and Louisa saw that Mrs May and Frederica were already waiting there for dinner. But no handsome marquess who plagued her thoughts more than was seemly.

Becca and Helen tugged her into the room.

'Frederica!' Becca called out loudly. 'Helen and I have solved the mystery.'

Their elder sister snorted and placed a hand on her hip. 'Of why Wick is late for dinner?'

'No, silly,' Helen replied. 'The mystery of Miss N—'

'Oh, there you are Wick!' Becca said in her exuberant voice. 'Where have you been all afternoon?'

The Marquess walked into the room dressed in fine evening clothes, but with his riding coat over the top of them, unbuttoned. He still looked handsome, but Louisa supposed he would be attractive even in a farmer's smock.

'I have been checking on the tenants, of course, and I've found someone who needs a home.'

Lord Cheswick reached into his coat pocket and gently lifted out a black kitten by its neck. He cradled it in his strong hands. She wondered what it would like to be held by such strong, gentle hands.

He placed the small creature into the eager arms of

his youngest sister and Becca brought the small animal against her face and kissed it several times. 'I love him so much!'

Helen narrowed her gaze at her brother, her arms crossed. 'It's a girl, Becca. And why am I not surprised that you gave *her* the kitten, Wick? She's always been your favourite.'

Louisa felt a pang of sympathy for Helen. She had never been the favourite in her home either. Aunt Rockingham only cared for her sons and never brought gifts for her.

'You're right,' Lord Cheswick said, reaching into his opposite coat pocket. 'Alas, Leech only had two other kittens to spare.'

He pulled out two more kittens. One was striped grey and white, and the other an orange ball of fur. Helen was practically climbing his arm to grab the orange kitten from him.

Louisa had misjudged him. Lord Cheswick was not treating his sisters differently.

'Oh, Wick, he's absolutely precious,' Frederica cooed as she took the grey-striped kitten. 'Forget all the nasty things I have ever said about you.'

The Marquess raised his eyebrows as he shrugged himself out of his riding coat and tossed it carelessly on a chair. 'That may take a while. There's been so many.'

His sisters laughed merrily as they cradled and stroked their new kittens. The Marquess watched them fondly and Louisa's chest filled with warmth. He was clearly a loving brother and a thoughtful man.

Mrs May sighed from behind them. 'I suppose you couldn't have waited until after dinner, my lord? Are we to eat with the kittens at the table?'

Lord Cheswick's lips twitched and then he threw back his head and laughed. 'Oh, dear, Mrs May. I didn't intend to bring them now, but one of them behaved badly in my dressing room and Older said that he would resign on the spot if I didn't get rid of them. And I'm afraid that a more superior valet would be hard to find.'

The Marquess had a wonderful laugh, Louisa thought. It made the hairs rise on her nape and arms.

The housekeeper sighed again, appearing resigned. Except Louisa could see that her eyes were smiling. Mrs May was obviously fond of the Stringham family, and Louisa couldn't help but be fond of them too. Even though she knew her time with them was coming to an end.

The Marquess's brown eyes shifted to her and Louisa flushed—again—underneath his scrutiny. She was already breathing hard, but when his eyes were on her she practically panted for air.

*So embarrassing.*

'Miss Nemo, are you all right?'

Louisa took a deep breath, trying to steady her voice. She wasn't all right. Certainly not when he was near. Her heart beat wildly and her hands felt hot and clammy. And there was a strange sort of pleasant burning in her stomach and a tenderness in her breasts. Sensations that she had never experienced before.

'She's not Miss Nemo any more, Wick,' Becca said, not bothering to look up from her kitten. 'She's Lady Louisa.'

He blinked at Louisa twice, before taking a step towards her. '*You're* Lady Louisa Bracken, daughter of the late Earl of Rockingham of Greystone Hall?'

His tone held scorn and her heart plummeted in her chest. Her title and true name meant something to him.

There was no point in denying the truth. Eventually she would have had to tell the Marquess and his sisters her true name anyway, if they were to help her find her Uncle Laybourne and the trustees named in her father's will. She would need those trustees to access her inheritance and have her London season. Besides, she trusted them. Even Lord Cheswick, who had eyed her with suspicion once he'd realised that she wasn't a governess. And made her feel hot and breathless and full of an unknown want…

'I am… How—how did you know my name?'

His lips turned into a sneer. 'I was unfortunately acquainted with Lord Barnabas Bracken before he was sent down from Oxford because of his gambling debts.'

Louisa touched her hot cheeks. It did not sound as if Wick was fond of her cousin. Not that she liked him either. He was a toad.

Becca cleared her throat. 'The villain enters the scene and the plot thickens!'

'Yes!' Helen's eyes grew wide. 'Is he trying to marry you against your will so that he can steal your fortune?'

'I daresay you're an heiress?' added Frederica.

Louisa swayed on her feet and held a hand against her stomach. She couldn't quite believe that the Stringham sisters had guessed her true circumstances. It was so unlikely. Almost unbelievable.

'How many times do I have to tell you?' Lord Cheswick said dismissively. 'She isn't the heroine in a gothic novel and you should call her Lady Louisa.'

Frederica tickled her kitten under his chin. 'And you should read more of them and then you'd know that a del-

icately nurtured young lady only flees her family home when she is being forced into a distasteful marriage. And why else would her evil aunt try to make her marry her bad cousin unless she was an heiress?'

'It's entirely obvious,' Helen said, lifting her chin defiantly.

Huffing, Lord Cheswick turned his eyes from his sisters to her. *'Is* it true?'

Louisa felt so mortified that she would have been happily swallowed up by floor. She'd hoped that when she told him the truth of her identity the Marquess would show her the same kindness he demonstrated with his sisters.

'It is.'

'I don't blame you for not wanting to marry Lord Barnabas,' he said, looking at her closely, his voice softening. 'He's a rum touch. But why did you not appeal to your other relatives? Surely there is someone in your family who would help you?'

She wasn't precisely sure what a 'rum touch' was, but by the tone of his voice Louisa was certain that her cousin was one. She rubbed at her forehead. 'I was trying to seek refuge with my uncle, the Canon of Sherborne, when you found me on the road and mistook me for your governess.'

'Then why the secrecy with your name? And why did you not wish to continue to find him this morning? I told you I would have provided you with a carriage and a proper escort.'

Louisa lowered her head, unable to meet his disapproving eyes. 'I am so sorry, my lord,' she whispered, her hands fidgeting against her gown. 'I should have left. Only, I feared being returned to my Aunt and Uncle

Rockingham. The servants at Greystone Hall helped me escape and I don't wish for them to get into trouble.'

'Are Lord and Lady Rockingham your guardians?' he asked.

Still gazing down, she shook her head. 'Not any more. I am turned one-and-twenty. They have never allowed me a season. And in the nearly eleven years they have been my guardians they have only permitted me to leave the estate to attend church. I have so longed for a season, and for an opportunity to be presented to the Queen.'

## Chapter Nine

When Lord Barnabas had bragged in his cups about marrying his wealthy and beautiful cousin who was an heiress, Wick had dismissed it as the idle boasting of a gambler whose pockets were always to let. If this Lady Louisa was so fetching, why hadn't she been brought to court and been presented at a come-out ball? Why had she not attended *ton* parties? He'd thought the poor woman must be an antidote or a halfwit.

The fact that she was neither made him almost believe his sister's wild theories about villains. Whatever the case, he couldn't hide nor harbour a runaway. Particularly one of such high birth. It would not look good to the *ton*. And if he wasn't careful he would be forced into marrying her. The last thing he wanted to do.

She would have to go to her uncle's house in the morning.

There was no other option.

Otherwise, by law, she'd have to be returned to her former guardians. Something he could not do after Lady Louisa had worked so hard to escape them. He would have to appeal to her maternal uncle, and hopefully he

would help her. It was her uncle's responsibility and not his. Wick had enough on his plate, trying to find a new governess for his wayward sisters. The sooner the better.

'Mrs May and I will escort you to your uncle's home first thing in the morning. There you can explain the situation to him and request his assistance in locating your trustees and arranging a proper come-out and season for you.'

She glanced up at him, her countenance trusting. It touched something in his heart. 'Thank you, my lord.'

'Girls, take the kittens to the kitchen and wash your hands before you return for dinner,' he said, moving to the door and opening it.

They filed out, oldest to youngest.

'Don't say anything interesting without us,' Becca reminded them as she left.

One side of Wick's mouth quirked up into a half-smile. 'I promise we won't.'

His sisters returned shortly after, with clean hands and large appetites. Wick was relieved that they were too busy eating to squabble with each other or him. Conversation passed by amicably, with the help of Mrs May and Lady Louisa. He couldn't help but be impressed by the young lady's excellent manners and thoughtful listening.

Frederica stood up first, tossing her napkin onto her dessert plate. 'It's time for dancing lessons!'

Wick balled up his napkin in his hands. 'I don't have time tonight.'

'Please, Wick,' Becca said, scrunching up her nose at him. 'Helen is a horrible partner. Poor Louisa won't know how to be properly led in the dance.'

This was true. He could only be grateful that Lady

Louisa's personality was neither stubborn nor wilful like his little sisters'.

'I'm a better lead than you,' Helen said.

Becca lifted her chin and sniffed. 'Hardly.'

'Besides, Wick,' Frederica said, 'if she is leaving first thing in the morning we won't have another opportunity to be her teachers.'

'I always enjoy watching a good dance,' Mrs May said, with a twinkle in her smile underneath her cap. 'And it is such good practice for your sisters. As well as keeping them out of mischief.'

*The housekeeper is in league with my sisters!*

Yet the prospect of dancing with Lady Louisa was not as repugnant to him as it should have been. He liked talking with her, and perhaps holding her in his arms for an hour would cure him of his unwanted desire for her.

He held up his forefinger. 'One hour. I will give you one hour of my time.'

Becca grabbed his arm. 'He said yes!'

Helen took his other arm and his sisters frogmarched him to the blue saloon, Frederica in the lead. She took her spot at the pianoforte. Mrs May sat next to her, ready to turn the pages. Helen partnered Becca, leaving Wick standing by Lady Louisa. He held out his hand to her and she placed her shaking fingers in his. Her eyes were on his cravat, as if she didn't dare look up into his eyes. He hoped that he had not been too terse with her. She was a very comely young woman, and in other circumstances he might have liked her very much, but she was just another responsibility that he did not want, foisted upon him.

Helen folded her arms. Despite being the sister who looked the least like their mother, she had all the same

mannerisms. 'The first dance we'll teach you is the Roger de Coverley. It's a very popular country dance. Now, you and Wick will stand across from each other. Becca and I will be the other couple.'

Wick was only half listening to Helen's instructions on how the bottom man and the top lady should advance, link arms, and then weave their way to the end of the group before joining hands and promenading up. He was focused on her shallow breathing and the way it made her chest rise and fall quickly. How her surprisingly dark eyelashes brushed against her freckle-kissed cheeks.

He watched her concentrate on following each of Helen's instructions as she held tightly to his hand and then his arm. Her slender fingers shook. With excitement? Embarrassment? Attraction? Or all of them together?

His eyes kept darting to her lips and the freckle just above them that he longed to kiss. But he wouldn't.

'Very good,' Helen said, dropping Becca's hands. 'Frederica, play us some music and we'll try it again.'

Frederica's nimble fingers began to play a tune. Wick worried that it would be too fast for Lady Louisa's first lesson, but she took his hand. When they released their clasp she turned the wrong way and nearly ran into Becca. His littlest sister burst into giggles, but instead of stopping they kept dancing until Lady Louisa made the figure correctly and they promenaded together at the end.

Becca and Helen clapped their hands.

Wick found that he was reluctant to release his hold on her hand. It felt as if it fitted perfectly inside his own. The weight. The size. The shape. He rubbed his thumb over her knuckles, wishing that they weren't both wearing gloves. That he could feel her skin against his.

Becca placed both of her hands on her hips. 'Wick, you're supposed to let go of her hand.'

Helen sniffed in a superior manner. 'Maybe you need dancing lessons as much as Lady Louisa.'

Dropping her hand, he couldn't help but smile down at her as he clapped. 'It appears that I do.'

'Good,' Frederica said from the pianoforte. 'Because we still need to teach Lady Louisa the waltz. Every fashionable ball has at least one.'

Wick could only be thankful that he managed to miss most 'fashionable balls', which were little better than marriage markets for the wealthy and titled. Not that he didn't like pretty girls—he most certainly did. But matchmaking mamas were to be avoided at all costs. He wasn't interested in marriage, and he knew that his mother was the most determined matchmaker of the lot. She'd already caught a duke for her eldest daughter, and had all but arranged a marriage for Frederica to the heir to another dukedom. He could only be grateful that at present she was on another continent.

Becca cleared her throat. 'Now, you're the one following, so you allow your partner to place his hand on your upper back and you hold his other hand. Like this. Your other hand goes on his shoulder.'

Even though Becca was taller, she was allowing Helen to lead. A rare concession, thought Wick. He used the hand he was holding to pull Lady Louisa closer to him. He let go, but only to place his hand on her narrow waist, holding it just above where it dipped in. He longed to run both hands up and down her back. Instead, he took her other hand and clasped it with his. She tentatively reached out to touch his shoulder. Her fingers were as light as a butterfly perched there. He could barely feel

the weight of them through his coat. But he sensed her touch with all his body.

'A waltz is really quite easy,' Helen said, demonstrating the basic step with Becca. 'You're only making a box with your feet.'

Tightening his hold on Lady Louisa's waist, Wick said, 'I step forward with my left foot and you step back with your right.'

Lady Louisa bit her lower lip and gave a slight nod.

Leading her, he performed the first step with accuracy. 'Now, move your left foot sideways and I'll mirror you with my right.'

'All right…' she whispered.

She was a natural dancer, with grace and elegance.

'Next, slide your right foot next to your left, so that they are parallel but not touching.'

Lady Louisa followed him as if she trusted him instinctively—something that none of his sisters would have done. All four of them insisted on leading.

'Then you'll step forward with your left foot and I'll step back with my right,' Wick said as they continued through the movements. 'Now, move back with your right foot and sideways… That's it! The last step is to move your left foot so that your feet are parallel again.'

Still in his arms, she finally looked him in the eyes as she said, 'It is a box. A perfect little box.'

Wick couldn't help but smile down at her. 'Shall we try again?'

Lady Louisa grinned up at him with her kissable lips with that freckle just above their centre that he was so obsessed with.

'Please.'

He tightened his hold and repeated the box step once.

Then twice. And a third time. As they continued to spin around the room together Wick realised that Frederica had begun to play a waltz and he hadn't even noticed the sound. He'd been so intent on gazing at and dancing with Lady Louisa he'd even forgotten Becca and Helen, who were waltzing beside them, both attempting to lead, which was turning the dance into a wrestling match.

Wick turned his attention back to his beautiful partner. 'Did Lady Rockingham give you a reason for not giving you a presentation or a season in London?'

Lady Louisa's ears turned red again and her neck flushed. 'I am afraid that my aunt considers me a burden. I can do nothing to please her. My mother left her private fortune to me, but until I am twenty-five there is only a yearly allowance given from my trustees to my uncle for my keep. Aunt Rockingham says that it is not enough for my maintenance, nor for the hiring of a governess or dancing master. That is why my clothes are little more than rags and why my aunt refused to take me to London. She says that she could not bear the expense.'

Wick snorted in derision, shaking his head. 'According to your pernicious cousin Barnabas, you're the heiress to over one hundred and fifty thousand pounds. Even if your yearly allowance was only the interest, that would be easily over seven thousand pounds a year. More than enough to dress you like a duchess and employ a dozen governesses, dancing masters, and rent a house for the London season.'

'Truly?'

He couldn't help but pull her a little closer on their next turn. She looked so vulnerable. Her body gently brushed his chest and set his pulse racing.

'Your uncle owns your father's house in London and

I've never seen your aunt miss a season. Lady Rockingham is usually drowning in silks and jewels. She must be keeping all your allowance for her own use.'

Lady Louisa's eyes fell again to his cravat. There was a tell-tale pink in her cheeks. 'She said that I am too ugly to take to London and that I'm lucky that my cousin is willing to marry me.'

Wick stopped dancing, feeling a sort of primal anger run through his veins. What sort of woman would cheat her own niece out of her fortune? And treat her like less than a servant in the meantime?

'Believe me, Lady Louisa,' he said, breathing hard as he pulled her closer to him until their full bodies met together, his hardness to her softness. Her curves perfectly matching his dips. 'You are the most beautiful woman I have ever seen. You will be surrounded by suitors in London—and not just because of your fortune and your title.'

Lady Louisa's eyes were still focused on the folds of his cravat. 'Will you be one of them?'

'You won't need me,' he assured her, stepping back. Touching her was too tempting. 'There are plenty of other eligible young men who will appreciate your charms. But first we must take you to your uncle. There will be less gossip if you are staying with a family member, and he will know who your trustees are and how to reach them. Surely they cannot be aware of how you are being treated by your aunt? No man or woman of conscience would allow it.'

'Will—will you help me?'

He knew better than to give rash promises, but her countenance was so open and trusting that he couldn't help himself. 'I will.'

She gave him a shy smile. 'Lady Frederica said that your parents are in Africa—is this their first visit?'

Wick's jaw tightened. 'Their second. The last time was nearly a decade ago.'

'But your sisters would have been so young then... Still in the nursery.'

He nodded sharply. They had all been too young to be left in his care. 'Despite having a menagerie on Animal Island, my father doesn't believe in domesticating wild beasts. He only purchases animals that have already been taken out of their environment by travelling groups or wealthy peers. His trips to Africa, then and now, are to return the poor creatures to the wild. And my mother goes with him. Mostly because they do not like to be parted, but also because she's hoping to find a new plants or herbs to use in her perfumes. She has her own perfume company and a shop on Bond Street. She blends the new scents herself.'

Lady Louisa gave him another dazzling grin. 'I had no idea a lady could have her own business. How very thrilling!'

Wick tried not to return her smile, but his lips kept quirking upwards of their own volition. 'It is not precisely favourable in the eyes of the *ton*, but Mama comes from a trade background. Our maternal grandfather is one of the wealthiest tradesmen in England. There's not a banker or a broker in London who doesn't know his name. Or owe him money. I daresay we would all be shunned by society if Mama wasn't such good friends with the Prince Regent. She blends a cologne just for him, and usually sends him a bottle every month. Before she went to Africa she delivered Prinny a whole case.'

Lady Louisa fluttered her eyelashes and her green

eyes seemed to sparkle in the candlelight. 'What a marvellous family you have, my lord.'

'That's not the exact word I would use to describe it,' he said ruefully.

'Oh, but *I* would,' she said. 'I would...'

And he believed her. Lady Louisa seemed to fit perfectly into his crazy family. Perhaps a little too perfectly. Dancing with her had proved disastrous. Instead of curing him of his obsession with her, it had only stoked his passion. Talking with her... Touching her... He wanted her more than ever. Wanted her breathless and blushing in his arms. He imagined himself kissing her every freckle, one by one.

'I think we had better call it a night,' Mrs May said with a yawn. 'Lady Louisa and I have a journey in the morning.'

Relieved by the housekeeper's distraction, Wick left Lady Louisa's side and offered his hand to Mrs May to help her to her feet.

'You're such a thoughtful man, my lord.'

He was thinking of Lady Louisa entirely too much.

He could hardly wait to be rid of her tomorrow.

# Chapter Ten

Despite Lord Cheswick's reassuring words the previous night, Louisa felt anxious about seeing her mother's brother and his family. Her stomach roiled uncomfortably as the Marquess's carriage ambled over the country roads. She patted her curls, hoping that her family would approve of her…that her Aunt and Uncle Laybourne would help her gain her fortune and have the debut her mother had always dreamed of for her.

Lady Frederica, Lady Becca and Lady Helen, with a new, smaller snake, had all offered to accompany her. But Mrs May had been firm, telling them that there was not enough room in the carriage and they must stay at home.

Lord Cheswick sat across from her. He looked awfully handsome. He was so tall, and his build so muscular. The whiskers down the side of his cheeks framed his strong jaw and chiselled cheeks, even when he was frowning. She couldn't help but steal several glances at him. His mere presence gave her both strength and resolve.

She wished he could be one of her potential suitors, but he'd been quite adamant whilst they'd been dancing the night before that he would not. Yet he had pulled her

close to him. His body had pressed against hers and everywhere they'd met she had burned with an unknown need. She had longed to touch his skin with her own. His lips with hers.

'Are you quite well?' he asked now.

Louisa could feel a blush growing from her neck into her face. She'd been caught staring at him.

*How embarrassing!*

'Only a little nervous, my lord,' she said, turning her gaze towards Mrs May. 'I can only hope that my uncle's family is as open and caring as your own.'

Mrs May's eyes seemed to dance. She glanced from Louisa to Lord Cheswick and then back again. The housekeeper was clearly aware of Louisa's attraction to the young Marquess. Louisa could only be glad that the kindly older woman could not see her most intimate thoughts.

'Yes,' he agreed. 'But hopefully without reptiles or camel leopards.'

'Snakes are quite useful in the kitchens and in the cellar, my lord,' Mrs May said matter-of-factly. 'We have no problem with mice, thanks to Lady Helen's pets.'

Lord Cheswick gave a shudder that Louisa assumed was revulsion. Despite adoring Helen, Louisa found she was not fond of snakes either.

Straightening her new gown, Louisa was glad that at least she would not be facing her mother's brother in leftover curtain cloth. Mrs May had found her a gown that had once belonged to the Marquess's oldest sister, the Duchess of Glastonbury, and had altered it cleverly to fit Louisa's frame. The housekeeper had apologised that it was several years out of fashion, but to Louisa it was the finest piece of clothing she'd ever possessed.

The town of Sherborne looked as if it belonged in the medieval past. She loved the stone buildings, white-washed cottages, and the impressive abbey with its pointed windows. Louisa had never been to a large town before, and she hadn't realised how noisy they were. People, animals and carriages…all were going about their business. She was enjoying watching them from the window and was a little dismayed when the carriage came to a stop.

Lord Cheswick opened the door and assisted Louisa and Mrs May out. The Canon of Sherborne's house was large, without being ostentatious, but it was small compared to Hampford Castle. When a servant opened the door, the Marquess handed the man his card. The butler blinked, before opening the door wider and ushering them all into a formal parlour. Louisa assumed that future dukes were not left waiting on the doorstep to see if the family was at home or not.

Mrs May took a chair that faced the front windows, crossing her feet and placing her reticule in her lap. Louisa sat opposite her, next to Lord Cheswick. He was not only handsome, he made her feel safe.

The parlour looked very tidy. The fine chairs appeared as if they had never been sat on. The walls were strangely bare, giving the room an austere feel. Louisa felt unaccountably cold and rubbed her arms with her hands.

Suddenly the housekeeper's reticule moved, and Mrs May jumped in her seat. 'Oh, goodness!' she exclaimed.

Louisa watched as Mrs May took a deep breath and opened her small bag.

She shook her head and held it out for them to see. 'Lady Helen must have put a snake in my reticule because I wouldn't let her come.'

Lord Cheswick groaned and touched his head. 'I am so sorry, Mrs May.'

Louisa couldn't help but think that he was quite sweet and very attractive when he was flustered.

Mrs May closed the strings. 'If I were afraid of snakes, my lord, I couldn't work at the castle. Lady Helen is a veritable snake charmer.'

Louisa had to stifle her laughter. The Stringham sisters were irrepressible. She couldn't help but wish she was more like them. They were strong and fearless. They stood up to their brother in a way that she had never been able to stand up to her aunt. Louisa hoped that Uncle Laybourne's wife would be kinder to her than Aunt Rockingham. Mayhap she could even love Louisa, and help fill the void left by her mother's death.

The door opened and Louisa saw a man with brown, grey-streaked hair and a red beard. His frame was tall and slender, verging on gaunt. He wore unrelieved black, except for his stark white collar. His eyes were green, like hers, but that was the only resemblance between them. His wife was on his arm and she also wore black. Louisa wondered if they were in mourning.

Her Aunt Laybourne was nearly two heads shorter than her husband, and her square frame was not flattered by the high-waisted gown. She wore a white frilly cap, under which her brown hair was scraped back into a tight bun, giving her round face a severe look. Not the warm, maternal expression that Louisa had been hoping for.

Lord Cheswick and Mrs May stood and bowed to her aunt and uncle. Louisa could only stare.

Her Uncle Laybourne brought a handkerchief to his nose, sniffing twice. 'When Lady Rockingham came to see us yesterday, Louisa, claiming you had run away, I

was naturally shocked by such disobedient behaviour. I did not think that the daughter of my sister would conduct herself in such a heedless and wanton fashion.'

Louisa felt her eyes fill with tears, and a pain at the back of her throat. She clutched her arms around her middle, hiding her palms. She felt as if she were a child again, standing before Aunt Rockingham and being chided for not being more obedient, for asking too many questions. Desperate to please, but unable to do so.

'Now, see here, sir,' said Lord Cheswick, stepping towards her uncle. They were about the same height, but the Marquess was twice as wide and more intimidating. 'How dare you make assumptions about your niece without even hearing her side of the story?'

Her uncle sniffed again. 'She is in the presence of a notorious young marquess—which is damaging enough without hearing what she has to say.'

*Notorious?* Louisa could well believe it, for he was achingly handsome and painfully sweet. She could not be the only woman in the world to have noticed it.

She watched Lord Cheswick's hands curl into fists. 'I would hardly compromise a young woman in the company of my three sisters. And my housekeeper, Mrs May, has proved to be a most efficient chaperone.'

'A servant cannot become a chaperone overnight,' her Aunt Laybourne said, touching her husband's arm as if for support.

Louisa could have fainted on the spot. So much for making a favourable first impression on her relatives. She rubbed her face and felt her throat constrict. She feared that after all her scheming and the help of the servants she was going to end up back at the hall, underneath Aunt Rockingham's thumb. She would never enjoy a

London season. She would never see the Marquess or his sisters again.

That thought alone brought tears to her eyes.

'Your home, I believe, is Hampford Castle,' said her Uncle Laybourne. 'Where my niece has spent two nights in your company without a suitable chaperone. You must marry her immediately or return Louisa to her guardians, Lord and Lady Rockingham, for appropriate punishment.'

'Oh, no!' Louisa couldn't help but say it. It would be a poor way to repay his kindness to force Lord Cheswick into a relationship not of his choosing. Even if, for her, marrying him would be a dream come true. 'The Stringhams have been nothing but kind to me. The Marquess should not be forced to do anything.'

Lord Cheswick glanced at her and gave her a reassuring look. 'I have no intention of being browbeaten into marrying anyone. Now, sir, you can listen quietly to your niece's side of the story, or I shall hold you down until you do.'

Her uncle sniffed into his handkerchief once more. 'I would have you know I am a canon and the grandson of a marquess.'

'Well, I *am* a marquess, and heir to a dukedom, with close connections with the royal family,' Lord Cheswick said, stepping menacingly towards him. 'And I won't ask you again.'

Aunt Laybourne whimpered from the seat she had taken on the sofa, but she didn't speak. Uncle Laybourne sat beside her and gave Louisa a cold stare.

She swallowed, and clutched at the sides of her new gown. Her head was lowered in deference, but her voice was clear. 'My aunt, Lady Rockingham, is no longer my

guardian. I turned one-and-twenty this week. I asked her for the names of my trustees, for I have never once seen a farthing of my yearly allowance. Aunt Rockingham refused to give me their names and said that my only choice was to marry her son, whenever they could persuade him. My clothes are practically rags. The boots on my feet are second-hand, given by one of the maids. I have no others. I decided to come to you for help. I set off to find you, but I did not know that you were no longer at the Frome vicarage. When I arrived there, I was told that I would find you and your wife here. I began to walk, even though it was getting late. By chance, the Stringhams happened upon me and kindly took me to their home. They even provided this dress that I currently wear. They have been nothing but souls of generosity and goodness. I owe them an irreparable debt.'

'And what do you expect my husband to do?' asked her Aunt Laybourne, her beady eyes narrowing on Louisa.

Louisa slumped a little in her chair. 'I had hoped that my uncle would help me contact my trustees and find someone to present me to the Queen and chaperone me for a season. I wish to find a suitable match and therefore a home of my own.'

Aunt Laybourne's nostrils flared as she turned to address her husband. 'She certainly cannot stay here. We already have nine daughters to find husbands for, without taking in a niece of questionable moral standards with a prodigious number of freckles. She would bring disgrace on our dearest daughters.'

Her freckles again.

Would her blemishes always keep her family from accepting her? Loving her?

'Of course she cannot stay here,' her Uncle Laybourne agreed, clutching his sodden handkerchief. 'And nor do I have time to go to London and see about the legal matter of her inheritance. I know nothing about the trustees named in the late Lord Rockingham's will. Louisa, you would be best served returning to Greystone Hall and begging for your aunt's forgiveness. Perhaps your cousin will refuse to marry you after this escapade—then you'll have no need to vacate the home of your youth. But I can do nothing for you. The scandal of your leaving home is enough to cause damage to my position.'

Louisa opened her mouth and then shut it. The sinking feeling in her stomach was growing with each passing moment. What was she to do now? She could not—*would* not—return to Greystone Hall. Would she have to run away again? Where would she go without any money or friends?

'If you are determined to be derelict in your duties to your niece,' Lord Cheswick said, 'then Mrs May, my sisters and I will take Lady Louisa to London. We won't leave a stone unturned until we find her trustees.'

His words filled the hole in her heart. She stood up to her full height and lifted her chin. Unlike her family, he would not take advantage of her fortune. He would not abandon her. The Stringham sisters didn't expect her to lower herself to earn their approval. Or for her to try and change into someone she was not.

'As you must be already aware,' her uncle said, wiping his running nose with his monogramed handkerchief, 'your servant is hardly an appropriate chaperone.'

Lord Cheswick flexed his arm muscles as he straightened his cuff. It was hardly an appropriate time for her to notice, but he was certainly a powerfully built man.

'But my sister, the Duchess of Glastonbury, is. No one will dare say a word against her chaperonage. Let us take our leave, Lady Louisa… Mrs May.'

Louisa did not have to be told twice. She all but ran for the door to escape her horrible family. Mrs May linked her arm with Louisa's and patted it reassuringly. Louisa felt giddy with relief. Her heart expanded in her chest. Somehow she had been blessed enough to discover true friends at Hampford Castle.

Before she reached the door, Mrs May clutched at her chest theatrically and said, 'Oh, no—is that a snake on the floor?'

From the look of satisfaction on the housekeeper's face, Louisa felt certain that the snake had not been let go from her reticule by accident. Her Aunt Laybourne shrieked even louder than before and her uncle stepped onto a sofa.

'Don't put your feet on the furniture!' Aunt Laybourne yelled at her husband, but then practically jumped on the sofa herself as the snake slithered by her feet. It hissed at her and she shrieked some more.

Lord Cheswick opened the door and they walked out of the room together, leaving her aunt and uncle still standing on top of the furniture.

Mrs May did not laugh until they were all inside the carriage and he had closed the door behind them.

The Marquess grinned at her. 'That was brilliant, Mrs May.'

The housekeeper adjusted her hat on her head. 'Never underestimate a *mere* servant.'

Louisa couldn't help but agree. The servants at Greystone Hall had made her life bearable and helped her escape.

She'd been foolish to think that her Uncle Laybourne

would help her. Perhaps she didn't deserve his help or his time. It had been wicked of her to demand so much from a stranger. Maybe she really was a selfish as Aunt Rockingham had always said.

'I am so sorry to be a burden to you,' she said now, wringing her hands together, wishing to weep in despair. 'If it is easier, you may return me to Greystone Hall.'

## Chapter Eleven

'I have made you a promise, Lady Louisa, and I mean to keep it,' Wick said.

Her head sank even lower, until her chin was touching her chest. 'But I have already been a great inconvenience to you…and you have your three sisters to take care of already. I could not ask you to travel to London. Nor could I presume so much of your sister, Lady Glastonbury, who has never even met me.'

Wick had never before felt such pure anger. His blood twitched in his veins and his pulse was thunderous. He half regretted not punching the sanctimonious clergyman right on his long, skinny and running nose. How anyone could treat Lady Louisa so poorly was beyond his reasoning. This beautiful young woman's actions were nothing but kind and considerate. Her manners were excellent. She hadn't demanded anything much of her relatives; she'd only asked for help in a world that rendered a daughter powerless.

'You needn't worry about Mantheria—she loves to boss people around, and the only person she has now is her three-year-old son. Our sisters have long since stopped obeying her.'

A tear ran down Louisa's cheek and she wiped it away with her gloved hand. 'Your sisters are all very strong young women.'

'It is why they are alive,' he whispered, thinking of poor, frail Elizabeth, who had been unable to fight off scarlet fever. 'Perhaps, in return, you can continue to keep them occupied until I can find them a proper governess.'

'I don't think you can afford to be particular, my lord,' Mrs May said with the same irrepressible twinkle in her eyes. 'You might need to choose an improper one.'

Lady Louisa let out a watery chuckle. 'Proper or improper governess—I should be glad to help you in any way that I am able, my lord.'

Wick clenched his fists tightly until he couldn't feel his fingers. If Lady Louisa's late father hadn't trusted his brother and wife with his daughter's fortune, why in heaven's name had he trusted them with her person? The dead Earl had taken better care of his wife's money than his child... But Wick would change all that.

Several minutes passed before he glanced up to see Lady Louisa's eyes on him. Blushing, she looked down at her hands. He saw that Mrs May had dozed off with her mouth open. The poor woman had probably not got much sleep since his sisters had been sent home. He needed a governess so that the housekeeper wasn't in effect holding two positions at the same time. He knew from personal experience that taking care of his sisters was a thankless and often dangerous task. It was enough to keep a person up late at night and make them rise early the next day.

Lady Louisa peeked up at him again. 'May I ask you about Lady Glastonbury?'

Exhaling, Wick lifted his shoulders and let them fall. 'What would you like to know about my sister?'

She smiled even wider, and he tried not to fix his gaze on the kissable freckle above her lips.

'You have said that she has a little son; does she have any other children?'

'No, only the one—but she's still young. Not even one-and-twenty for another fortnight.'

'She is only twenty and already a duchess?'

Wick shifted in his seat. 'Mantheria was seventeen when she made her debut, and she became engaged to the Duke of Glastonbury after only a few weeks. It was a bit of a whirlwind courtship. They married at the end of the season and left for a wedding trip to France.'

Lady Louisa breathed in and out. 'Oh, I hope that I am as lucky if I get a season of my own.'

'Lucky enough to marry a duke?' he asked sardonically.

She shook her head and a red curl came free of her chignon and fell over her shoulder. He wanted to touch it. Her gorgeous hair looked like liquid flame.

'Oh, no. Or at least not necessarily. It is just that I have always wished to be married and have a family of my own. A home of my own, where I feel I belong. I do not mind if my suitors do not have titles, as long as they have good hearts.'

He had misjudged her aspirations. The sweet young woman wasn't being socially ambitious in her wishes. She merely wanted to have a home of her own and a husband who loved her. Such little things that were often took for granted.

'I suppose most young women wish for marriage and a family.'

A little colour stole into Lady Louisa's cheeks. 'It is what we are taught to look forward to. But ever since my father died I have longed to have a family of my own. Someone to love and someone who loves me.'

That someone would not be him.

Clearing his throat, Wick doggedly continued their conversation. 'I shall send an express message to Mantheria as soon as we get back to the castle. She'll receive it tonight and we can be off first thing in the morning, after I make the arrangements.'

'She won't mind four more guests for the remainder of the season?'

Wick furrowed his brow. 'Four?'

'Myself and your three sisters.'

He could have swallowed his tongue. Of *course* he would have to bring Frederica, Helen and Becca with him. They couldn't be left at the castle without the housekeeper, and Mrs May would have to accompany them to chaperone Louisa until they reached Mantheria's house. Wick couldn't afford even a whiff of indiscretion over the daughter of the late Earl or he'd be forced to marry her.

'Five guests,' he said.

'Will you be staying with your sister as well?'

'Oh, no. I meant Mrs May. I have my own rooms in London,' he explained. 'My parents have a house in Berkley Square, but I prefer the comforts of my bachelor suite.'

The young lady nodded. 'Your sisters mentioned that you have a brother living in London. Do you share accommodations?'

'Matthew's a great gun…but he has his own apartments, closer to the financial district. If anyone can find your trustees and help with your father's will it is he. Matthew makes the pen a dangerous weapon.'

Lady Louisa leaned forward in her seat. 'Do you really think so? Will he be able to help me gain access to my fortune?'

Wick felt himself move towards her, propelled by more than the movements of the carriage…by a need he did not recognise and did not want. 'Yes, Matthew's a legal genius.'

She smiled at him again. 'He is not a naturalist like your father?'

*Like Charles.*

Wick moved back, folding his arms. His heart was sinking in his chest. 'No, he is not,' he said sharply.

Lady Louisa sat back too, her face looking red, as if someone had slapped her. Wick didn't know how to explain that her words had bruised him but that he hadn't meant to snap at her.

She moved in her seat, bumping into Mrs May, who was startled awake.

'We were talking about governesses?' she said, rubbing her sleepy eyes.

'Yes, Mrs May,' he said.

The housekeeper yawned. 'The sooner the better.'

And the sooner he got rid of Lady Louisa the better. He hadn't meant to tell her so much about his family. It reminded him of Charles and thinking about his little brother was like touching a tender bruise that never healed. He only felt raw pain.

# Chapter Twelve

Louisa didn't know what she had said that had made Lord Cheswick so angry, but he'd barely spoken a word to her on their journey home. Perhaps she had been impertinent, asking personal questions about his family. She longed to know him better, but he seemed determined to keep her at arm's length. Her regard for him was clearly not returned. She needed to stop thinking about him so much and focus on her season and the suitors she would meet.

A London season that would take place thanks to *his* kindness.

But ridding her thoughts of him was proving quite impossible.

Mrs May, who was now wide awake, conversed merrily with her about the duties of running a household. Louisa wondered if the housekeeper was quizzing her about her capabilities. Luckily, Mrs Barker had taught her well, and Louisa knew more about managing servants than any feminine accomplishments.

When they arrived at the castle Lord Cheswick helped them out of the carriage and then immediately excused

himself to make arrangements for London. Instead of going with them to the house, he went towards the stables.

Louisa spared him one last glance, before Mrs May took her arm and led her inside. The butler opened the door for them and the three Stringham sisters sprang upon them. Literally.

'You're back!' Becca said, hugging Louisa tightly. 'You came back. I am so very glad.'

'What happened?' Frederica demanded, as she patted Louisa on the shoulder. 'Was your family not at home?'

Louisa pulled at her collar, feeling sweat form on her brow. 'They were at home. However, they are not inclined to help me.'

'What fustian!' Frederica said with a growl.

Louisa felt light-headed, and longed to flee rather than tell them the truth. 'Wick... Lord Cheswick...thought that perhaps your sister Lady Glastonbury might let me stay with her whilst he contacts my trustees.'

'So we're all to go to London,' Mrs May said, clapping her hands. 'Now, you'd best stop pestering poor Lady Louisa and start packing.'

'London!' Becca squealed.

Frederica grabbed Helen's hands and they jumped up and down together. 'What fun we will have there.'

'I can feel my hair turning greyer already,' the housekeeper said drily, which sent the Stringham sisters into hysterical laughter.

Sobering after a few moments, Helen cleared her throat and gave Mrs May a sharp look. 'Where is my new snake?'

Mrs May blinked; pretending to be surprised. 'I do not know what you mean, Lady Helen. What snake would that be?'

Louisa had to bite down on her lower lip to keep in her laugh. The housekeeper was not going to let her charge know that her prank had been successful. Nor of her own exploits with the reptile.

The older woman breathed in deeply. 'No more dallying. It's time for you all to go to your rooms and get ready for our trip to London. I'll send up the maids.'

Louisa smiled. Mrs May was more than a match for the young ladies in her charge. She doubted that she could have handled them half so well. Whoever they found for a governess would need a sturdy constitution and a well of patience.

After dinner that night, Frederica declared that they were going to practise curtsying. Louisa was grateful for the help—if a little nervous. She didn't want to embarrass herself or Lord Cheswick in front of his sister the Duchess of Glastonbury the next day. She longed to earn the young woman's good opinion, and it would be entirely lovely to have a friend her own age.

Frederica cleared her throat. 'Place one foot slightly behind the other and then open your hands, bow your head, and slightly bend your knees.'

Helen curtsied to her brother. 'Like this, Louisa.'

'*Lady* Louisa,' Lord Cheswick reminded his sister.

'Oh, I have told your sisters that their calling me just Louisa is fine,' she said, her cheeks warm. 'My lord.'

'*Just Louisa* it is,' Becca said with a giggle. 'You can drop Wick's title as well. If you keep calling in "my lord" he will get terribly toplofty.'

Louisa's face felt as if it was on fire when she turned to look at the Marquess. 'I couldn't...'

'Please,' he said in a low, attractive voice. 'My sisters will tease me abominably if you do not.'

'That's true,' Helen chimed in.

'Louisa, if your rank is beneath theirs, you lower your eyes when you curtsy,' Frederica explained. 'But if it is the same, or higher, you don't have to. *We* only lower our eyes for royalty.'

'Now you try,' Becca said.

Louisa stood in front of Wick—it felt so intimate even to think of him by that name. He bowed to her, one hand on his waist, in a graceful bend. His brown eyes never left hers. Taking a quick breath, Louisa placed one foot behind the other and sank into a deep curtsy. She was too shy to keep eye contact with him when he was smiling at her.

'Too low,' Helen said, shaking her head.

'He's not royal, Louisa,' Frederica said, wagging her finger at her. 'Don't give him any self-aggrandising ideas. You only need to do a slight bend of your knees.'

Her face even redder, Louisa stood up. Her pulse was racing and her heart beating loudly in her chest. Loud enough that she was sure that the Stringhams could hear it.

'Try again?' Becca suggested.

Helen touched the bottom of Louisa's chin. 'And keep your chin up. He's only a *courtesy* marquess. Not even the real thing.'

Wick barked out a laugh and gave Louisa another perfect bow. Biting her lower lip, Louisa kept her eyes and chin up and made a shaky bounce with her knees, barely dipping. Her body felt stiff and unnatural. Aunt Rockingham had been right: Louisa was terribly awkward.

Frederica clicked her tongue and folded her arms

across her chest. 'Not bad, but not good… Louisa, you need to try again.'

'Why don't you three go and play a game of cards over at the table near Mrs May?' Wick suggested, clearing his throat. 'I think having three demanding tutors is rather overwhelming *Just Louisa*.'

Louisa's lips twitched upwards when he said her name. 'Just Louisa' almost felt like an endearment. But that was ridiculous. He'd made his lack of interest in her plain.

'Her face is very red,' Becca remarked with painful honesty.

Louisa touched both of her cheeks with her gloved hands. They did feel hot—but then so did the rest of her. Oh, how she wished she were a polished and accomplished young lady.

'All right, Wick. I suppose we can play some *Speculation*,' Helen said, the last word dripping with innuendo.

All the Stringhams laughed—even Wick. The three sisters moved to the round table on the other side of the room and sat down. Mrs May brought them a pack of cards but did not join their game.

Wick grinned at Louisa and her heart jumped inside her chest. Her pulse felt erratic, and even the blood in her veins seemed to heat under his scrutiny.

'There's no need to be nervous,' he said, with a smile that melted away what was left of her sense. 'I don't bite…despite what my sisters say.'

But Louisa had already been bitten. This young, handsome, loving, kind and perfectly wonderful marquess had quite captured her heart. But Aunt Rockingham had been right. Such a man would not be interested in her romantically. Not even her fortune would tempt him.

Her eyes fell to her borrowed slippers. 'I don't want to disgrace you or myself in public.'

He shook his head, giving her the same sweet, tender look he gave his little sisters. 'You couldn't. You're every inch a lady.'

Louisa released a shuddering breath, daring to move her gaze from her feet to his boots. 'I've been dreaming of having a London season since I was a little girl. My mother died when I was seven years old, and my strongest memory of her is the story she told me of her presentation to the Queen.'

'I take it the event was memorable?'

She managed a small smile as she touched the back of her neck. 'Queen Charlotte had a strong reaction to my mother's perfume…it caused her to sneeze. And, according to my mother, her second sneeze was so strong that it blew off one of the feathers in Mama's hair. The Lord Chamberlain had to fetch it for her. Mama said that she was so embarrassed, but Queen Charlotte smiled at her and said, *"Well, I shan't forget you."* And she didn't. When Mama married Papa she was presented again, as the Countess of Rockingham. Queen Charlotte gave her another rare smile and told Papa that they were old acquaintances. When I was little, my mother would put a feather in my hair and we would pretend that I was being introduced to the Queen.'

'I am afraid that Queen Charlotte is not quite as fond of our family,' Wick said with a smirk. 'She and the King did not get on very well with their eldest son and heir, the Prince Regent, even before King George III went mad. And, like I told you, my mama is a great friend of the Regent's…despite their different views on almost every political subject.'

Louisa couldn't help but meet his gaze, leaning closer to him. 'Really?'

He took a few steps towards her, closing the distance between them. 'I can tell you from first-hand experience that I have never met a more personable man than the Prince Regent—nor a more juvenile one. But he's an odd mixture of parts and will probably make a terrible king.'

Louisa gasped at his honesty and covered her mouth with one shaking hand. He was standing close enough that she could smell him: a musky mixture of vanilla and vetiver. His nearness filled all her senses.

Wick laughed and rendered her breathless by gently tucking a curl behind Louisa's ear. 'I wouldn't say so to my mother, of course.'

He had touched her!

Gloved... But still, he had *touched* her.

'Never,' she whispered.

He stepped back and bowed to her again.

Without thinking, Louisa curtsied in return.

Wick took her hand and pressed a soft kiss to the back of her glove. She could have happily died on the spot.

'Perfect,' he said. 'All you needed was a little distraction to settle your nerves. Now you'll be the most elegant lady at all the *ton* parties.'

Her chest swelled with pride. She had done it. The gawky girl without a proper governess had managed a curtsy worthy of a lady. If only Aunt Rockingham could see her now. But she would still probably find something about Louisa to criticise.

Glancing over her shoulder, she asked, 'Should we join your sisters at cards?'

'Oh, please, no. They are not currently arguing, and I would hate to interrupt a perfectly harmonious game.'

Louisa couldn't help but giggle. She was relieved that he wanted to stay with her. She doubted that she would ever tire of his conversation or company.

Wick gestured with his hand to the sofa nearest the fire. 'Shall we sit? We can talk…or I can fetch a couple of books.'

'I should l-like to talk,' she managed to say, before sitting down. She knew it was foolish, but she wanted to get to know him better.

He sat down beside her, not quite touching her leg, but close enough for her to enjoy his masculine scent again. Louisa's breathing was irregular and her face felt hot again. She needed to focus on something else— anything else but him.

Leaning down, she pulled the needle out of the inside of her hem. 'Would you mind if I finished embroidering these handkerchiefs while we converse?'

'Not at all,' he said, grinning at her. 'Do you always keep a needle in the hem of your gown?'

Louisa threaded the needle and pulled the first stitch through. The steady tension of the thread helped calm her racing pulse, but her hands were still shaking from his nearness.

'I was always mending at Greystone Hall…it seemed wise to have my favourite needle handy.'

'To make a plain cloth beautiful or to mend something that is torn is truly a wonderful gift. Few people have the ability to repair what is wrong in the world.'

She kept her head lowered, unable to look him in the face. 'You give my skill too much credit.'

'Or perhaps you give yourself too little,' he said, bumping his knee with hers.

It felt warm and hard. She wished he would rest his knee against hers.

'Besides, we are all more than the measure of our talents. How we treat others… Who we are kind to… How we fulfil our responsibilities to those who depend upon us… My parents taught me that those are truly the things that must be measured.'

'You are clearly not a seamstress,' Louisa said, glancing up at him with a half-smile. 'For everything must be measured precisely if a garment is to fit properly.'

Wick laughed. It was a deep but soft sound. It made her heartbeat quicken and the blood pump through her body. She wished again for the impossible…

Focusing on her sewing, Louisa pulled another stitch through. 'But I believe you are right,' she said. 'What is truly important about a person's soul cannot be measured… But I have never heard of a gentleman being introduced with a list of his accomplishments. Only ladies.'

Interlocking his fingers, he stretched out his arms. 'It's because our accomplishments aren't quite as impressive or presentable as those of the fairer sex.'

Louisa toyed with her needle between two fingers. 'Nonsense. I daresay that your talents could take up a whole page.'

'At least my good intentions.'

Louisa chuckled, and he grinned back at her. His face was close enough that if she leaned forward a little her lips would brush his. Blushing, she realised that she wasn't the only one looking at lips. Wick's eyes were lowered and he was gazing at her mouth as if there was nothing else in the room.

How badly she wanted him to kiss her! It would be even more wonderful in reality than it was in her dreams.

But he could hardly do so with his three little sisters and Mrs May in the room. Even though the girls were now yelling at each other on the other side. Their harmonious card game had not lasted long.

Shakily, she got to her feet, clutching her embroidery. 'I think I shall retire to bed. It has been a long day and I know we make an early start in the morning.'

Wick stood up and bowed to her. 'Of course. Sleep well.'

Louisa took only one step away from him, but it already felt too far. She bade goodnight to Mrs May and the Stringham sisters and made her way up the candlelit staircase to her room.

Alone.

It reminded her that she wasn't truly a part of their family. She was only a temporary guest.

## Chapter Thirteen

Wick rode beside the carriage on their way to London the next morning, after ensuring that his little sisters had not brought with them any reptiles or vermin. He had handed all the extra pets to Harper before they'd departed—Helen had another 'new' snake and Becca a mouse—and he even had the forethought to check their trunks. Happily, there were no stowaways there.

He had let them bring their kittens, because Frederica had told him that the dear creatures would be full-grown cats by the time they returned to the castle. Wick sincerely hoped that he wouldn't have charge of his three little sisters and their three kittens in London for *that* long. He planned to conclude Louisa's business in less than a week and interview governesses from a respectable agency.

They stopped at an inn for a midday meal, and then continued the long drive to London. Both Wick's backside and his temper were in need of a rest by the time they reached his sister's townhouse in Mayfair. Servants streamed out through the front doors to meet the carriage,

followed by his sister Mantheria and his nephew Andrew. His brother-in-law was strangely absent.

The three-year-old squirmed out of his mother's arms and ran down the stairs towards his uncle and aunts. Wick and all three of his sisters had their arms outstretched to the little boy with wild black curls. All competing for his favour, begging him to come to them first.

Andrew launched himself at his uncle. Wick grabbed him by the waist and swung him round. He couldn't miss his words.

'I want an ice!'

His bribery was working well.

'And Uncle Wick will take you to Gunter's to get one.'

His adorable nephew reached out his chubby little arms to Frederica and Wick reluctantly relinquished him. Andrew was his favourite member of the family. One he could love and spoil without having any responsibility over his health and happiness.

Andrew squeezed Helen and Becca, before hugging Louisa's legs. Then his little head tipped up and his blue eyes became wide circles. He let go of Louisa and pointed up at her. 'Who is she?'

Louisa touched the very noticeable red curls that had escaped from her bonnet and turned pink as she smiled. It wasn't an embarrassed blush, he thought, but rather a pleased one. He noticed that she often blushed—no doubt it was caused by her fair skin. But he had begun to recognise the different emotions behind her blushing. If her ears and neck were red, Louisa felt embarrassed. If her cheeks were pink, she was happy. And if her entire countenance was flushed, she was trying hard not to cry.

Life, it would seem, had not been kind to her since

her parents' deaths. It made his blood boil just thinking of the Rockinghams.

Becca knelt down next to their nephew. 'This is our new friend Louisa.'

Andrew pointed at Louisa. 'Loo-ee-*zah*!'

Becca clapped and hugged her nephew. 'That's right. You clever boy.'

Mantheria hugged all her sisters and Wick, before picking up her son and placing him on her hip. She bowed her head to Louisa. 'It's a pleasure to make your acquaintance, Lady Louisa.'

She gave Mantheria a shaky curtsy. Not at all like the graceful one she'd given Wick the night before. 'Thank you for letting me stay, Lady Glastonbury. I hope that it is not too great an imposition.'

'It is no imposition at all, and please call me Mantheria,' she said, waving her hand towards the house. 'Come inside, everyone. I've had my housekeeper prepare rooms for all of you—including you, Mrs May. I've chosen my very best…although Wick's letter said nothing about kittens.'

Wick ignored this sally, grateful that his sister was being so welcoming to Louisa.

Andrew reached out his hands towards Becca. 'Kitty!'

Becca grinned and handed over the black kitten to her nephew. Andrew cradled it like a baby. Helen handed Wick her kitten, the little orange ball of fur. Instinctively, he stroked the little animal's back.

'I want a kitty, Mama,' Andrew said.

Mantheria groaned. 'He's a Stringham through and through.'

Becca and Helen retrieved their kittens before dashing inside the house. Frederica linked arms with Louisa,

leaving Wick and Mantheria, still carrying Andrew to take up the rear. His sister was six years younger than him, but in some ways she felt older. She was married with a child and ran several households of her own. Even though she was the same age as Louisa…only a few weeks younger.

When she had made her debut the *ton* had declared her 'a diamond of the first water'. And his sister *was* beautiful. Mantheria's person combined the best characteristics of his parents: Papa's blond, aristocratic features and complexion, and their mother's curvaceous figure.

'I hope Glastonbury doesn't mind our visit,' he said.

His sister glanced away from him as they entered her large and opulent home. 'Of course he doesn't mind. Alexander doesn't even know. He left three days ago for a house party in the company of Lady Dutton. I don't expect to see him for at least a fortnight—probably longer.'

Wick cursed underneath his breath. Mantheria had been too young to marry that lecherous old goat. Even if he *was* a duke. Lord Alexander Spooner, the Duke of Glastonbury, had been forty-five to his sister's seventeen years. Only among the *ton* could that sort of disparity in age be seen as acceptable. Or even desirable. When the Duke had married Mantheria the rumour had been that he wanted an heir. And he'd got one.

Wick felt a surge of protectiveness. 'Do you want me to have a talk with him?'

Mantheria set down Andrew, whose little legs were pumping before they even hit the marble floor. The lad was clearly anxious to catch up with his aunts.

Wick followed his sister into a parlour with dark maroon walls and matching furniture. She didn't sit down

and so neither did he. They stood awkwardly next to each other. Their usual camaraderie gone.

'Do you think me a child?' she asked him. 'Incapable of handling my own affairs?'

He held up his hands. 'Of course not. I only thought to help. Forgive me for intruding where I am not wanted.'

His sister took his arm and rested her head on his shoulder. She had the same golden curls and blue eyes as their father and Matthew, also Charles, Helen and Elizabeth.

'I know you mean well, but I am not your responsibility any more. And I prefer things the way they are.'

Wick scoffed, shaking his head. 'You prefer your husband to be with another woman?'

She sighed, rubbing her face into his sleeve. 'Glastonbury's brief infatuation with me barely lasted past our wedding trip, when I became pregnant with Andrew. He has been with Lady Dutton ever since. Any jealousy I once felt is now long gone.'

Wick's fingers touched his parted lips. For over three years his sister had borne this terrible situation on her own. 'The villain!'

His sister's tense posture loosened and she let out a long breath. 'I do not hate him any more, but I cannot love him either, and I do not want him here. But at least he is good with Andrew. He positively dotes on him. And Lady Dutton is scarcely less friendly. She brings him a present every time she visits, and I know that Glastonbury takes Andrew to see her. He calls her Aunt Cressida.'

Wick's entire body stiffened. 'So you live together as strangers?'

'Glastonbury is always polite, and we tend to spend

very little time together outside of the London season,' Mantheria said, her face pale. 'He is often at house parties or overseeing his other estates. He only visits to spend time with Andrew.'

'Do Mama and Papa know? Did you tell them before they left?'

'How can I tell them when they pushed for the match? They thought I would grow to love Glastonbury, like Mama did with Papa... And from a material point of view I could not have done better. I am a duchess, and one of the wealthiest women in England.'

Wick spoke between his clenched teeth. 'And the loneliest.'

He realised he did not want Louisa to make a similar loveless match. She deserved a loving husband and family after all her suffering at the hands of her aunt and the neglect of her uncle.

His sister forced a smile. 'Nonsense. How could anyone be lonely with Andrew around? And now that my sisters, Mrs May and Lady Louisa have come to visit, I am quite overburdened with company.'

'Does Glastonbury wish for more children?'

Wick knew that most peers wanted 'an heir and a spare', just in case something happened to the firstborn son.

Mantheria stepped away from him, a look of revulsion on her face. 'Despite his many flaws, Alexander would never force himself on me. He has an heir to his dukedom, and he knows that he will have no other children from me.'

Wick picked up a figurine from the table and squeezed it with all the anger he felt for his brother-in-law. A man he'd once respected and admired. 'Would you consider

a divorce? It's common knowledge that he is unfaithful to you. It wouldn't be hard to prove.'

'A woman cannot obtain a divorce unless there is cruelty—which there has not been. Only a man can divorce for infidelity. Men are given all the privileges and never held to the same standards as women.'

'I could always shoot him.'

Mantheria burst into laughter, breaking the tense feeling in the room. 'Yes, but I wouldn't want you to hang.'

Wick huffed. 'In a proper duel—not in the middle of the street. I wouldn't hang.'

She lifted her hands and dropped them. 'What if you were the one who died? And anyway it's no matter. I could never deprive Andrew of his father. He adores Alexander and Andrew adores him... Now, let's focus on your own problems.'

'I need another governess.'

'Obviously—a lady who will get on well with Becca, Frederica and Helen. I'll ask around my friends to see if they know of any young woman who would suit our family. Someone who isn't averse to kittens, snakes or emus.'

Wick bit the side of his cheek. 'And I want Lady Louisa to be presented to Queen Charlotte and enjoy a London season. One of her only memories of her mother is being told about her presentation. Matthew and I will track down her trustees and sort out her finances.'

Mantheria laughed again, raising her eyebrows. 'You don't ask for much. Just a come-out wardrobe for a debutante, a royal presentation, and an introduction to the *ton* with absolutely no notice at all. It is something I cannot do on my own. In my husband's absence I will need a proper escort.'

A shiver of panic ran down his spine; he feared where

this conversation was heading. 'I hope you don't want *me* to accompany you to these society squeezes.'

His sister patted his arm. 'Yes, dearest brother. You must come to all the parties with us and lend our group your countenance.'

Wick stepped away from his sister and held up his hands as if he'd been waylaid by highwaymen. 'I will get eaten alive. The debutantes will swarm around me like killer bees. I will be of no use to you or Louisa.'

Mantheria lifted her chin. 'If you don't, then I won't.'

He was half tempted to test his sister's threats, but he'd promised Louisa that he would help her and he couldn't without Mantheria's assistance.

'You drive a harder bargain than Mama,' he said, putting down his hands. 'Fine. I will escort you to the presentation and to a couple of balls. But I won't dance. And you will have to help me find a new governess for the girls.'

His sister held out her hand. 'It's an agreement.'

'Agreement,' he echoed, shaking it and knowing that he would regret this pact.

# Chapter Fourteen

Louisa had never been shopping before, so she didn't know what to expect. The stylish premises that Mantheria took her to the next day did not have any prices displayed. Nor any dresses. They were taken to a parlour with several chairs and given tea from a silver tea tray with small cakes. The modiste, a Madame Brunet, sat with them and chatted merrily about the weather with a pleasing French accent.

She was a petite, dark-haired beauty with an olive-skinned complexion. Her dress was cut fashionably, but sensibly. And nothing about her demeanour suggested that they were about to spend any money. Nor did Madame Brunet rush them at all. She waited for Louisa and Mantheria to finish their tea before she stood up.

'If you are ready, Your Grace?' Madame Brunet said, looking at Mantheria, who was the highest-ranking woman in the room. 'I shall have my assistants model the latest fashions from Paris. If any dress strikes your fancy, I can have it made up in the colour and material of your choice.'

Mantheria nodded and smiled at the other woman. 'Yes, Lady Louisa's colouring might prove a bit tricky

on some of the shades. But I am sure that we can rely on your good taste to guide us to the best you have to offer. My mother would expect nothing less.'

'Of course, Your Grace,' said Madame Brunet, bowing. 'I am honoured by your family's custom.'

Louisa bit her lower lip. Mantheria wasn't asking for a price reduction. She was telling the modiste to show her only the most expensive wares. Louisa knew that Mantheria and her sisters were very wealthy, but she had no idea when she would be able to repay them for their kindness —nor for Parisian gowns. She prayed that Wick would be able to locate her trustees quickly.

She cleared her throat. 'May I speak alone with the Duchess?'

Madame Brunet curtsied. 'But of course, *mademoiselle*. I shall go and help my assistants prepare. *Au revoir.*'

Louisa waited until the modiste had left the room to open her mouth. Although they were the same age, she still felt nervous in Lady Glastonbury's company. She was afraid to disappoint the Duchess, as she had Aunt Rockingham and Aunt Laybourne. And she wanted so badly for them to be friends.

'I appreciate that you want the very finest for me… but the thing is…although I am an heiress…truly… I don't have any money yet, and I would hate to impose upon you further.'

Mantheria moved from her chair on the opposite side of the room to the one next to Louisa. She placed a lace-gloved hand on hers. 'My dear Louisa, I trust that you will repay me whenever you can. I am not in any hurry. Besides, the bills will be sent to my unfaithful husband, and nothing would please me more than to spend thousands of pounds in his name.'

It was an obvious question, but Louisa couldn't help but ask, 'You aren't happy in your marriage?'

The Duchess squeezed Louisa's wrist. 'Sometimes I forget that you haven't been a part of the family for long. My marriage to the Duke of Glastonbury is not a happy one. He spends his nights and most of his days with his mistress, Lady Dutton. And, like a good little wife, I am supposed to smile and pretend in front of society that I do not know that he is with Cressida. My marriage is an elegant lie.'

Louisa gulped, shaking her head in disbelief. 'His mistress couldn't possibly be more beautiful than you.'

Mantheria's grip on Louisa's wrist tightened until it hurt. It was clear that the Duchess had already known a great deal of pain in her marriage. The Duke's betrayal was even worse than her own aunt and uncle's treatment of her.

'Beauty has little to do with love.' Mantheria released her hold on Louisa. 'Do not be in too much of a hurry to marry, my dear. A lifetime can feel like an eternity with the wrong person at your side. Especially if your heart belongs to another.'

Louisa didn't know if Mantheria was referring to herself or to the Duke. She worried about her own choices. Would any man love her if she didn't have money or a title? She feared that Wick held more of her heart than was good for either of them. But he kept on making it abundantly clear that he would not be her suitor, and she couldn't let her feelings for him stop her from making a suitable match.

'I will do my best.'

Picking up the bell, Mantheria rang it. 'That is all you can do.'

Madame Brunet came into the room, followed by three women wearing the most delicate and beautiful ball gowns Louisa had ever seen. She couldn't stop herself from standing up and examining one more closely. The seams on the bodice of the gown formed a diamond shape in front. Walking behind the assistant, she saw that the sewing style made the back of the dress look very small, emphasising the oversleeves.

'It's called a tight back style,' Madame Brunet said.

Glancing over her shoulder, Louisa saw the modiste standing there.

'Do you sew, Lady Louisa?'

She bit her lower lip, nodding her head. 'But nothing as fine as this.'

Madame Brunet smiled. '*Non.* It is all in the pattern, my lady. I am sure you could sew something just as fine. You see the inverted pleats at the centre of the back? They give the dress shape and fullness to the skirt. Some ladies add a small roll or pad to create a subtle roundness, but with your lovely shape no such tricks are needed.'

Louisa blushed as she looked at the next model's gown. It was trimmed with festooned flounces and interspersed with puffs of net forming rosettes. The final assistant wore yellow crêpe embroidered with floral sprigs and applied shell designs that threw the hem into a three-dimensional relief. Every gown was a work of art. Louisa longed to run her fingers over the embroidery and the perfect little stitches. She wanted to untangle all the secrets of their sewing.

'One of each gown would be perfect,' Mantheria said from behind her, still sitting on her chair. 'But I don't think yellow would flatter Louisa. It would make her skin look rather sallow.'

Madame Brunet nodded her head vigorously. 'Yes, yes… Yellow would quite wash out her glorious colouring. But a bright green would look divine on the lady.'

'And blue,' Louisa added. 'Any shade.'

'One of her dresses must be white,' the young Duchess said. 'Every debutante has to have a white dress, and that won't clash with her red hair.'

Louisa would finally be a debutante. Something she'd always dreamed of being. She pinched herself to make sure that she was truly awake. She felt a brief stab of pain, but it was quickly replaced with pleasure. Wick would see her in these beautiful dresses. They might even dance. Her pulse quickened at the thought of being in his arms again.

'Why don't we get her light silk slips in white, pale blue and pink?' Mantheria said, fiddling with the braided lace. 'Then she can wear a white net gown or crêpe *lissé* over them for a new look each time.'

Louisa clapped her hands. 'Oh, I love that idea.'

She could mix and match and use her own skill with the needle to expand her wardrobe without costing the Duchess or her philandering husband any more money. She had no idea how long it would take for Wick to find her trustees, or for them to release to her the yearly allowance.

Mantheria cleared her throat. 'And any partially finished gown you have on hand that can be altered quickly and sent to my home would be much appreciated, *madame*. Lady Louisa needs a wardrobe immediately.'

'I am writing it down now, Your Grace,' Madame Brunet said, scribbling into a small book. 'I shall take down your entire order and then we can measure *ma-*

*demoiselle* to ensure that each piece of clothing fits her form perfectly.'

Mantheria smiled. 'Very good, Madame Brunet. Now, about a court gown… We will need it by the end of the week.'

The modiste shook her head. 'I am afraid that a court gown would take several weeks to complete, Your Grace. Even if my seamstresses sewed through the night we could not complete it in time.'

'Blast!' the Duchess said, and exhaled loudly. 'I have managed to weasel a spot at St James's on Thursday evening by calling in a favour. Is there nothing you can do?'

'Perhaps I could help? Another pair of hands?' Louisa said, holding her knees together, feeling the blood rush to her face. She felt awful, putting the unhappily married Duchess to more work.

Madame Brunet waved a hand. 'That will not be necessary. But your words do remind me that we have had a court gown returned because it did not meet Lady Rutledge's exacting approval. She is about the same size as Lady Louisa, and the gown could be altered in time. If my suggestion is not offensive?'

'We can hardly be particular,' Mantheria said, with a wink to Louisa. 'But we will be. Please show it to us, Madame Brunet. I am sure your work was exceptional. Lady Rutledge probably couldn't afford the bill for the gown—she runs through her quarterly allowance faster than a racehorse at Ascot.'

A few moments later the modiste returned with two seamstresses holding a dark green gown between them. It was the most ornate piece of clothing Louisa had ever seen. The train had to be at least eight feet long, and the skirt was wide, as if it had been made for an old-

fashioned hoop. Flounces crisscrossed the skirts and were embellished by point lace.

Giggling, Mantheria gave Louisa a little push on her arm. 'You look overwhelmed by its sumptuousness, but I must assure you that this gown is quite perfect for a presentation to the Queen. The more ostentatious your dress is the better, and when in doubt you must add another flounce and two tassels.'

Louisa did feel overwhelmed—but by its beauty.

'It's magnificent,' she whispered. 'It must cost a fortune.'

'Three hundred pounds, my lady,' Madame Brunet said with another obsequious curtsy.

Louisa could only blink. She'd had no idea that one gown could cost so much. It was a small fortune!

But the Duchess of Glastonbury did not appear at all surprised by the price. 'We will take it. Now, Louisa, I'll wait here while you go with the seamstresses to be measured. And then we will be off to buy hats, gloves, slippers and everything else a debutante needs for the season.'

Louisa was in a daze as she followed the sewing women behind a curtain and they helped her out of her day dress. She felt embarrassed that her chemise did not even reach her knees and was practically threadbare. Madame Brunet did not mention it, but simply took out her tape measure and put it around Louisa's waist, chest and hips. She called out several numbers to one of her assistants.

Gulping, Louisa watched as the two seamstresses brought the beautiful gown towards her. 'Perhaps you will be so kind as to add underclothing to the order?' she said.

'Of course, my lady,' she said, squeezing Louisa's waist with her hands, 'and a hoop for your presentation gown.'

Glancing over her shoulder, Louisa saw another woman bringing a large hoop contraption to tie around her waist. She held herself still as the woman attached it with ties, letting the hoop fall almost to the floor. Then the two other seamstresses pulled the emerald gown over her head. It felt like a second skin as Madame Brunet did the buttons in the back.

'What do you think, Lady Louisa?'

The modiste gently turned Louisa's shoulders until she was looking into a mirror. She almost didn't recognise her own reflection.

'It's perfect,' she whispered. 'Perfect...'

If this was a dream, Louisa did not wish to wake up.

# *Chapter Fifteen*

Wick knew better than to visit Mantheria before noon. His sister was not a morning person. She was positively prickly until she'd had her hot chocolate and read the morning news. He was reasonably sure that his three little sisters would be awake. But they couldn't get into too much mischief at Mantheria's townhouse, could they?

A cold sweat covered his forehead as he entered White's club. His younger sisters could and often did get into a great deal of mischief.

He allowed a footman to open the door to an adjacent room and ordered coffee. Sitting down, he was about to lean back in his chair when his best friend Lord Sunderland—'Sunny'—sat beside him.

'I didn't expect to see you in town again so soon. I thought you were rusticating in the country. Determined to avoid the desperate debs.'

Wick didn't bother covering his yawn. Sunny had been the one sent home to 'rusticate'. They'd been to Eton and then Oxford together, each staying at the other's homes during the summer holidays. Such old friends didn't need to stand on ceremony.

'My sisters need another governess.'

Sunny chortled. 'What does this make? Their seventh or eighth since the battle-axe Miss Nix retired? I'll say this for your old governess...she walloped just as hard as any man.'

Wick smiled wryly. Both he and Sunny had deserved the spanking she'd given them after letting out all the chickens. 'Only the sixth.'

'Give it time... I am sure there will be a seventh and eighth.'

He shook his head. 'Please don't talk about my sisters. They are Mantheria's problem for a few hours. I need a break from all the drama—just for a little while.'

Sunny grinned, emphasising his nose, slightly crooked above his straight white teeth. 'You have brought your little sisters to London? Surely there is more to this story.'

Wick closed his eyes, rubbing his temples. 'I couldn't leave them at home alone.'

'I should have thought Mrs May and Harper more than capable of containing them for a few days.'

Reluctantly, Wick dropped his hands and opened his eyes. 'Mrs May had to come to London.'

'Tell me the true reason why—and no more Banbury stories, Wick,' Sunny said. 'I am your oldest friend, and I can tell when you're lying or misdirecting.'

Huffing, Wick sat forward in his seat and said in a low whisper, 'The girls sent me on a wild goose chase in the wrong direction after their last governess and I happened upon another young lady and mistook her for the errant governess.'

Wincing, Sunny said, 'Oh, dear. You didn't try to kidnap the wrong woman, did you?'

'No! I mean, I did bring her home…but she was willing to come.'

'Of course she was.' His friend chuckled. 'When's the wedding?'

Wick's fingers clenched into fists. 'Don't make me break your nose again.'

Sunny held up his hands in surrender. 'Truce, old friend. Tell me the rest of your sad tale.'

'My sisters pointed out that she wasn't the governess, and then the blasted young lady wouldn't tell us her true name.'

'A lady? Wick, you *are* in the basket. Is she pretty, at least?'

'Ravishing,' he admitted, 'but I had the forethought to have Mrs May play chaperone, and when we discovered that she was Lady Louisa Bracken I tried to fob her off on her uncle, the Canon of Sherborne.'

Sunny clenched his teeth, shaking his head. 'Worse and worse.'

'The fellow wanted to send her back to the Rockinghams, who were treating her like a drudge, which I'd already promised her that I wouldn't do… When she ran away from her relatives her clothing was threadbare—and she's a blasted heiress. And she's twenty-one, so legally they are no longer her guardians. And all she wants is a proper season and to be given her yearly allowance.'

'Your soft heart is going to get you into trouble.'

'It already has,' Wick said.

Sunny shook his head. 'And Mantheria too. I take it you have dumped your mystery lady, Mrs May and your three little sisters on her doorstep?'

Wick felt the blood rush to his face. His friend was right. He'd literally dropped all his problems and respon-

sibilities on his sister, who had enough on her plate with her own child and an unfaithful husband.

'I'm a wretch.'

'No, you're a softie, and all four of your sisters pull your heartstrings like a harp. You can't say no to any of them,' Sunny said. 'Except maybe Helen. I adore her bluntness. Did she bring her snake to London?'

'No.'

His friend grinned, then laughed. 'You know she'll just find another one. She's got a sixth sense about them.'

Wick dropped his head into his hands. 'Can you stop talking? Or at the very least change the subject?'

'What if I were to tell you there are a couple of prime 'uns at Tattersalls that you'll be interested in? I'd buy the chestnuts myself if I had a feather to fly with.'

'Are they beauties?'

'They prettiest set of goers I ever laid my eyes on,' his friend assured him. 'I think they could even beat your greys in a race.'

Wick's pair of matched greys were a splendid team, and he'd raced with them several times, never losing. But his father had purchased them when Wick was only eighteen, and the horses were growing older and slower. They still had several years in them, but their racing days were coming to an end.

'I'll go and give them a look later today.'

Sunny stood up and held out his hand. 'I'll come with you. I have nothing else to do except stop at Jem Belcher's. He's promised to show me how to block your bruising left hook.'

'Let's stop at Jem's first,' Wick said, getting to his feet. 'In my current mood I could pound even the champion into the wall.'

Sunny's upper lip curled. 'Jem's only let you hit him once.'

'He didn't *let* me.'

Sunny shook his head, linking his arm with Wick's. 'He did.'

They walked out of the room together, talking more loudly than they should in the gentlemen's club. Especially in the reading room, where they nearly ran into a gentleman with dark greying hair.

Wick was about to apologise when he saw the man's face. It was Alexander. Mantheria's husband. But no one in his family called the jackanapes by his first name any more. Only by his title—Glastonbury. His sister's unfaithful husband was supposed to be at a party in the country. He clearly was not. No doubt he hadn't left London at all, but had spent the last few days at Lady Dutton's townhouse. What Glastonbury saw in the woman Wick would never know. She had to be fifty, at least. And the widowed Lady Dutton couldn't be called pretty. At her age, handsome was the only epithet she could hope for. But, according to *ton* gossip, Glastonbury had loved her for thirty years—even before her husband had died.

The other man smiled, touching his hat. 'Wick, it is good to see you.'

Wick clenched his hands into fists. He wanted nothing more than to punch his brother-in-law in the face. To slap his glove across his cheek and demand the satisfaction of a duel. But Mantheria had told him not to, and he had to respect her wishes or he would be a villain like her husband.

'I take it that your house party broke up early, Glastonbury? Where was it again? Shropshire?'

A tinge of colour entered Alexander's cheeks. And

to think Wick had once idolised him. Envied him for being a notable whip and a renowned Corinthian. What a difference four years made—and it wasn't just the additional grey hairs on the man's head. Wick now knew that Glastonbury wasn't a man of honour, despite his friendly nature.

Four years ago Glastonbury had put Wick's name up at White's, Watier's, and even the Four Horse Club. With such a sponsor Wick had had no difficulty being accepted to any club in London. His own father didn't belong to any clubs. Nor was Papa at all interested in society.

Wick had been a young man, fresh out of university and looking for a mentor. He might have fallen prey to the sharks and hangers-on, but Glastonbury had taken him under his wing. Taught him how to race his greys. Which gaming hells to avoid. And once lent him money when he'd overrun his quarterly allowance. Wick had been eager to pay him back, but Glastonbury had refused to accept it. He'd become Mantheria's husband by then. Something that had made Wick feel proud.

Now he only felt shame for telling his sister what a great gun Alexander was and encouraging the match. He'd known about Lady Dutton—but many men about town had affairs. Particularly with willing widows. The *ton* usually closed its eyes to them. And so had Wick. He'd never thought that Glastonbury would be unfaithful to his beautiful sister. He'd let Mantheria down again.

Glastonbury cleared his throat. 'Yes. Well… It turned out that the daughter of the house caught the measles, and I felt it unwise to risk carrying them back to Andrew.'

'He dotes on you.'

The older man smiled slightly. 'I am very lucky to be his father.'

Sunny put on a fake smile. 'Glad I'm not a father—at least not that I am aware of.'

Wick should have passed by, but he couldn't leave without saying something more. 'You're very lucky that Andrew is too young to understand what kind of man you are. What kind of husband you truly are. But someday he will, and then your son will despise you as much as I do.'

Glastonbury flinched as if Wick had indeed struck him across the face with his glove.

Wick pulled his friend away from his brother-in-law. 'Come, Sunny, my fists are itching to hit something.'

'I hope you don't mean me,' Sunny said. 'You've already made my nose crooked.'

'You gave me a black eye first.'

His friend laughed. 'You're right. What was the fight over, anyway? I can't remember.'

They walked out of White's together.

Wick shook his head. 'A buxom barmaid in Eton, who was twice our age and considered us to be nothing but little schoolboys.'

Sunny grabbed his chest. 'I remember now. Molly was a tasty woman.'

'Whom neither of us tasted.'

His friend laughed loudly, and Wick couldn't help but join him. They didn't call for his carriage or hire a hack—instead they walked to Jem Belcher's boxing house.

The former champion met them at the door with a crooked smile.

Sunny waved to him. 'I'm here to learn that block against Wick's left hook. You promised me that you would teach me how to beat him.'

Jem shrugged, shaking his head. 'That will take a great many more lessons, my lord.'

Wick's friend was at least a head shorter and two stones lighter than him. Sunny had been taller than him at one time, but Wick had more than caught up. Wick laughed and went to change his clothes.

In a loose smock and breeches, he was able to land punches on his friend's stomach, shoulder, and even his chin.

Sunny touched his red jaw. 'Keep the punches lower, Wick. I've got to catch an heiress with this face.'

'*You're* participating in the season?'

'My mother insists upon it,' his friend said in a funerary tone. 'She says it's high time I found myself a wife and secured the family line by fathering sons. If only she had been kind enough to provide me with a brother, like yours did. Another heir…'

Sunny's father had died when he was only three years old, making him the Duke of Sunderland. Wick had only ever known him by his title. Now, at the age of six-and-twenty, Sunny was contemplating marriage and heirs. Wick would also inherit a dukedom—but *he* was in no hurry to produce offspring.

# Chapter Sixteen

Louisa put on the dress of emerald velvet and wondered if it might be too elaborate. The style was not unlike her mother's own court gown, over twenty years before.

Mantheria assured her that it was how all court dresses looked, and that the Queen insisted on young women wearing the old-fashioned style. Their necks and shoulders had to be bare unless they had a doctor's certificate. Which she didn't. Even the corset was different. Instead of pushing up her breasts, it flattened them most uncomfortably.

Chandler, her new lady's maid, added another large white plume to her already enormous coiffure. Her head appeared to be twice its normal size because of all the ostrich feathers that were attached to lappets which hung below her shoulders.

Louisa made a face at herself in the mirror and thought perhaps her dress was too spectacular. 'I look like a prancing peacock showing off its fine feathers.'

'Peahen,' Becca corrected from behind her. 'Peacocks are the males of the breed. Peahens are the females, and their plumage aren't nearly as impressive.'

'But they're all fowl,' Helen said with a wink.

The sisters all laughed, but it took Louisa a moment or two to understand the play on words. 'I *feel* foul,' she said.

Frederica touched her shoulder. 'You look stunning.'

'And only a decade out of fashion,' Helen said.

'Don't be rude!' Mantheria scolded.

Her own dress was just as wide. The silk was a rather stunning shade of pink that set off her pale complexion. Even the ostrich feathers in her hair were dyed pink. The sleeves and underskirt were turquoise, and everything was trimmed in wide gold braid. She had tassels artistically draped around her artificially large hips.

'Now, *your* dress, Mantheria,' Helen said, 'looks two decades out of fashion. I daresay Mama had one just like it when she was first married.'

Mantheria dived for her sister. 'You little snake.'

Helen dodged out of her way. 'I take that as a compliment.'

'I think we've had enough compliments this evening,' Frederica said, handing Louisa a pair of lace gloves. 'Wick is already waiting for you two, and you know the Queen of England waits for no one.'

'Even those who wear flamingo-pink dresses,' Helen added, but wisely was already at the door, ready for her escape.

'Don't listen to her,' Becca said, touching her sister's puffed sleeve. 'It's more the soft pink of a newly born piglet.'

Louisa couldn't help but laugh. 'And my green dress?'

'The colour of an alligator or a crocodile,' Becca said, taking the question seriously. 'I can never remember the difference between the two creatures.'

'They both have sharp teeth—like Helen,' Mantheria said, offering her arm to Louisa, who took it. 'We shall have a marvellous time.'

Louisa's stomach roiled. 'What if I have to use the privy? I couldn't possibly, whilst wearing this gown.'

Mantheria wrinkled her nose. 'There are no privies at St James's court. If you need to relieve yourself, your maid will give you a sort of dish called a *bourdaloue* to put underneath your dress.'

Her insides clenched. 'I am supposed to relieve myself while standing?'

Colour stole into Mantheria's cheeks. 'Well, yes... Sometimes you must stand for hours at court before you are presented to the Queen.'

'I don't see what all the fuss is about,' Becca said. 'Animals relieve themselves standing. I cannot think of even one that sits to complete its business.'

Louisa watched Mantheria make a creditable effort at keeping in her laugh. Her face went red and her cheeks puffed out. Her lips were pinched together tightly.

'They don't even use a dish,' Becca added.

It was too much for the young Duchess. She burst into laughter. Louisa couldn't help but giggle with her. Wick's little sisters were positively incorrigible.

'Can we not discuss the habits of animals relieving themselves just now?' Mantheria said, but there was still a smile on her lips. 'Come, Louisa. Miss Chandler will bring the *bordaloue*, just in case... Most ladies try to drink and eat as little as possible at social events to avoid such a need.'

'I don't know why you're so missish about it, Mantheria,' Helen said, from the hall. ''Tis only a part of nature, and there will be a screen to go behind.'

The Duchess waddled towards Helen in her enormous dress, but Helen was easily able to escape her—not being hampered by hoops and trains.

Louisa followed behind Mantheria, and had to turn sideways to fit through the door frame. When she reached the front staircase she saw Wick, standing at the bottom. He was looking particularly handsome in knee breeches, an intricately tied cravat, a golden waistcoat and an embroidered green coat with long tails. The same colour as her own dress. She couldn't help but wonder if the choice had been intentional. She hoped so.

Wick smiled up at her as she walked carefully down each stair. 'Louisa, you are a vision of loveliness and sure to be this season's diamond of the first water.'

Louisa grinned back at him and decided that her gown was the perfect amount of sumptuousness. She hoped that if she looked pretty enough he would change his mind about courting her.

'And me, Wick?' Mantheria asked, holding up her fan as if it were a weapon. 'Where is *my* compliment?'

'It's still trying to find its way out of all that silk.'

Mantheria whacked him on the arm with her fan. 'You're as rude as Helen.'

'No one is as rude as Helen.'

Louisa saw his sister's head peek out from above the stair railings. 'I heard that!'

'Come,' Mantheria said, sweeping past him to the foyer. 'I daresay we are going to hurry to get there just to stand and wait. But that is the way of court.'

The butler opened the front door and Wick offered his arm to Louisa. She happily took it, but they were unable to walk together through the entrance. Her skirt was

simply too wide. After their second failed attempt, Wick spun Louisa around and pulled her through after him.

He helped both Mantheria and Louisa into the carriage, but they had to sit on opposite seats because their dresses were simply too wide to accommodate a second lady. Wick was forced to lift up part of Mantheria's skirt in order to sit down beside her on the carriage seat.

'Ooh! I have found the compliment. You look as pretty and delectable as a French *macaron*… Also, you're the same colours.'

His sister tried to whack him again with her fan, but this time his hand came up to block it.

'And Louisa looks like a *langue de chat* dipped in green icing.'

'Oh, please stop talking about cakes,' Louisa said, clutching her rumbling middle. 'My stomach is already in knots and I feel rather sick.'

When they arrived at St James's Palace, a footman opened the door. Mantheria helped Louisa wrap her long train over her left arm, and then did the same with her own gown. They were led into the redbrick castle towards the drawing rooms, and then to a long gallery. Louisa was relieved to see that every young lady there—and some not so young—was wearing the same kind of ornate court dress.

Mantheria touched Louisa's cheek. 'You look beautiful. Now, all we can do is wait until you are summoned to the Presence Chamber. The Lord Chamberlain will announce your name. You will then enter the Queen's presence and make the deep curtsy that we have practised. Because you are the daughter of a peer, you do not kiss her hand. She will kiss your forehead. Then you may arise. Queen Charlotte may want to exchange

pleasantries. But if she does not, you will curtsy deeply again and walk backwards slowly. You must never turn your back on a queen.'

Louisa looked down, once more clutching her rumbling tummy. 'I don't know if I can do this…'

'I know you can,' the young Duchess said with an encouraging look. 'You are one of the bravest people I know, Louisa. You left your home and your family, all on your own, and set off on an adventure to make your dreams come true. I am proud to consider you one of my friends.'

Louisa's eyes filled with tears, for this was what she had hoped for. Longed for. A friend of her own age. 'Truly? You consider me a friend?'

'Of course,' Mantheria said, leaning forward and kissing Louisa's cheek. 'I am so glad that Wick brought you to me.'

Wick cleared his throat and both Louisa and Mantheria turned their heads to see what he wanted to say. 'We are almost at the front of the gallery.'

Mantheria gave a small nod. 'Louisa, let go of your train.'

Louisa dropped the fabric in her left hand. Two footmen came forward and pulled the train gently to its full length. Then they did the same for Mantheria's pink silk robe. Even Wick straightened his coat. Louisa could barely breathe. She took quick, short gasps as her stomach continued to roil most uncomfortably. She longed to flee, but her feet would not move.

Wick took her arm and pulled her forward to the entrance of the Presence Chamber. Mantheria followed behind them, her fan around her wrist.

The Lord Chamberlain cleared his throat as they en-

tered. 'May I present Lady Louisa Bracken, daughter of the late Earl of Rockingham?'

Wick dropped his arm and Louisa walked forward alone. The Queen sat on a throne at the front of the room. Her hair was white, but it might be a wig. Louisa knew that underneath her powder and cosmetics Queen Charlotte was in her sixties. Her expression was solemn, but not unkind.

Louisa continued to step forward, unsure of where she should stop and make her deep curtsy. Was she too far back? Or if she got closer would she be performing a solecism? Louisa took a few more short breaths and matching steps before sinking down into a deep curtsy. This at least she had practised several times with Mantheria and the girls. Becca tended to lose her balance and bring all of them to the floor like a row of dominoes.

Unconsciously, Louisa smiled at the memory.

She felt the brief contact of dry lips against her forehead. Then, still keeping her eyes to the floor, continued to stay in her low curtsy.

'You have the look of your mother,' Queen Charlotte said with a slight accent. 'But you don't make me sneeze.'

Louisa slowly came up to stand. Her eyes shone with unshed tears and her heart was full. If only her mother could see her now. If only her mother could have been with her to experience this day that they had practised for and dreamed of together. But she knew she was not alone. Wick and Mantheria were with her.

'Thank you, Your Majesty.'

Queen Charlotte gave her a benign smile, but she did not open her mouth again.

After a moment or two, Louisa realised that her audi-

ence was over. She swept into another deep curtsy before slowly backing away from the Queen.

Mantheria and Wick met her at the entrance and escorted her out of the Presence Chamber and through the long gallery to the drawing rooms. Wick stooped down and picked up both Louisa's and his sister's trains for them to put over their left arms. Louisa wondered why they couldn't hold them with their right, but did not ask. Court rules didn't seem to have much to do with logic.

Louisa exhaled slowly. 'I've waited for that presentation my whole life, and now I am so glad it is over.'

'Me too,' Wick said. 'My knees were knocking for you.'

Mantheria hit him on the back of the head with her fan. 'She was perfect.'

He raised his hand. 'If you touch me one more time with that accursed fan, I will snap it in two.'

'But it's made of mahogany.'

'I'll find a way.'

Louisa couldn't believe it, but felt a laugh bubble out of her. Wick gave her a slow smile and Louisa reached out to him with trembling hands. He held both of hers in his strong ones, squeezing them gently.

'You were marvellous.'

'And you didn't even need the *bourdaloue*,' Mantheria added from their side.

Wick blinked. 'What's a *bourdaloue*?'

Louisa gave another shaky laugh.

## Chapter Seventeen

The next evening all four Stringham sisters watched Louisa as her maid, Chandler, pulled, laced, primped and then arranged her hair. Louisa couldn't help but be surprised at how well the white gown with the lace over-lay fitted her. It had been a readymade garment that had been altered specifically for her frame. Madame Brunet and her assistants were truly talented with their needles.

'Isn't white the colour for young debutantes?' Louisa couldn't help but ask.

She didn't want to make any mistakes. She mustn't give society any reason to reject her as her own family had.

'We will be turning tradition on its head,' Mantheria assured her. 'With such stunning hair as yours, it would be a pity for any colour to compete with it.'

She watched Becca and Helen dig through a chest of jewellery that looked like a pirate's hoard, with many jewels of all colours set in different metals.

'Garnets?' Becca asked.

Helen shook her head. 'No, rubies. Nothing cheap for Louisa's first party.'

Frederica held out her hand. 'Give them to me.'

Louisa sat still while Frederica clasped a ruby necklace around her throat. One large ruby was surrounded by small diamonds and two more additional small rubies. It had to be worth at least a thousand pounds! The Stringhams didn't seem to notice or care for its value. Then Becca placed two ruby earrings in her hand, and with shaking fingers Louisa put them in her ears. Helen added two diamond combs to her red curls.

Chandler helped Louisa put on long, white satin gloves. Becca wrapped the lace shawl that Mrs Barker had given to her around her shoulders. It was the only item of clothing she had that was exquisite enough to go with the clothes the Duchess had bought her.

'One last touch,' Mantheria said, adding diamond bangles to Louisa's wrist.

Frederica smiled at her. 'You look stunning.'

Louisa glanced down at the bangles on her wrist and fiddled with one. She was not used to compliments and had to bite her lower lip to stop herself from decrying their kind words. How she loved being with them. It felt like belonging to a family.

Helen tugged the shawl into the right place. 'Beautiful.'

Becca gave her a tight hug around the waist. 'You'll dance wonderfully. Just remember everything we said and try to let the man lead. Even if he is dreadful at it like Helen.'

*Dancing.*

Louisa's growing confidence deflated like the flying balloon she'd once seen pictured in a book. 'But I've only had a few lessons with you and the dancing master. I can't possibly dance. I will make a fool of myself.'

'You can't waltz until an Almack's patroness gives you

permission, so don't worry about that,' Frederica said, hugging her with one arm around her shoulders. 'And you'll be fine during the country dances. Simply follow the lead of the person in front of you. No one will notice if you make a mistake on a figure.'

'We are already unconscionably late,' Mantheria said, pointing to a clock on the mantel. 'Come, Louisa, before my sisters overload you with more well-meaning advice that makes you feel quite ill.'

Louisa's heart beat against the rubies on her breast as she walked down the stairs with Mantheria. Wick was standing waiting at the bottom. She caught her breath. Everything about him seemed polished and sparkling. The brass buttons on his blue coat reflected the lamp-light. He wore the tails over knee breeches, which showed his defined calves to admiration. Even his brown hair seemed to glint and shine.

His coffee-coloured eyes stared at her intently. She could have happily lost herself inside them. His lips looked as if he'd just licked them. Blushing, she thought of how much *she* would like to lick his lips.

Wick bowed to them. 'My ladies, you both look too exquisite for mere words.'

Mantheria rapped his knuckles playfully with her fan and then linked her arm with his. He turned and offered his other elbow to Louisa. She placed her hand on his muscular forearm. She noticed that the dark blue coat fitted him so well that it looked a second skin.

Wick led them out to the carriage. They didn't speak much on the way to the ball. Louisa's throat felt too con-stricted for words. But once the vehicle stopped in front of a grey stone townhouse she found her tongue. 'What if they refuse me entry because I don't have an invitation?'

'I don't have one either,' Wick admitted. 'They will not ask for one at the door.'

'You are with me,' Mantheria said with a reassuring smile. 'And no one says no to a duchess.'

Wick took Louisa's hand and helped her out of the carriage. 'Not even our father.'

The young Duchess giggled behind her. 'Papa may be eccentric, but he isn't stupid.'

He assisted his sister out next, and escorted them both into Lady Dennard's home. Mantheria had been right. Lady Dennard didn't even raise an eyebrow at her extra lady guest, and her smile was all too wide when she saw Wick entering behind them.

'Lord Cheswick,' the lady said, fawning. 'I am deeply honoured that you have chosen to attend my small party. You are a rare guest at such events. This is quite a social coup for your hostess.'

Louisa almost laughed at the look of chagrin on Wick's face.

But he bowed over the lady's hand. 'I wouldn't have missed your party for the world.'

Lady Dennard tittered with laughter and they walked on. They were among the last guests to arrive, and it seemed to Louisa that an enormous number of aristocrats had been squeezed into several small rooms. Wick nodded to acquaintances as they weaved through the ballroom, which was as hot and crowded as a country fête.

'Oh, good,' Mantheria said. 'We've missed the first quadrille. It's such a long, slow dance.'

A fair gentleman walked up to them and bowed. He was the same height as Mantheria and had a pleasing countenance, a crooked nose and a winning smile. 'Lady

Glastonbury, may I have the pleasure of dancing the first waltz with you?'

Mantheria offered her hand and the man bowed over it, bringing it to his lips. 'I would be delighted to dance with you,' she said. 'Allow me to present my dear friend, Lady Louisa Bracken. Lady Louisa, this is Lord Sunderland. The best dancer in all of England.'

Louisa tentatively held out her hand and Lord Sunderland took it lightly, bending over it. 'Bracken? Any relation to Lord Barnabas?'

'He is my cousin,' she said, pulling her hand back. 'The current Earl of Rockingham is my uncle.'

'You poor thing.'

Louisa felt herself blushing with embarrassment. She had no idea how well her cousin or her uncle fitted into society. Would her connection with them hurt her own social standing?

Mantheria hit Lord Sunderland's shoulder with her fan and tipped her head towards Louisa.

Blinking, Lord Sunderland cleared his throat. 'Ah, Lady Louisa…might I reserve the set after next?'

Louisa looked at Wick, who gave her a slight nod. 'I should be pleased to accept, Your Grace.'

The music ended and the couples on the dance floor began to clap. Lord Sunderland held out his hand to Mantheria, who took it. Leaving Louisa alone with Wick in a room full of people, many of whom were openly staring at her.

Louisa touched the curls at her neck. 'Is something wrong with my face or my hair?'

Wick tweaked a red curl with two gloved fingers. 'You look beautiful. They are staring because you are the most arresting woman in the room.'

She couldn't stop her lips from forming a smile. If she hadn't been beautiful before, his words would have made her so.

Louisa felt herself beaming at him. 'Are you sure that they aren't looking at you? You are devastatingly handsome in evening clothes.'

'Oh, no!' Wick said, briefly touching his chest and turning his body towards her. He placed a hand over one side of his face, as if to hide his identity. 'They've spotted me. I am done for.'

'Who has spotted you?'

'Lady Ashton and Mrs Nells. Between them they have at least half a dozen daughters they're desperately trying to fob off on to any unsuspecting gentleman of means.'

She glanced over her shoulder and, sure enough, there were two matrons eyeing Wick as if he were a plum pudding at Christmas. 'Surely they can't make you ask their daughters to dance—let alone marry them.'

'You'd be surprised at how many tender young maidens hurt their ankles when I am near. Or drop their handkerchief or their fan.'

'Do you pick them up?'

He raised one eyebrow. 'The maidens or their fans?'

'Either?'

Wick took her arm and led her in the opposite direction from Lady Ashton and Mrs Nells. 'Neither. I walk by and pretend not to hear their calls for help. I have no intention of being trapped into marriage any time soon.'

Louisa's lips had quirked upwards at his jest, but his last words wiped the smile off her face. Wick did not want to get married. Perhaps that was why he refused to be her suitor. Maybe there was nothing too wrong with her after all.

Taking a deep breath, she tried to come up with a suitable sally. 'Then it appears that you have nothing to fear from being here.'

He shook his head, frowning. 'You're wrong. I have walked willingly into the lions' den. I will not escape without scratches and possibly a bite or two.'

'If you are to be bitten, I hope that it is at least by a pretty young lady and not by her mama.'

Wick groaned, but there was a smile in his eyes. 'I told Mantheria how it would be, but she insisted that I accompany you two.'

Her heart sank a little. He didn't want to be here. With her. She knew it, of course. Yet his words still stung like a wasp's sting.

'Cheswick, is that you? I thought you hibernated during the season with your father's beasts.'

Wick manoeuvred both himself and Louisa to face a man whose looks were arresting. His curly golden locks were longer than most men's. His eyes were a startling light blue in his slim, pale face. His suit was also golden, and he wore lace on his sleeves and around his throat. On his feet were golden heels with large brass buckles.

Louisa had never seen a more beautiful gentleman, or any person more sumptuously dressed. But he appeared fashionably bored and indolent.

The man held an ornate golden quizzing glass surrounded by diamonds and he brought up to his right eye and feigned surprise. When he spoke again his voice was surprisingly high and soft. 'It *is* you! I do believe you once told me at a curricle race that polite society was not your natural habitat.'

Louisa could feel the muscles in Wick's arms tighten underneath her fingers as he gave the man a painful smile

that looked more like a grimace. He inclined his head slightly. 'Lord Norwich.'

The golden man dropped his quizzing glass. 'Would you do me the honour of presenting me to your companion? Word has spread quickly of her beauty and her identity. And how she was singled out by the Queen for conversation.'

Louisa couldn't help but look from the dazzling man to Wick and back again in surprise. Rumours about her were spreading through town! She wondered how long it would be until they reached her family.

Taking a step, Louisa moved closer to Wick.

Sighing, Wick gave another grimacing smile. 'Lady Louisa, may I present the Earl of Norwich?'

Louisa curtsied slightly and the golden man, with a speed belied by his previous indolence, took her free hand in his and gently kissed it. Her pulse quickened in fear or attraction—she was not sure which emotion.

'Lady Louisa, would you do me the honour of joining the set?'

She glanced at Wick and he gave her another sharp nod. Releasing her hold on his arm, she allowed Norwich to lead her away from him. She couldn't help stealing a glance over her shoulder to look back at Wick. He was no longer alone, but surrounded by a crowd of women. Some, she guessed, were the matchmaking mamas, and the others their daughters. A sharp pang of jealousy cut through her.

Turning back to her partner, she knew that she had no right to be jealous. Wick was not hers. And he never would be.

Lord Norwich led her to the dance floor and to their correct place. Louisa's pulse continued to race. She was

finally dancing at a *ton* ball and she prayed that she wouldn't make a cake of herself. She saw that several eyes were upon them. She couldn't help but think it was her partner's elaborate suit in its shocking golden shade that made them look. But not all the eyes were female. Men of all ages were looking at them. At her.

Louisa's hands shook as she clasped hands with Lord Norwich for the first figure of the set. She tried to block out the people around her and focus solely on the music and the dancing. She desperately wished that she'd had more time with the dancing master Mantheria had employed to prepare her.

Taking another gentleman's hand, she glanced up to see that it was Wick.

He smiled at her, with no grimace. 'You're dancing superbly.'

But before she could answer he had moved to his next partner in the set and she was back with Lord Norwich. The look he gave her felt predatory… Shaking her head, she thought that perhaps she'd spent too much time with the younger Stringham sisters. She looked for Wick and saw that he was partnered with a pretty brunette with a heart-shaped face. The young woman was smiling, but Wick looked as if he'd had all his teeth pulled out.

'Would you be willing to indulge my curiosity, my lady?' Lord Norwich asked, his voice so soft that she could barely hear him over the lively music.

They spun together in a circle. 'I do not know, my lord. Ask your question and I will do my best to answer.'

Norwich laughed softly. It was more a breath of air than a sound. 'Despite having the countenance of an ingénue, you play the game like a dowager. Why were you

not presented before now? You are older than most of the debutantes.'

Louisa was grateful that the figure caused them to separate at that moment, giving her time to come up with an answer. She could tell him the truth—but she did not wish to confide in him. Lord Norwich was certainly beautiful, yet he felt cold. Mocking. Indolent. None of the things that she hoped for in a suitor and a husband.

They clasped hands again. She gave him her most dazzling smile. 'I was thinking the same thing about you, my lord.'

One of his eyebrow's quirked up. 'I beg your pardon?'

'That you look older than most of the debutantes.'

Norwich gave another of his nearly soundless laughs. Louisa was glad that her sally had not insulted him.

The music ended and they bowed to each other. Lord Norwich took her hand and led her to the side of the room, where Mantheria was standing next to Lord Sunderland. He relinquished her hand and bowed to them both. Mantheria snapped her fan open to hide her face and Louisa guessed that she disliked the Earl.

Sunderland inclined his head. 'Norwich.'

The Earl took a deep breath before slowly picking up his quizzing glass and gazing at Mantheria and Lord Sunderland. 'Sunny…still pining for the one who got away?'

Louisa saw Mantheria's face pale at his insinuation, and Lord Sunderland's cheeks coloured. Louisa touched her throat and wondered if there was something between her friend and the young Duke who was most certainly *not* her husband.

'After another heiress, Norwich?' Sunderland said be-

tween clenched teeth. 'I suppose someone must pay for your many tailors. Lady Louisa, shall we?'

Sunderland offered his hand to Louisa and she took it. They returned to the dance floor and performed the Roger de Coverley. The young Duke did not speak much, for which Louisa was most grateful. It took all her concentration to follow the steps of the figures with only occasional glances at Wick. His partner this time was a small, beautiful blonde, with the sort of curvaceous figure Louisa had always wished for. Instead, she was a beanpole, with small breasts and not many curves to speak of.

Wick, however, didn't seem too impressed by his lovely partner. His expression was one of long suffering.

'I see I am not the only one besotted with a Stringham,' Sunderland said as they clasped arms. 'Happily, not the same one. How awkward that would be.'

His words surprised Louisa into a laugh, and then she blushed. She'd hoped that her feelings for Wick were not too obvious.

'They're not,' he said, as if he were reading her thoughts. 'I simply recognise the look of another sufferer.'

Sunderland's eyes moved from her to Mantheria, who was dancing with an older gentleman. 'Mayhap your story will have a happier ending than mine. I can assure you that I will do all in my power to assist you. Although Wick is as stubborn as a mule and twice as stupid when it comes to his heart.'

Louisa blinked at him, her own heart sinking a little. 'Lord Cheswick has made it very clear that he does not wish to court me.'

'I did that to a lady once too—to my eternal regret.'

She was now sure that he was speaking of Mantheria, who had married another man. Another duke, even.

'Don't give in too easily,' Sunderland said, bowing over her hand at the end of the dance. 'Love is worth fighting for.'

The Duke led her to the opposite side of the room, where Wick was releasing the hand of the beautiful blonde.

Sunderland bowed to them. 'Wick, I have brought you your partner for the next dance. Lady Laetitia, would you do me the honour?'

The young Duke then placed Louisa's hand into Wick's and offered his arm to the young blonde. They walked away.

Louisa felt a burning heat where their fingers touched and it spread throughout her entire body. She glanced up at Wick, but his expression was unreadable. Perhaps he did not wish to be forced to dance with her by his friend. Embarrassed, Louisa tried to pull back her arm. She didn't want his pity.

Wick's larger hand tightened around hers. 'Shall we?'

She glanced down. 'Only if you wish to.'

'I'd rather dance with you than any other woman in the room.'

Shaking her head, she smiled, bemused. 'I am not sure that is a very high compliment, for I know that you do not wish to be here.'

His eyes met hers. 'I find that at this moment there is no other place I wish to be.'

Louisa pursed her lips and tried to swallow down her joy. She didn't want anyone besides Lord Sunderland to know of her *tendre* for Wick.

The country dance was a vigorous one. With lots of

hopping, clapping and spinning. And every time their hands touched she felt as if she were on fire. A candle burning brightly in the night. Hot and dangerous. When his eyes met hers, she could almost imagine the sparks between them.

The dance, like all perfect things, ended too quickly. Although it had to have been at least a half an hour.

'What do you think of your first ball so far?' Wick asked, leading her off the dance floor. 'You've already surpassed every other lady here. You have danced with the three highest-ranking gentlemen in the room.'

She fluttered her eyelashes in surprise. 'I did not think you held Lord Norwich in high esteem?'

'The man is made by his tailors.'

'Is he what they call a Bond Street Beau?'

Wick snorted derisively. 'A more apt phrase would be a Bond Street Buffoon.'

Louisa couldn't keep in a trill of laughter.

He glanced down at her, his lips twitching into an almost-smile. Something intangible was still simmering between them even now, after the dance was over. She was certain that he felt it too.

Wick cleared his throat and turned his head away from her. 'Come, let me escort you back to Mantheria, who can find you more eligible partners before I am besieged by the matchmaking mamas.'

Swallowing down her disappointment, Louisa managed to rally a little. 'Have you been scratched or bitten by one of them yet?'

His lips twitched again, but she saw him suppress the smile. He led her over to Mantheria, who was surrounded by gentlemen.

Wick bowed over her hand before letting her go. 'The only scratch I've received has been from you.'

Before Louisa could interpret the meaning of his words, Mantheria had linked arms with her.

'My dear Lady Louisa,' she said in a bright voice. 'All of these gentlemen are waiting eagerly to be introduced to the diamond of the season.'

She stopped watching Wick walk away from her and focused on the four gentlemen standing around her friend.

'Oh, dear,' Louisa said, shaking her head and touching her flaming red hair. 'I thought I was a ruby.'

The gentlemen laughed politely, and she tried not to feel too disappointed that Wick was not among them.

# Chapter Eighteen

The next night, Wick groaned audibly and tried to shake Sunny's hand from his arm. But despite being smaller and lighter his friend had a surprisingly strong grip.

'Let go of me, you idiot.'

Sunny's fingers pinched into Wick's flesh further through his evening coat as they walked down the street, passing carriages waiting to unload their passengers.

'Mantheria asked me to make sure that you attended this ball.'

For the third night in a row, Wick would be stuck at a *ton* squeeze. A fate he did not feel he deserved. 'I suppose we could look into Lady Kensington's ball for a little while. I've agreed to go. Now let go of me—before I make your nose even more crooked than it already is.'

His friend released his arm. 'Just another street away.'

They walked a few more feet before Wick sighed and asked, 'Why are you so determined to get me to this ball?'

Sunny, whose countenance was usually as light and happy as his nickname suggested, looked grave and serious. 'I gave your sister my word.'

'She shouldn't have asked you to.'

'Mantheria could ask me anything and I would do it gladly.'

His friend's words caused him to stop in his tracks. 'What do you mean by that?'

Sunny took a deep breath and then exhaled. 'I never thought I would tell you this… I never thought I would want to. But when we were twenty-one and still at Oxford, do you remember, we went home to Hampford Castle for Christmas? Mantheria was only sixteen, but she was the most beautiful woman I had ever seen. So, being my stupid self, I tried to avoid her—but she caught me underneath the mistletoe and kissed me. There are only a handful of moments in my life that are transcending and that was one of mine. I promised to dance with her at her come-out ball in the spring, when she would turn seventeen and have her first season.'

Wick didn't know what to think or what to say. Despite being best friends for years, he and Sunny rarely spoke of their feelings. It was even more awkward to hear that Sunny seemed to harbour emotions for Wick's sister.

He shook his head. 'You didn't come to her ball.'

'I know. Mantheria cornered me the day after, wanting to know why,' Sunny said, bringing his hands to cover his eyes. 'I told her that I had no intention of getting married any time soon and therefore would not be attending *any* of the debutante balls. The expression on her face is one I will never forget. She didn't cry. She didn't try to argue with me. She simply became coldly polite. And three weeks later she was engaged to the Duke of Glastonbury—the greatest catch on the marriage mart with a fortune ten times the size of my own. I told myself that I was happy for her. I went to her blasted wedding and watched her walk away with another man. I

thought it would break my heart, but I was still a young fool. My heart was only bruised. It wouldn't truly break until I saw how unhappy she was in her marriage and could do nothing about it. It was too late.'

Wick patted his friend on the shoulder awkwardly, attempting to show his compassion. 'I am sorry, Sunny, but I don't understand why you're telling me this now and on the way to a ball.'

He watched Sunny's gloved hands tighten into fists. 'I don't want to watch my best friend make the same mistake.'

'What do you mean?'

'Don't be obtuse, Wick. You care for Lady Louisa. I can see it. Your sisters can see it.'

Wick began to walk again and could hear Sunny's footfalls behind him. They passed several houses before he spoke. 'I am not ready for marriage yet.'

'I don't know any man who is. But believe me, you won't want to see her married to someone else. Someone like Lord Norwich.'

'Or Lord Glastonbury?'

Sunny nodded slowly.

Wick hadn't liked watching Norwich dance with Louisa. Or with Sunny for that matter. Or even the eligible and not so eligible gentlemen who had claimed her hand for a set the night before. It had been torture. But nothing like the pain of losing someone he loved. Of feeling partially responsible for their death.

'I am not interested in marriage.'

Sighing, Sunny bumped Wick's arm with his elbow. 'You've got to let them go, mate. It's been nearly ten years. You have to let your grief for Charles and Elizabeth stop dragging you down. There was nothing you could have done. Scarlet fever killed them—not you. And you're the

reason your other five siblings are still alive. You rode to London and got a proper doctor to take care of them instead of a country quack.'

'It wasn't enough.'

What Wick was really saying was that *he* wasn't enough.

'You were only sixteen. Still a child. And, as much as I love your parents, they should never have asked you to bear such a heavy weight. You weren't ready for it then, but you are now. You're doing a bang-up job of taking care of your sisters.'

He huffed. 'I've already lost a governess and have yet to find a suitable replacement.'

'And your parents have lost five governesses—six if you count the old battle-axe Nix, who retired. Give yourself some credit... And sooner or later you'll have to settle down and make heirs. It might as well be with someone you love.'

Wick was saved from giving Sunny an answer because they had arrived in front of Lady Kensington's redbrick townhouse. Footmen lined the front façade and eagerly ran to open carriage doors and assist the guests into the well-lit house. Wick and Sunny passed two footmen on the way to the front door. They followed the line of guests into the hall, where Lord and Lady Kensington stood greeting them.

Lady Kensington's eyes widened, and she grinned when she saw the pair of them. She stepped towards them with her hands outstretched and squeezed each of their hands. 'Lord Sunderland... Lord Cheswick, how delighted I am that you were able to come. I am sure all the young ladies will be thrilled as well.'

'It is my pleasure,' Sunny said with his polished smile.

'Ah, Kensington, we have missed you the last few days at Parliament. Are you quite recovered from your cold?'

Wick didn't hear the lord's answer, because Lady Kensington had stepped in front of him. 'Rumour has it, Lord Cheswick, that you are here for the lovely Lady Louisa Bracken. The latest heiress who is strangely not in possession of her own fortune.'

His jaw clenched. 'No. It is in the control of her relatives, the Rockinghams.'

Lady Kensington gave him a glittering smile and nodded. 'Yes, your dear sister Lady Glastonbury asked me personally to invite them tonight. And Lady Cowper so dear Lady Louisa could get a voucher to Almack's and permission to waltz.'

Wick bowed, groaning inwardly. He fervently hoped his sister wasn't planning on creating a scene with the Rockinghams. 'I pray it has not been a great inconvenience?' he said.

'Nonsense. I am hedging my bets upon it making my party the most talked of event of the season.'

He gave her a perfunctory smile and walked past her husband to catch up with Sunny. They were among the last guests to arrive. The rooms were already so full that it was hard to walk to where Mantheria and Louisa were standing. Wick had to apologise more than once for bumping into a sir or a lord. Lady Kensington's party was truly deserving of the epithet 'a squeeze'.

Mantheria gave them both a glittering smile and Sunny a pointed look.

He nodded, and held out his hand to Louisa. 'May I have the first dance, my lady?'

Louisa's eyes were on Wick as she said, 'Yes.'

Sunny managed to lead her through the throng to the crowded dance floor. It was only then that Wick re-

alised his friend usually danced first with Mantheria at every ball. He gazed at his sister and wondered if she returned Sunny's regard. Not that it mattered. She had a husband. A husband who was having an affair with another woman…

Mantheria gently tapped his arm with her fan. 'Thank you for coming, Wick. I should love to stand and chat, but I must go and procure more partners for Louisa.'

He grabbed at her hand to stop her. 'Wait, I need to tell you something.'

Mantheria turned on her heel to look at him. Her eyes were hooded. 'What?'

'Glastonbury isn't away in the country,' Wick said slowly. 'I ran into him at White's… He has never left London. I don't think you'll see him here tonight, at Lady Kensington's party, but just in case I don't want you to be surprised. Or embarrassed if someone mentions seeing him.'

'You're warning me not to give the excuse that my husband is out of town,' Mantheria said, waving her painted fan at him. 'But you needn't have bothered. For reasons unknown, the beau monde never minds if a man has an affair. They will not think less of me for coming alone to a party. Obedient wives are praised for their understanding natures. My popularity will only grow. There will not be a dance for which I won't have a partner.'

Wick took a deep breath. 'I'm sorry, Mantheria. I didn't call him out, but I did insult him. I couldn't help myself. I once idolised him, for goodness' sake. I even aped his ways…trying to flick my snuffbox open with only my thumb.'

She touched his shoulder. 'You don't even like snuff.'

'I was only pretending.'

'And so was I when I thought I could love him.'

He shook his head, clenching his teeth painfully together. 'But you have been faithful to him. You have done nothing wrong.'

Mantheria smiled sadly. 'Nor have I done much right in my marriage besides Andrew. You can ignore your feelings, like I did, but that will not make them go away. Be wiser with your heart than I have been, my dearest brother.'

Wick's heart already felt rather battered, and the pain didn't lessen as he watched Louisa dance with Sunny, Lord Carlisle, Mr Peterson and Lord Norwich. Despite being approached by several matrons who dropped extremely obvious hints, he did not dance.

He couldn't.

Standing at the side of the room, his eyes followed Louisa and Mantheria through the figures of the dance. His sister Helen had the same colouring as Mantheria and Elizabeth before she'd died, but if Lizzy had lived she would have matured like Mantheria and been a beauty in her own right. Would Elizabeth have wed and become a mother by now, too? Had she survived, would she have stopped Mantheria from marrying a man she didn't love? Would Elizabeth have seen past Glastonbury's wealth and title to his soul?

Elizabeth had been sensitive like that. She had sensed other people's emotions, and more than once soothed Wick's pride or bruised ego. How different all their lives might have been if she and Charles had lived. If he could have saved them both. Then maybe he could have courted Louisa. Loved her.

Instead, he watched her twirl around the dance floor with another man.

# Chapter Nineteen

Despite wearing another beautiful new gown of celestial blue with a matching silk slip, Louisa felt rather flat. Wick had arrived late to the Kensington ball and he had not asked her to dance. It was some solace, but not much, that he had not asked any other young lady to dance either. He was making it clear to the world—and to Louisa—that he hated these things and everything to do with the marriage mart.

She needed to stop hoping for him to change. For him to love her. Besides, she was not worthy of his love. The gentlemen who had asked her to dance seemed to be fonder of her fortune than of her face. It was just as Aunt Rockingham had warned her. Without her title and her money, Louisa was nothing.

Her partner Mr Snow bowed to her and took her hand to lead her to the crowded side of the ballroom, where Mantheria stood next to two young gentlemen. Louisa assumed that they would be her next partners. The young and beautiful Duchess had made sure that Louisa had a partner for every set.

A step away from Mantheria, Louisa felt someone grab

her free arm and step on the hem of her gown. Louisa thought it might be Wick, but when she turned her head she saw that it was Cousin Barnabas. 'Louisa, what are you doing here?' he said, in a loud voice that caused several pairs of eyes to turn in their direction. 'Mother has been looking everywhere for you.'

'Let go of me!' she said, twisting out of his grip and tearing the flounce on her gown.

Barnabas reached for her arm again—but this time Wick stood between them. 'If you lay a finger on her I will knock you to the floor. Then beat you senseless.'

Her cousin blinked and his bulbous eyes focused on Wick's muscular arms. Louisa knew that it was no idle threat and felt her own confidence rising. She was no longer friendless and helpless. All the Stringhams had accepted her into their pack, and Wick's sisters would have fought for her as viciously as he did.

'Louisa!' Aunt Rockingham practically yelled from the other side of the dance floor and rushed towards her. The crowd parted to make way for her and all eyes fell on Louisa.

Her aunt tried to brush past Wick, but still he stood between them. 'No, Lady Rockingham. You are not to touch her.'

'She is my niece. I am her guardian.'

The once loud ballroom was now as silent as a church on a Thursday afternoon.

Louisa found her backbone and her tongue. 'I am of age, Aunt Rockingham. You have no further hold on me.'

Aunt Rockingham clutched at the diamonds around her neck. 'Is this how I am to be treated after taking care of you for over ten years? For loving and protecting you?

I would not have thought you so ungrateful as to run away with a stranger. I have been so worried.'

There were several gasps. Louisa glanced around the room and saw that the dancing had stopped. Everyone was watching the scene her cousin and her aunt were making as if they were in a play on the stage.

Wick stepped menacingly towards her relatives but Louisa placed a hand on his arm. The Stringham sisters didn't need anyone to stand up for them. They stood up for themselves and she could do that too. She stepped forward to challenge them head-on.

'I was tired of being your servant, Aunt Rockingham,' Louisa said loudly. 'I was weary of wearing rags while you were dressed in diamonds. You claimed that my allowance would not cover better clothing, or even boots that did not pinch. You said that you could not afford to bring me to London for my debut. If that is the case, then you need not worry about spending another farthing on me. I have friends who do not begrudge me the basic necessities of life, and they treat me with the honour that I should have received in my own home, as befits my birth and station in life.'

'How dare you speak to my mother that way?' Barnabas said, raising his hand as if to slap her.

Louisa briefly closed her eyes, but the blow did not fall. Instead, she saw Wick standing over her cousin, who was flat on his back on the floor. Wick delivered another punch to Barnabas's face and then grabbed his coat collar, dragging him across the ballroom floor and out of the room. The expression on his countenance was murderous. She almost felt sorry for her cousin. *Almost.*

'This is not over,' Aunt Rockingham said.

'I should think not,' Mantheria said, linking her arm

with Louisa's. 'You will be hearing from my lawyers to-morrow about the misappropriation of your ward's funds. I suggest that you contact your own solicitors.'

For the first time in Louisa's life she thought she saw fear on her aunt's face. The woman's left eye twitched and her mouth was set in a grim line.

'You will regret this, Louisa.'

'The only regret that *I* have, Lady Rockingham,' Mantheria said loftily, 'is wasting even a minute in your tedious company. Come, Lady Louisa, there are more important people to speak with.'

Louisa's heart raced as she and Mantheria walked away from her livid aunt. She supposed that her aunt knew better than to cross swords with a duchess. Even one as young as her friend.

She exhaled slowly. 'I hope we haven't ruined Lady Kensington's ball.'

Mantheria laughed, patting Louisa's arm reassuringly. 'Oh, no, Louisa. If anything, we have made it the most talked about event of the season. She will be ecstatic—I promised her fireworks. Lady Kensington really ought to send us a thank-you note.'

A small, nervous giggle escaped Louisa's lips, but she sobered when she glanced down at the torn flounce that was dragging on the floor. 'I am afraid Barnabas stepped on my hem and tore it. Do you mind if I go to the retiring room and repair it quickly?'

'I shall come with you,' Mantheria said. 'But I must warn you that I have no skill with a needle. I am coming only to offer emotional support.'

Together they walked into the retiring room, and Louisa let go of her friend's arm to kneel down and reach the needle she had stuck inside her hem.

'You have brought your own needle?' the Duchess said with a little laugh.

Louisa tied a knot in the end of the thread and poked the needle through the inside of her gown, to attach it to the torn flounce. 'I never go anywhere without one. You never know when you might need a needle.'

'I am duly chastened,' Mantheria said solemnly, but her eyes danced with laughter. 'However, I would more likely prick my thumb than actually accomplish anything if I carried a needle around. My old governess, Miss Nix, was always saying, "Don't bleed on the cloth." She was always more concerned for the material than for my poor injuries.'

Louisa made several tight little stitches to secure the flounce to her gown. She made one last loop and knotted it. 'Then perhaps it is best that you don't carry anything sharp.'

Mantheria let out a trill of laughter and Louisa found herself smiling, despite everything.

She poked the needle through her hem and stood up. 'I am ready.'

'To be the belle of the ball?'

'Yes.'

Mantheria looped her arm with Louisa's. 'Good. For you deserve to be, my friend.'

They left the retiring room just as the musicians began to play a new tune, and Mantheria took her to where Lord Sunderland stood.

He bowed to her. 'My lady… Shall we dance? Or would you prefer I fetch you a glass of punch after that unfortunate ordeal?'

Louisa would have loved a drink, but she had waited

her whole life to go to parties and dance. Holding out her hand, she smiled. 'Dance, please.'

Lord Sunderland led her to the front of the dance floor, the most prominent position. He was a duke, after all, and for the first time she saw his countenance wore a hauteur equal to his rank. He stared down several matrons, and even a lord. Louisa might have lost a little of her heart to him if she hadn't known that he was doing it all for Mantheria. The woman he loved and could never have.

He put his hand on her waist and then they twirled together. 'I'd say our plan is working extraordinarily well. It is obvious that Wick cares for you. He has never made a public scene before, and he's now nursing his dignity out on the terrace.'

'Lord Sunderland—'

'Sunny, please.'

They switched hands in the dance. 'Sunny, just because Wick cares for me, it doesn't mean that he's ready for marriage.'

'Don't give up on him yet. I haven't. You should ask him about his brother and sister.'

Louisa didn't know to which sister Sunny was referring. Frederica? Helen? Becca? It seemed odd for him to tell her to ask him about his brother Matthew, whom she had never had the pleasure of meeting. Mantheria said he avoided society balls even more assiduously than Wick.

After the dance ended he returned her to Mantheria, who kissed both of Louisa's cheeks. 'You were marvellous and so self-possessed. You are the envy of every lady in the room. Let me find you another partner. It would be quite a different sort of scandal if Sunny danced with you three times.'

Louisa held up her hand to stop her well-meaning

friend. 'I am very thirsty and quite out of breath. I think I shall go to the refreshment table and rest for this set.'

Mantheria smiled. 'I will come with you.'

'Oh, no you don't,' Sunny said, possessing himself of Mantheria's hand. 'I have danced with every single lady you have told me to. Now it is my choice and I choose you.'

A pretty pink stole into Mantheria's cheeks as she allowed Sunny to escort her away from Louisa. How she wished her friend could have the happy ending she so richly deserved! But Louisa knew from her own experience that life was not fair. And happy endings were rare.

Several people openly ogled her as she made her way to the refreshment table. A few ladies even looked at her and talked behind their hands. Sighing, she picked up a ladle and poured some lemonade into a glass tumbler. Her throat felt rather dry and scratchy. She had not been fibbing to Mantheria when she'd said that she was out of breath. Louisa was not used to dancing vigorously for several hours at a time.

After draining her cup, she immediately refilled it.

'I see that you are fond of lemonade.'

She didn't have to look up to know that voice—it was Wick's. He was standing near her, the ladle now in his hand as he poured himself a drink.

Louisa knew that several eyes were on them, but she couldn't quite keep in her smile. 'As are you.'

Wick took a sip of the sour concoction and made a face. 'I would infinitely prefer something stronger.'

Sipping, she nodded slightly. 'So should I after that awful scene with my family... I feel I am constantly thanking you, but please accept my gratitude for protecting me from my cousin. He's never tried to hit me before.'

'You've never defied him before.'

Louisa didn't know how Wick knew that, but it was accurate. She'd been nothing but a doormat for her relatives to wipe their feet on. 'I wish it had been me who had punched him.'

Wick lifted his glass to his lips. 'He's not worth bloodying your knuckles over.'

Her eyes went to his white gloves as he took a drink and she saw that they were discoloured around his knuckles. 'Oh, dear. I didn't know that you had been hurt. I am so terribly sorry.'

He drained the rest of his lemonade in one big gulp. 'Don't be. My fists have been itching to hit your cousin's face ever since I learned your true name. I haven't felt this good in weeks. The only thing that would make my night better would be to dance with you.'

Louisa's heart expanded in her chest in forlorn hope. His eyes were gazing intensely into hers; she could have happily lost herself in them. Then Wick leaned slightly towards her and she revelled in his scent—spicy and masculine with a hint of vanilla. His gaze dropped to her lips, and she couldn't help but lick them. How she longed to be kissed by him!

But Wick shook his head and stepped back. 'It is best not to. I have no wish to cause further scandal, and the entire *ton* is now aware that you are not in possession of your fortune. I will go and see my grandfather first thing on Monday, and discover if he has learned who your trustees are. There's not a better businessman in all of England. Your inheritance will be yours soon, and you will need have no further connection or communication with your tedious relatives.'

Louisa brought the tumbler to her lips and choked down

a little lemonade. Wick was back to keeping her at arm's length.

'Ah, there you are, Lady Louisa,' a soft voice droned.

Wick jerked his head and gave the man a sharp bow. 'Norwich.'

The Earl of Norwich was not dressed in gold tonight, but in a stunning shade of salmon. Louisa was certain that no other gentleman could have worn such a suit of clothing and still appeared handsome. No, that wasn't a strong enough word: he was beautiful.

Louisa curtsied. 'My lord.'

'Lady Glastonbury assures me that you would be in raptures to dance with me again,' he said, with a slight sneer on his lips, as if he were addressing the question to Wick instead of herself. 'Unless you are already claimed…for this next set?'

The meaning behind Norwich's pause had to be as obvious to Wick as it was to Louisa. She stole a glance at him. Wick was wearing his grimacing grin that looked more painful than joyful.

'Happily, she is not.'

He took the glass from her hands and the hope from her heart.

Taking a deep breath, she put on her own grin. Louisa held out her hand for Lord Norwich to take. 'I *am* in raptures, my lord. Thank you for your kindness.'

Lord Norwich took her fingers and lifted them to his lips, placing a lingering kiss on top of her hand.

Louisa heard Wick groan, but he said nothing.

Did nothing.

As another man led her away from him.

# Chapter Twenty

On Monday morning, Wick drove his phaeton to pick Matthew up at his rooms. His brother was waiting on the steps of the building. He resembled Papa, with blond hair and blue eyes, and it irked him to admit that his little brother was four inches taller than him and considered to be the handsomer of the two. Despite being the Duke's 'spare' heir, Matthew was chased by matchmaking mamas even more than Wick was. Probably because he rarely left London.

Climbing into the phaeton, his brother smiled mischievously. 'I hear that you attended two balls last week—and a presentation at St James's Court.'

Wick flicked the reins. 'Yes.'

His brother elbowed him in the side. 'You went to the marriage mart…on purpose?'

'I escorted our sister and Lady Louisa to a couple of balls,' Wick said stiffly. 'Nothing more.'

'Did you dance?'

He was not about to give his little brother ammunition with which to tease him. He was almost as bad as his sisters. So Wick played the dunce. 'Is *that* what you're supposed to do at a ball? I am so glad somebody has told me.'

Matthew chortled merrily. 'If only I had seen you before Saturday. It is said that you didn't dance even once at Lady Kensington's ball. Although that might have been awkward for your partner after you'd bloodied your gloves on Lord Barnabas's face.'

Tightening his hold on the reins, Wick forced himself not to rise to his brother's baiting. 'I have been wanting to punch him in the nose since Eton.'

'You *did* punch him in the nose at Eton. I was there.'

A reluctant smile formed on his lips. Wick had forgotten that episode, having endured—and fought—several bullies while at school. Lord Barnabas was one of many who had picked a fight with him. If only Wick had broken his nose like he had Sunny's.

'I did hear that you danced with several eligible young ladies at Lady Dennard's ball,' said Matthew. 'But none so beautiful as a certain runaway heiress.'

Wick turned the corner quickly, causing his brother to hold on to the side of the phaeton. 'Say another word and I will flatten your nose next.'

Matthew only laughed.

They arrived at their Grandfather Stubbs's business premises and a groom took the horse's reins. Wick and Matthew entered his office. The old man sat behind his desk, his cane leaning against his chair. His white hair obscured his face as he studied the document in front of him. He didn't look up as they entered. Wick watched his maternal grandfather read for several more minutes before the man glanced up at them.

'You only visit me when you need something, Wick.'

He flushed, pulling at his collar. 'That's not true, Grandfather.'

'Your grandmother and I haven't seen hide nor hair of you in two months.'

Wick took off his hat and hung it on the rack. 'I've been busy trying to take care of my little sisters. They cannot seem to stay out of trouble for longer than a day. Not even that.'

'I hear they are in need of a governess *again*.'

He shrugged his shoulders and sighed. 'It would appear so.'

'Your Grandmother Stubbs thinks that one of her great-nieces might be of use.'

Wick cleared his throat. Anyone his starchy step-grandmother might select would not approve of his wild sisters, nor their pets. 'As much as I appreciate Grandmother Stubbs's offer, Mantheria is already handling it.'

Matthew laughed. 'Anyone want to lay odds on how long the new governess will last? I'll give you ten to one that she doesn't last a full day. Twenty to one she doesn't last more than three hours.'

Wick gave his brother a blistering glare, which only caused him to laugh harder. Even Grandfather Stubbs guffawed. Wick's lips quirked up of their own volition.

'Well, since you've brought the girls to London,' Grandfather Stubbs said, 'don't forget to bring them to visit us. I'd like to hear first-hand about their latest mischief. Frederica is the best storyteller of them all.'

'You'll need to reserve an entire afternoon,' Wick said dryly. 'Possibly two.'

'I wouldn't be averse to meeting your Lady Louisa, either. Rumour has it that she is a very lovely young woman.'

Matthew tried to elbow Wick again, but this time he wasn't driving his carriage. He grabbed his brother's

elbow and twisted his arm behind his brother's back, pushing his face against the wall. 'Not another word from you.'

'No fisticuffs in the office, boys,' their grandfather said, as if they were still children.

Wick released Matthew's arm and they sat down in chairs set on opposite sides of the room.

Grandfather Stubbs held up the document on his desk. 'I am particularly good friends with the head of Fordham's Bank…' he said. In other words, the man was terrified of his grandfather. 'He has been kind enough to send me a copy of the late Earl of Rockingham's will. I'll have my solicitors comb over it later, but it is straightforward. The late Earl's wife left her personal fortune of one hundred and fifty thousand pounds to her only daughter, Lady Louisa Bracken.'

Matthew let out a low whistle. 'You really do know how to choose them.'

Wick was scarcely less surprised. He'd thought Barnabas was exaggerating when he'd said that his cousin was set to inherit such a large fortune.

'She was meant to receive a yearly allowance of seventy-five hundred pounds for her maintenance While she was left in the guardianship of her uncle, the new Earl of Rockingham. Over the last ten years the amount would have come to seventy-five thousand pounds.'

Wick clenched his hands into fists. Her aunt and the current Earl had been stealing her allowance. 'The way Lady Rockingham has treated Louisa is robbery. She must have used the funds to support her own family and lifestyle, while keeping her niece in penury.'

Grandfather Stubbs set down the paper. 'Unfortunately, I don't think we will ever be able to recover those

funds. The late Earl didn't seem to realise that his brother and sister-in-law would treat his daughter poorly. He must have known that they were not good with money, for he appointed three trustees to invest her fortune: Mr Pickett, Lord Waller and Mr Biggs. As far as I can tell, they have done a bang-up job. Lady Louisa's fortune has grown under their management to one hundred and eighty thousand pounds.'

This time Wick whistled. 'No wonder Lady Rockingham wanted to keep Louisa in the family—or at least her fortune.'

'Yes,' Grandfather Stubbs said, rubbing the end of his beard. 'According to the will, Lady Louisa's fortune becomes her own when she reaches five-and-twenty years of age or when she marries someone of whom her guardians approves.'

'What can we do?'

Matthew cleared his throat. 'Nothing until she is married. The will is quite clear that she is to have no control over her fortune before her marriage or until she is five-and-twenty. I have sent letters to all three of Lady Louisa's trustees. Mr Biggs has already responded by sending a note with his servant. From what he says, that they will agree not to send this quarter of her yearly allowance to the Rockinghams, but they will not allow her to touch a penny of her fortune until there is a ring on her finger.'

Wick's hands curled into fists. This was not the answer he'd hoped for. Wick had wanted Louisa to be in full control of her fortune immediately. He didn't wish her to have to marry a rotter like Lord Norwich to receive her inheritance.

'At least the Rockinghams won't get their grimy fingers on another shilling of her fortune,' he said.

Matthew slumped in his chair. 'It might turn into a nasty scandal. I've heard rumours of the Rockinghams' financial difficulties in certain less respectable quarters. The Earl's heir seems to be drowning in gambling loans. He's tangled with a particularly villainous moneylender named Marcus Sullivan. If Lord Barnabas isn't careful, he'll end up being murdered and thrown into the Thames.'

Wick's grandfather grunted. 'The head of Fordham's also hinted that the Earl of Rockingham is in debt. He would not tell me how much. I could put pressure on him to do so…'

Wick shook his head. 'It doesn't matter. Perhaps it is best for Louisa to make a clean break from them.'

Matthew tapped his fingers on the wooden armrest of his chair. 'I wouldn't want to let them off that easily… We could threaten legal action if Lord Rockingham refuses to approve of the man Lady Louisa wishes to marry.'

Wick knew they meant *him*.

Grandfather Stubbs smiled and Matthew smirked.

He blushed like a blasted debutante at her first ball. 'I have no intention of marrying Lady Louisa. Of marrying anyone.'

'Then you haven't asked her yet?' his grandfather asked.

'Wick has always been a bit slow.'

He jumped out of his chair and charged at his annoying little brother. Matthew might be taller, but Wick was broader and stronger. His brother tried to push Wick off as he got to his feet. But Wick wrapped his arms around Matthew and, after receiving a few hits to the shoulder and face, soon had him in a choke hold.

Matthew tapped the arm that was around his neck. 'Give!'

Wick released his brother. They were both breathing hard. Grandfather Stubbs chuckled. Matthew shrugged and then laughed, clapping Wick on the back.

And then Wick couldn't hold it in any longer—he laughed too.

## Chapter Twenty-One

Wick wished that he had better news to bring to Louisa and his sisters. In fact, he would have preferred to break the news of the conditions in her father's will to only Louisa and Mantheria. But Becca, Helen and Frederica would not leave the room without bodily violence. And, while he was more than happy to wrestle Matthew, he wasn't about to give his little sisters the same treatment. Especially since he knew that they fought with their fingernails.

Clearing his throat, he forced himself to look at Louisa. She was looking a little pale. There were shadows underneath her luminous green eyes. He wished the words that he was about to speak were better tidings.

'My grandfather has procured a copy of your father's will, Louisa, and he has been in touch with all three of your trustees.'

Becca clapped her hands. 'I knew he could do it!'

Helen hushed her, and then Mantheria hushed them both.

Louisa's gaze never left his face.

'Unfortunately, the late Earl's will specifically states

that Louisa is not to have control of her mother's fortune until her five-and-twentieth birthday or until she is—'

'Married.' Louisa finished the phrase for him.

'What rot!' Frederica said, grinding her teeth.

For once, Wick was entirely in agreement with his most wilful sister. But it didn't change the facts.

'My grandfather is certain he will be able to convince the trustees not to issue any more of Louisa's yearly allowance to the Rockinghams. So at least they will no longer profit from their exploitation of her and treating her like a servant in her own home.'

Louisa leaned forward, and it was as if her eyes were devouring him whole. 'And the money they've already taken from me?'

Sighing, he admitted, 'It is lost. There was nothing in your father's will to stipulate exactly how the yearly allowance for your maintenance should be spent by his brother and his wife.'

All his sisters were talking at once. Wick couldn't follow all the conversations, but the expressions on his sisters' faces were murderous.

He held up both of his hands. 'Quiet!'

One by one his sisters stopped talking and looked at him.

'I know that this is not the news any of us hoped for, but Grandfather and Matthew are still working on it. And if anyone can twist a situation to his advantage, it's Matt. Now, we can stay here, arguing over what cannot be currently changed, or I can take you all for ices.'

His nephew Andrew had been playing in the corner of the room with his boat, but at the sound of the word 'ices' he dropped the wooden toy. 'I would like an ice!'

'I'll call for Mantheria's barouche,' said Wick, eager

to leave the room and no longer be followed by Louisa's disappointed eyes.

All six of them squashed into the large carriage, and none of his little sisters argued on the way. A rare trip.

When they arrived at Gunter's, Wick ordered Andrew's raspberry ice first. Then ordered for all his sisters. He would have given Louisa the next choice, but she was still trying to decide on the flavour, and whether she wanted a sweet or a savoury one. Wick ordered both: one parmesan ice and one strawberry ice—his personal favourite.

They all sat down at a table in the centre of the room. Every eye was on them. His family drew attention wherever they went. They were infamously wealthy, and notorious for not caring about the *ton*'s rules.

Andrew's ice came first, and his nephew did not wait for the others to receive their own treats before he began spooning it into his mouth. Wick was the last to receive his strawberry ice, but he didn't mind. He was enjoying himself watching Louisa.

'Try the strawberry one first,' he told her.

She dipped her spoon into the pink ice and took a very small bite. He watched her touch the spoon to her lips. How he burned to touch those lips with his fingers. His mouth. His tongue. Louisa licked her lips and her eyes were on his. She took another small bite, this time of the parmesan ice. Never before had Wick thought that the eating of an ice could be seductive. But it was when Louisa used both her lips and her tongue to take such a small bite off the spoon.

'Why aren't you eating, Uncle Wick?' Andrew asked.

Wick had been so absorbed in watching Louisa that he had not started on his own ice. Feeling the blood rush

to his face, he picked up his spoon and took a large cooling bite. The ice made his tongue cold, but the rest of his body was still on fire. Longing for Louisa. Wanting to kiss her over and over again.

Mantheria smiled with knowing eyes at both of them. 'Louisa, what do you think of your first ices? Do you prefer sweet or savoury?'

Louisa lowered her eyes, her cheeks turning a pretty shade of pink. 'The sweet—but the parmesan is also nice, and an unexpected taste.'

'It was our brother Charles's favourite.'

Wick choked on the ice in his mouth, feeling cold all over.

'Charles was our third brother,' Mantheria explained. 'Just two years older than myself and my twin sister.'

Louisa set down her spoon. 'I am sorry. I did not know that you had a twin...or a brother named Charles.'

Wick's sisters rarely talked about Charles and Elizabeth around him. They knew how painful he found it. But Mantheria seemed determined to open that old wound today.

'I don't remember them very well,' Becca admitted, her lips drooping. 'I was only three when they died.'

Mantheria's eyes were full of unshed tears, but she smiled. 'Oh, they would not wish for you to be sad that they are gone. Both Charles and Elizabeth were the happiest children I ever knew. Charles was so sweet, and he loved animals—just like you and Helen. He taught Sadie the elephant all her parlour tricks—like putting on her own cloak and kneeling to allow rides. And he didn't like sweet foods at all. Not even fruits. That is why the parmesan ice was his favourite.'

'Charles was usually good-natured,' Wick said. 'But

Papa called him Char Bear, because occasionally you'd poke him and he'd get really angry, like a bear. I was teasing him one night at dinner and he picked up his plate and pushed it into my face. There were carrots in my hair and gravy on my nose.'

'And mashed potatoes in Wick's eyebrows,' Mantheria added.

Helen put her elbows on the table and leaned forward. 'What did Mama and Papa do?'

Wick shook his head. 'Nothing.'

'Nothing?' Becca repeated.

Wick couldn't help but smile at the memory. 'Mama said that justice had been served and told Harper to bring me another plate. We continued eating dinner as if nothing were amiss.'

Helen shook her head. 'And you say *we* are wild animals!'

'What about Elizabeth?' Becca asked eagerly, her ice quite forgotten.

'Elizabeth loved sweet things,' Frederica said, sniffing. 'She was the only one who could steal biscuits from the kitchens without getting into trouble. Papa said that her tongue was sweeter than sugar. No one could stay cross with her for long.'

'She was very slight…bordering on frail,' Wick found himself saying. 'Cook was always trying to fatten her up. It wouldn't surprise me if Cook had brought her the biscuits.'

'Or Mrs May!' Mantheria said with a little laugh. 'They both doted on her. She was the good twin and I was the naughty one.'

'That hasn't changed,' Helen said, giggling.

But it had. Wick had been the only one old enough

at the time to see it. Mantheria had changed after Elizabeth's death. She had become serious, obedient and eager to please, as if trying to take the place of her twin in the family. She had carried a heavy burden as the oldest daughter.

Wick's eyes filled with tears and he got to his feet abruptly. 'Come with me, Andrew. I'll buy you another ice. Yours is all gone.'

His sticky nephew dropped his spoon on the table with a clatter and eagerly placed his hand in Wick's. They walked away from their seats, but he could still hear his sisters' voices.

'Wick blames himself for their deaths,' Mantheria said. 'He was the oldest, and our parents were away in Africa when scarlet fever hit the family. He rode all night to London, to fetch a specialist for Charles, but it was too late. The fever had taken his strength and his heart. Wick stayed up with both of them, night after night. Charles died a few days later and Elizabeth did not outlast him by more than an hour... I know it sounds strange, but I was glad of that. I had always been with Elizabeth, and I was happy to know that neither of them was alone— even in heaven.'

'Mama and Papa didn't blame Wick,' Frederica said. 'They blamed themselves for leaving us. I suppose we all feel the guilt of surviving when they didn't.'

Unconsciously, Wick tightened his hold on Andrew's wrist. His sisters had put his feelings into words that he never could. As he'd held Charles's slender hand in those final hours, he had prayed that God would take his life instead. But his prayers had not been answered.

'Too tight, Uncle Wick!' Andrew protested, yanking his hand away.

'Sorry,' he said with a sniff.

Wick would always be sorry.

# Chapter Twenty-Two

They finished their ices and Mantheria suggested they stroll in the park before heading back home. Louisa was grateful for the extra time with a certain marquess, and the younger Stringham sisters also took up this suggestion with enthusiasm.

Once they reached the park, they began running along the path. Andrew tried to keep up with them, and Mantheria followed her son. Louisa slowly walked behind them and found Wick by her side. The familiar thrill of his nearness caused her pulse to quicken and her mind to reel. She wished she knew what to say to him. How to comfort so great a loss.

Wick cleared his throat. 'I suppose I won't see you again until tomorrow night at Sunny's ball. He's promised actual fireworks, after I assured him that we were not going to offer another free drama or more fighting for his guests. He confessed his keen disappointment, but still wishes us to come.'

A smile played on his lips and made him look breathtakingly handsome. Wick was so dear to her. Too dear, perhaps.

'How forbearing of him,' she teased gently. 'Who is hostess for the ball? A gentleman doesn't host a party alone, I believe?'

He nodded. 'Sunny's mother, the Dowager Duchess of Sunderland, will be the formal hostess, but I can assure you that Sunny, or at least his secretary, has done all the work. The Dowager has spent the last twenty-three years making mourning a profession. She wears only black, and often a veil over her face. The clocks in Sunderland House have not been set since the death of the late Duke, and she keeps black curtains on all the windows. She only bestirs herself from her coffin-like house during the season, when she half-heartedly tries to marry Sunny off to an heiress.'

Louisa felt a pang of sympathy for Sunny; her own father had not been the same after her mother had died. It had been as if he were a shell of the person he once was. He'd no longer read to her or played with her. She had felt as if he'd died three years before he actually had.

'I suppose she'll like me, then,' she said with a forced laugh. 'My title and my money are quite the best things about me.'

Wick stopped walking and touched her arm. 'I know she will like you—and not just because you are an heiress. Your fortune is the least interesting thing about you.'

She sighed ruefully. 'Or lack thereof. I am probably the only penniless heiress. I hate it that I have imposed so much upon Mantheria. It makes me want to accept the first offer of marriage I receive so that I will be able to repay her.'

His hand tightened on her arm. 'Do not rush into a marriage that you may some day regret. If you're worried about the bills, *I* will repay her.'

'I am not your responsibility either. You have quite enough of that, with your little sisters, and in my humble opinion you are doing a wonderful job. You clearly love them, and you listen to them. I know that you have their best interests at heart and will find the perfect governess for them.'

Wick dropped his hand. 'I do love them dearly, and I wish that I could protect them from all the dangers in the world.'

Louisa shook her head. 'You cannot protect them, but you can prepare them...and catch them when they fall.'

Wick's brown eyes gazed intently into hers. 'Who catches you, Louisa?'

*You,* she thought.

That day on the road, when he'd mistaken her for the governess and brought her to Hampford Castle with his sisters, he had saved her from a life of not knowing a loving family or a happy home. An existence without friends her own age. Wick had made her dreams of being presented to the Queen and having a London season come true—everything her mother had planned for her.

She spun her parasol. 'Your sisters,' she said. 'Becca, I would say, caught me first, when she begged you to let me stay, but no doubt Frederica and Helen would argue that it was them. And I don't know what I would do without Mantheria. She is like the sister I always wanted but never had.'

Louisa had tried to lighten the mood, but Wick continued to frown, his countenance serious. Blushing, she wondered if he thought she was trying to take Elizabeth's place in Mantheria's life. Her words had been so thoughtless!

'Not that I am her real sister,' she said. 'I could never

be that. And I would never presume to fill the void left by her twin… I only meant to convey that Mantheria has treated me better than anyone of my own family and I will never be able to repay her goodness to me.'

Wick shook his head. 'I do not think you are being presumptuous. If I appear stern, it has nothing to do with you. It is the weight of loss and guilt. Because I didn't realise how much Mantheria has had to bear on her own. I thought… I thought I was shouldering the burden. I didn't know how much responsibility she was taking. If you are providing her with a confidante and friend of her own age, I can only be grateful to you. She needs one now more than ever, with her philandering husband.'

'Must you carry your burden alone?' Louisa whispered. 'My housekeeper, Mrs Barker, always said that we share our burdens so that they may be lighter. I know that each of your sisters would happily share yours with you, and I would help you in any way that I can. When you carry your burden alone, it makes you lonely.'

He turned his head away from her. 'Why should they have to carry the burden of my guilt when it wasn't their fault? They were only children. Becca and Helen don't even remember the night Charles and Elizabeth died. But it's emblazoned in my memory. I have never felt more helpless in my life. I knew that I had let them down, but I didn't know what else to do. I didn't— I couldn't—'

Wick stopped mid-sentence, his voice choked with emotion.

Louisa longed to throw her arms around him. To hold him. To comfort him. To share the burden that caused him to push her and everyone he loved away. But he wouldn't let her.

Clearing his throat, Wick offered his arm. 'Shall we

catch up with my sisters? I can't have them falling into any scrapes before we return to Hampford Castle at the end of the week.'

Louisa gently placed her hand in the crook of his elbow and they continued walking. She felt more sorrowful with every step. He was leaving.

'Have you found a governess yet?' she asked.

'No,' he said. 'I will be interviewing several candidates tomorrow, that Mantheria has found from an agency. I am hopeful that one of them will be good enough.'

Taking a deep breath, Louisa couldn't help but give him some unwanted advice. 'You should ask Mantheria and Mrs May to go with you for the interviews. Mantheria will know who will prepare the girls best for society. Mrs May can get the girls to look after Andrew.'

Wick didn't say anything, so Louisa tumbled on in her speech, 'After we arrived home from my Uncle Laybourne's, Helen asked Mrs May where her new snake was, and your housekeeper pretended that she didn't know what your sister was talking about. But I knew she did. She had let the snake out in my aunt's best parlour. I realised then and there that Mrs May doesn't let your sisters flummery her, and that she has a great affection for them. I know that she is not their mother, but I think if you asked her she would help. With a governess, of course. She already has her duties as housekeeper. Then you'd be free to conduct your business affairs.'

'I appreciate your suggestion,' he said in a low voice. 'I shall ask them both if they'd be willing to attend the interviews with me.'

Louisa couldn't help but smile. He was taking *her* advice. He was going to let others help carry the burden of his little sisters' care whilst his parents were away. Maybe,

just maybe, he would let her help carry the burden of his grief. The loss of his two younger siblings. She would happily share in any of his burdens if only he would open his heart to her.

A phaeton stopped by them on the path and she saw it was the Earl of Norwich. Today he was dressed in an exquisite crimson driving coat with no less than fifteen capes. Louisa counted. His tall beaver hat shone in the light and his hessian boots sparkled as if they'd just been buffed.

Lord Norwich's lips curved into his usual sneering smile. 'Lord Cheswick, Lady Louisa…what a pleasure, seeing you here.'

Wick gave the man a curt nod.

Louisa curtsied deeply, still holding on to the support of Wick's strong arm. 'Lord Norwich, shall you be at Lord Sunderland's ball tomorrow?'

Norwich switched the reins from one gloved hand to the other. 'I shall indeed, my lady. And, if I may be so bold, might I request from you the first two dances?'

She glanced at Wick's profile, but it was as if his face had been carved from granite. There was no emotion there. Nothing to show that he cared for her or that he had any intention of dancing with her at the ball at all.

'I should be pleased to reserve them for you, my lord.'

The Earl touched his hat. 'Until then.'

Louisa watched the Earl urge his team of horses forward and pass by. He gave her one last wave. Wick took no notice of it, or of her. He started walking again at a quick pace and Louisa trailed along at his side like a rag doll.

'Should I not have said yes?' she said breathlessly. 'Your sisters have said that a lady is not supposed to say

no when a gentleman asks her to dance at a ball. I did not know how to refuse politely.'

'You needn't refuse Norwich. He's not a bad match, as long as you don't mind that he will love his clothes more than you.'

Wick's curt words cut at her heart. Did he not care for her at all?

She swallowed. 'Then you approve of Lord Norwich as a suitor for me?'

His jaw clenched, but he didn't look her in the eye. 'There's only one better catch this season on the marriage market, and that is Sunny.'

Louisa's lips drooped. 'I do not think Sunny is truly on the market. He's only playing at it. His heart has already been taken.'

'Regret is a cold bedfellow.'

Wick's tone was harsh and she knew he was speaking from his own experience. Louisa's soul ached for the pain she knew Wick had felt and would always feel about the loss of Charles and Elizabeth. She understood now why he wasn't interested in marriage. He did not want to love another person he could lose. He didn't wish to feel helpless again.

But Louisa had felt helpless her entire life until leaving Greystone Hall, and at this moment she was hopeless. Wick was not ready for her love. And she was tired of loving those who did not love her back. Like her Aunt and Uncle Rockingham. Her cousins.

And now Wick.

She would not give her heart to anyone who did not love her in return.

# Chapter Twenty-Three

Louisa and Mantheria sat in the elegant barouche on their way to Lord Sunderland's ball. They looked like opposites.

Mantheria wore a black gown, low-cut, with scalloped sleeves and several flounces on the skirt. Her silver necklace held three large black diamonds with matching earbobs, and in her hair were tall black feathers that contrasted greatly with her yellow curls.

Louisa's dress was simpler, with no ornamentation besides a lace overlay of creamy white. Her neckline was also higher, and around her throat was a set of three rows of pearls on loan from the young Duchess. Louisa's hair did not have any feathers, but Chandler had woven in baby's breath from the bouquet Wick had sent for her.

Mantheria took Louisa's hand and they intertwined gloved fingers like the keys of a piano. 'How were the girls today?' she asked.

Louisa snorted, and then laughed. 'Becca rescued a mouse from her kitten and I think she believes it is her newest pet.'

The Duchess closed her eyes and shook her head. 'No

doubt she'll cause an infestation in my house before they leave for Hampford.'

'Did you find a new governess?'

'They were all awful,' Mantheria said with a sigh. 'Even Wick thought so. The first one, a Miss Thornburgh, flinched whenever we spoke to her. Can you imagine how she would handle the girls? Let alone the animals in the menagerie?'

Louisa giggled, covering her mouth with one hand. 'They would frighten her to death.'

'My sisters or the animals?'

'Your sisters.'

They laughed together until tears started falling out of Mantheria's eyes and she shook her head. 'Then a Miss Meadows talked of using the strap as if it were some great personal pleasure.'

Louisa shuddered. 'Oh, no!'

'Don't worry, Wick would never let anyone beat our sisters. The next candidate from the agency was a lady in her sixties, clearly not in good health. Mrs May didn't think she would have the stamina to keep up with them.'

Louisa found herself nodding in agreement. The Stringham sisters needed someone young and vibrant.

'And the last, a Miss Tucker, positively frightened me during the interview. I sat up so straight that my neck still hurts.'

'Perhaps she would be better suited as a drill sergeant rather than a governess.'

Mantheria shrugged, slumping a little in her seat. 'None of them will do.'

Trying to appear nonchalant, Louisa asked, 'And what did Wick say? Will he stay in London longer? Until he finds the right one?'

'He swears that he won't stay even one extra day,' his

sister said with a harrumph. 'He is more stubborn than any animal Papa has ever owned.'

Louisa bit her lower lip to stop it from trembling. She had hoped that Wick would be near her longer. But he was determined to leave.

A footman opened the door of the carriage and escorted them into a beautiful grey stone London mansion with countless candelabra lit, making it appear almost as bright as day. Lord Sunderland's blond locks looked golden in the candlelight, and he beamed when he saw them. Or rather when he saw Mantheria. His eyes seemed to eat her whole.

Louisa wondered, if she married another, whether her traitorous heart would continue to long for Wick. But it didn't matter. Without her fortune she had no money and nowhere to go, and the only way to receive her inheritance early was for her to marry. She could not continue to take advantage of Mantheria's charity and wait for a man who had openly refused her.

A woman stood next to Sunny. She was a petite little thing, whose head did not even reach his shoulder. She was dressed in black bombazine—a material known for not reflecting the light. Her face was covered by a black lace veil, as if she were attending a funeral.

'Lady Glastonbury… Lady Louisa,' Sunny said, showing his usual endearing smile beneath his crooked nose. 'Now my ball can begin. But where is Wick? He said that he would be escorting you.'

Louisa's eyes darted to Mantheria, whose cheeks had turned a pretty pink as Sunny took her hand and lifted it to his lips. 'I am sure he is coming. Perhaps he is late. We had a rather dismal afternoon interviewing for a new governess.'

The Dowager Lady Sunderland removed her veil to

show a surprisingly young-looking face. Her skin was smooth, except for the fine lines around her mouth and eyes. She pointed a black gloved finger at him. 'Lord Cheswick should be interviewing candidates for a wife. He's not getting any younger and neither are you, Alphonse.'

Sunny's given name was Alphonse. The nickname fitted him much better, Louisa thought.

Sunny's smile turned rather hard. 'That is why I am here, Mama. But let us not hold up the line any longer. Lady Glastonbury, will you please save me the supper waltz?'

Before Mantheria could answer, Lady Sunderland spoke again. 'There's no point in asking *her*—she's already married. You ought to have asked Lady Louisa. Not a bad-looking girl, even with the freckles, and she has a fortune besides.'

Louisa could have happily sunk down to the floor at the Dowager's words.

Mantheria linked her arms with Louisa's. 'Alas, Lady Louisa, you are too late for the supper waltz, for I accept your offer, Lord Sunderland. But perhaps you might want to reserve another dance with our fair Louisa?'

Sunny took Louisa's hand briefly, bowing over it before letting go. 'Shall we say the first set?'

Louisa felt the blood rush to her face as she answered, 'The first two dances are already claimed, my lord.'

'The third, then?' he said, his eyes bright.

'Very good.'

'Phew. I am glad I got in early.'

Mantheria gave a little laugh and guided Louisa away from the receiving line. 'Oh, please tell me that my brother has reserved those dances.'

Louisa swallowed and shook her head. 'Alas, no. They were reserved by Lord Norwich.'

Her friend appeared almost as disappointed as Louisa. 'Perhaps Wick, like Sunny, wants to save his dances for the supper waltz. That way he will also be able to escort you to dinner and sit by you during it.'

'I don't think he intends to dance with me at all.'

Mantheria sniffed, shaking her head. 'That will not do. He is not going to spend another ball skulking around the sides and snubbing every young lady here. My mother would not have stood for it and neither will I.'

Louisa's eyes filled with tears and she cursed her uncontrollable emotions. 'Please do not ask Wick to dance with me. I shall die of shame on the spot if you do.'

The young Duchess stuck out her chin. 'Very well. There are plenty of handsome young men who would happily queue up to dance with a beautiful young lady like you.'

Louisa wiped away an errant tear from her cheek and attempted a small joke. 'According to Lady Sunderland, I am not a bad-looking girl. Even with my freckles.'

'Don't listen to that old prune! You are gorgeous.'

'I'm skinny and freckled.'

'Your figure is willowy—which is the prevailing style, I'll have you know. And your skin is perfectly lovely. Your freckles give your face character.'

Louisa glanced down. 'My Aunt Rockingham always said that they made me ugly.'

Mantheria's hand touched Louisa's cheek. 'Nothing could make you ugly, my friend. You have the purest heart and the kindest soul I have ever known. And they shine through your eyes.'

Louisa's eyes threatened to fill with tears again, but

she shook her head. 'What do you think of the Earl of Norwich?'

Mantheria gave a little gurgle of laughter. 'Oh, I never think about men who are prettier than me. How lowering it is!'

Louisa felt her lips tug upwards into a smile. 'Lord Norwich is very beautiful.'

'And dresses like a god. Beau Brummell mocks his flamboyant style, but I think it suits Norwich down to his high-heeled boots.'

'Yes!'

Mantheria's smile slipped for a minute, but then it was back on her face. 'He has a lovely estate in Norwich, and two smaller ones, I believe. One near Bath and the other near Brighton. The *on dit* is that he's in debt because of gambling with the Duke of York. But that was last year. I have not once seen him at a card table this season. Perhaps he has learned the lesson that fortunes are only lost at gaming and never won. I start to break out into a cold sweat if my losses rise above fifty guineas.'

'I've never gambled before.'

'*Life* is a gamble, my dear Louisa, and you don't always get to choose the cards you are dealt,' Mantheria said, and then curtsied to Lord Norwich. 'Ah, you are here to steal our lovely Lady Louisa away for a dance.'

The Earl wore an intricately embroidered silver suit that gleamed in the light like freshly polished silver. He looked cold and perfect enough to be a marble statue. 'How clever of you, Lady Glastonbury, for I do indeed intend to steal Lady Louisa—and her heart.'

He offered Louisa his hand and she placed hers inside it. How different it felt from Wick's. Lord Norwich's fingers were long and slender. They lacked the size and strength of Wick's. And the warmth.

They spoke very little during the quadrille—the dance most fashionable balls started with. She found Lord Norwich to be an excellent dancer and a thoughtful partner. He was always where he should be, and more than once helped her through a mistake in the figure without bringing attention to it.

The next dance was a country jig. Louisa was a little breathless as she hopped about, but words spilled from her mouth when he took her hands. 'Are you interested in my heart or my inheritance?'

Lord Norwich's perpetual sneer turned into a grin. 'Oh, I do like you, Lady Louisa. Straight to the point.'

The figure caused them to part, but when they came back together, he answered, 'Both, I am afraid. Like yourself, I am in desperate need of funds. I believe you are currently living on the generosity of Lady Glastonbury and will not see your fortune until you are married?'

'I do not wish to be courted for my inheritance.'

'Nor do I for my title. But it is what people first notice.'

She turned away again and followed the line, his words sinking in with each step. She could not blame him for being interested in her money when she wanted a husband with an estate and home. Perhaps pecuniary reasons were not entirely wrong to consider in a marriage partner.

Lord Norwich held out his hands and she took them.

'You are wrong, Lord Norwich. It was not your title that first brought you to my notice, but your suit of clothes.'

He gave a soundless laugh as they twirled together in a circle. They returned to their own sides of the line and bowed to each other as the music ended.

Lord Norwich took her hand and began leading her back to Mantheria. 'A word of warning, my dear,' he whis-

pered in a soft, cold voice. 'You are not the first woman to set your cap at Lord Cheswick, and nor will you be the last. But he has no need to marry. Do not turn down a real offer for a forlorn hope.'

He let go of her hand and Louisa gave a full-body shiver, despite feeling a little overheated. His words crawled down her spine. Had they been a threat? A warning? Or honest advice? Had she not told herself something similar?

Before she could confide in Mantheria, Sunny appeared at her elbow. 'This is our set, I believe, Lady Louisa?'

Mantheria blew them a kiss—or perhaps just Sunny. His jaw was tight and his usual smile absent. The set was a waltz (which she could now participate in after receiving Lady Cowper's permission), and Louisa thought it was like dancing with a stranger. Sunny appeared to be in a grim mood. She wondered if it was his mother's words about Mantheria or his own misery.

'My housekeeper always said that misery loves company,' Louisa said quietly. 'If you need company in your misery, I am here.'

Sunny took a deep breath and guided them around another couple. 'I do not want company in my misery. Yet I fear my bloody idiot of a best friend will soon be joining me, because he is too stubborn and stupid to allow himself to be happy.'

Louisa knew that he was speaking of Wick. 'He's not coming, is he?'

He huffed, shaking his head. 'I don't know. He hates balls. He hates the season. But he came here for you—he even had Mantheria secure you a presentation with the Queen. I have never seen him bestir himself so much for a person who is not part of his family. I had hoped that

he had finally forgiven himself for Charlie and Lizzy's deaths, but the fool seems determined to live in his own personal purgatory.'

His words ought to have stung, but rather they were a balm to her battered heart. She, Louisa Bracken, was not the problem. She was not unworthy of love. Undeserving of happiness. She was none of the awful things her Aunt and Uncle Rockingham had told her that she was as a child and a young woman. And believing those lies was keeping her in her own personal purgatory. She could not save Wick, but she could save herself.

'I am sorry if I have put Lord Cheswick to so much effort,' she said, her voice a little shaky. 'I can only promise that I will not be a burden upon him for much longer.'

The music stopped and Sunny faced her. 'You were never a burden, Louisa. You are his salvation. If only he is not too blind to see it.'

Louisa did not know what to say, so she didn't say anything at all.

When Sunny returned her to Mantheria her friend had already lined up several more partners for her: Mr Beesley, Lord Thorley and Mr King. She noticed that Mantheria had not found her a partner for the supper dance.

Mantheria briefly squeezed Louisa's hand. 'I am sorry, Louisa. I thought he would be here by now.'

She didn't need to ask who her friend meant.

She watched Sunny lead Mantheria away and then waltz with her. Their dancing together was so beautiful that it brought tears to her eyes again. She could see that they loved each other. Every movement was a graceful give and take…a stolen happiness that would end with the music.

Then Louisa felt a hand on her lower back and turned to find herself in Wick's arms. His usually perfectly

tamed locks were dishevelled. His cheeks were red and his breath smelled of spirits. His always intricately tied cravat was rumpled. His other hand took hers and he started waltzing with her before they had even reached the dance floor. Over his shoulder, Louisa could see several eyes upon them.

'Are you intoxicated?' she asked.

He closed his eyes and then opened them again. 'Completely foxed.'

'Should you be dancing?'

'Probably not,' he said, pulling her closer to him. 'Perhaps you could steer?'

Louisa was tired of him toying with her emotions. Pulling her to him and then pushing her away. 'I am not sailing a boat.'

Wick's hand pressed into her back until their bodies were touching. He gazed intensely into her eyes. 'No, you're my Louisa, with hundreds of sweet freckles, and I want to kiss every single one. I'd start with the one just above the curve of your lips.'

Despite her best intentions, she melted in his arms. His words soothed a thousand of her Aunt Rockingham's slights about her looks. The spots on her skin weren't blemishes—they were sweet freckles. She felt her temperature rise at the thought of Wick's lips on every single one of them.

Then he twirled her around and Louisa quite forgot everyone else. He was uncharacteristically silent, but she didn't mind. She lost herself in the pleasure of waltzing with the man she loved. In the thrill of his hand on her back. The scent of vanilla and leather that characterised his person. There was nowhere in the world that she'd rather be.

The waltz ended all too soon, and Louisa was afraid

that Wick was going to pass her off to another man to dance with.

'Shall I fetch you a drink?' he asked.

Louisa touched one of her hot cheeks. 'Perhaps a little fresh air?'

Wick offered her his arm and they wove through the room. She watched him nod at several acquaintances, almost challenging them to give him the social cut. But none did. Maybe because some day he would be a duke.

He led her out to a small garden lit by hanging lanterns. Louisa had thought that there couldn't be anything more romantic and lovely than a ballroom, but she'd been wrong. This little garden smelled of roses and mint. The warm lights of the lanterns transformed it into a fairyland, like in one of the stories her governess had told her before she'd been dismissed.

Louisa's knees were shaking and so were her hands. Her heartbeat felt loud in her ears. If it hadn't been for his firm hold on her elbow she would probably have fallen to the ground.

Wick released her. Louisa felt unbalanced and fell forward against his hard chest. Her arms naturally wrapped around his neck. She heard the thunderous sound of his heartbeat.

Wick's hands clutched her waist, pressing her even closer to his body. Louisa felt his sweet breath on her lips. Tilting her head back, she offered her mouth in open invitation. Wick did not keep her waiting long. His soft lips first brushed that freckle above her mouth, and then her lips. Over. And over. And over again. Then he increased the pressure of his mouth against hers and Louisa tightened her arms around him. She didn't want this kiss to end. Or *kisses*, as he continued to explore the shape of her mouth.

Then she felt something wet and soft against her mouth. His tongue. He was licking her lips! Louisa opened her mouth in surprise and felt his tongue slip between her lips. She felt hot all over and a growing need deep in her belly. Wick deepened the kiss, and Louisa was sure that there could be no greater pleasure in the world than kissing. She gasped, and he pressed his tongue farther inside her mouth. It felt wanton and wickedly wonderful. She opened her lips wider and felt his tongue teasingly touching all over her mouth, sending sparks of pleasure through her entire body.

Taking a breath, Wick kissed her again and nuzzled her neck. Louisa clung to him, knowing she would fall without his touch. He raised his eyes to look at her, but Louisa didn't wish to talk. She pressed her lips to his mouth and then licked his lips to make him open them. Capturing his bottom lip with her teeth, she tugged on it gently. Then she released it and opened her mouth for another decadent kiss. She felt Wick's tongue enter again and she could not resist sucking on it.

She felt his body stiffen against hers.

He released her and stepped back.

Louisa touched her hot neck, unsteady on her feet. 'Did I do something wrong?'

Wick shook his head and brought his hands to his face. 'No. You could never do anything wrong. The fault is all mine. I should not have brought you out here. I should not have kissed you. You deserve so much better. Someone who is worthy of you.'

She reached out her hand to touch him, but he flinched and she dropped it to her side. 'You are the worthiest man I have ever met...'

'I'm a wreck, Louisa... A wreck held together by re-

sponsibilities and mostly good intentions,' he said, turning his back to her. 'I am not the man for you. For anyone.'

Every word was like a needle-prick on her sore soul. Unbidden, her eyes filled with tears and her throat felt full of emotion. She swallowed it down.

'We are all wrecks, Wick. Ships beaten about by the storms of our past. Every single one of us. My parents died. My aunt and uncle stole my fortune and my self-esteem. I was a complete and total wreck. Then you picked me up off the road and took me home to your sisters. And I learned that even wrecks can be worthy of love. That a person can be imperfect and still cherished. I learned that from you. From the way you treated your wild, flawed and entirely loveable little sisters. To be loved by you would be the greatest gift in all the world.'

Wick took another step back from her. 'I just can't...'

Sniffing, she wiped the tears from her cheeks. 'Fine. Stay in your personal purgatory and may your regrets keep you company—for I will no longer.'

Her legs shook as she walked away from him, back inside the house. Wick did not follow her.

Louisa swallowed her sadness and slipped into the crowd heading to the supper room, her heart shattered.

# Chapter Twenty-Four

Wick waited a few minutes after Louisa went inside. His mind was still a little fuzzy, but kissing Louisa had sobered him. He knew that it would be a bad idea to walk back into the room at the same time as her. People would think that he had done exactly what he had—kissed her. Some members of the *ton* would even think that he'd compromised her.

*Fustian!*

He raked his hands through his hair. What a mess he'd made of his life—and of hers. He oughtn't have come to London and attended these balls. He wasn't interested in marriage. Not yet. Maybe not ever. His brother Matthew could inherit the dukedom for all he cared. He'd never wanted the responsibility of being the head of the family. The oldest. The one in charge when something went terribly wrong.

Charles and Elizabeth's deaths would always haunt him. He'd spend the rest of his life wondering whether, if he'd done something different, they would have lived. Elizabeth should have been at this ball with Mantheria. She should have danced every single dance. Maybe she

would even have been married, with a child of her own. Charles should have been in Africa with their parents, learning more about the animals that they all loved. He would have been old enough now to sail all over the world, looking for new specimens. He should have been making a name for himself as a naturalist.

Oh, how Wick wished things had turned out differently. Wished that he could have been the sort of free man who could give his heart to Louisa and take responsibility for a wife and a family of his own.

Shaking his head, Wick knew in his heart that he was not good enough for her. Louisa deserved to be loved by someone whole. Someone who could give her the family and home she'd lost when her parents had died.

The sound of footsteps on the gravel behind him caused him to turn. Even in the dim fairy lights of the garden he easily recognised the features of his best friend.

'Getting some air?' Sunny asked.

Wick gave him a jerky nod.

'You're higher than a kite.'

He took a deep breath. 'Just a little in the wind.'

'What's wrong, old friend?' Sunny said in a low voice. 'It's not like you to get blind drunk, let alone arrive in that state at a ball.'

Wick blinked at Sunny. He didn't know what had come over his best friend lately. He'd shared his personal feelings and wanted Wick to talk about his. That was not how Englishmen behaved. They punched their friends and were polite to their enemies. They were stoic and strong and didn't cry in public. Not even when they wanted to. And they most certainly did not confide in other men.

'I'm fine.'

'You look terrible,' Sunny said, pointing at him. 'Your appearance would make your valet weep. Your hair is a mess and your clothes are rumpled.'

Wick snorted. 'If my appearance offends you, then I shall leave.'

He spun on his foot to go, and nearly lost his balance on the loose gravel.

'You can't just waltz with her once and leave,' Sunny said, grabbing Wick's shoulder and forcing him to face him. 'You'll have every tabby coupling your names together. You need to dance with other ladies.'

'I don't want to,' Wick said, sounding like a child even to his own ears.

Sunny's free hand went to Wick's other shoulder. 'I don't care what you want, you idiot. I care about Lady Louisa's reputation—which is already a little shaky, thanks to her horrid relations. You will make her the talk of the town. You waltzed with her as if she was a serving wench you could hold as close to you as you liked. Then you escorted her out of the ballroom. Many a matron will be expecting an engagement announcement in the *Gazette* tomorrow.'

Swallowing heavily, Wick shook his head. 'I can't. I can't marry her. It's too much—*too much.*'

His friend huffed in frustration. 'Well, if you won't marry Lady Louisa, then you will restore her reputation, and yours, by dancing every set until this cursed ball ends.'

'You said I look a fright.'

'Oh, you do,' Sunny said sharply. 'But after my valet has had you for a half an hour I expect you to return to

the ballroom as fresh as a daisy and ready to dance. Am I clear?'

'Yes.'

Sunny moved his hands from Wick's shoulders and grabbed him by the elbow. He hauled him through the back of the house and went with him up the servants' staircase—which wasn't necessary because Wick knew his friend's house as if it were his own. Then Sunny opened the door to his bedchamber and shoved Wick inside. He stumbled a few steps, still trying to clear his foggy, pounding head.

If Mr Mayhew was surprised to see either lord during the middle of a ball, he gave no such sign. He was a young man about their own age. Slim, pale and unassuming, with light brown hair and a hooked nose.

He bowed. 'May I be of assistance, Your Grace?'

'Tidy his clothes and his hair and sober him up, if you please, Mayhew,' Sunny said. 'I don't expect a miracle—just do your best. Then escort him back to the ballroom.'

Wick sighed. 'I know the way.'

'You know nothing,' Sunny said, shutting the door behind him.

Mayhew came up to Wick. 'Why don't you take a seat, my lord? I'll find you a drink that will help clear your mind, and then we can tidy up your appearance.'

Unsteady on his feet, Wick was grateful for the chance to sit down. The valet led him to a chair and Wick closed his eyes. He must have dozed off, for suddenly Mayhew shook his shoulder roughly.

'Lord Cheswick, here is your drink.'

His eyes flickered open and he accepted the glass from the man. Lifting it to his nostrils, he winced. It smelled horrendous. 'What's in this thing?'

''Tis best if you don't know,' Mayhew said, with a faint look of amusement on his face. 'Just swallow the whole thing down as quickly as possible.'

Wick followed his directions, and the concoction tasted even worse than it smelled. For a few moments he feared that he would be sick all over his shoes. But slowly the fog in his brain began to clear, leaving only a pounding headache and a heart full of regret.

Sunny had been right. Drunk or sober, Wick's behaviour at the ball towards Louisa was unpardonable.

He allowed Mayhew to comb his hair and replace his crumpled cravat with a new one belonging to Sunny. Wick usually tied his own cravat, but his hands were shaking too much for him to do a creditable job. Mayhew confided that Sunny never tied his own cravat, and carefully folded Wick's into the mathematical style. Then the valet brushed out the wrinkles in his coat and polished his shoes.

Finally Mayhew helped him to his feet and escorted him down the main staircase and back to the public rooms. Wick wanted to wish the fellow to the devil, but on the stairs he was grateful for his steadying hand underneath his elbow. The valet took him all the way to Sunny, who was standing in the doorway to the ballroom.

'Thank you, Mayhew,' he said with a nod. 'Cheswick, you have arrived at the most opportune time. I was just telling Lady Ashton how eager you are to dance.'

Wick groaned, and Sunny elbowed him sharply in the ribs. Lady Ashton had three unmarried daughters who were all out at the same time, and she was desperately trying to fob them off upon any unsuspecting gentlemen of means. As the wealthy heir to a dukedom, Wick was well worth pursuing.

He glanced at the matron and, sure enough, she was grinning at him. Behind her were three young women who all had blonde hair and willowy figures.

Wick bowed stiffly, still unsteady on his feet. 'Lady Ashton, it is always a pleasure to see you. And you too, Lady Nancy, Lady Eliza and Lady Caroline. Now I have the delightful dilemma of choosing which young lady to lead out first.'

Lady Ashton grabbed the eldest daughter's arm and all but shoved her at him. 'Nancy is particularly fond of the waltz.'

Sunny gave him a little push and Wick held out his hand to Lady Nancy, who accepted it. He led her to the dance floor and took her into his arms. She was pretty enough, but she kept giggling. Waltzing with her felt nothing like dancing with Louisa. It was a slow march of death and he could barely wait for the end of the tune to arrive. Especially when he eyed Louisa waltzing with Lord Fulton. She was giggling too. How he *hated* that perfect dandy.

The tune finally ended, but Wick was only granted a brief reprieve before he had to dance the Roger de Coverley with Lady Eliza. His only solace was that Lady Eliza did not laugh. If anything, she looked disappointed to be stuck with him as a partner. He tried more than once to make eye contact with Louisa, who was now dancing with Mr Beesley. He was a second son, with a respectable reputation and even more respectable fortune. Louisa determinedly wouldn't look in his direction, even when they touched hands in the dance.

But that was what he had wanted—for her to marry someone else. Someone worthy of her.

Wasn't it?

## Chapter Twenty-Five

A man was standing near Mantheria when Louisa came into the breakfast room the following morning. His hair was silvered at the sides and his countenance handsome, if a bit wrinkled around his eyes and forehead. Mantheria wore a frown and appeared pale. Even her usually pink lips were devoid of all colour.

She held out her hand to Louisa. 'You've finally awoken, sleepyhead. Allow me to introduce my husband to you. Lord Glastonbury, this is my dear friend Lady Louisa, who is staying with us for the season.'

Louisa took Mantheria's hand and was not sure which of them required the most support from the connection. She was certainly glad to be holding her friend's hand.

Louisa bowed her head. 'It is a pleasure to make your acquaintance, Your Grace.'

Lord Glastonbury bowed to her, but he looked stern. Disapproving. 'I have received a visit from the Earl of Rockingham, my lady. He was most distressed to learn from his wife that you had fled your family home and were in London without the protection of your guardians.'

Louisa could feel the blood drain from her face, and was certain that she was just as pale as the young Duchess. 'Lady Glastonbury has been so very good to me—unlike my own family, who have treated me as if I were a servant in my own home.'

The Duke gave an impatient sigh. 'Be that as it may, it is not proper for my wife—'

'To have not introduced you to our *dearest* friend Lady Dutton.' Mantheria cut him off. 'Something that will have to be remedied immediately. But first, Andrew and my sisters are waiting to go on a walk with us to the park. We must bid you a brief farewell, my dear husband.'

Louisa stood stunned. She knew from Mantheria that Lady Dutton was her husband's long-time mistress. She feared her presence in their home was causing more problems in Mantheria's already troubled marriage.

Still holding her hand, Mantheria dragged Louisa from the room. Louisa wanted to beg for her forgiveness, but they were met in the hall by Andrew, who hugged Mantheria and then Louisa around the legs. The small embrace filled her heart. The little boy had accepted her into the family.

Andrew tugged on her hand. 'You said we were going to the park!'

Mantheria smiled down at her son. 'And we shall. Let us fetch our hats and wraps and we can be on our way.'

They met the other Stringham sisters in the hall. They were already dressed for their walk to Hyde Park. The butler must have been expecting them, for he held both Mantheria's wrap and her own. Their hats were on the table beside him.

Louisa's hands were shaking as she tied the ribbon of her bonnet. She couldn't...*wouldn't* go back to

Greystone Hall and her Aunt and Uncle Rockingham. Her soul could not bear such an existence again. But it appeared that she could not rest on Mantheria's kindness for much longer.

Her only option was to marry—and soon. She needed to repay her friend for the expensive wardrobe they had purchased together. But how could she accept an offer of marriage when she loved Wick? And would her Uncle Rockingham even approve of any of her suitors after she had abandoned her family's home and protection?

'You have all been so very good to me,' Louisa said as they entered the park, chewing on her lower lip. 'I do not know how I will ever repay you.'

Frederica smiled. 'I suggest gold sovereigns.'

'I'll take an exotic snake from South America,' Helen said. 'And I don't mind if it's poisonous. I'd actually prefer it if it was.'

Becca grinned and wiggled her fingers. 'Diamonds. Only diamonds.'

Mantheria laughed. 'I hope you know we are jesting. There is no repayment for friendship, and you needn't feel any rush to pay for your clothing. The money I used was my own, not my husband's. He cannot protest at how I spend my allowance.'

The young Duchess briefly touched Louisa's arm, but it did not make her feel any better. She felt worse to have taken Mantheria's money. She would have much preferred to have borrowed from her unfaithful husband.

Several people waved at them. A few carriages wound their way through the park, and several ladies and gentlemen were on horseback. One of the riders was Sunny, who tipped his hat to them.

He focused on Mantheria's pale countenance. 'Are

you quite well this morning, Your Grace?' he asked solicitously.

'Why are you being so stuffy this morning, Sunny?' Frederica asked. 'You never call Mantheria by her title.'

'Hush,' Mantheria said, giving her sister a little shove on the shoulder. 'We're in public and he's addressing me correctly.'

'You may call me *Lady* Helen, then,' her other little sister said with a cheeky grin.

Becca giggled. 'Yes, and I am *Lady* Rebecca. You are only a duke after all, Sunny. You mustn't get above yourself.'

Louisa found herself laughing, despite her worries.

Sunny winked at the girl, and said solemnly, 'Thank you for the reminder—Lady Rebecca.'

His eyes went back to Mantheria. Louisa saw her friend's cheeks turn a pretty pink.

'Glastonbury is at home,' she told him. 'One can only pray that he will be invited to another house party soon.'

All the light faded from Sunny's face and Louisa mourned for both of them. For the impossibility of their love.

Touching his hat, Sunny said, 'You may be assured of my support should you ever require it, Your Grace.'

He didn't wait for her answer, but turned his horse and cantered away.

Frederica furrowed her brow. 'What was he talking about, Mantheria?'

But her elder sister only said, 'Hush.'

A carriage pulled up beside them. A woman with dark curls and a pretty face looked at them with interest. Beside her sat an older female companion.

'Lady Glastonbury, what a delight to have run into you this morning.'

'Lady Jersey.' Mantheria nodded like a queen, her face as pale as marble again. 'Allow me to introduce you to my new friend, Lady Louisa Bracken.'

Louisa kept her eyes up and performed a small curtsy.

The woman smiled at them, her eyes positively sparkling with interest. 'Yes. I have heard *everything* about you, my dear young lady. The reports do not do your beauty justice.'

'Thank you, my lady,' Louisa said breathlessly, a little surprised that such a fashionable lady should take an interest in her.

Mantheria gestured with one hand. 'And these are my sisters, Lady Frederica, Lady Helen, Lady Rebecca, and my son Viscount Chambers.'

Andrew beamed up at the woman and pointed at himself. 'I'm going to be a dook.'

'Of course you are,' Lady Jersey said with a winning smile. 'I know your papa—and I knew yours too, Lady Louisa. He was a fine man.'

Louisa's eyes watered. 'That he was.'

Lady Jersey's gaze moved back to Mantheria. 'I shall send Lady Louisa a voucher for Almack's.'

Mantheria bowed her head again, a hint of a smile on her lips. 'You are too kind, Sally. But also too late. Emily has already sent Louisa one and given her permission to waltz.'

Lady Jersey nodded and said her goodbyes. Her driver urged the horses on.

Becca waited until they were out of earshot to ask, 'What is Almack's and why does Louisa need a voucher?'

'The Almack's Assembly Rooms is only the most ex-

clusive club in London,' Frederica said excitedly. 'And only the *crème de la crème* of society are allowed to attend.'

Helen beamed at her. 'Seven lady patrons decide who is admitted, and they only give those people vouchers.'

Mantheria patted Louisa's arm. 'It is quite a compliment to you that Lady Jersey has singled you out. Usually one asks for a voucher. It is rarely offered without being requested.'

Louisa couldn't help but puff her chest out a little bit. Her Aunt Rockingham had been entirely wrong. Louisa was not ill-favoured and floundering in society. She was being included by the highest sticklers.

Helen squealed. 'You are going to be the toast of London society.'

Becca's stomach grumbled. 'Must you mention food? I am starving.'

Frederica poked her. 'We have only just eaten breakfast.'

Louisa's own stomach turned, but it had nothing to do with hunger. More with anticipation for her long wished-for London season.

Becca grabbed her sister's finger and was twisting it when another carriage pulled up. The Stringham sisters released each other and smiled, as if they hadn't been fighting moments before.

'Viscount Duncannon... Viscountess Duncannon,' Mantheria said with a deferential nod.

'Lady Glastonbury—and your sisters,' a vivacious lady said, looking at them all with great interest. 'Your parents are still in Africa, I believe?'

'Yes,' Mantheria said. 'Mama is hoping to find new plants for her perfumes.'

'Next time you write to her, be sure to mention that I asked after her.'

'I will.'

As they drove away, Frederica whispered. 'Lady Duncannon is Lady Jersey's sister. She is still angling for Mama to make her a scent of her very own.'

'Mama only gives them to her *particular* friends,' Becca explained with a sniff. 'It's quite a social coup to have a perfume made specifically for you.'

The wind picked up and Andrew's little hat flew off his head. It tumbled along the grass towards the Serpentine. Instinctively, Louisa ran after the errant hat. She ducked down to grab it, but the wind took it away again. Holding on to her own bonnet, she chased Andrew's to the rocky shore of the lake. She stepped on it with one foot, before reaching down to pick it up.

She waved the hat. 'I've got it!'

Before she could walk back to Mantheria and the girls, a man wearing black rode his horse in front of her. With one strong hand he hauled her onto his lap. His arm was around her neck, making it hard to breathe.

She dropped Andrew's hat as she tried to scream and kick to free herself. Faintly, she heard the shouts of the Stringham sisters, but the horse's rider urged his steed forward, away from her friends. Twisting to see his face, she saw that it was masked. Whoever it was, he clearly meant her harm.

Using the last of her strength, she jabbed her elbow between the man's legs. He gasped and released his hold on her. Louisa slid off the horse and hit the ground hard, knocking the wind out of her body.

The masked man stopped his horse and turned the animal around, ready to come back for her. Louisa forced

herself to her feet and began to run back towards her friends. The sound of the horse's hooves caused her pulse to beat frantically.

She took two more steps before she felt a stunning blow to the back of her head—and then she knew no more.

## Chapter Twenty-Six

Wick didn't expect Mantheria's house to be quiet when he arrived. That would be too much to hope for. But he certainly didn't expect to enter a room where Andrew was sobbing and clutching his hat while Mantheria held him, hyperventilating. Frederica was stamping on the floor. Helen was sniffling, tears running freely down her cheeks as her fingers tapped the side of her chair. And Becca held a pencil and paper and was sketching as if her life depended on it. She was a good caricaturist—accurate and unflattering.

'What in heaven's name is the matter?'

Mantheria handed Andrew to his nurse and came towards Wick, taking his hands. 'Louisa's been abducted!'

He squeezed his eyelids shut, shaking his head. 'That's ridiculous. Such things only happen in trashy novels. There must be a logical reason for her disappearance. Perhaps she is visiting a friend.'

Frederica snorted. 'A man dressed in black and on a horse grabbed her right in the middle of Hyde Park.'

Becca set down her pencil. 'She put up a fight and was able to escape his first attempt, but the villain knocked her out cold and carried her off.'

Wick blinked, trying to make sense of their outrageous story. 'In broad daylight?'

'Yes!' all four of his sisters yelled.

Stumbling to a chair, Wick sat down, still trying to process their words. 'Why didn't anyone help her?'

He blinked rapidly, trying to understand who would abduct Lady Louisa and why. And then he remembered his grandfather's words… The current Lord and Lady Rockingham were in debt and Louisa would inherit a fortune. Of course they wouldn't want to let her go. But would they go to such lengths to secure her money?

Helen stopped tapping the chair and put a gentle hand on his forearm. 'We were nearly twenty feet away. Louisa had gone to chase Andrew's hat. It had flown off in the wind. We ran to reach them, but the villain had already got away with Louisa.'

'What are we going to do, Wick?' Mantheria asked.

It was just him and his sisters. He wished his parents weren't on another continent. He would have valued both their experience and their wisdom at this moment.

Wick wet his lips, feeling more vulnerable than he had before in his entire life. Louisa had stolen his heart and now she'd been stolen. It was the thing he'd feared most—losing another person he loved. If only he had accompanied his sisters to the park. He might have stopped the assailant. He was sure of it. Instead, he'd been nursing a hangover. Again, he'd let down someone who trusted him and he cared for.

'You are all going to stay here,' he said, getting to his feet. 'I'll go and speak to Lord and Lady Rockingham and see if they know anything about where Louisa has been taken.'

Mantheria released a long breath. 'That is a prudent place to start.'

'Take my sketch.'

Becca held out her drawing: it was of a man on a horse. The man's face was obscured by a mask, but she had captured with her pencil-tip the horse's bald face and the white mark that reached past its eyes. One of the horse's legs had a white sock.

'You can show my sketch to people and ask if they've seen this horse or this man.'

Mantheria pulled the cord for a servant. 'Please have a carriage brought round immediately for myself and my brother.'

The butler bowed. 'Very good, Your Grace.'

Wick raked his hands through his hair. 'I don't need you to come with me and hold my hand, Mantheria.'

'Good, for I have no intention of holding your hand. I am coming as a chaperone for Louisa. She is my friend, and she will need me to preserve her reputation.'

Chagrined, Wick muttered, 'Sorry.' He hadn't thought about the propriety of being alone with Louisa after she'd been rescued.

'But why would they abduct Louisa?' Helen asked.

Wick was about to answer, but Frederica beat him to it. 'It's obvious to anyone who reads gothic fiction. Clearly they want to force her to marry their horrendous son, so that they'll be able to keep her fortune. A woman's inheritance becomes her husband's upon marriage.'

'That's true,' said Wick, rubbing his chin. 'But what I cannot understand is why an abduction? Unless Lord Barnabas and his parents plan to travel to Scotland a marriage in England takes several weeks to arrange. The

banns must be called, or a special licence obtained. But they can hardly extract a special licence for an unwilling bride. The Archbishop of Canterbury would not countenance such a thing.'

'Scotland is an awfully long way away…' Mantheria said dubiously, wrapping the string of her reticule over her wrist. 'The journey there would take a week, even with fast horses and dry roads. It would be hard to transport a prisoner that far without being seen or questioned by local innkeepers.'

Becca leaned forward, her eyes wide. 'Maybe the villain isn't trying to marry her, but to compromise her. So that she *must* marry him.'

Wick's jaw dropped. If Lord Barnabas or any other villain tried to force himself upon Louisa, he would tear them into pieces as a lion ripped apart its prey.

'You don't even know what that means,' Helen said haughtily.

His youngest sister sniffed. 'I asked Frederica, and she explained to me that if a young woman of reputation is alone with a man it is believed that they have behaved like a married couple. And the only way to preserve her good name is for them to marry.'

Frederica rested her chin on her elbow. 'Becca has a point. It would certainly be cheaper, and they would not have to travel as far. And if the man has a cottage or a house within a few hours' ride, then it would be harder for us to track them. The great north road to Scotland is infamous, and a lady without baggage would be memorable. And Louisa's red hair is very noticeable. Every innkeeper on the way would recall her.'

Wick ran his hands through his hair. His sisters were hardly comforting him, but they did make some very

good points. And if...no, *when* he found Louisa, at least *he* would not be compromising her by being alone with her. As much as he wanted to.

The door opened and the butler intoned, 'The carriage is ready, Your Grace.'

Wick stood up and Becca launched herself into his arms. Followed by Frederica, Helen and Mantheria. They all piled into the embrace, squeezing the life out of him.

Becca stepped back first. 'Whoever did this is going to regret tangling with the Stringhams.'

Wick could only blink at his sisters. All four of them. Foolishly, he had thought to bear all his grief and problems on his own. But he needn't. In fact, they wouldn't let him. Just as Louisa had told him, his sisters were eager to share his burdens. To lighten them. If only he would let them. Let *her*.

'Forgive me for entering unannounced,' Sunny said, walking through the door. He was still wearing his blue riding coat, but took off his hat. 'I saw what happened at the park. I was too far away to stop the villain, but I chased after him. I watched him put Louisa into a carriage and four that was waiting for them just outside the park. He took off his mask. It was Lord Barnabas Bracken. I followed for several miles, but my horse was already spent. They were headed east, on the road to Windsor and Slough. I decided it was best to come back and get you. But you weren't in your rooms, so I came here.'

Wick stepped forward and hugged his friend. He didn't know which of them was the more surprised by his action. He let go.

'Sunny, I don't know how to—'

'No need, old friend,' Sunny said, clapping a hand on his shoulder. 'I will always be here for you.'

Mantheria touched Sunny's arm and Wick saw the searing look that they shared.

'Will you go and notify Matthew and Grandfather Stubbs about what has happened?' she asked. 'Perhaps they can go and speak to Lord and Lady Rockingham instead of us.'

Sunny nodded. 'As you wish.'

His sister let go of Sunny and Wick almost thought he must have imagined the intense connection between them, but then he saw Mantheria's eyes, full of unshed tears. How would he feel if Louisa was married to another man? The thought made him see red.

'Come, Wick,' Mantheria said, tugging on his arm.

He glanced over his shoulder at his three other sisters. 'But the girls…?'

Mrs May stood at the door. 'Do not worry, my lord. I'll watch over them and keep them out of mischief.'

'Thank you, Mrs May,' Mantheria said. 'You're a treasure.'

Wick could only nod in agreement as he followed his sister out of her house. When they reached the carriage door, he gave the driver instructions to take them to Slough, a village over five-and-twenty miles west of London. There, they would try to discover in which direction the hired carriage had gone.

He thought his heart would explode from his chest before they reached there. He couldn't endure the possibility that her cousin had violated Louisa. Hurt her. If Barnabas had so much as laid a finger on her, Wick would kill him. With or without a duel.

## Chapter Twenty-Seven

Louisa opened her eyes, but all she could see was blackness. Had she lost her eyesight from the terrible blow she'd received to the back of her head? Tentatively, she touched the bump with her fingertips and gasped in pain. Her head was aching. She wanted to scream for help—or simply just to scream.

Covering her mouth with her hands, Louisa forced herself to breathe slowly through her nose. She couldn't allow whoever had kidnapped her to know that she was awake. Even though she could not see, she could feel. Her hands and her feet were not bound, nor her mouth. Wherever the man had taken her must be remote, for he did not care if she cried out.

She felt around with her hands, down to her knees and the edge of her gown, pricking her finger on the needle in her hem. It was small and sharp. Hardly a weapon. But it was all she had. She touched the floor; it was made of earth. She reached out her hands around her and felt a couple of wooden barrels and some sort of leafy vegetable in a basket. She closed her fingers on what felt like a carrot.

Her stomach grumbled. Her mouth and throat were dry and sore. She hadn't eaten since breakfast, and she felt positively famished. Wiping the unknown vegetable on her dress, she brought it to her mouth and took a bite. It was indeed a carrot, and even raw it tasted delicious. Louisa chewed as quietly as she could, not wanting to alert her attacker.

Once she had finished the carrot, she felt for the wall and managed to get to her feet. Touching the wall, she followed it until her knee hit some wooden stairs. She cursed beneath her breath and grabbed her sore leg.

'What did you bring your fancy piece here for?' a woman's shrill voice demanded. 'Aren't I enough for you?'

''Course you are, Belinda,' a man said.

Louisa recognised her Cousin Barnabas's voice. She gave a full-body shiver. *The rogue!* She should have known it was him from the start.

'Then why did you bring her to my house?' the woman asked. 'I thought you loved me. *Only* me.'

'I do. I swear it,' he said. 'My cousin is a freckled, ugly woman, and if I didn't need her money she wouldn't be here. But I do. Without Louisa I could not have paid for your cottage or for your fine dresses.'

Louisa gritted her teeth. Her allowance had been used to pay for Barnabas's mistress to wear fine clothes and jewels, whilst Louisa had been given rags. If she hadn't already disliked and distrusted her cousin, she would have hated him now. And she was sure her aunt had known it and not cared. Her villainy seemed to know no bounds.

She blushed as she heard the unmistakable sound of

kissing above her. She supposed that Belinda had for-
given Barnabas for bringing Louisa to her house.

Pressing her ear to the wall, she waited to hear more
words instead of amorous embraces.

'What do you mean to do with her?'

Barnabas cleared his throat; the sound caused Louisa
to shiver again.

'I will have to make it so she must marry me.'

'No, sir. I won't allow a woman to be taken against
her will in my house. Even *I* have morals.'

At least that was something to be thankful for. Lou-
isa would rather die than allow her cousin to touch her.
Kissing Wick had felt beautiful. Pleasurable. The thought
of Barnabas's hands on her filled her mouth with bile.

'I won't lay a finger on her—I swear it,' he said. 'All
I have to do is spend the night in the same house as
her alone and her reputation will be ruined. Louisa will
have no choice but to marry me, and when she does
all of her money will become mine. I need that money,
Belinda—desperately. I have borrowed from a particu-
larly nasty moneylender named Marcus Sullivan, and he
says that if I don't give him what he's owed by the end
of the month he'll murder me. And he ain't the sort of
chap to make idle threats.'

Louisa covered her mouth with her hands to stifle a
gasp. Barnabas would not let her go because his life de-
pended on it.

Louisa heard a few footsteps come closer to where
she stood in the cellar.

'I can't say that I approve, my lord,' the woman named
Belinda said. 'But I suppose it won't do her no harm to
stay a night in my cellar… I've never had a real diamond
necklace, afore… I daresay you'll want to show me how

grateful ye are after I helps you to a fortune and saves your life.'

'I'll buy you a dozen jewels once she is my wife.'

Holding her breath, Louisa tried to keep in her tears. But it was no use. Barnabas was right. He didn't have to touch her to ruin her. Merely the hint of scandal would be enough to have Louisa expelled from society and spurned by the *ton*.

Wiping her running nose with the back of her hand, Louisa knew she would never meet the Queen again.

*And Wick.*

Just thinking of him made her silently sob harder. She loved him. *Loved* him. And she was pretty sure that he cared for her as well. If only he would allow himself to be happy.

But they would never marry now.

With one blow to her head, Barnabas had dashed all hope of that. Even though it was not her fault Louisa would be ruined. Her reputation would be in tatters. Lady Jersey, Viscountess Duncannon and several other fashionable people had seen her being taken by a man in the middle of Hyde Park. There was no way she could quash the rumours or hope that it would be forgotten. Mantheria had told her that Lady Jersey's nickname was 'Silence' because she could not stop talking. The woman had probably already told people about Louisa's kidnapping…

And even if Wick was willing to believe that nothing had happened, her reputation would be irrevocably ruined. If he married her, Wick would be ruined too. Even his sisters: Mantheria, Frederica, Helen and Becca. All who had treated her with such love and kindness would be tarnished by association. They had become the family she had lost. The friends she had longed for. She

couldn't possibly injure them so deeply after all they had done for her.

Louisa laid her head in her lap and cried until there were no more tears inside her. And no hope.

# Chapter Twenty-Eight

Several hours in a carriage had not improved Wick's temper. He wished that he had ridden his horse, and knew that he could have made better time without his meddling sister. But she had proved helpful in the search. More helpful than he liked to admit.

It was Mantheria who had learned from another lady in the posting inn where they had stopped that Lord Barnabas's carriage had taken the road to Cookham. Wick nearly exploded with impatience as they waited for a change of horses. Mantheria insisted that he drink something. She drank milk, but he had ale.

Once the horses had been changed, they set off at a spanking pace towards Cookham. Wick told Mantheria's driver to spring the horses. If they needed to get a new set at the next posting inn, then so be it.

If he'd been feeling better, he might have appreciated the quaint Tudor village, with its beautiful redbrick buildings and beam work. The tallest building was Cookham Church, a grey stone edifice that resembled a castle from another era. It sat near a river.

Mantheria pointed out of the window. 'Oh, look, there's

an inn called the Crown. I dare say it is large enough to have a private parlour for refreshments.'

Wick opened the carriage window. 'Stop at the Crown.' He closed it with a loud snap. 'You can rest safely in a private parlour and I'll continue my search alone.'

'I'm not giving up on the search, ninny,' his sister said indignantly. 'Who better than the proprietor of a coaching in to know if Lord Barnabas has passed through? Or if he has any haunts nearby.'

The driver opened the door of the carriage and Wick reluctantly followed his sister out and into the Tudor-style inn. The first floor was made from redbrick and the second was whitewashed, with triangular wooden beams, three gables and windows. A short man who was nearly as broad as he was tall bowed to them. He had a head full of black hair and a beard that reached past his stomach.

'Can I offer you a private parlour, my lord?' he asked. 'I can tell that you and the lady are members of the quality.'

'Have you seen a carriage and four come through your town this afternoon?' Mantheria asked.

The innkeeper stroked his beard, shaking his head. 'They didn't stop here if they did...'

What if they had already passed them? What if Louisa was in mortal danger and he had gone the wrong way?

Wick's muscles were strained and his neck stiff as he pulled Becca's sketch from his pocket. 'Have you seen this man or his horse? The horse is brown with a bald face and a white sock.'

He stroked his beard again. 'I reckon I have, my lord. It belongs to a gentleman by the name of Mr Barnabas Brecks, who keeps a cottage with a woman of dubious

morals. He often stops at the Crown when he visits the village.'

So Lord Barnabas had been clever enough not to use his real name or his title.

Wick felt his hands clenching into fists again. 'Have you seen him today?'

The innkeeper shook his head. 'Haven't seen Mr Brecks in a fortnight.'

The villain had not been foolish enough to be seen with Louisa in the village. Lord Barnabas was proving to be not as stupid as Wick had always taken him for. But he was twice as dastardly.

'Where is his cottage?' Mantheria asked.

'I don't rightly know, my lady,' said the innkeeper, shaking his head. 'Somewhere on the opposite side of the river. It's not my business to be nosy.'

'Mr Brecks has abducted a young lady,' Wick said, stepping closer to the innkeeper. 'It is everyone's business to stop him and to rescue her from his clutches.'

The innkeeper's breath hitched. 'But I thought he was a proper toff.'

Mantheria scoffed. 'There's nothing "proper" about him. A true villain he is.'

The short man exhaled slowly and twirled the bottom of his beard around his index finger. 'I don't know where he lives, truly. But there's someone who might.'

'Who?' his sister asked, before Wick could.

'I'd ask at the vicarage.'

Wick rubbed his tired eyes. 'The vicar?'

The innkeeper barked a laugh. 'Nah. Old Reverend Perkins can't see past the end of his nose. But his wife, Mrs Perkins, is the greatest gossip in the county. Nought

happens within a ten-mile radius of Cookham that she don't know.'

'Where is the vicarage?' Wick demanded.

The older man pointed down the road towards the church. 'The house next to the church, my lord.'

Wick turned to the door. He had to find Louisa. Every moment counted. She might not have been violated yet. He could still save her.

'You go on foot,' Mantheria said. 'I'll wait with the coachman for the carriage to get a new team of horses and then follow you.'

Wick walked as quickly as he could without running. His heart was pounding and sweat poured down his face by the time he knocked on the door of the stone house next to the church. Taking out a handkerchief from his pocket, he wiped at his face.

A middle-aged woman answered the door. He took off his hat. 'Mrs Perkins?'

The woman shook her head. 'I am the housekeeper, Mrs Daily.'

Reaching into his pocket again, Wick pulled out a bent calling card. 'I am Lord Cheswick and I wish to see Mrs Perkins immediately.'

His title did the trick, and he was ushered into the front parlour.

'I'll go and fetch Mrs Perkins, my lord.'

Wick did not sit down. He could not stop himself from pacing back and forth through the room.

A young woman opened the door, carrying a book in her hands. She appeared to be reading as she walked. Her hair was light brown, and a delicate pair of spectacles were perched at the end of her nose. She had a pretty face with large brown eyes, a petite nose and a prim mouth.

'Forgive me, sir. I did not know that we had company.'

'Then you are not Mrs Perkins?'

'She is my mother. I am Miss Perkins.' The young woman held out her left hand, showing a slim gold band around her third finger. 'But I will be Mrs Wallace in a year or two. Once my fiancé has his own living.'

Wick could not care less about the woman, or her fiancé. 'I wish to speak to your mother about a serious matter. The man known to your village as Mr Brecks is truly Lord Barnabas Bracken, and he has abducted his cousin, Lady Louisa.'

She dropped the book in her hands. 'Good saints!'

An older woman stepped through the open door. 'What is this about Mr Brecks?'

The woman had the same brown hair, and a matching pair of spectacles, but there were lines around her eyes and mouth. She had to be Mrs Perkins.

'I believe that a man named Mr Brecks keeps a cottage near Cookham for a...' *could he say mistress in front of a vicar's wife?* '...a kept woman. I also believe that it is where he has taken his cousin, Lady Louisa, after abducting her in a London park.'

Mrs Perkins gasped and brought her hands to her chin. 'I always knew there was evil in that young man.' She curtsied to Wick. 'It is a great pleasure to make your acquaintance, Lord Cheswick.'

Wick didn't have time to be toad-eaten. He cleared his throat. 'Do you know where the cottage is?'

The vicar's wife moved her hand from her chin to her neck. 'Cross the bridge and head west for a mile. You'll see a road. No, it is barely more than a path... The path will lead you another two miles until you reach a white-washed cottage.'

Miss Perkins pushed her spectacles up her nose. 'I had better come with you. It is already getting dark. You'll never find the path on your own.'

Mrs Perkins nodded. 'Yes, daughter.'

Wick thanked them both profusely, wishing that they could leave that very second.

The sound of horses caused him to look out through the front window. By some miracle, Mantheria's carriage was in front of the vicarage.

'I'll grab my bonnet,' Miss Perkins said, dashing from the room.

Wick walked out of the house and opened the door to see the carriage was being drawn by a fresh team of horses. He opened the carriage door and saw Mantheria, sitting in the middle of the seat, eating a sprig of grapes.

'Would you like one? The innkeeper said I was looking peaky.'

Wick could only shake his head and turn back to the house as he heard Miss Perkins's footsteps. Her bonnet was already tied securely around her neck and there was a shawl around her shoulders. The young woman was certainly efficient.

'I shall ride with the driver,' she informed him. 'It will be impossible for me to see the way from inside the carriage.'

'Very well.'

Wick helped Miss Perkins up to the driver's perch and climbed into the carriage next to his sister. He opened the window so that he could hear the young woman's brisk voice, giving instructions to the driver.

Somehow it seemed that the last couple of miles of their trip were taking as long as their entire journey to Cookham.

# Chapter Twenty-Nine

Belinda giggled loudly and Louisa stood up, covering her ears with her hands. She'd heard quite enough, and she had no intention of sitting in the cellar and waiting for Barnabas to fetch her in the morning. None of the Stringhams would sit and accept their fate. They would fight for what they wanted. And Louisa would too!

She'd found the stairs again. Once it was quiet above her, and she could be reasonably sure that it was night-time—it was impossible to tell in the dark—she would escape the cellar and make a run for it. Neither Barnabas, her aunt, nor her Uncle Rockingham were going to get another penny of her money. She was going to return to London. To her season. To the courtship she'd waited for her entire life. She wasn't going to let her aunt, her uncle or her cousin take another dream from her.

*Never again.*

Listening to her cousin and Belinda eat was making her stomach grumble. Louisa ate two more carrots, but they did not taste as nice. Delicious smells were wafting from the kitchen. Trust her cousin to choose a mistress who was as good in the kitchen as in the bedroom. She

heard the scraping of forks and knives, but not their conversation. She did not think it was a great loss.

Leaning her head against a stair, she waited until there were no more sounds in the house. Then, crawling up the wooden stairs, she held a hand in front of her face so that she wouldn't hit her head on the cellar door. One more step up and she felt wood above her. Taking a deep breath, she pushed against the door. It didn't move at all. It must be locked.

Louisa used both hands to feel around the door for a lock. The wood was rough, and she felt more than one splinter enter her fingertips, but she did not stop until she felt metal. Touching it with her sore fingers, she found the keyhole. Obviously she didn't have a key. Or a weapon of any kind.

All she had was her needle. It would have to do.

One side of her mouth quirked up into a half-smile as she thought, *A lady doesn't need a sword as long as she has a sewing needle handy.*

Louisa pulled the needle out of her hem and carefully held the eye of it, while placing the sharp point into the lock. She stabbed and pressed with it. Nothing happened. Her eyes filled with tears and she longed to cry out her heart at the injustice of it all. She had finally reached London, had been presented to the Queen and attended *ton* parties. She had friends and fine gowns and handsome suitors…

Wick was unlike the men in her family in every way. He listened to and respected the women in his life. He bore his sisters' teasing and gave them their own back again. And he was thoughtful. She would never forget the soft expression on his face when he'd pulled out of his pockets the kittens for his little sisters. It was clear

that he loved them just as they were. He didn't expect them to change into someone else to be worthy of being loved. Wick wanted the very best for them.

Oh, how Louisa longed to be loved by Wick too.

Blast Barnabas!

Louisa might be ruined, but she would not give him the satisfaction of marrying her for her money. If anyone would be buying jewels with her inheritance, it would be her. She was not the same docile creature who had left her aunt and uncle's home. Louisa felt strong and free. She would never cower before her relatives again, begging for a scrap of affection.

She pressed the needle into the lock once more. She felt it catch something. Pushing harder with the needle, she felt the eye stabbing at her finger, but she could not stop. Would not stop. At last, she heard a click. Louisa dropped the needle. There was no way to find it in the dark, so she didn't bother to try. She placed both hands on the cellar door and slowly lifted it up. The door was heavy, but she was determined. Louisa stepped on the highest stair and used her whole body's weight to push the door open. The hinges creaked loudly, and before Louisa could stop it the door fell backwards with a loud crash.

Blinking, she let her eyes adjust to the dim light. She wasn't blind. It was growing dark outside. She needed a weapon. Something to defend herself with. Louisa grabbed the kettle off the stove.

She ran across the kitchen towards the front door, but her cousin Barnabas was standing in front of it, wearing only his breeches. His bare stomach was hanging over his waistband. It was more of him than she'd ever wished to see.

He held a candle up to her face. 'How'd you get out?'

'It doesn't matter,' Louisa spat, holding the kettle like a cricket bat. 'I'd rather die than marry you, and I don't give a fig about my reputation.'

Barnabas sneered at her. 'No one will marry you after this. You're damaged goods now. Your only choice is to marry me. And don't worry—I'll leave you well enough alone. You can take care of Greystone Hall, as you have your whole life.'

'But will you leave me alone, cousin?' Louisa said loudly, so that his mistress would hear. 'Won't you need a son and heir for the earldom?'

'Shouldn't take too long. My aunt had you nine months after her marriage to my uncle.'

'A girl—not a son and heir. If you have any hope of continuing your line, you'll have to give up Belinda—and your other mistress who lives in Tunbridge Wells.'

The 'other mistress' was a fabrication, for Louisa had seen that Belinda now stood in the bedroom door. Happily, the woman was wearing more clothes than her cousin.

'You've got another girl in Tunbridge Wells?' Belinda said, throwing one of her boots at Barnabas's head. 'You gib-faced villain.'

The boot hit her cousin in the ear. Barnabas dropped the candle and covered his head with his arms. 'I never have, Belinda, love. She's lying to you.'

The mistress eyed Louisa with suspicion. Louisa held up the kettle. 'He's already planning to marry me—surely you don't think he'll stay faithful to you for long? Nor give you a diamond necklace? He'll pay off Mr Sullivan and leave you high and dry. I hope the deed to this

cottage is in your name. Or he'll throw you out of it for his next mistress.'

Belinda hurled the second boot at Barnabas and it, too, caught him on his ear. The candle he'd dropped had now started a fire on the rug at his feet.

Louisa held up the kettle and advanced on her cousin. 'Let me out or I will strike you.'

Barnabas put a hand on each side of the door. 'I'll be dead before I let you out of my sight.'

'I will not marry you. *Ever!*'

'You have to. Mother says so,' he said. 'I owe over one hundred thousand pounds. Besides, you don't want the moneylender to kill me, do you? Your own cousin.'

Gaming. Her idiot cousin must have lost a fortune on cards and he'd been too stupid to stop after his staggering losses.

Louisa's swallowed. 'Your debts are not my responsibility.'

Her mind felt foggy…it was probably all the smoke in the room. The fire was growing. She had to do something.

Taking the kettle in her hands, she poured the contents onto the burning rug. It doused most of the flames, but didn't quite put them out. Then Louisa felt a strong arm push her away and saw Belinda throwing a blanket over the rug to smother the remaining flames. Belinda stamped on the blanket until Louisa was fairly certain that the fire was out.

'Some help you were, rum 'un!' Belinda yelled at Barnabas. 'Ye nearly burned down my cottage and did nothing to put the fire out.'

Barnabas opened his arms to his mistress. 'I swear,

I love none but you, my darling. But I had to guard the door. I couldn't let my cousin escape.'

Her cousin's broad form still blocked Louisa's way out as Belinda allowed him to put his arms around her. Then Louisa heard a clunk and a thud and her cousin's body hit the floor.

Belinda was holding the kettle. She must have struck Barnabas with it. He was sprawled out at her feet.

Louisa gulped, touching the column of her throat. 'Is he dead?'

Belinda pushed back her hair with her free hand. 'Nah... He'll wake with a bloody headache in a bit, and then I'll kick him out. I've got no need for a broke protector.'

Louisa's eyes stung from the smoke, and she couldn't quite believe what she saw. 'I am glad. He is quite odious, but I didn't want him dead.'

'Run for it, love,' Belinda said with a wink. 'Before he wakes up and tries to stop you. Thanks for saving my cottage. 'Tis bought and paid for in my name.'

Louisa didn't have to be told twice. She gave a thankful nod to Belinda and dashed out through the front door. Outside the cottage it was dark and wooded, and she didn't know which way to go. But the farther she was from her cousin when he woke up, the better.

She continued to run, her throat dry and her lungs burning.

# Chapter Thirty

The sound of Mantheria's chewing grated on Wick's nerves. How could she eat at a time like this?

He kept glancing out of the window—not that it helped much. It was growing too dark to see anything more than the outlines of trees. He was glad that Miss Perkins had accompanied them. He doubted if Mantheria's driver would have been able to find a rarely used path at this time of night with only the light from the carriage lanterns.

Suddenly the carriage turned sharply and his sister gasped as they almost slid off the seat. The path seemed to be made of stones, for they all bumped up and down for a most uncomfortable mile or two.

Wick knew they must be close when he smelled smoke. When the vehicle came to a stop, he swung the door open and saw a cottage with its front door ajar and a lantern lit on the table. Pulling his pistol out, he cocked it. He rushed in to see Lord Barnabas on the floor and a pretty buxom woman sweeping up what appeared to be the remnants of a fire. Even with the door open, the smell of smoke was strong in the room.

'If you're looking for the lady,' the woman said, pointing, 'she dashed out five minutes ago. I told her to hop to it before he awoke.'

Wick swallowed; his mouth tasted of ash. 'Was she harmed in any way?'

The woman shook her head and leaned against her broom. 'A regular firecracker, that one. Escaped the cellar and stood up to His Lordship. Then the clunch dropped a candle and she helped put out the fire. So I knocked him out and told her to run for it. 'Twere the least I could do after she saved my cottage.'

Louisa had been locked up. Had she also been ravished? He had to find her.

Miss Perkins entered the cottage and pushed up her spectacles. 'Miss, do you know in which direction she went?'

'No.'

'Thank you,' Miss Perkins said, and then gestured to the prone Lord Barnabas on the floor. 'Do you require any assistance with Mr Brecks?'

The mistress snorted. 'Nah. I'll send him on his way as soon as he can stand upright. 'Tis my cottage, after all.'

Wick had no sympathy for an abductor and possible rapist. 'Thank you for your information, madam.'

The woman winked at him. 'It's *miss*.'

He could only nod and make good his escape from the smoky cottage.

Miss Perkins trailed behind him. The door to the carriage was still ajar and Mantheria was sitting on the edge of her seat.

'Where's Louisa?'

Wick took a deep breath, his chest swelling with pride. 'Escaped on her own.'

Mantheria clapped her hands. 'Bravo!'

'But we do not know where,' Miss Perkins reminded him.

He stretched out his hand to help his sister out of the carriage. 'Miss Perkins, may I introduce you to my sister, the Duchess of Glastonbury?'

Miss Perkins curtsied, but didn't appear overly awed by his sister's title. 'It appears that Lady Louisa has gone into the woods. I think it would be best if we were to go in pairs, taking the lanterns from the carriage, and spread out about twenty feet so that we may cover the largest amount of ground. Each group can take a pistol, and if one group locates her they can fire a shot in the air to let us all know to come back to the carriage.'

'Excellent,' Mantheria said. 'Miss Perkins, would you like to go with my brother or my driver?'

The young woman took a deep breath. 'Your coachman, Your Grace.'

Mantheria instructed her coachman to take down the lanterns and bring his pistol. Miss Perkins sent him and Mantheria in a north-western direction, whilst she and the driver went off in south-east. It was efficient and effective. Wick couldn't help but be impressed with her skills in managing a duchess and an irritable marquess.

Mantheria held the lantern in one hand and Wick's hand in the other. She squeezed it tightly as they stepped into the unfamiliar woods.

Wick cleared his throat. 'Louisa! Louisa!'

His sister's voice echoed his and she held up the lantern like a beacon. The forest was thick with trees, and Wick hoped that Louisa would see their light through them.

He called her name again, and then waited for a response.

Nothing.

Goosebumps formed on Wick's arms as he worried that she might have fallen and been hurt. That she wouldn't be able to see their light or hear their words. But then he remembered the saucy woman's words. Louisa had escaped the cellar *and* the cottage. She was strong.

'Louisa!' Mantheria yelled.

After a short pause, Wick heard a voice in the distance.

'I'm here.'

He dropped Mantheria's hand and cupped his fingers around his mouth. 'Keep talking so that we can find you,' he shouted.

Taking his sister's hand again, he followed Louisa's voice until he saw her sitting on the ground, leaning against a tree. The lantern's light shone on her face, which was dirty with soot and dust.

Louisa's hand was on her side and she was breathing heavily. 'I'm so thirsty. I haven't had anything to drink since before we went to the park.'

Wick stooped down beside her, desperate to touch her. Hold her. 'We will get you some water as soon as possible. Would you like me to carry you?'

Before Louisa could answer, he felt a tap on his shoulder. Glancing over, he saw Mantheria.

'Miss Perkins said we had to fire a shot when we found Louisa, so that the other search parties would know to return to the carriage.'

Again, he was amazed by how well thought-out Miss Perkins's plans were. Wick took the pistol out of his pocket and handed it to her. 'Care to do the honours?'

Mantheria nodded eagerly, setting down her lantern and taking the weapon from him. Like all his sisters, Mantheria knew how to handle a shooting piece. She

cocked the hammer back and fired a shot in the air. The sound echoed in the night.

Louisa took a deep breath and then released it. 'Did Belinda tell you where I was?'

'Who is Belinda?' Mantheria asked.

Louisa took another breath before she answered. 'My cousin's mistress. Although I doubt she will be for much longer. He is in debt for over one hundred thousand pounds to a moneylender, and without coin Barnabas is of no interest to her.'

Wick let out a low whistle. He had known that Lord Barnabas played high; but he'd never have guessed his debts would amount to that.

'Shall I carry you?' he asked, for the second time.

She shook her head. 'I can walk, but I won't say no to leaning on your arm.'

Wick helped Louisa to her feet and she leaned heavily against him. Mantheria picked up the lantern and walked in front of them, back towards the cottage. He wrapped his arm around her waist, half carrying her. When they arrived at the carriage Miss Perkins and the driver had already returned.

Miss Perkins climbed up into the carriage seat. 'Hand her up to me.'

Wick did so, and Louisa leaned against the stranger.

Miss Perkins pointed to Mantheria. 'Do you have any water or wine?'

'In the basket on the seat behind you,' his sister said, climbing into the carriage to hold Louisa while the other woman uncorked the wine and placed it to Louisa's pale lips.

Wick was glad that she didn't force too much down Louisa's throat, only small sips.

'Shall we take her back to the Crown?' Mantheria asked him.

Wick said, 'Yes.'

Just as Miss Perkins said, 'No.'

'Excuse me, my lord,' she said, 'but I believe that there will be less talk if she spends the night at the vicarage rather than a coaching inn. Your sister as well. I promise that my mother and I will take care of them both.'

A surge of gratitude filled his heart. 'Thank you, Miss Perkins. You truly are an exemplar of Christian kindness. I'll give direction to the driver.'

He closed the door to the carriage and climbed up on the perch next to the coachman. 'The Cookham vicarage, if you please. And you can take it a little slower this time.'

The man touched his hat. 'Aye, my lord.'

The trip back to the vicarage passed by in a blur. Wick hoped—prayed—that Louisa had not been violated. That her injuries were only from her escape and the smoke and not from the body of her cousin. But even if she had been violated it would not change how he thought of her. Her virtue and her worth were not like chicken drumsticks, to be chewed up and discarded only once. Besides, his concern was not for her reputation, but for her heart. Her feelings. For the emotional scars that people could not see. Scars like the ones he possessed...

He climbed off the perch and opened the carriage door for Mantheria and Miss Perkins.

'Wick, stay with Louisa whilst we get her room ready,' his sister told him, and then followed Miss Perkins into the house.

Stepping into the carriage, he saw that Louisa was sitting up, but leaning against the squabs. 'I am quite fine, Wick. Only very dirty and very tired. The next time I

escape I will make sure to drink some of the water from the kettle before I douse any fire.'

Wick sat beside her, his knee touching hers. 'I hope that there will never be a next time.'

Louisa bit her lower lip. 'I can't help but agree with you. Being abducted gives one a terrible headache.'

His hand gently touched her hair, caressing it lightly. 'I dare say you have a large bruise. My little sisters said that you were hit quite hard in the park.'

She inclined her head forward slightly and winced. 'Yes. Barnabas knocked me out. I didn't wake up until I was in the cellar.'

'Then he didn't--?'

'Oh, no. Belinda told Barnabas that she would not allow a woman to be taken against her will in her cottage. I find that I like her a great deal more than my cousin.'

Wick knew that Louisa was attempting to lighten the situation with humour, but it was too soon for him. His feelings were raw and his heart felt as if it had been scraped over a washboard.

'How did you escape from the knave?' he asked.

'With my sewing needle,' Louisa explained. 'Barnabas had planned to keep me in the cellar until morning and then claim to have compromised me. But I was able to use the needle from the hem of my dress to pick the lock. Except I made too much noise, and my cousin blocked the front door. I said some things to make his mistress jealous, and she threw her boots at him, causing him to drop a candle and set fire to a rug. But he still blocked the door, so I helped put out the fire. In gratitude for my efforts, Belinda knocked out my cousin and helped me escape.'

'She knew that he had locked you in the cellar?'

Louisa swallowed, her throat dry. 'Well, yes...'

'Then she is an accessory to the kidnapping,' Wick said. 'And should be reported to a justice of the peace.'

Louisa brought her hands together, wringing them. 'Oh, please don't. Belinda helped me, and Barnabas will get his comeuppance soon enough from his creditors.'

Wick only wished Barnabas's comeuppance could be at his own hands. Or rather fists.

'Louisa, I—I don't know how to express how sorry I am that this has happened. That I was not there for you. That I didn't protect you from your pernicious cousin.'

She placed her scratched and dirty hand on top of his. 'I protected myself, Wick—something I would not have dared to do if it hadn't been for you and your sisters. You showed me that I am strong. That I am capable. You need not feel any guilt on my account. You carry too much guilt already.'

Turning his hand so that his palm was underneath hers, he intertwined their fingers. 'I don't deserve your absolution. But I promise if you ever need me, I will come.'

'You have my absolution all the same,' she whispered. 'And I think both Charles and Elizabeth would give you theirs as well... I can tell when you speak of them how much you loved them, and I am sure they loved you too. They would want you to be happy, healthy—and whole. Yes, you should miss them, and mourn them. But you must let go of the guilt that is dragging you down. Live a life worthy of their love.'

*Worthy.*

Louisa had used that word again. She had said last night that he was worthy of her love, but the events of today proved that he wasn't.

'The room's ready, Wick,' Mantheria said from outside the carriage.

Wick half carried Louisa into the house and up to the room that Mrs Perkins and her daughter had prepared for her. He saw two female servants carrying buckets of water to Louisa's room for a bath. He would have been happy to help, but he was shown, politely, to the door.

He climbed back into the carriage alone and told the driver to take him to the Crown. Uncorking the wine, he took a long swig. Louisa had already spent most of her life unloved and neglected—he didn't want anything to hurt her again.

He should have protected her.

Wick had failed her as he had failed Charles and Elizabeth.

He was not in any way *worthy* of her.

# Chapter Thirty-One

*Never has a bath felt better,* Louisa thought, sinking underneath the hot water until it reached her nose.

Leaning her head back against the copper tub, she took a ragged breath. Her throat felt as if she had swallowed stones. She coughed, and the door to her room opened. The bespectacled young woman walked in with a glass of water.

The stranger gave Louisa a reassuring smile. 'I thought you might be thirsty.'

Louisa greedily accepted the glass, and quickly emptied the contents down her dry throat. She swallowed. 'I am afraid that we have not been properly introduced. Although it seems a little silly to have an introduction when I am in the bath. I am Lady Louisa Bracken—but you are welcome to call me Louisa.'

The pretty young woman pushed her spectacles up the bridge of her nose. 'I am Mary Perkins. I would be pleased if you would call me Mary. We might as well be on a Christian name basis, for you are about to wear one of my nightdresses.'

'We have both stolen Mary's clothes, I'm afraid,' Mantheria said from the door.

She came into the room, her long blonde hair in one plait over her shoulder. Her face was still pale in the candlelight. She was wearing a prim white nightgown that buttoned up to her neck. The hem of the gown reached the floor.

Mantheria pushed up the long white sleeves and knelt beside the copper tub. She picked up a sponge and set it in the soapy water.

'I can do that,' Louisa said, quickly. She was embarrassed to be waited upon by the Duchess and naked in front of a stranger.

Mantheria squeezed out the sponge. 'I'll have you know that Andrew gives me high marks for my scrubbing. Andrew is my son, Mary. Now, lean forward like a good girl and I'll scrub your back.'

Too tired to protest, Louisa leaned forward in the tub and allowed Mantheria to wash her neck, her back, her arms and even her hair. Then her friend handed her the sponge and Louisa washed the front of herself, before stepping out of the tub and into a robe held by Mary. Mantheria handed her a towel and Louisa dried herself as best as she could.

Both ladies helped her into a nightgown and tucked her into bed as if she were a small child like Andrew.

Louisa took both Mantheria's and Mary's hands. 'I cannot thank you enough for finding me and helping me.'

'It was my pleasure, my lady,' said Mary.

'Louisa.'

Mary curtsied to Mantheria and then pushed up her glasses with her free hand. 'Louisa. I will leave you two alone. I am sure you have much to discuss.'

She watched Mary walk to the door and quietly close it behind her.

Mantheria sat down on the edge of the bed, still lightly holding Louisa's hand. 'Of course I would come to find you. I am your chaperone, after all, and your friend. Although I seem to have been doing a poor job of being both. I should have protected you better. If only I had taken a footman with us to the park.'

Louisa shook her head against the pillow. 'Nonsense. Both you and your brother take too much responsibility upon yourselves and give yourselves too little credit in return. No one, especially myself, could blame you for my cousin's actions. And, as I have already told your brother, I was not ravished.'

A tear slid down Mantheria's cheek. 'I believe you, dearest Louisa, but that doesn't change the circumstances. Nor the rumours that will spread about your reputation.'

'You mean that I have been compromised?'

Sniffing, her friend nodded. 'The *ton* doesn't care about the truth—they only care about appearances. The only way to save your reputation and good name is to have the protection of a gentleman's name.'

*Marriage.*

But she didn't want a loveless marriage like Mantheria's. Nor did she wish to rely so heavily on her friend in the future. Louisa wanted to be independent. To forge her own destiny. She had finally awoken from the dream that was the Stringham clan. She loved them, but she would never be one of them. Not truly.

'I am so sorry if my presence in your home has caused more problems in your marriage,' Louisa said. 'What a poor way to repay your many kindnesses. I will find a new situation as soon as possible.'

Mantheria sniffed, shaking her head. 'Glastonbury and I were not arguing about you... I finally confronted

him about Lady Dutton and asked if we could have a *divortium a mensa et thoro*.'

Louisa coughed. 'I don't know what that means.'

'It's Latin. Roughly translated, it means a separation of bed and board.'

Louisa brought a hand to cover her mouth. 'And what did he say?'

'Alexander told me the same thing my solicitors had— that we cannot have a legal separation because he has not beaten me nor treated me cruelly.'

Louisa knew all too well that words could inflict as much violence upon a person as fists. 'Flaunting his mistress in front of your face is cruelty enough.'

Mantheria held up a hand and Louisa closed her mouth.

'Glastonbury also does not want to cut me and Andrew off financially, which must be a part of an ecclesiastical separation. He suggested that instead we honour the spirit of the law. That he will find a separate living situation.'

'No doubt with Lady Dutton?'

'Most likely,' she said, exhaling. 'But he said that I can keep our London house for myself and Andrew, as well as use any of the Glastonbury estates. His only request was that he is to be able to visit Andrew frequently. Which I acceded to. He deserves to have his father in her life.'

Louisa thought of Sunny. 'And you deserve to have your own life.'

More tears fell down her cheeks. 'My life will have to be my son. Once my husband and I are separated, I will have to be more circumspect than ever in my social inter-

actions in order to keep my position. I can't afford to give the gossips any reason to have my name on their lips.'

'I understand,' Louisa said, swallowing down a lump in her throat. 'I will not besmirch your name.'

Mantheria shook her head and tears fell on the coverlet. 'No, you do not understand. I meant Sunny, not you, Louisa. You are welcome to stay with us forever. Only, I am not sure how many invitations I will receive after the news of the breakdown of my marriage becomes known. Or if I will still be considered a proper chaperone for you.'

'Wherever I live, you must allow me to repay the monies you lent me,' Louisa said, sitting up. 'You shall need them now more than ever. And I will beg upon my knees to my trustees if I have to.'

Mantheria wiped her nose with her sleeve—very un-duchess-like. 'I don't think that will be necessary quite yet. After the behaviour of Lord Barnabas, I believe your trustees will see how unsuitable your Aunt and Uncle Rockingham have been as your guardians. I am sure my grandfather and Matthew will be able to wrest control of your fortune from them and pass it to you. No one is equal to my brother Matthew with a pen. If you gave him enough paper he could write the stars down from the sky and sell you the moon at a discount.'

Louisa forced herself to smile. 'I've always wanted the moon.'

'And I a bright and particular star,' Mantheria whispered, pressing her lips against Louisa's forehead before leaving the room with the candle.

Louisa leaned back against the pillow and closed her eyes. Sunny was Mantheria's bright particular star, yet they could never be together. Sunny had foolishly thought

himself too young to court her, and Mantheria had married another. Despite being compromised, Louisa would not make the same mistake. For in her mind nothing could be worse than to be married to one gentleman and in love with another.

She would be much better off on her own. With or without proper society.

# Chapter Thirty-Two

Wick's legs and arm muscles tightened, as if he were about to run. He took a deep, calming breath, reminding himself that Louisa was safe now. But still he only felt relief when the carriage ride was over and he stood in front of the vicarage. The housekeeper from the day before led him into a small parlour, where Mantheria sat with both Mrs and Miss Perkins.

'Where's Louisa?'

Mantheria stood up and offered her hands. 'Still sleeping.'

Wick squeezed her hands before letting go of them and recalling his manners. He bowed to the other ladies, who had also risen to their feet because of his entrance. 'I hope I haven't called at an inconvenient time.'

'Of course not, my lord,' Mrs Perkins said, giving him a friendly smile.

Miss Perkins pushed up her spectacles and gave him a wide-eyed stare. 'Perhaps we should go and check on Lady Louisa, Mama? I am sure Lord Cheswick would like to speak to his sister in private.'

Mrs Perkins touched her chest. 'Of course, my dear.

How thoughtful you are. And shall I call for some tea, my lord?'

Wick's stomach grumbled, but he didn't want tea. 'None for myself, thank you. But I am sure Lady Louisa would be glad of a cup.'

'Yes,' Miss Perkins said, and guided her mother out of the room by her elbow.

Once the door was closed, Wick sat down on the sofa next to Mantheria. She was wearing the same dress as the day before and it looked a little worse for wear. 'How is she truly?'

'Shaken, yet determined to assert her independence,' his sister said. 'One can hardly blame her with a family like the Rockinghams… But we both know that it will not do. There is no true independence for women in our society. She cannot remain unmarried long.'

Wick nodded his head gravely. 'I intend to propose to her. I will offer her the protection of my name.'

'I think Louisa would prefer the protection of your heart.'

His throat tightened. 'I cannot offer what I do not have.'

'A heart?' she said, shaking her head. 'Of course you do not have a heart—you've already given it to Louisa, if only you weren't too stubborn to see it.'

Wick scrambled to his feet and walked to the window. His feelings were too raw to be shared.

'And I have solved your other problem,' Mantheria continued. 'I think that Miss Perkins would be an ideal governess for our sisters. Mary—Miss Perkins—said something last night about having to wait a few years for marriage. I am sure that some additional income would

be welcome before her wedding, and I am sure you would pay her well.'

Turning back to face his sister, he asked, 'Does she have any experience teaching?'

Mantheria waved that consideration aside with one hand. 'You don't need a scholar, Wick. You need someone to teach our sisters who doesn't go into hysterics over their pets or feel shocked over their behaviour... Miss Perkins didn't bat an eye over an abduction or a fire. She's perfect.'

'You have strange requirements in a governess,' Wick said, trying hard not to smile. 'No wonder none of the candidates from the agency fits the bill.'

Mantheria jumped to her feet. 'I had better ask Mary how she feels about snakes.'

'And elephants,' Wick added.

'Giraffes.'

'Bloodsucking ichneumons.'

Mantheria giggled and her shoulders shook. 'Kangaroos.'

'Cockatoos.'

'Ostriches and emus.'

'And don't forget the llama or the monkeys,' he said. 'If she is willing to put up with all the animals, we had better employ her on the spot.'

His sister threw back her head and laughed again, loudly. 'Little does the poor woman know that the animals are much better behaved than our sisters.'

The door opened again several minutes later, and Mrs and Miss Perkins came back into the room. Miss Perkins chose a seat next to her mother on the settee.

Wick cleared his throat. 'Miss Perkins, my sister and I have been impressed by your competence and charac-

ter. We are wondering if you would be willing to accept as position as governess to my three little sisters, aged thirteen, fifteen and nearly seventeen.'

Mrs Perkins blinked and looked at her daughter. 'Governess?'

Miss Perkins didn't bat an eyelash. She sat perfectly still, as if considering his proposition.

Wick knew that a typical governess only received between ten and twenty pounds per annum. He would offer five times that.

'I should pay you the wage of one hundred pounds a year, in addition to your room and board. I am sure that such funds will be of use in your upcoming marriage.'

'I have never been a governess before,' Miss Perkins said. 'I fear, my lord, that my lack of experience would be a disappointment to you.'

Wick stood up taller. 'I don't give a fig about your experience. I am looking for someone who will have a degree of influence over my sisters. I know that they will never be controlled. It isn't their nature and I wouldn't want it to be. I only wish for a kind and well-mannered woman who can curb their more dangerous expeditions and will not have hysterics when they bring home snakes or other wild beasts.'

'I am not prone to hysterics.'

Mantheria smiled at the young woman. 'I noticed how calm and collected you were during last night's crisis. That is why I suggested the idea to my brother. I think you will be the perfect governess for my younger sisters.'

A little colour stole into Miss Perkins's cheeks and her glasses fogged up. 'I am well-versed in the Bible and English literature, but I do not speak French or Italian.

And, whilst I can play the pianoforte, I would not consider my skill anything worth mentioning.'

Wick waved his hand. 'Frederica already speaks both French and Italian, and she can play the pianoforte very well. You would only need to encourage her to practise. And Helen has no interest in music—she is a naturalist at heart. She would enjoy it most if you read the same books as her and collected insects. She doesn't believe in pinning them to boards, though. She thinks it's rather barbaric and so do I. And Becca... Well, my Becca is a sharp and talented young artist. But she has difficulty reading and she was teased at her former school. Her last governess called her slow.'

Mrs Perkins gasped, bringing her hands to her cheeks. 'The nerve of the woman, to speak to your sister that way. I hope that you sent her packing?'

'She left of her own accord,' he admitted. 'And she wasn't the first governess to find my sisters' strong natures too difficult to handle.'

'I do believe that I would be happy as their governess as long as you do not have any unrealistic expectations of my abilities,' Miss Perkins said slowly.

Mantheria clapped her hands. 'Hurrah!'

'And Becca?' he couldn't help but clarify. 'You'll be kind to her and help her with her reading?'

'I shall certainly never call her names,' Miss Perkins said, taking off her glasses and rubbing the lenses clean with her handkerchief. 'And I would be happy to help her with her reading. But I do not know that I will be any more successful at it than the previous governesses.'

He appreciated her honesty. 'Excellent—you shall be our new governess... Are you able to come to London

with us today, or shall we send a carriage for you in a few days?'

Mrs Perkins stood up quickly. 'I shall go and have the servants prepare my daughter's trunk at once.'

She bustled out of the room and they could hear her voice in the hall, calling for a maid.

'I do not think we are in that great deal of a hurry, Mary,' Mantheria said with a little chuckle. 'We must wait for Louisa as well.'

But Miss Perkins had also got to her feet. 'Lady Glastonbury… Lord Cheswick, I should like to be ready to leave when you are. If you will excuse me? I must say my goodbyes to my father.'

Miss Perkins reached the door just as Louisa walked into the room. Wick did not recognise the gown she wore, and it looked as ill-fitting on her as Miss Young's dress had, that first night she'd arrived at Hampford Castle. It was tight on her shoulders and at least six inches too short on her legs. Her face, however, looked pink and fresh and healthy.

'I am afraid I was a bit of a slugabed this morning,' she said. 'Where are you off to, Mary?'

Miss Perkins pushed up her slipping spectacles with her index finger. 'Louisa, I have been offered the position of governess to the Stringham sisters.'

Louisa beamed at her. 'Oh, I am sure the girls will love you—and you them.'

Mantheria got to her feet as well, and walked to the door. 'I will help Miss Perkins pack.'

She closed the door behind her, leaving Louisa alone with Wick. Something that she had never done before, since she was supposed to be acting as her chaperone.

It took him only a few seconds to realise that his sister expected him to propose to Louisa right now.

Taking a deep breath, he wished he'd had a little more time to prepare. He walked back to the window and looked outside. What should he say? Should he kneel?

'Perhaps I should go and help Mary and Mantheria,' Louisa said, fidgeting with the material of her skirt. 'I'll leave you to your thoughts, Wick.'

Spinning on his foot, he held out his hand, although she was too far away for him to touch her. 'No. Don't go. Forgive me. I am trying to compose myself—words—speech...'

Louisa raised one eyebrow and it was as if her green eyes devoured him whole. Wick wished he was brave enough to offer his heart as well as his hand.

'The thing is... Well, you see... You can't go back to London. Or anywhere. Despite your bravery and your clever wielding of a needle, you have been compromised... And now I am making a total hash of my proposal...'

'Your what?'

Wick decided that he should kneel. Dropping to one knee, he said, 'Louisa, will you do me the honour of accepting my hand in marriage?'

# Chapter Thirty-Three

Louisa's heart soared at his words. This was the happy ending that she had dared not even hope for. Wick was asking her to marry him! This handsome man whom she loved with all her heart. She would be a true member of the crazy and entirely loveable Stringham family. She and Mantheria would be real sisters. Her trustees would release her inheritance upon her marriage and she would pay back her dear friend, whose loveless marriage was ending.

Except…

Wick hadn't mentioned love.

He'd praised her bravery and her cleverness, but that wasn't enough. She had seen with her own two eyes the misery of being married to a person who didn't love you. She would rather live with the Rockinghams again than marry Wick without love.

'Dear friend, please stand up,' she whispered, not trusting her voice to be steady at a normal tone.

She watched him slowly get to his feet. His eyes were no longer meeting her own. He didn't wish to marry her. She was just another responsibility that he didn't want.

He was only proposing out of duty, because her reputation had been compromised.

'Did Mantheria tell you that she is separating from Lord Glastonbury?'

Wick shook his head.

'She will no longer stay in a loveless marriage,' Louisa said. 'And I will not settle for such a match either. I will wait as long as it takes, until I find a sensible, good man who can love me and I can love in return.'

'But your reputation has been ruined!'

'My reputation is not as important as my happiness.' Although speaking the words made Louisa feel as if her heart was breaking into little pieces too small to sew back together.

He finally lifted his eyes to meet hers. 'I've always wanted your happiness.'

Louisa nodded her head, knowing that if she tried to speak she would sob.

She turned and left the room. Like Mantheria, she was learning that independence came at a steep price.

Despite the excellent company of Mantheria and Mary on the way back to London, Louisa couldn't help but feel solemn. Wick rode beside them on a horse he'd hired from the innkeeper, claiming that the carriage was too full. But Louisa knew the real reason. He was avoiding her.

The carriage stopped first at Lady Glastonbury's house. Frederica ran out through the front door to meet them. 'Did you find Louisa?'

She was followed by Helen, Becca, Andrew and Mrs May.

'I am here,' Louisa said, leaning her head out of the carriage window.

The Stringham girls pulled her out of the carriage and surrounded her in a hug.

'I am so glad! I didn't sleep a wink. I have been worried sick,' Helen said.

'Me too,' Becca echoed.

Louisa felt another pang of regret that they would not be her sisters. Her new family.

Mantheria stepped out of the carriage and picked up her son. Andrew scrunched up his little nose and pointed a chubby finger at his uncle on the horse. 'You no get ices, Uncle Wick.'

He laughed.

Oh, how she loved that sound.

'I shall take you tomorrow, Andy. I promise,' Wick said. 'But today I need to go to my rooms and freshen up. I smell of horse.'

'I like horses,' Andrew said.

Louisa found her tongue. 'Before you go, Lord Cheswick, would you and Mantheria escort me to my Uncle and Aunt Rockingham's house? I have some unfinished business there.'

Mantheria set down her son with a kiss on top of his head. 'Andrew, can you keep an eye on your aunts whilst I am gone? And will you promise not to let them get into any mischief?'

The little boy sniggered, nodding. 'I will.'

'Oh, Mrs May, please allow me to introduce you to my new friend,' she said, as Mary got out of the carriage. 'This is Miss Perkins, and she will be the new governess. She likes snakes.'

Helen's eyes widened and she bounded towards Mary. 'Really? Which is your favourite type?'

'A grass snake.'

Frederica and Becca crowded around the new gov-

erness too, asking Mary questions faster than she could possibly answer them. Louisa saw that Andrew was in the capable hands of Mrs May.

Mantheria touched her elbow and a groom helped them back into the carriage. Louisa was sorry to ask her friend to travel farther, but she needed to confront her aunt and uncle once and for all.

Mantheria took Louisa's hand in hers. 'I know this interview will be unpleasant for you. If there is anything I can do or say to help you, please let me know.'

She squeezed her hand back. 'Thank you, dearest friend. Just having you there with me will make all the difference.'

And it was true. Mantheria held her hand until they arrived at her aunt and uncle's London house. Wick assisted them both out of the carriage and they were escorted into a parlour. Her aunt and uncle were both there. Her uncle was reading and her aunt was doing needlework.

Her Uncle Rockingham stood and walked towards her, hands outstretched, when she entered the room. 'My dear niece, you are safe. Lord Sunderland has been claiming the most outrageous things about my son abducting you. Has it all been an unfortunate misunderstanding?'

Louisa half wanted to say that it had. But Barnabas's actions had not been a misunderstanding. He had meant to force her into a hateful marriage.

'It has not. Barnabas hit me on the head in the park and dragged me all the way to Cookham, where he locked me in his mistress's cellar without food or water.'

Her uncle recoiled. 'It can't be true.'

'I wish it were not, Uncle,' Louisa said. 'However, from today I shall have nothing to do with any of you again—familial or financial. I won't sue you for the mis-

spent funds of my allowance, but nor will I help you pay Barnabas's debts.'

'All we need is a brief loan to meet his most pressing creditors,' Uncle Rockingham said. 'We have cared for you for these last ten years, and I am sure your father would have wanted you to help his only brother.'

Wick grunted, but didn't say a word. Mantheria gritted her teeth. Louisa was in no doubt of their feelings on the matter.

Aunt Rockingham clasped her hands together beseechingly. 'How can you be so heartless to your own family? We will be ruined. Ruined!'

Louisa straightened to her full height. 'I *could* ruin you. I could press kidnapping charges against your son and have him hung or transported. But I will not. As long as you leave me alone. If you so much as speak to me again, I will be forced to take legal action… Come, Your Grace…my lord. It is time to leave.'

Louisa was grateful to be sandwiched between them as she left her aunt and uncle's house on her own two feet. For the first time she had no desire for their approval.

# Chapter Thirty-Four

Wick could hardly believe that a week had passed since he'd left London for Hampford Castle with his little sisters and Miss Perkins. It had been the longest seven days of his life, and perhaps the most transformative. He felt like a new man. A lighter one.

One day, after his sisters' lessons, they had insisted he go with them to pick flowers and place them on Charles and Elizabeth's names in the crypt.

Wick had expected it to be a solemn outpouring of mutual grief.

It was not.

Somehow his little sisters had made it a celebration of their lost siblings' lives. They'd laughed, cried and shared stories. Frederica and Helen remembered things that he did not. Like the fact that Elizabeth had been a champion pincher and had been able to leave bruises. Or that it had been Charles and not Frederica who had broken a bottle of his mother's perfume in one his few temper tantrums. He'd felt so sorry that his little sister had happily taken the blame. Frederica had always been getting into trouble anyway.

Becca had asked Wick to tell the 'plate in the face' story again and he did, as well as sharing a dozen other reminiscences. Including one about a large swan that had chased poor Charles all around Animal Island, trying to peck him.

On the walk back to the castle Becca and Helen had each taken one of his hands, and Frederica had looped her arm to Helen's. And in that moment he couldn't help but think of Louisa and her wise words about sharing burdens to make them light.

Wick still experienced sadness over his siblings' deaths, but he no longer felt overwhelming grief. And after a few days of observing Miss Perkins with the girls, as well as noticing the benevolent hand of Mrs May over them all, he realised that his sisters didn't need him. Miss Perkins had a knack of making lessons fun and indulging them in their passions. Nearly half of every day was spent out of doors, and he noticed how the governess allowed his sisters to teach her too.

It had not taken Miss Perkins long to rise high—not only in his esteem, but his little sisters' too.

Wick went on long rides, overseeing the land, but also thinking. He missed Louisa with an ache as real as any ailment. She had refused his offer of marriage, but he still believed—hoped—that she loved him. The more he thought about it, the more he realised that Mantheria had been right. If he had offered Louisa his heart she would have accepted him. He would not wish for a loveless marriage based on duty either.

He told his sisters at dinner that night that he intended to go back to London to visit Sunny.

'You mean Louisa,' Frederica said, dropping her fork and grinning at him.

Helen folded her arms across her chest. 'Try to do a better job of your proposal this time.'

'Did you kneel?' Becca asked, spilling her drink in her apparent excitement. 'You should kneel and take her flowers. Lots of flowers. Miss Perkins, what flower means love?'

The governess didn't smile, but her spectacles fogged up a little as she said, 'Red roses.'

Becca beamed at him. 'Take vases of red roses.'

'How is he supposed to carry them?' Helen pointed out.

'While kneeling?' Mrs May said from the opposite end of the table, and they all chuckled.

Now, Wick couldn't help but smile as he remembered their well-meaning rose-laden advice as he rode to Hyde Park, hoping to see Sunny. He pulled his horse to a stop, and was looking around him when two riders approached: Sunny and Matthew.

'Oi!' his brother called out. 'The triumphant rescuer returns.'

Smirking, Wick shook his head.

'I assume you have heard?' Sunny said in a lower voice, as he pulled his horse to a stop next to Wick's.

He nodded. 'Mantheria has told me that she intends to separate from Glastonbury.'

'Yes, she already has,' Matthew said, waving a hand. 'But that's not what we're talking about.'

Wick didn't let his little brother change the subject. 'Do you think Papa and Mama will be disappointed?' he asked.

'In Mantheria's marriage dissolving?'

Wick felt a sinking feeling in his stomach. 'In me. Should I have perhaps done something more? Tried to

help patch it up instead of telling Mantheria that Glaston-bury was not out of town as he had told her?'

Sunny turned his head away, his jaw clenched. He knew his best friend had feelings for Mantheria, and that he would not wish for her to stay in an unhappy relation-ship. But Matthew had no such bias, and even less tact.

'Our parents are never disappointed in you, Wick,' Matthew said, without his usual mocking tone. 'You are the ideal eldest son. A good property manager. Beloved by all of your younger siblings. And you bear the re-sponsibility well. Better than you know and better than I would. I would have let the girls join a travelling perfor-mance company and washed my hands of them. I would not have crossed half of England trying to find them the perfect governess.'

Wick's lips twitched, but he knew he could not allow his brother to amuse him now. 'But—'

'No buts, Wick,' Matthew interrupted. 'Despite you being annoyingly perfect, even *I* love you. And our par-ents and the rest of the motley Stringham crew don't hold you responsible for our own choices. Mantheria is a grown woman and a mother.'

Wick's entire body relaxed in the saddle. His brother's words had relieved his worries regarding his care of the family.

'Matthew was referring to Lady Louisa,' Sunny said from his side. 'She has received a most flattering offer of marriage from Norwich.'

Stiffening, Wick found it hard to breathe as he asked, 'And has she accepted him?'

Sunny shook his head. 'Not yet—but she might. She fears that her presence in Mantheria's home is feeding the unpleasant rumours regarding her separation. Not that

Mantheria agrees with her, but they have both received letters withdrawing their invitations to parties and routs. They are social pariahs at the moment.'

Wick's hands tightened on the bridle.

'Poor Louisa was also feeling terribly guilty over borrowing money for her wardrobe from Mantheria,' Matthew said, riding up to Wick's other side. 'However, I have solved *that* particular difficulty. After the Rockinghams' bankruptcy was announced in the *London Gazette*, I paid a call to all three of her trustees and pointed out how they had failed in their fiduciary duties to protect Louisa's yearly allowance from her aunt and uncle. I may or may not have threatened legal action if they did not immediately release to Louisa control of her yearly allowance. Happily, they saw the weight of my arguments and I left with all the necessary legal documents in my hand. Louisa should no longer feel obliged to marry in order to repay her debt to Mantheria, but she might still feel obliged to marry a gentleman to restore her lost reputation.'

'Someone like Norwich,' Sunny added unhelpfully.

'Oh, dear me,' Matthew said in a light mocking voice, putting his free hand on his chest. 'Is that my sister's carriage near the Serpentine?'

'I believe it is,' Sunny said gravely, shading his eyes with one hand. 'And what luck! There is Lady Louisa inside it.'

Wick knew what his best friend and brother were doing, but he didn't need their urging. He knew now that he loved Louisa. That he had done for almost every moment they had been together since he had pulled her into his curricle after mistaking her for his sisters' governess. He'd first been bewitched by her beauty, and then

he'd been pricked by her sewing needle, her intelligence and her kindness. He would do anything for her. She was everything he wanted in a wife and he wished to spend the rest of his life with her. To love her and cherish her. Protect her.

He didn't dare wait another moment; he spurred his horse forward.

## Chapter Thirty-Five

Louisa made eye contact with Lady Jersey, who put a gloved hand in front of her mouth and whispered to the lady beside her in the carriage. The social cut. Blushing, Louisa glanced away. Why was she being punished for her cousin's actions? She had done nothing wrong. She was not ruined. Her worth did not depend upon one day or one event. Or one person's opinion and approval.

Tilting her chin up, Louisa determined to show the *ton* that she didn't care for their narrow minds, nor for their terrible treatment of women.

'It might not be you they're whispering about,' Mantheria said in an undertone. 'I am sure it is common gossip now that Glastonbury has moved out of the house… Perhaps we should have waited until next year before making our return to London society.'

Louisa could only be glad when Lady Jersey's carriage passed by them and moved out of sight. From the corner of her eye she saw Lord Norwich, driving his phaeton towards them. He was wearing the same elaborately caped driving coat as before. She hoped that he was not coming to ask for her answer. She wasn't quite ready to give it yet.

Only a week ago she had painfully refused Wick's offer of a marriage without love, so how could she accept another lord's proposal without love? The only difference in her mind was that she loved Wick and she did not love Norwich, although he was an amusing companion.

She couldn't decide what would be the worst torture: to be married to a man she loved who didn't love her back, or to be trapped in a marriage where neither person loved the other. Perhaps they would grow fond of each other? Or perhaps his gaming debts would swallow her fortune as well as his own? Norwich claimed to have learned his lesson at the tables, but Louisa didn't want to save her fortune from her cousin only to lose it to another gambler.

Lord Norwich's smart equipage pulled up beside their carriage and both vehicles came to a halt.

'Ladies,' he said, tipping his hat to them.

Louisa looked down at her hands in her lap.

She heard Mantheria clear her throat. 'Lord Norwich, what a pleasure it is to see you.'

Louisa stole a glance at the gentleman and saw his lips form their usual sneer. 'And to be seen by me… I fear many of our fond society matrons appear not to be able to see either you or your carriage.'

Mantheria gave a little laugh. 'Oh, and don't forget the horses and my driver.'

Lord Norwich gave his soundless laugh.

Louisa was all but certain she was going to refuse his offer, but she didn't wish to be a burden upon her friend. And she didn't want to spend the rest of her youth ostracised by the *ton* and unable to join the London season entertainments she'd always dreamed of.

'Lady Louisa, dare I ask if it is a pleasure for *you* to see me?' asked Lord Norwich.

She swallowed. Her answer to this question would be almost the same as accepting or rejecting his offer of marriage. She took a deep breath, trying to organise the chaos of her mind.

The sound of galloping hooves caused her eyes to turn. Mantheria had told her that no one was supposed to gallop in Hyde Park during the promenade—the fashionable hours of three to five o'clock. Yet this gentleman was openly disregarding the rules.

He lifted his face and she saw that it was Wick! Her heart skipped a beat. He was back. She hadn't thought that he would return to London for the rest of the season.

'Ah, I see that Lord Cheswick has returned, and it is certainly a pleasure for you to see *him*,' Lord Norwich said sardonically.

'Forgive me, my lord,' she said in a state of confusion, glancing back at him. 'I did not mean to offend.'

He gave her a rueful look. 'Sometimes being fashionably late is a liability; it appears your affections have already been engaged. I do wish you every happiness in proving me wrong about Cheswick. Now I shall bid you lovely ladies adieu. I have no wish to hinder the grand reunion. But please be assured of my continued friendship and support.'

Norwich lifted his whip and snapped it above his horses' heads as they cantered forward.

Louisa had never liked the Earl so well as in that moment.

'Against my will, I am growing fond of Lord Norwich,' Mantheria said with a half-smile.

Before Louisa could answer, Wick pulled his horse to a stop beside them. 'Louisa, may we go for a walk?'

Mantheria raised her eyebrows. 'But what of your horse, Wick?'

He swung out of the saddle, looking handsomer than ever. Grabbing the bridle, he tied it to the back of her carriage before opening the door.

Wick held out his hand to her. 'Shall we?'

'I should be pleased to walk with you,' Louisa said, in a breathy voice that was not quite her own.

She placed her hand in his and a sweet warmth flooded through her entire body. He helped her down from the carriage and then offered his arm. Louisa briefly placed her fingers on the crook of his elbow, and again she experienced a flushed heat and a feeling of rightness.

'You can walk down by the Serpentine,' Mantheria said. 'But stay in sight, Wick. I am her chaperone, after all. And Louisa—don't go too easy on him.'

Louisa had to bite her lower lip to keep in her grin.

Wick gave his sister a menacing glance before leading Louisa away from the carriage towards the glistening blue waters of the lake. They stepped on to the pebbled shore and he turned to look her in the eyes.

'Louisa, please say that I am not too late.'

'Too late for what?' she countered, hoping for but not daring to assume his renewed attentions.

'Too late to tell you—tell you how I feel. That I— That I love you and I have always loved you. And that I will do anything in my power to make myself worthy of you if you'll be my wife.'

Her eyes filled with tears. 'You are already worthy. You are the best man I have ever known.'

Wick stepped closer and gently brushed a curl back from her face and behind her ear. 'Does that mean yes?'

Louisa leaned towards him. 'Yes.'

She licked her lips in anticipation. He was so close to her she was sure that he would kiss her again. Waiting for his mouth to touch hers felt like an exquisite torture. Her gaze fell to his lips. Wick brought his gloved hand to her face, cupping her cheek. His eyes searched hers.

'I wish that I could kiss you again,' he whispered. 'But I suppose I will have to wait until we are married.'

Wick might be willing to wait, but Louisa was not.

Standing on her tiptoes, she gently pressed her lips to his. Lightly. Softly. She felt his other hand on her back, pressing her closer to him, against his muscular body. He moved the hand on her face to her neck, and then his fingers into her hair. Not once breaking the kiss. Gaining courage, Louisa wrapped her arms around his neck and pressed her lips harder to his. She heard him give a slight moan and felt her power over him. Wick wanted her as much as she wanted him.

His mouth moved over hers with more pressure. Louisa gasped, and she felt his mouth close over her lower lip and gently suck on it. She felt heat in her belly and her whole body tingled. Her eyes popped open and she saw his smiling face. Moving her hand from his neck, she traced his lips with her finger. He closed his eyes and made a sound not unlike his sister's kittens when they were being stroked. Wick clearly enjoyed her caresses as much as she had his kisses.

Leaning forward, she opened her mouth slightly as they kissed again. Wick responded in kind. She felt the heat from his mouth and the wetness of his lips. It was even more deliciously wicked and wonderful than their

first kiss. She captured his lower lip between hers and sucked. He tasted sweet, like honey.

Reluctantly, she let his lip go. Wick did not move back from her, but returned his mouth to hers, deepening the kiss. His hands moved up and down her back and shoulders, overwhelming her senses and overturning her good manners. So much so that Louisa allowed one of her hands to drift from his neck down to his cravat, and then to the hardness of his chest.

Louisa felt Wick's hand cover hers. 'Perhaps we'd better stop giving the *ton* a show. I think there's been enough scandal for both our families already.'

The blood rushed to her face and she tried to pull her hand back, but Wick held it firmly.

'I didn't mean... I am sorry...'

'I hope that you *did* mean to kiss me and that you are *not* sorry,' he whispered, bringing her hand to his lips and kissing it. 'For this is the happiest day of my life.'

'You don't think I am too forward?'

He kissed her hand again. 'I think you are perfect just as you are. My only fear is that you have a sewing needle somewhere upon your person and that I am about to be pricked.'

Louisa giggled. 'You're quite safe. The needle is on the inside of my hem.'

'And you are inside my heart. Always.'

She couldn't help herself. Standing on her tiptoes, Louisa pressed a kiss to his cheek. 'And you are in mine.'

# *Epilogue*

Wick walked into the dimly lit Hampford Chapel. He didn't think his body could take any more joy. Filling one side of the pews, he saw Mrs May, all the maids, the butler, the footmen, the grooms, the gardeners, the keepers and Merrell, the head animal keeper. They had all come to support him.

Wick's father didn't believe in making his employees attend church. He left the matter of their souls entirely to themselves. The fact that every single one of them had chosen to attend his wedding warmed his soul.

Vases of red roses lined the aisle and adorned the altar. His little sisters must have been hard at work all morning. He sincerely hoped that they didn't want him to kneel in front of Louisa now.

The other side of the chapel was more sparsely filled. Grandmother Stubbs sat in the front row with Andrew perched on her lap. Behind them were Helen and Becca, holding their kittens. Miss Perkins was handing Frederica a handkerchief. Wick was floored—he hadn't seen Frederica cry in years.

Matthew and Sunny stood at the front of the chapel

by the chaplain. They were both his best men. When he reached their side, they shook his hands. Mrs Berry, the chaplain's wife, began to play the organ.

Wick looked at his best friend and prayed that some-day he too would have a happy ending with Mantheria, even if he didn't know how. But life was full of surprises and second chances, he'd discovered, and sometimes being a wreck brought you to the right shore.

Behind them was a large circular stained-glass win-dow of the archangel Michael slaying the dragon. It wasn't the most romantic of illustrations for a wedding, but the soft coloured light that it shed into the chapel felt holy.

Then Louisa entered the chapel on his grandfather's arm and all other thoughts fled his mind. She followed Mantheria, her matron of honour, and she was holding a bouquet of red roses, but none were as bright and as brilliant as her own red curls. Her dress was seafoam-green, and on her shoulders was the delicate lace shawl that Mrs Barker had made for her.

Slowly, she came towards him, and with each step his heart grew fuller. When she reached him, Louisa let go of Grandfather Stubbs's arm. They turned to face each other and Wick couldn't help but smile at his beautiful bride. Louisa beamed back at him and she practically sparkled.

The Reverend Berry, the Duke's elderly personal chaplain, opened his book and began the ceremony. Wick heard maybe one word in ten. His eyes and concentra-tion were on Louisa. He did, however, manage to say 'I will' at the appropriate moment, as did Louisa.

'I pronounce that they be man and wife together, in the name of the father, and of the son, and of the Holy Ghost. Amen,' Mr Berry said.

Wick could wait no longer. He swept Louisa into his arms and slanted his mouth towards hers. Louisa's lips were warm and insistent against his. The kiss ended to the sound of cheering.

Matthew clapped him on the back. 'Well done. But you'd better sign the register to make it all legal.'

Mantheria handed Wick a pen. He signed his name: *Lord Simon Anthony Peregrine Stringham, Marquess of Cheswick.*

'That's quite a mouthful,' Louisa teased, taking the pen and signing her own name beneath his. 'I think I shall stick to calling you Wick. But you can call me the Marchioness of Cheswick.'

'Or my wife.'

She beamed at him. 'That would be accurate too.'

They left the chapel arm in arm. Once out of the holy place his sisters descended upon both him and Louisa with hugs and kisses and kittens.

Andrew tugged on his knee breeches. 'Up, Uncle Wick.'

He laughed and swung the boy up to his shoulder.

Frederica punched his arm. 'I told you that Louisa was a lady. You should have trusted my instincts from the first.'

'Well, *I* thought she was a princess,' Helen said loftily, her long snake Theodosia curling around her right arm.

Becca smiled. 'And I thought she was beautiful.'

Wick kissed the top of his sister's head. 'Thank you, Becca, my heart.'

'I suppose Louisa is your heart now,' she said with a laugh, and followed Helen and Frederica to the Great Hall where a dessert table that had been set out.

Turning, he watched his grandmother kiss Louisa on both cheeks and his grandfather give her a bear hug.

His grandfather leaned heavily on his cane as he pulled a document out of his pocket.

'Wick wanted to ensure that your inheritance remained your own after your marriage,' he said in a gruff voice. 'And thanks to Matthew's devious talent with words it is thus. Louisa, your mother's money is still yours in a separate estate overseen by the Chancery Court.'

Louisa's green eyes widened and she looked at him. 'You have done that for me?'

Andrew pulled at his hair and Wick gave a painful gasp. 'Yes. Yes, I have. I want only you. Not your fortune.'

Grandfather Stubbs held out one hand to Andrew. 'Come here, Andy.'

His nephew managed to pull Wick's hair once more and kick his ear, before landing in his great-grandfather's strong arm.

'Shall we have some cake?' he asked the child.

Andrew giggled. 'And an ice!'

'Anything for you,' Grandfather Stubbs said, holding Andrew with one arm and his cane with the other.

Wick's little nephew had no idea that he was in the arms of one of the most powerful businessmen in England. One who could literally give him whatever he wished.

Wick felt Louisa's arms wrap around his waist. Smiling, he pulled her closer to him and rested his head on her hair. She fitted perfectly there.

Louisa snuggled her face against his chest. 'I can't imagine a more perfect day. Can you?'

'Actually, I can.'

She leaned back. 'What's wrong?'

He kissed her nose. 'This is only the beginning. I plan to keep you up for the rest of the day and most of the

night.' Wick released his hold on his wife and held out his hand. 'Come, let's go.'

Louisa placed hers into his, but said, 'We cannot leave in the middle of the wedding party. Everyone will know why and what we are doing.'

Wick laughed wickedly. 'But they won't be able to find us.'

He pulled her out of the room, down to the hall and into the courtyard...stopping only once to give her a long, seeking kiss.

\* \* \* \* \*

# ACCIDENTAL COURTSHIP WITH THE EARL

'Well-behaved women seldom make history.'
– Laurel Thatcher Ulrich

To: Debbie Welch

# *Chapter One*

*Hampford Castle, England—*
*1817*

The snake slithered down the steps before her in the secret passageway. Lady Helen Stringham preferred it that way. She didn't like mice and her pet snake, Theodosia, ensured that not a mouse could be found in the dark hall. Turning the corner, she realised that she was not alone.

It wasn't a mouse—it was her little sister, Rebecca.

Helen breathed in sharply. 'What are you doing here?'

Becca shook her head in the dim light. 'The same thing you are. Eavesdropping on Mama and Papa.'

Helen sat next to her sister, near the secret door that led to her mother's dressing room. The door that neither of her parents knew about. They both leaned against it, pressing their ears close to the age-old wood. Linking arms, they eagerly waited to hear what their parents had decided about their London Season.

'Why must they go to London at all?' Papa asked from the other side. 'I don't see why they need to get married. I would much prefer that they stayed with us for ever.'

'You didn't mind when the older children left,' Mama pointed out.

'Because they weren't half as interesting as the two youngest.'

Helen nudged Becca and they both grinned at each other. *Dear Papa.*

They heard Papa clear his throat. 'I…uh… Well, the thing is…you see… Becca is not getting any younger… and she is very mature for her age…certainly…uh…more mature than most debutantes. I do believe with all of my—*head* that it would be a marvellous idea. Or was it a great idea? It's both! For her to accompany Helen this Season.'

Helen couldn't hold in her smirk. Papa had just ruined Becca's carefully prepared speech that she'd composed for him.

*The word was supposed to be* heart, *darling Papa.*

'I see that Becca has put you up to asking me if she can go with Helen to London and debut at the same time.'

Mama had seen right through the charade and their father had no guile in his scientific soul.

'That's the ticket,' he admitted.

'The answer is still no.'

Both Helen and her little sister groaned. Becca rubbed her eyes and Helen's throat felt dry and sore as if her disappointment was stuck inside it. She adored her little sister's company and Becca accompanying them to London would have been like bringing a piece of home with her. They were both peculiar girls and they belonged together.

Mama set down something that clattered on the table, making Helen jump. 'A pair of Bow Street Runners couldn't keep track of them both in London. You know it would be a complete disaster. I dare say the Great Fire of 1666 would dim in comparison.'

Helen shrugged. 'Unflattering, but fair.'

Becca pursed her lips to one side and nodded.

Papa cleared his throat again. It was now time for Helen's speech for him. She hoped her father would do better at hers than he had at poor Becca's.

'If two girls are too much to bring to London,' he said, 'why doesn't Helen stay home with me and Becca can go and have her very own presentation? Helen has no interest in it and she would be happier here studying her reptiles. She feels out of place in London and loves being at home where she belongs.'

Helen sat up straighter. Papa hadn't flubbed her speech. *She* had made him repeat it at least a half-dozen times.

'Helen put you up to that, too, I suppose,' Mama said. She grimaced.

*Why did Mama have to be so shrewd?*

Hopefully, Papa remembered the second part of their argument. She waited a few moments before he said, 'Her book is coming out this summer and that is enough stimulation for this year. Scientists believe it is unwise for a young female to feel too much excitement. It can quite overturn her delicate constitution.'

They heard their mother get to her feet. Never a good sign. It usually signalled the end of a discussion. 'There are porcupines that are more delicate than our second-youngest daughter. She doesn't want to stay home for her book or her reptiles. Helen wants to stay home and make eyes at Jason, who needs more to do than being his father's curate and grinning at all the young ladies in the parish. Helen should have the chance to meet a man with better prospects than Jason. Besides, Becca must stay here as I've already arranged for a young scholar from Oxford to visit Hampford and help Becca with her spelling. I am sure if she applies herself, her reading difficulties will be over.'

Helen let her head fall on Becca's shoulder and they both groaned.

'Do you mean Helen likes Mr Robertson's eldest son? The one with the large canines and the ears that stick out?'

Jason Robertson's ears *did* stick out a trifle, but there was nothing wrong with his teeth. They were straight and strong. Perhaps they were slightly large. Oh, dear, thanks to Papa she would now think of the line from *Little Red Riding Hood* every time that she saw him: *Oh, what large teeth you've got.*

'I believe that they may be secretly engaged,' Mama said.

*How did she know that?*

The only person Helen had told was Becca.

'Mama must have second sight,' Helen whispered into her sister's ear. 'There is no other way that she could have known.'

Becca sighed and then bit her lower lip. 'I really am applying myself to spelling and reading. The letters on the page just don't stay in the right places.'

Her little sister's difficulties with reading and writing were of long standing and none of the eight governesses they had previously engaged could help her overcome it.

Helen held up a hand to silence her sister. Her parents were talking again.

'You'd better take Helen to London after all,' Papa said. 'We don't want her marrying a curate whose ears stick out. It's a hereditary trait that he'd probably pass on to all of their children.'

Helen could have screamed in frustration. But she was unsure if Papa objected to his lack of fortune, or his ears more. She was the daughter of a duke and Jason was only the son of the local rector. It would be an unequal match. But it wasn't as if Helen was young and impressionable.

She was one and twenty. She had briefly and disastrously attended school, where she had not made even one friend. She had travelled abroad to Greece and failed to create new acquaintances. And at home, the only humans who seemed to like her were her own family and Jason. She was simply too different from other people.

London society would be a nightmare! She would perpetually be the one fiddle that was out of tune with the rest of the chamber orchestra. No matter how hard she tried, she was simply odd. And was abysmal at pretence. Even in their family theatricals, she'd never been given a speaking role and sometimes her sister Frederica had made her be a part of the background set so as to not ruin the play.

Helen could never fit in with the *ton*, nor become a peer's wife. Her suitors would expect her conversation to be on normal feminine topics like the weather and fashion, not about the natural sciences and the mating habits of different species of snakes. And a peer would expect her to be obedient to him, which was never going to happen. Helen was bossy like her mother. She wished to be a scientist, not a hostess. The thought of planning social gatherings—which she hated—for the rest of her life was enough to make her feel queasy.

No. She couldn't marry an aristocrat with a title.

Jason didn't mind that she was peculiar and, if they married, she would not have to suffer through the London Season. They could stay in Ashbury village near Hampford Castle. Her natural habitat and where she was the happiest.

Helen was old enough to make her own decisions and it grated on her that she wasn't allowed to. She stood up and grabbed her little sister's hand. 'Come on, Becca. It's not over yet.'

\* \* \*

Mama set her wine glass on the table. 'This discussion is over.'

Helen grumbled. 'I don't wish to have a London Season. I am simply not the debutante type. I am a naturalist. Papa, tell her.'

She cast a look of entreaty at her father.

Papa, bless him, looked from her to her mother and shrugged. Mama, the Duchess of Hampford, was the alpha of their family. Not that Papa was the beta—that was Wick's wife, Louisa, who was too kind for her own good—but he wouldn't go up against her. She was the queen bee and Papa didn't want to get stung.

Her father cleared his throat. 'Helen, I think your mother is right. Why don't you go to London and meet more young men…with ears that don't stick out…you might decide that you like them better after all?'

'And if I don't?'

Her father looked to her mother and waited for *her* to answer. Thirty years of marriage made him wise enough to know when not to speak.

Mama took another sip of her wine. 'We are not heartless. If you do not find another man whom you like better, we will not oppose an engagement to Jason.'

Helen pulled at a loose curl in her coiffure. 'Can I get that in writing? Like the contract you had with Grandfather when you married, Papa?'

'You write it up and I'll sign it. But you must promise, Helen, to smile and attend every single event whose invitation I accept. You will dance with whomever I choose and you must promise to keep an open mind with your suitors.'

Becca cleared her throat and gave Helen a speaking glance.

'And Becca,' Helen said stoutly. 'Becca must be allowed to come with me for the Season.'

Her mother set down the goblet. 'Absolutely not.'

'You let Frederica debut at nineteen,' Becca protested. 'The same age that I am.'

'Yes, but she had no elder sister who was unmarried,' Mama said, giving Helen a penetrating glare. 'Becca, you will have your turn next year.'

Becca harrumphed, but Helen held her tongue. Once Mama made up her mind there was no moving her. And if Helen went to London and was agreeable, her parents would approve her match with Jason. Then she would never have to leave Ashbury and Hampford Castle again. It was more than she could have hoped for. Now all she had to do was ensure that every eligible young man in London wanted nothing to do with her.

That shouldn't be a problem.

# Chapter Two

Mark Wallace did not want the title of Earl of Inverness. He didn't want the Scottish estates. And he didn't want the town houses in Edinburgh and London. Mostly, he didn't want his elder brother to be dead.

Two years ago, he'd lost his leg at the Battle of Waterloo, the same battle where all his close friends had also perished. Then to lose his brother a year later, from a digestion complaint, was the final nail in his coffin. He was a walking ghost.

Mark felt the phantom itch in his missing leg. He knew it wasn't there, but he still reached down and scratched the wood of his prosthetic leg. He had been carried safely off the battlefield and taken straight to a surgeon. Yet, it felt as though part of him was still on the fields of Belgium. Scratching the wood didn't relieve the feeling, nothing did. Mark felt a leg that was no longer there.

Like his heart.

No matter how hard he tried, he could not be the lighthearted fellow he was before the battle. That young man was gone.

Nor could he marry his young cousin. A match that both his mother and his maternal aunt were actively promoting. Niamh was only seventeen and a bonny lass with red hair

and sparkling green eyes. She deserved someone young and happy. She wanted more than he could give. The only thing that he could do was escape to London and pretend to be looking for a wife there. Edinburgh was too close to home and Aunt Fiona would simply bring his cousin there.

No.

He had to make a fresh start in a new city.

Not that Mark could marry any woman. His body and soul were too damaged from the war. And if he didn't strangle his bride in his sleep, he would scare the wits out of her with his screaming. He had hoped that the night terrors would lessen over time, but more often than not he woke up drenched in his own sweat and in a living nightmare. And he hadn't found pleasure in anything or anyone since the Battle of Waterloo. He was not husband material.

Jason's usually large toothy grin was absent from his face. 'You're leaving?'

Helen placed her hand on his arm to comfort him. Touch had always been her favourite way to communicate. Animals used it more effectively than humans and she'd often found it difficult to express herself with words. She could never find the right ones. 'I have to go for the London Season. There is no other way for us to be together.'

And live in Ashbury for the rest of their lives near everything that was familiar and where people were used to her oddities.

He raked his fingers through his fair hair and she couldn't help but notice how much his ears *did* stick out. But it wasn't unattractive, it was adorable. Jason was tall and had an athletic figure, with dazzling grey eyes and thick, curly brown hair. Every young lady for twenty miles around admired him.

He had a pleasant disposition that was always hoped for in a member of the clergy. He had a smile and kind word for everyone. Jason had known Helen his entire life and had not once ever compared her to one of her better-behaved and prettier sisters. Nor did he criticise her behaviour or blunt manner. He was a dear!

Jason sighed, his shoulders slumping. 'I know that I am not a great match for you, Helen. You deserve to marry a prince.'

Bravely, Helen wrapped her arms around his neck. It felt both familiar and strange to be so close to him. They had been friends for so long. 'You are a good match for me. You are my best friend. And I made a bargain with my mother. If I go and enjoy the London Season, she will let us become engaged when I return in the summer. And I'll never have to leave Ashbury again.'

His lower lip stuck out petulantly. 'You'll forget me.'

'I won't. I couldn't.'

Jason put his hands tentatively on her waist. His hold was light as if he was trying to touch a butterfly. 'Can I kiss you before you go?'

Helen nodded. She'd been waiting her whole life for her first kiss. She'd always been fascinated by how animals showed affection and mated. Closing her eyes, she puckered her lips and tipped them upwards to him. She waited for what seemed like several minutes, before he bumped his dry lips against hers.

Then he released her, stepping back.

*That was it?*

Blinking, she couldn't help but feel a keen pang of disappointment. Helen had expected something quite different. Her sister Frederica and her husband, Samuel, were constantly kissing, even after two years of marriage. Helen

had to knock before she entered *any* room when they were visiting. Their kisses weren't at all like the brief embrace she'd just experienced with Jason. Their hands were all over each other and their faces red with exertion.

'Will you at least write to me?' he asked.

Her heart felt as if it were shrinking inside her chest. There was a heaviness in the air and in her body. 'Mama wouldn't permit it, you know. Because we are not formally engaged. But I know that Becca will. I'll send your letters enclosed in hers and she can deliver them to you.'

Jason took her hand and kissed the back of it with more passion than he had her lips. Perhaps it had been his first kiss, too. It was natural for it to be rather awkward. Neither of them knew what they were doing. It didn't mean anything that she'd felt cold after. No. Their next kiss would be much better. They had cared each other since they were children. Such a feeling could only grow into something more.

He smiled at her with all of his large white teeth. 'You have made me the happiest of men, Helen.'

She bit her lower lip. She was happy, she really was. The lowness she was currently feeling must have to do with her leaving him and her home. 'I had better go.'

'I will think of you every moment of every day.'

Helen doubted that she would give him that much time in her own thoughts, but she felt the warmth in her heart again. Her relationship with Jason was like with an old pair of slippers: well-worn and comfortable. Smiling, she squeezed his hands one last time. 'And I will think of you often.'

The heaviness that had weighed her down seemed to lessen as she walked back to Hampford Castle. She found

Becca in her room with Mademoiselle Jaune, their yellow macaw, on her shoulder.

The bird spoke first. 'Small treasure chest. Small treasure chest.'

Helen glanced down at her rather small endowment. Unlike her mother and three sisters, her figure was not voluptuous. She was straight like a rail. Her hair was flaxen and so pale that it almost looked white. Her eyes were a light blue, like her father's. Her features were very similar to her paternal grandmother's, the previous Duchess of Hampford, whom she only knew through a painting in the hall. The poor lady had died young. Wick, her eldest brother, used to tease her that she had been switched at birth with a fairy child, that she was a changeling. But the painting had always assured her that she did look like someone in her family. Even if they were long dead.

'Oh, be quiet, Bird!'

Mademoiselle Jaune flew around the room and landed near Becca. 'Large treasure chest. Large treasure chest.'

Helen couldn't help but laugh. Becca *did* have a large chest and she was amply curved. It was no wonder that their mother hadn't wanted them to debut at the same time. With her more vibrant complexion, rich brown hair and voluptuous figure, she would have received all the male attention. And even though Becca was two years younger than Helen, strangers usually thought that Becca was older. Perhaps because of her curves and her poise or the fact that she was six inches taller.

Becca's cheeks turned red. 'Am I too plump?'

Helen sat next to her sister, bumping her shoulder playfully with her own. 'Of course not! I would kill for your curves.'

Her little sister touched her sides and then slid her hands

down to her wide hips. 'Do you think the size of my waist is why Mama will not let me debut this year?'

Helen elbowed Becca sharply. All of the Stringhams were natural elbowers. 'Now, none of that! Mama is only afraid that you will take all the eligible young men from me and I will have to marry Jason after all.'

Becca looked Helen square in the eyes. 'Are you sure that you want to marry him? I know that he is your dearest friend, but is that enough to begin a marriage with?'

A bubble of uncertainty filled her chest, but Helen pushed it down resolutely. She loved Hampford Castle and its surrounding fields. They were her home, her natural habitat, and if she married Jason she would never have to leave. They would live in the neighbouring village of Ashbury and she would not constantly stick out like a sore thumb, as she would in London society.

'What greater love could there be than friendship? It won't fade with beauty or time... Becca, I have a favour to ask of you since you will be staying home. Don't roll your eyes yet. I was hoping that I could include a letter for Jason inside your letters and that you would deliver it to him.'

'I would be happy to be your personal mail delivery service to one very smiley curate. I only wish I could read well enough to understand the words. I should dearly love to snoop.'

Helen gave her sister a quick hug. 'Perhaps with the help of your new tutor, you will be able to devour every scandalous detail and society snub.'

Becca embraced her sister again and stepped down, dancing around the room. She spun with her arms out for an imaginary suitor. 'Thank you for the dance, Lord Tall-upon-Handsome.'

Helen laughed. Her little sister could have all of the

lords. 'I wish you could come as well. I am sure every handsome peer would pursue you.'

Her little sister bowed to her as if Helen was her dance partner, with a great flourish of one hand. 'Nonsense. I will hold your nosegays while you dance with several dashing admirers.'

'The only flower I'll have is a wallflower. Because that's what I'll be.'

Becca smiled, wrinkling her nose. 'Oh, pish posh! Every handsome young man will wish to dance with you and you need to enjoy yourself while you can. Like Frederica did before she married Samuel. For soon you'll be a vicar's wife and expected to keep chickens and set a good example in the parish.'

This image did not please her at all. One of Jason's greatest attractions was that he lived in Ashbury where all the villagers were used to her peculiar behaviours. Helen stuck her tongue out at her sister and Becca laughed. 'Theodosia would probably eat the chickens.'

'Besides that, do you intend to be the perfect vicar's wife?'

Helen's insides squirmed. 'I intend to be the perfect wife for Jason.'

Her little sister shook her head, folding her arms across her chest. 'I am not sure that they are the same thing. A vicar's wife should be seen and not heard.'

'That phrase refers to children,' Helen said tartly.

'Have you ever heard Mrs Robertson offer an unsolicited opinion?'

Jason's mother was a kind woman with rather weary eyelids that were always half-shut. She did have a great number of children to keep her busy. 'Perhaps she has nothing to say.'

'Or she knows her place as the vicar's wife.'

'Now you're the one spouting nonsense,' Helen said, leaving Becca's room. But she couldn't forget her little sister's words and wondered if she could become the type of person who was a good wife to a rector. She wished to explore the countryside and the forests and continue her studies in natural history. She was not at all obedient and she insisted on being heard. And she didn't want to stay home and watch her children and chickens.

# Chapter Three

If Mark had hoped to live quietly in London, he'd been much mistaken. Since he became Lord Inverness, matchmaking mothers seemed to jump out of the woodwork to introduce him to their daughters. Brothers and fathers wanted to befriend him at gentlemen's clubs, only to mention that they happened to have a most beautiful and accomplished sister or daughter, with a good dowry, whom they would like him to meet.

He tried to put them off with talk of enjoying his bachelorhood. Mark could hardly explain that his anatomy did not work properly since the war and that he could not perform a husband's duties. Nor did he have the emotional capacity to tie his soul to another's. His heart was a dry well and he did not wish for company in his misery.

Mark shook his head. The same people would have discouraged his suit a few years ago as a fortune-hunting second son. He was used to people toad-eating his elder brother, Jamie, because he had a title and a solvent estate. How he wished his brother were still alive. He would have laughed at Mark's predicament and perhaps helped him find the humour in it as well.

Even the London house had not met Mark's expectations. His family had let it for over ten years since his father's

death. Jamie hadn't had any interest in visiting. Either the tenants or his servants had quite let the property go. The back garden was an overgrown jungle. All the walls inside the house were stained with smoke. The carpets had scorch holes in them. The curtains were all ragged and the linens full of tears.

He had no choice but to dismiss all the servants and hire new ones, as well as a range of tradesman to remove and replace the carpets and wash or wallpaper the walls. He also had the foreman move the master bedchamber to the back parlour on the ground floor. It was difficult to go up the stairs with his wooden leg.

The inside of his house was a cacophony of workers.

He had to escape.

Limping to the back door, he carried a chair out into the long grass of the garden. There was a crooked tree that gave quite a bit of shade. He placed the chair under it and took out his sketching book. In Scotland, he'd loved to go bird watching and to draw the ones he saw. He doubted he would see much variety of birds in London. The sky was mostly grey with smoke from all the chimneys.

He looked up at the tree and saw a common red robin, sticking out his breast as if to challenge the world. Mark began to sketch the fellow's chest and then the tail feathers, claws and, lastly, his face and beak. If the bird could survive in such an inhospitable city, perhaps it was not so common after all. The robin squawked as if it understood his thoughts. But, no, he was claiming his territory from another bird.

Mark had to blink a few times to assure himself of what he was seeing.

The bird flying around his garden was not indigenous to England. It was a beautiful, brightly coloured, tropi-

cal bird. The chest was a golden yellow and the wingspan was wide. Scribbling furiously, Mark tried to capture this exotic creature. The bird's beak was black and curved like a hooked nose. The back of the bird was turquoise blue and there was a tuft of green feathers on the head. Around the eyes, the feathers were white and possibly black.

It had to be a parrot or a macaw.

But what was a macaw doing in London?

Sketching the claws, he saw that the bird was missing his left foot, like himself. He dropped his pencil. The macaw had successfully scared the robin away and was circling around him, before landing on the armrest of his chair.

'Pegleg. Pegleg.'

Mark glanced down at his legs. His wooden leg was hidden inside his trousers. It was not apparent that he was missing the lower half of it. He even wore a matching boot on the fake foot.

'Mademoiselle Jaune, you come back here right now!' a feminine voice called from over the fence directly south of him. 'You're not supposed to leave the conservatory.'

The macaw made a trilling sound. 'Small treasure chest. Small treasure chest.'

'Stop calling me that.'

He glanced over his shoulder and saw a young woman climbing over the top of the five-foot stone fence. Her hair streamed down her back in the palest shades of blonde. Nearly white. Her skin was practically translucent and the delicate white gown that she wore was spun like gossamer. Her shape from the back was willowy, but quite lovely as well. So much so that he longed to see her face.

The phantom itch returned. The need to scratch his long-gone leg.

What was he thinking? Fairy, woman or witch. She cer-

tainly wasn't for him. No female was. And he didn't even wish to speak to her. Closing his eyes, he leaned his head back and pretended to be asleep just as he heard her feet land on the grass behind him.

'You naughty, naughty bird,' the voice said. It was polished and aristocratic. He could tell that she was used to giving orders.

The macaw's wings flapped, causing Mark's hair to stir. 'You naughty. Naughty. Naughty.'

'I am not going to exchange insults with a bird. If you don't come at once, I am going to feed you to Theodosia.'

'Pegleg. Small treasure chest. Pegleg. Small treasure chest.'

Mark resolutely kept his eyes closed, mortified that the bird had known about his missing limb. If he just pretended to be asleep, maybe the beautiful young woman would disappear over the back fence the same way that she'd come.

'He does rather look like a pirate, Mademoiselle Jaune,' she said in a softer tone of voice.

His black hair was too long and he hadn't allowed his valet to shave his face in several days. He let his hair grow to cover the long scar on the edge of his left jaw.

She leaned over him and glanced at the sketchbook in his lap. The young woman was certainly not shy of strangers.

'Oh, what excellent illustrations,' she exclaimed. 'Do wake up, sir. I know that you are not sleeping. I have five siblings and I can tell when someone is only pretending.'

Chagrined, Mark reluctantly opened his eyes. He'd been wrong. She wasn't merely beautiful, she was as ephemerally delicate as the morning dew. Her form was slender, but not without gentle curves in the right places. Her white dress was stained with dirt from her climbing. Her eyes were the lightest blue he'd ever seen and she moved with the grace

of a bird. If she hadn't taken his sketching book, he'd have been half tempted to draw her, for she seemed otherworldly.

Then she smiled at him. It was blinding in its intensity and heat collected in his belly for the first time in years. 'I'm Helen. I see that you've already met Mademoiselle Jaune. She's a complete rascal. I can only blame her upbringing. She belonged to a horrible man in a rookery before Papa purchased her and tried to set her free, but she was too domesticated at that point.'

Mark knew he should stand up and bow to her, but he didn't want her to know about his leg. He didn't want this beautiful fairy creature who made his blood hot to pity him like the other women did. And he didn't give his surname or his title. He was never going to see her again anyway. 'I'm Mark.'

'Have you ever sketched snakes, Mark?'

He could only blink at her. Was this some sort of hallucination brought on by the laudanum? But he hadn't taken it in weeks. It didn't numb the chronic pain, nor stop him from waking up soaked in sweat from his nightmares of the war.

She laughed, a floating sound that trilled in the air. 'Maybe you were actually asleep after all. But since I've already awoken you, I might as well continue. I am Helen Stringham and I'm publishing a book on snakes and I do believe that your sketches would improve the work. Pictures can be so much more helpful than words.'

His entire body tightened at the thought of spending more time with her. He rubbed his eyes, still half convinced that this was all a fever dream. 'You're publishing a book on snakes?'

Helen grinned, nodding her head. 'Actually, Gibbs and Thomas are the publishers. I wrote it, though. And I think

that snake illustrations would greatly improve it. Would you be interested in drawing them?'

'Snakes?' he repeated stupidly.

'Yes.'

Mark should not spend more time with her. She was a lady and he had no interest in becoming her suitor. 'No.'

Helen gestured around the overgrown garden. 'By the looks of things, you shouldn't say no either.'

'I don't need your money.'

*Or your pity.*

She sighed, shrugging her narrow shoulders. 'All right. I shan't pay you in coins, but in garden work.'

'I doubt you've done a day's work in your life, my lady,' he scoffed.

'You would be wrong.' Helen took off her gloves and showed him the calluses on her hands. 'One does not become a leading naturalist on snakes by staying inside. I will return tomorrow with my snake, Theodosia, and I will tame your back garden while you draw her.'

Mark opened his mouth to tell her no for a second time, but she'd already reached out an arm out for the macaw, who dutifully hopped on it. Helen didn't wait for his answer, but walked to the fence, lifting her pet over first, before stepping on a tree branch and scaling it as easily as a staircase. He felt a tingling at the back of his neck as his blood gathered most inconveniently in uncomfortable places. Apparently, he was not dead quite yet.

And the fairy queen would be back.

'Where have you been, Helen?' her mother asked.

Helen lifted her arm for the macaw to fly away inside the greenhouse room at the back of their town home. 'Ma-

demoiselle Jaune escaped from the conservatory and I had to go and retrieve her.'

Mama shook her head. 'You're covered in mud from head to toe. Come, you must have a bath before your presentation to the Queen.'

She dutifully followed her mother and spent the next three hours being poked, pinned, prodded and covered in tall feathers like a bird. She couldn't help but think of their mercurial neighbour, Mark. He had made her heart beat most irregularly. Maybe he would like her now that she was covered in white feathers. He seemed quite interested in birds, but not in her. Blushing, she remembered how handsome he was, so unlike the other men of her acquaintance. His appearance was rumpled and careless. His manners non-existent. He'd not even stood in her presence, like a peer would.

Perhaps he truly was a pirate. The idea thrilled her. He was so much more intriguing than the buffoons dressed in pastel coats with their high shirt collars, who were looking for society wives to become hostesses for their guests and mothers for their progeny.

The door to the room burst open and her elder sisters came in. Both Mantheria and Frederica were dressed in the same outrageous court gowns with feathers, stoles and hoops. The elderly Queen Charlotte insisted that ladies dress in the same fashions as their grandmothers had for court and they were ridiculous.

'You two look like tiered cakes,' Helen said.

Frederica laughed, kissing her cheek. 'Thank you! I know that I look good enough to eat.'

'Don't encourage her, Helen,' Mantheria said, half smiling. 'I am in the same carriage as her and Samuel and the

way they look at each other is enough to make one blush scarlet.'

Helen couldn't help but grin. The Horrible Samuel of their childhood had somehow turned into a handsome young duke who doted on her sister. Frederica and Samuel were always kissing or quarrelling, sometimes at the same time. They played and loved roughly like a pair of foxes in spring.

'Did you bring Arthur down from the nursery?' Helen asked.

Her one-year-old nephew was adorably roly-poly, with the chubbiest cheeks that you couldn't help but kiss.

Frederica shook her head. 'Samuel offered to stay home with him, but Nurse wouldn't stand for it. I've finally found someone who intimidates my husband.'

Mantheria giggled. 'Nurse?'

Eyes dancing, Frederica nodded.

Sighing, Helen said, 'I'll happily stay home with them as well.'

Frederica and Mantheria each took one of her arms and marched her to the door. Older sisters were overbearing that way.

Mantheria squeezed her elbow. 'You're not getting out of your presentation to the Queen.'

Frederica gave her a sympathetic grin. 'Don't forget your bargain with Mama. You have to go to every event she says, if you hope to marry your curate and live an idyllic life in the country.'

'Very well,' Helen said, frowning. 'But I don't have to like it.'

# Chapter Four

Mark sat fidgeting in his club. It would have been foolish to stay home. He had no desire to see Helen Stringham again or her pet snake. That was if she even came back to his garden. A proper young lady did not do such a thing.

He dropped the book in his hand.

The stocky man in the chair across from him bolted upright, as if he'd been awakened. He rubbed the back of his wrist against his eyes.

Mark stooped over to pick up the book. 'Sorry. I didn't mean to wake you, sir.'

He yawned, shaking his head. 'Not your fault. My son is teething and I am getting hardly any sleep at home. Captain Mark Wallace, isn't it?'

Mark suddenly recognised the man sitting across from him was none other than the soldier who had saved his life by carrying him off the battlefield. He was a powerfully built young man with broad shoulders. He'd been an aide-de-camp to General Lord Wellington. 'Colonel Lord Pelford?'

He smiled. 'Just Pelford now.'

'And I'm Lord Inverness… You have a son?'

Pelford's smile widened. 'Yes. I held him most of the night. The poor lad has three teeth coming through. We are

staying with my wife's family for the Season and I needed to go somewhere I could rest.'

Mark remembered the Duke's beautiful and fearless fiancée who had helped nurse him back to life with the help of her red soap. 'And how is Lady Frederica? I mean the Duchess.'

'Excellent. She is preparing for her sister's coming-out ball this Friday. You should come. I'll send you a card. I'm sure Frederica would be pleased to see you.'

That was the last thing in the world he wanted to do. Something of his thoughts must have shown on his face, for Pelford laughed out loud. 'You don't have to come and I promise that I'm not matchmaking. I'll still have my wife send you a card, though. We should go shooting sometime at Manton's.'

Mark hadn't held a gun since Waterloo, but he wasn't about to turn down Pelford's offer of friendship. All his other mates were dead and buried. He held out his hand for the Duke to shake. 'I should like that.'

He watched the stocky young man walk away and slumped back in his chair. He couldn't help but wonder what it would be like to have a son of his own. Few fathers would have stayed up the entire night with an infant—that was traditionally the role of the nurse or the mother. But Pelford didn't seem to have minded at all. He appeared proud and happy to spend time with his child. Somehow, he'd returned from the war unscathed. Unlike Mark. But to be a father, he would have to be a husband first, which he couldn't be. He didn't have a whole heart or body to give to a wife.

The young Duke didn't act as if some dark cloud followed him around, blocking the sun out from his life. Not that Lady Frederica would have allowed him to. Pelford's

wife was a very assertive young woman, not unlike the one who had invaded his garden, Helen Stringham.

Sitting up in his chair, he grabbed his face as it dawned on him. Lady Frederica's surname before marriage had been Stringham. The party she was preparing for was for none other than *Lady* Helen Stringham. The snake charmer from his garden that had made his skin tingle. But she had not introduced herself as a lady. And the two sisters looked nothing alike, but there was something similar in their mannerisms. How they moved their hands when they spoke, that was the same.

Slowly, he got up and limped to the door.

He had hailed a hack to his home and passed through the workers tearing out the carpet. Opening the back door, he saw that she was already in his garden.

Today, her hair was braided down her back like a long snake. Her long-sleeved cotton dress was appropriately printed with green thorny vines. She wore a wide-brimmed straw hat and was efficiently wielding a pair of sheers at what once had been an enormous bush. The snake she called Theodosia slithered around her and looked at him. Its beady eyes unnerved him a little.

'Lady Helen.'

She looked at him over her dainty shoulder. She was more beautiful than he had remembered. More fairylike. 'Just Helen.'

'Why is the daughter of a duke trimming my garden?'

Helen waved the sheers at him. 'Because it needs it… and we have a bargain. Theodosia is ready for her likeness to be taken. I could ask for her to stay still, but I can't guarantee it. She's a little shy. And snakes don't do anything that they don't want to do. I envy them that.'

She started to trim the bush again.

Mark took a few limping steps closer to her, intrigued against his inclination. His blood thrumming in his veins. 'What is it that you do not wish to do?'

'Be here,' Helen said, pointing to the ground. 'I had no wish to come to London at all. But Mama insisted and we made a bargain of sorts. If I had a Season, she would let me stay home at Hampford and marry my best friend.'

His heartbeat quickened. 'And who is that?'

'A boy I've known my entire life,' she said, unabashedly looking him in the eyes. 'He's currently the curate of a nearby parish that he will one day be the vicar of. So, you see why titles and position don't mean anything to me. I am like the creatures I study that way: they respect those who are stronger or cleverer than themselves. They care nothing for names or titles.'

'And what of money?'

Helen turned and continued to prune the bush. 'I have plenty of my own and, hopefully, more from the sales of my book.'

Mark didn't miss the hint. Pulling out the sketchbook that he always kept in his pocket, he turned to a fresh page before taking a seat on the chair that he'd left outside. He began to sketch. The snake was nearly four feet long. 'What sort of snake is Theodosia?'

'A Ball Python.'

'Is she indigenous?'

Helen shook her head. 'Oh, no. She is from Western Africa. My father brought her back from his expedition nearly ten years ago. He purchased her from the ship's captain who was using her to keep down the mice.'

He couldn't keep himself from asking the next question. 'How do you know that she's a girl?'

'Her size for one thing. Female Ball Pythons can grow to three or four feet long. Male Ball Pythons only reach two or three feet.'

Mark sketched the spots on the snake's back that resembled a giraffe. Carefully, he added the scale-like skin of the body. It was an exotic, beautiful creature. Not unlike its owner. 'What made you interested in snakes?'

Helen pulled out a weed and tossed it into a pile. 'My father is a naturalist and, out of his six living children, only Becca and myself took an interest.'

'Does he like snakes, too?'

'Papa prefers larger animals to study. But he always returns them to their natural habitats if he can. Some become too domesticated, like our elephant, Sadie, and cannot be released back into the wild. They would not be able to take care of themselves.'

Mark had felt the same way after returning from the war. He needed help now to accomplish the simplest of tasks. 'I am sorry for your elephant.'

'Sadie would appreciate that. Animals have feelings just like people do.'

Intrigued, Mark leaned closer to where she was weeding. 'Really?'

'You like birds, right?'

'Birdwatching.'

'Swans are the most loyal of birds. They mate for life and when their mate dies they do not take another. I often wonder if the human concept of love ever reaches that sort of devotion.'

He felt the blood rushing to his face. A young gentleman didn't typically speak about the mating of animals with an attractive young woman. Not even to an intriguing one like Lady Helen. 'Hopefully, it does with your curate friend.'

'Friendship is the purest form of love.'

She returned to her weeding and he to his sketching. Mark tried not to notice how much her very presence affected him, but he couldn't block her out, no matter how hard he tried to. She was like a fierce light in the darkness that refused to be dimmed. He finished his sketch of the snake and then turned the page and began to draw her. Among the overgrown flowers and bushes, she was a fairy in the garden.

'Your brother-in-law invited me to your coming-out ball.'

Glancing over her shoulder, Helen smiled, her eyebrows raised. 'You know Samuel?'

'I fought with Pelford at Waterloo.'

Helen nodded, smiling. 'And shall you come?'

Mark shrugged, ripping out the picture of the snake and handed it to her. 'I haven't decided yet.'

'Oh, don't be a Broody Byron and stay home,' she complained, waving her spade around in the air. 'That poet's quite gone out of fashion since he was more wanton with his favours than a male lion with a pack of lionesses.'

A laugh broke from him. What would Helen say next? Shaking his head, he said, 'I will try to look in to your party.'

'I'll save you a waltz.'

She had no idea how much those words stung.

Mark had only one leg.

He couldn't dance. He wasn't a whole man.

Still, he watched her lift Theodosia over the fence and follow behind her, stepping on a branch with her pruning shears. Helen had been in his garden for but an hour, possibly two, yet it already looked transformed. The dead branches and weeds were gone. He could see new sprouts of life poking through the black dirt, resiliently fighting for life.

# Chapter Five

Helen had never particularly liked the colour white, except for the one time she'd seen it worn quite fashionably on a polar bear. Now *that* white had been spectacular, even though she had wished the bear could have been freed. But the dull white colour that debutantes wore was nothing like it and Helen was a good four years older than most of her peers. After her sister Mantheria's disastrous marriage at seventeen—the appropriate age of presentation in the *ton*—her parents had waited with their other daughters. Frederica had not debuted until nineteen and married when she was over one and twenty.

Mama had offered to present Helen at nineteen as well, but instead, Helen had chosen to go to Greece with Mantheria, her estranged spouse who was in ill health, his mistress, Lady Dutton, her father and Becca. Helen had wanted to hate the Duke of Glastonbury for ruining his marriage to her sister, but she couldn't. Somehow, they had all become family. An odd, unconventional sort of family. And she hadn't regretted her decision to travel. She loved everything about Greece, from the animals to the mythology.

The ringlet curls escaping from her chignon looked a bit like snakes, but her stare would not turn young men—and some not so young—into stone.

*A pity, that.*

Her nephew, a young boy of ten, dashed into her dressing room. 'Aunt Helen, you look like a princess.'

Helen kissed the top of her nephew's head. 'Thank you, my love. But I'd prefer to be a gorgon.'

Andrew laughed merrily. 'Great-Grandmother Stubbs's stare can turn people into stone. I've seen her do it. They can't even speak.'

A chuckle escaped Helen's lips as she pictured it. 'Unfortunately, such a gift is hereditary.'

'What does hair territory mean?'

'It means that Great-Grandmother Stubbs married Great-Grandfather, but that we don't share any blood with her. Therefore, we cannot inherit any of her marvellous gorgon abilities.'

Her nephew's face was a study of consternation for a few moments, but then he smiled. 'I still think that you could turn men into stone, Aunt Helen.'

She swooped over and hugged Andrew, dropping another kiss in his dark curls. 'Now, you could inherit that from me. We do share blood and, therefore, the same hereditary traits. Although not the same hair colour.'

Andrew laughed.

Linking arms, they left her dressing room and descended to the lower parlour where all her family was assembled, except for her other niece and nephews. Andrew hugged her mother and Mantheria. Her eldest brother, Wick, and his wife, Louisa, were sitting together on a sofa, both with their hands on her growing belly. Helen was pretty sure that it would be a fourth boy. Wick and Louisa seemed to wish to singlehandedly repopulate the human species.

Her brother Matthew and his wife, Nancy, were sitting on a sofa with a giraffe-length space between them. Poor

Nancy's usually gorgeous Scottish complexion was rather pale with a tinge of green. She was also holding a bowl in her lap. Helen supposed that she was also expecting again and, like last time, her sense of smell had heightened like a cat's and she couldn't abide any scent. Including her husband's.

Frederica and Samuel were standing in the corner of the room, smiling stupidly at each other. She could only be glad that they weren't kissing. After two years of marriage, their infatuation only seemed to grow. They were always touching each other. A hand on the elbow, the shoulder, the waist, or holding the other's fingers. The connection between them was very physical. They often reminded her of a pair of monkeys, constantly touching and grooming each other.

She couldn't help but wonder if the touches between herself and Jason would become less stilted. More natural. Surely, their kissing would improve with practice? She couldn't see herself wishing for more of the dry brushing of lips. But even if it didn't, she would have her woods and her rivers. Her stars and her streams. And Jason would never expect her to be a society hostess or broodmare.

Mama swept into the room like the Duchess she was, smiling at her children. 'This is going to be a memorable occasion. The Prince Regent has even promised to stop in.'

Since the Prince Regent was a particular friend of their mother's, it wasn't too surprising or exciting. And Prinny could never get their names right. Unfortunately, the Prince's attendance would set her coming-out ball apart from similar such parties. Which was the last thing Helen could wish for. She wanted to be a failure and a wallflower, while still upholding her end of the bargain with her mother.

Leaning her chin on her hand, Helen sighed. 'I wish Becca and Papa were here.'

Wick laughed. 'Papa is lucky to be missing it.'

Shaking her head, Mama cleared her throat. 'Becca couldn't be left unchaperoned with her new tutor. It is a man this time. University educated. Top of his class. He received a double first like Matthew.'

'But Papa doesn't truly care about that,' Matthew said with a grin. 'Any excuse to not have to come to London is good enough for him.'

Helen nodded into her palm, sighing again. How she wished to be with him at Hampford Castle. 'True. It's probably why he agreed to make me come and made Becca stay home. The selfish wretch.'

Her mother stiffened, humming imperiously. 'Helen. Remember our bargain.'

Lifting her head, she put on a fake smile and curled her fingers into claws. 'Yes, Mama. Do you have a list of suitors I am to dance with? Or shall we see if anyone comes up to scratch?'

Her siblings laughed. They had all suffered from their mother's matchmaking attempts when they were single.

'As a matter of fact,' Mama said in a dignified tone, ignoring her progeny, 'I have *not* prearranged your partners. In the past, it has been most unsuccessful. I did not want you to be like your siblings and use it as the list of eligible people to hate.'

Her siblings and their spouses laughed again and Helen's lips tilted upwards despite herself.

'Nonsense, Mama,' Frederica said, kissing Samuel's cheek. 'I was very obedient. I married the man you chose for me.'

Mama put her hands on her hips. 'You eloped with him and I didn't get to come to your wedding. Even though I was

in the same city and could have easily attended it without getting in the way of your spying for Wellington.'

Frederica shrugged, beaming. 'You can't have everything your way, Mama. Even if you are a duchess.'

'I beg to differ,' Samuel said, lifting Frederica's hand and kissing it reverently. 'You *always* get your way, my Duchess.'

They grinned at each other in a special way. It was so *disgustingly* sweet. She couldn't help but wish Jason was more circumspect with his smiles. He smiled at everybody. It was something that she both loved and hated about him. Jason was all smiles and Helen was all scowls.

Mama clapped her hands to get everyone's attention. 'Wick, you will take your father's place at my side to welcome the guests.'

He groaned as though he was still a boy and not a grown man with three sons and another babe on the way. 'Must I?'

'You must.'

Matthew laughed.

Mama rounded on him, wagging her finger. 'Matthew, your job is to make sure that your sister never lacks for a partner.'

He looked at his three sisters. 'Which one?'

Helen giggled. Matthew knew very well whom Mama meant.

Their mother ignored his sally. 'Mantheria and Frederica, you will ensure that Helen does not escape the party.'

'We are to be your jailers,' Mantheria said with a wink as she took Helen's arm and squeezed it.

'What about Louisa and Nancy?' Helen asked, yanking her arm away from her eldest sister. 'Aren't you going to give them a task for my ball?'

The stern look on Mama's face softened. 'They are doing quite enough already.'

Louisa held her baby bump. Helen glanced at Nancy, who blushed. She was now sure that her sister-in-law was expecting a child.

'And Samuel?' Helen pressed, pointing at him. 'Does he not have to do anything?'

'I have to keep track of Frederica,' he said, grinning at his wife. 'And that proves to be a full-time task.'

No one disagreed with him.

'Samuel will open the ball by dancing with you,' Mama commanded. 'He is by far the best dancer in the family.'

Helen dutifully took her place by Mama and Wick, welcoming the guests for the early dinner. The only two visitors she smiled at were Grandfather and Grandmother Stubbs. She kissed Grandfather on the cheek and he slipped a necklace into her hand.

'Grandpapa, you didn't have to do anything.'

He beamed at her. 'I wanted to.'

Helen looked down at the necklace in her hand—it was one of a kind. It looked like a serpent, with turquoise, silver, gold, rubies, pearls and diamonds set in a scale-like pattern. The end of the necklace had the face of a snake. She loved it with all of her heart. 'Put it on. Put it on.'

Turning her back to her grandfather, she handed him the necklace and he clasped it around her throat. Helen gave him another hug and kiss for good measure and, in her good spirits, gave one to Grandmother Stubbs as well. Her step-grandmother was a stern woman with definite ideas about appropriate behaviour, but she smiled as Helen kissed her cheek. 'There. There, now. Only your best behaviour tonight. Yes? And the snake necklace around your throat is the only one on your person?'

Helen touched the turquoise snake. 'It is the only one, Grandmother. I promise.'

Grandmother Stubbs nodded, wagging a finger at her. 'Your best behaviour.'

Wick snorted.

Helen elbowed him in the gut. 'Why does everyone assume I will behave badly?'

'Because you always do,' Wick said, dodging her second blow.

Despite her eldest brother's ominous prediction, Helen behaved very prettily during the early supper and after, as they greeted more guests, including the Prince Regent, who kissed Mama on both cheeks and exclaimed that she was more beautiful than she'd ever been. Happily, Helen was given only a handshake and a compliment. She didn't want the lecherous old Prince's kisses.

Helen opened the ball by dancing with her brother-in-law Samuel. As the Duke of Pelford, he was also the highest-ranking person at the ball after the Prince Regent and the Duke of Glastonbury. But neither of them danced— Glastonbury because he was unfortunately confined to a chair and the Prince Regent because he was too important. It was rare for him to dignify a party by dancing.

After the dance, Lady Dutton wheeled Glastonbury over to her. Lady Dutton was his mistress, Mantheria his wife and the mother of his son, Andrew. They lived in separate residences in England.

Glastonbury held out his hand. In it was a golden snake arm cuff that twisted around a lady's arm. He must have purchased it for her in Greece. 'For you, Helen of Troy. The face that launched a thousand ships.'

Helen gave him a quick hug and then Lady Dutton, who was almost like an aunt to her, before sliding the cuff over

her long gloves and up her arm above her elbow. 'Well, now you know why the ships left so quickly. When they saw this face, they wisely made a run for it.'

Lady Dutton put a hand on Helen's arm. 'Nonsense, Helen. You are very beautiful. You shine like a beacon in the night.'

Helen thanked them and was whisked away for several country dances. Matthew seemed to be taking his role of finding her partners seriously. He had practically made a queue of them.

Breathless and thirsty, Helen escaped the ballroom for some punch. Both of her elder sisters followed her.

Frederica took her elbow. 'Back to the ballroom with you. The night is not half over yet.'

'But I'm tired and my feet hurt.'

'I've seen you stay awake all night for the birth of an animal,' Mantheria said. 'Surely you can handle staying awake for your own ball.'

Helen opened her mouth to complain, but her breath caught at a glimpse of black hair, too long to be stylish. Its wildness and unconventionality were arresting and, though he'd shaved, Mark somehow still had the air of a pirate. His black suit of clothes was very fashionable and not at all crumpled. Instead of the knee-breeches that most men had worn to the ball, he had full-length trousers on. Even his linen shirt and cravat were black. They made his blue eyes stand out and something inside her belly melt.

Leaving her sisters without a word, she walked up to him. 'You came, Mark! I didn't think that you would.'

He turned from the gentleman he was speaking to, to look at her, bowing his head. 'Lady Helen.'

Remembering her manners, Helen gave an obligatory curtsy.

Mark gestured to the man at his side. 'Allow me to introduce my cousin, Lord Watford. Lady Helen Stringham. Watty is the son of the Earl and Countess of Glencannon.'

She gave the other man a brief nod. His colouring was similar to Mark's, but his build was quite different. Mark was tall, slender, melancholy and achingly handsome. Lord Watford was short, angular, and his jaw was as square as his forehead.

'You call my cousin by his first name?' Lord Watford said, a condescending smile on his lips. 'Wouldn't it be more proper to refer to him by his title, Lord Inverness?'

Helen blinked. 'You're a lord then, *Mark*? I suppose your title is not a courtesy one, like Lord Watford's. No wonder you were so stuffy when I broke into your garden.'

The corner of Mark's lips twitched upwards, but it wasn't quite a smile.

Lord Watford guffawed. 'And what was the penalty for breaking into his garden?'

She smiled, her eyes on Mark alone. 'A waltz.'

'But my cousin can't dance,' Lord Watford said loud enough for all the people around them to hear. 'He doesn't have a leg.'

*Peg-leg.*

*Oh, Mademoiselle Jaune, you clever, clever bird.*

Poor Mark. It was no wonder he was surly. He'd lost a part of himself and, unlike a reptile, he couldn't grow it back.

The expression on Mark's face was stormy. 'I release you from our waltz, Lady Helen.'

Helen took his arm, twining her own through it. Her pulse quickened. 'But I do not release you.'

'Don't make a fool of my cousin. He's a cripple. If you want to waltz, I'd be happy to oblige you,' Lord Watford said.

She pressed her free hand to her chest. 'But you do *not* oblige me.'

Lord Watford blanched and touched his perfectly arranged cravat. 'You don't even know me, Lady Helen.'

She gave him her best snake stare. It had been a rude thing to say, but he'd just humiliated Mark and it wasn't nearly as bad as the naughty words Helen had been thinking. 'I know you quite well enough to be sure that I would rather sit out the dance with him than take a step with you. Come on, Mark. I have the perfect seat.'

He allowed her to escort him through the crowd to a secluded sofa near the stairs that was still in sight of ballroom. She walked slowly, unsure of what pace to set. She had no wish to embarrass him. Quite the reverse, he was her only friend in London who wasn't a member of her family. Helen sat down first. Mark lowered himself with his arms down to the sofa.

Helen bumped her shoulder to his. 'I hope I didn't embarrass you. Your cousin is more pompous and obnoxious than an orangutan in a troop of monkeys.'

Mark did his half-smile. 'You don't have to sit by me, you know. I won't be offended if you'd rather dance.'

'Truly, I am exhausted and my feet ache. I don't want to dance another step. Nor attempt to make civil conversation. I've quite finished my reserves.'

'Is it exhausting to make polite conversation?'

She briefly closed her eyes. 'It is tedious.'

'Shall we have an impolite conversation, then?'

Helen laughed and bumped his arm with her elbow in a friendly gesture. But the feeling in her body wasn't friendly

at all. Her pulse quickened and her temperature rose. The sort of thing a female animal experienced before being mated. It was a signal to the male that the female was interested and willing. But why was her body behaving like this? It had never done so with Jason. She had felt warm and happy in his presence, not this heat that spooled in her belly and a pressure tightening in her torso.

What did it mean?

She leaned a little away from him. 'My family will tell you that my conversation is always impolite.'

Mark took a deep breath. She noticed that his colour was higher as well. His blood circulation had increased. Was he suffering from the same strange bodily reaction that she had from their brief touch?

'And why is that?'

'I suppose I am honest to a fault. Human society would prefer that we pretend to be something we are not. Especially young women. We are not to let the world know how clever we are. Or how disagreeable we can be. That is why I hate society. I plan to live the rest of my life in Ashbury near Hampford Castle doing precisely what I please and never being polite again.'

He smiled.

They weren't even touching this time and she experienced the same physical sensations. There was heat everywhere in her body, burning through her veins. A sensitivity in her breasts and her pulse was racing as if she'd been running a marathon like the ancient Greeks.

'Are all young women secretly disagreeable?'

Helen couldn't help but smile back at him. It was a natural response that she couldn't suppress. 'When I was in Greece, an old man told me a story about a snake.'

'Tell me.'

'He said that a young man went high into the mountains and a snake talked to him. The snake begged the young man to wrap him in his warm coat and to take him down the mountain, lest he should die. The young man had a tender heart, so he lifted the snake in his arms, warmed the snake in his coat and carried him down the mountain. When they reached the bottom, the snake bit him. The snake's venom raced through the young man's body, killing him. The young man gasped in pain and asked the snake why it would hurt him after he had helped him. The snake slithered away, saying, *"You knew what I was when you picked me up."*'

Mark blinked, tilting his head to one side. 'That was not quite the ending I expected.'

'That's why I liked it so much,' Helen explained, grinning. 'Snakes will always behave like snakes. But humans, you never know what they'll do. How they'll react. When they will bite or betray you.'

She forced her eyes away from his to see her two sisters coming towards them.

Mantheria held out her hand. 'There you are, Helen. Matthew has a partner waiting for you in the ballroom. It is your come-out ball, you cannot hide in the shadows.'

Frederica smiled as she curtsied. 'Lord Inverness, how good it is to see you. The last time I saw you was in the hospital.'

'Now I am death walking,' he said with a thin-lipped smile.

Mantheria tugged on her hand. Helen reluctantly followed, looking over her shoulder at Melancholy Mark. She had wanted to stay with him. He didn't make her feel odd or different.

# Chapter Six

It was beyond foolish to have attended the ball the evening before when he had only one leg. Especially because he wanted to see a girl who was secretly engaged to someone else. Mark had made a cake of himself without his starchy cousin's help, yet he'd been unable to resist viewing Helen in all her finery. She was a rare beauty. Even with her hair tamed and her dress tidy, there had been a sort of fae wildness about her. She would never be truly domesticated. And he couldn't help but think how sad a thing it would be if she were.

He waited in his carriage while the footman went up to the door of Hampford House to get the Duke of Pelford. They were to go shooting at Manton's this morning, something that he had never done before. Having been a captain in His Majesty's army, Mark was a very good shot. Pelford climbed into the carriage with a smile. He was shorter than him, but nearly twice as wide. A strong and muscular man who had been an incredible soldier. Mark could see a small jam handprint on his dark blue sleeve, but didn't mention it. His baby son had clearly left his mark on his father that morning.

'Shooting clay pigeons isn't real sport,' Pelford said with

an easy smile. 'But it's the closest thing a man can do in London.'

'I haven't held a gun since Waterloo,' Mark admitted. 'I will probably be a bit rusty.'

'Excellent. Then I shall win. I must confess that my wife used to always beat me at marksmanship.'

'The Stringham sisters are certainly intrepid young ladies.'

He laughed. 'That is a polite way to put it.'

The carriage came to a stop and Pelford got out. He waited for Mark, but made no attempt to assist him. Mark liked the Duke more for it. Together they walked into Manton's shooting range. The footman had barely opened the door when Mark heard the sound of a shot and the acrid smell of gunpowder filled his senses. Instinctively, he ducked down, covering his ears with his hands. He couldn't breathe. The sounds of more bullets filled the air and he cringed, the faces of his men flashing before his eyes. Shaking his head, he cleared the images from his mind. He was no longer at the Battle of Waterloo. He needed to stand up and behave like a man. But his good leg would not support him and he could not move.

'Inverness,' Pelford said. 'Inverness, are you all right?'

Mark couldn't answer. He couldn't even move a muscle.

For the second time in his life, Pelford lifted him up and took Mark to safety. He'd been the one to carry Mark's limp body off the battlefield. It was humiliating to repeat that experience in London at a popular shooting club. Pelford put him in his carriage, as if his weight were nothing to the man. Shame trickled down Mark's neck as he finally was able to open his eyes. He was a wreck of an earl.

'You're not the only former soldier to respond to gunshots that way,' Pelford said quietly. 'War affects every-

one differently and there is nothing to be ashamed of. You served honourably and sacrificed for your country. I am privileged to consider you a friend.'

'I feel unmanned,' Mark admitted, covering his eyes with his hands. 'Or rather like half of a man.'

Pelford exhaled slowly. 'I have felt the same way. Sometimes I wake up in the night screaming and my wife holds me until I can calm down. No one who hasn't lived through the horror of a battle can ever truly understand what it does to a person.'

Mark wouldn't trust himself with a woman. Let alone a lady wife. Taking a deep breath, he dropped his hands. 'Yet you are not afraid of the sound of a gunshot.'

'No,' he said, shaking his head. 'But now the sight of blood makes me swoon. Not very manly, eh? I blacked out when Frederica bore our son. It was terrifying to see her covered in her own blood. It reminded me of when I nearly lost her in Belgium.'

Mark could only nod his head forward, his throat closing on all the words he could have said. But for the first time since his brother's death, Mark thought someone truly did understand what he was going through. And he did not judge him for it.

The carriage arrived at his house and Mark slowly got out. Pelford followed him to the door without a word. He could not meet the other man's gaze even to thank him. The Duke did not seem to want thanks, for he waited until Mark was inside his house to leave.

Limping out to his garden, Mark sat down in the chair that had become a permanent fixture back there. Helen had come back to the garden without him. The grass was perfectly trimmed. New wooden bark was in the flower beds and the bushes had been cut back. His chair had been set

underneath the only tree in the garden, which had also been pruned. It was like his own private haven from the world.

He took out his sketchbook and had no difficulty drawing Helen from his memory of last night. The braided circlet of her hair with escaping curls. The snake around her neck and her arm. The movement of her white gown with its overlay of lace. The gossamer shawl floating over her shoulders and arms.

'Is that how you see me?' a voice said from behind him.

Mark didn't have to turn to know that it was hers. Snapping his sketchbook closed, he sat up in his chair. He placed his hands on the armrests to help him lift his body to standing.

'There is no need to stand, Mark,' Helen said from in front of him. 'There is no formality between friends.'

'Are we friends?'

She surprised him by taking a seat on the ground by his chair and leaning her back against its side. Perilously close to him. 'I think we're friends.'

He attempted a little humour. 'I'm not sure that I want to pick you up. You might bite me at the bottom of the hill after I carried you down.'

Helen laughed, a high, unearthly sound. 'You entirely missed the point of the story. Of course I am going to bite you. I am a snake. It is who I am and, no matter how many times I shed my skin, it is who I will always be.'

'Then what animal am I?'

She didn't hesitate. 'A bird with a broken wing.'

'Flightless.'

'Not all birds were meant to fly.'

He clenched his teeth. 'I don't know any bird that does not.'

Helen sighed, leaning her head against the hand rest of

his chair, so close to his hand. 'It's because you haven't been to South America. Neither have I for that matter, but I want to go. In South America they have a species of bird called penguins and they do not fly, but swim in the icy waters.'

'I've never heard of a penguin.'

'You look like one, too,' she retorted. 'They have white bellies and black backs, making them look as though they are always wearing a tuxedo.'

'What else do you know about them?'

Her forehead wrinkled as if she was trying to remember something. 'The males sit on the eggs and not the females.'

'What do the females do?'

'They hunt for fish, of course.'

Mark grimaced. That was all very well for the animal kingdom, but human men were supposed to be the hunters. The protectors. Not patiently sit back and care for the offspring.

'Why are you here, Helen? Surely you have several bouquets from suitors this morning and a line of them out your door, waiting to call on you.'

She pulled her knees against her chest, resting her head on them. 'I don't like clipped flowers. It kills them prematurely. Such a waste. If they knew me at all, they would have sent me a flower in a pot that I could put in my room or plant in my garden.'

'You clipped several bushes and flowers in my back garden.'

'Sometimes you have to cut something down, so that it can grow in a new direction.' Helen opened her reticule and two small snakes slithered out of it. 'A smooth snake and a grass snake. The only other native species of snakes in Britain is an adder, which is poisonous. I did not bring

one for obvious reasons. Would you care to draw these two snakes?'

Mark opened his sketch book and began to draw the small snake. The yellow and black collar behind its head and the black spots down the side of the body. The snake hissed at him and he couldn't help but flinch.

'How do you know it's not poisonous?'

Helen lifted her head to look at him. 'The adder has a dark zigzag pattern on its back and a dark V-shape on its head. As you can see, there are only black markings on its body signifying that it is a grass snake.'

Mark was discovering that he did not like snakes at all. He quickly finished the first sketch and turned the page to start the other. This snake was grey with a dark butterfly wing shape on the top of its head. 'Will there only be three snake illustrations in your book?'

She shook her head, her hair loose down her back, shimmering like the waves in a pond. 'Oh, no. But we'll have to go to the Tower of London Menagerie to sketch the rest of them.'

Dropping his pencil, he stooped to pick it up only to touch her hand instead of the graphite. It was so pale that her blue veins were translucent through the skin. She was impossibly delicate. Unable to resist, he ran his finger over her hand and up the tender flesh of her arm. Her hand had calluses and small white scars, but the skin on her arm was as soft as silk.

Helen closed her eyes and made a contented noise with her mouth, drawing his eyes there. He had not kissed a woman since before the Battle of Waterloo. Yet he longed for nothing more than to lean over and press his lips to hers. Were they as soft as the skin on her arm? He wished to be chest to chest, hip to hip with her.

Mark released his hold and her eyes popped open.

She swallowed and stared at him, before handing him the pencil. 'Will you come with me to the Tower of London tomorrow?'

'Yes.' The words were out of him before he could think. Before he remembered that he needed to keep her at a proper distance.

Helen smiled, and instead of leaning her head against her knees again, she laid it on the side of his leg, as though she was a cat. He was tempted to stroke her hair and the curve of her long neck. Something inside him told him that she would make a purring sound if he did. But it would change their soft friendship into something else. Something his heart and body were not ready for. He was too broken to love her. To be a husband to any woman.

Yet surprisingly, she was leaning her head against his bad leg. The one that was cut off below the knee. The one he hid underneath long trousers. Did Helen know that it was his missing leg? Would she have cared? Would she be disgusted if she saw the scars on his knee and the others on his belly? His long hair covered the scar on his forehead and the damage to his soul was hidden underneath his skin.

Helen wore her scars on her hands, unashamed for everyone to see.

# Chapter Seven

Helen did not know why she liked spending time with Mark so much. It was as if there was an affinity between them. He never seemed shocked by what she said. Nor did they have to speak. Yesterday afternoon, she had fallen asleep against his leg. Helen could not understand why she had leaned against it in the first place. She had been awfully tired from the ball, but that wasn't it. She'd simply wanted to touch him. To be near him. She felt so marvellous when she touched him. It made her blood thrum quite delightfully.

Helen asked her lady's maid to prepare her blue walking habit and hat. Dressed and pressed, she descended the stairs. Samuel and Arthur were waiting for her in the foyer. Her brother-in-law was bent over, holding the hands of his little son. Arthur waddled back and forth, giggling. Helen saw that his two top teeth had finally come in. The one on the bottom was still just beneath the skin of his gums.

'Where are you going?' Samuel asked.

She stepped passed him and said over her shoulder, 'To the Tower of London to sketch snakes.'

He nodded, following her. 'And who is going with you?'

*Oh, dear. Propriety was about to bite her and it was going to sting.*

'A friend.'

'Nnnn…' Arthur cooed, walking towards her.

Helen scooped him up and covered him with kisses until he squealed with giggles. She truly couldn't help herself. Arthur's chubby cheeks were made for kisses. She set her nephew back down on his small feet and walked him the few steps to his father.

Samuel gave her a quelling look. 'What species is the friend?'

It was at moments like this that she wished her brother-in-law had not known her for her whole life. 'Human.'

'Gender?'

Tying her bonnet, she looked down at the ribbon. 'Male.'

'You know that your mother would not approve of you travelling alone with a young man. You need to bring your lady's maid along.'

'Cartwright is a wonder with hair, but she is as stiff-necked and starchy as Grandmother Stubbs. She is tedious company and frowns at me the entire time.'

'Frederica and your mother are both at the perfume shop today, there is no other female to accompany you.'

'You could let me go alone, just this once. Or I could bring a footman.'

Samuel shook his head, blocking her exit with his broad shoulders. 'You know that your mother would have my head and Freddie would eat my gizzard, if I did.'

Helen huffed, letting her chin fall to her chest. 'I suppose you and Arthur can come, but don't hover over me like a nurse. And don't frown at me if I say or do something naughty. Mark is not my suitor so I don't have to pretend to be a proper debutante.'

'I never hover or frown,' Samuel said indignantly.

Arthur responded by blowing raspberries.

She waited for them to put on their coats and hats. Sam-

uel hailed a hack, because her mother had already taken the carriage.

'Where are we picking up the male human?'

Helen wrinkled her nose. 'I don't rightly know his address. He lives in the town house directly behind us.'

Samuel laughed. 'Do you happen to know his name? Or do you just refer to him by his place in the animal kingdom, family, phylum, genus and species?'

'His name is Mark—Lord Inverness.'

Samuel waggled his eyebrows. 'Ooh.'

Arthur who was sitting in his lap, cooed along with him. 'Ooh...'

'You're worse than Frederica,' Helen said, leaning back in her seat, unable to keep her mouth from forming a small smile. Not that she was romantically interested in Mark. She wasn't. He was a peer and he was from Scotland. She didn't want to be a countess, nor to be so far from the family and home that she loved.

Samuel only chuckled again and gave the driver the instructions for Mark's house.

If Mark was surprised to see Samuel with her, he didn't show it. Using a cane, he limped down the steps of his house. He paused before entering the carriage, switching the leg that went in first. Using his upper body strength, he lifted himself inside and then sat down beside her. His left leg stuck out straight.

Leaning over, he bent it back. 'Lady Helen. Pelford.'

'Inverness, allow me to introduce you to my son, Arthur,' Samuel said formally.

Mark tipped his hat. 'A pleasure, young master.'

Arthur waved one chubby fist and blew more raspberries.

Helen felt the invisible pull to slide closer to Mark. To

press the side of her body against his. To feel the thrill she experienced when they touched. So different from the comfort of Jason's skin.

She didn't move. Instead, she scowled at her brother-in-law. 'They insisted on being our chaperons. I told them I didn't need one. That this was a business meeting.'

'You don't,' Samuel said with a half-smile. 'Poor Inverness is the one who needs us. Otherwise, he'll be forced to offer marriage to you and what will your cheery curate who has followed you around for the last decade think?'

She had never thought about it that way. Having a chaperon protected the young man just as much as it did the young woman. 'Jason would trust me.'

It was the truth. But for some reason it made her feel guilty. Jason had no guile and her entire soul was made up of it.

Samuel only raised an eyebrow, but didn't reply.

Arthur nearly flopped out of Samuel's lap, leaning towards her with his arms outstretched.

Helen eagerly picked him up. 'Come here, monkey. I don't mind that *you're* here. Just your papa.'

She smothered his chubby cheeks with kisses and he called to her. 'Nnn…'

Arthur tugged on her hair, before diving for Mark's lap. She nearly dropped him and would have, if Mark hadn't put out his arm.

'Monkey, what do you want?'

Arthur reached out his hands to Mark. Helen looked at Mark and realised that he looked a little alarmed at the prospect of holding a baby. 'Do you mind holding, Arthur? He seems to be quite taken with you.'

Tentatively, Mark held out his arms and Arthur needed no further encouragement to tilt his entire body and weight

towards him. Once nestled on Mark's lap, Arthur grabbed the cane at his side and sucked on the silver ball at the end.

Samuel laughed, appearing proud and pleased. 'Pretentious, isn't he? Won't have a thing to do with a wooden rattle, only pure silver for this future Duke.'

Helen watched her nephew's drool slide down the cane. 'He gets his snobbery from your side of the family.'

Her brother-in-law shrugged, nonplussed. 'And the slobbering from yours.'

She turned her gaze back to Mark who seemed transfixed by Arthur. 'Do you want me to hold him?'

'Oh, no,' Mark said quickly, glancing up at her and smiling.

Helen wasn't sure if she'd ever seen him smile before. The expression had all the charm of a gentleman and the swagger of a pirate. It made her catch her breath. She was used to her dour, reluctant friend who didn't bother with civilities, not a man who was so handsome that she could think of little else. It made her heart skitter.

Mark unsettled her.

They arrived at the Tower of London. Samuel took both Arthur and Mark's cane. 'Are you sure you don't need it, Inverness?'

Mark shook his head. 'It's more an ornament than anything else.'

Helen put her hand through Mark's arm. 'I hope you don't mean to hover, Samuel. No one likes a gooseberry.'

Her brother-in-law laughed. 'Not at all. If you need us, we'll be playing on the green where Anne of Boleyn lost her head.'

Helen's lips couldn't help but quirk up on one side. It was the sort of macabre history Samuel knew that she was

fascinated by. And it was also the only lawn in the entire complex to play on.

She steered Mark towards Lion Tower to where the creatures were on display. They walked slowly, but his limp was barely noticeable.

'You don't have to hold my arm. I am not an invalid.'

Helen's eyes met his. 'I didn't think that you were.'

'Then why are you clinging to my arm?'

'Because I wanted to touch you.' It was the sort of honest statement that made her mother cringe in embarrassment and her brothers laugh. Helen didn't usually care what others thought of her, but now she felt strangely light-headed and there was a tightening in her chest.

'Why do you want to touch me?'

This time she didn't look him in the eye, but stared resolutely forward. He was not her suitor. 'I don't know. I simply wanted to. Don't you ever do things just because you want to?'

'Rarely.'

She stole a glance at his handsome countenance and her chest tightened again. 'Because of the war or because you're a lord?'

Mark stopped, glancing down at her. 'Both, I suppose.'

'Duty is dull. That is why I avoid it whenever possible.' *As well as proper society.*

'My brother was the original heir and I feel obliged to do my best in his place.'

Helen squeezed his arm. 'I am so sorry. How devastating for you. Have you any other siblings?'

He shook his head.

She leaned her head briefly against his shoulder. There were no good words for mourning in any human tongue. She

understood why wolves howled and crows cawed. Such intimate pain could not be expressed properly in any other way.

Mark allowed her to hold him for a minute or so, but then stepped back. 'Do you know the way to the reptiles?'

'Of course. It's my favourite part of the menagerie. I have visited it at least a hundred times.' Helen intertwined her fingers with his and pulled him towards the enclosure with the Indian boa. 'Isn't she gorgeous? And very poisonous.'

The boa was sixteen feet long and yellowish-brown in colour. Her back was elegantly marked with a series of large irregular brown blotches bordered with black and numerous smaller spots scattered along the sides.

Mark released her hand and stepped up to the cage for a closer view.

Helen hailed the nearest keeper and asked him to bring them a pair of chairs, wisely slipping the man a guinea. Doffing his hat to her, the keeper assured her that he'd be back in no time at all.

The keeper made excellent time and brought out two wooden chairs. Helen sat down first. Mark looked at the chair and his colour heightened. Did he think that it was because of his wooden leg? She'd simply wanted him to be comfortable while he sketched.

'Do lords not sit on chairs?'

One side of his lips quirked up. 'Never.'

'Very well then, I shall sit comfortably while you stand and draw,' Helen said, stretching out her arms above her head. 'We have the anaconda next, followed by a rattle-snake.'

With a sigh, he lowered himself down on the chair. Opening his sketchbook, he began to make long, decisive strokes.

'I've always wished that I were a rattlesnake.'

Mark lifted his pencil. 'And why is that?'

'People would fear me, simply by my sound. The rattle of my tail.'

He touched the top of his graphite to his lips. She wondered if they would be dry like Jason's or soft and moist. 'Why would you want people to fear you?'

Helen shook her head slightly, clearing the image of her lips pressed against his from her mind. 'I want them to leave me alone.'

Putting his pencil back to the paper, Mark continued to sketch in silence. She watched in amazement how a few strokes of black could somehow so accurately represent the reptile in front of them. Helen had no artistic abilities herself. Becca had managed to steal all the drawing skills of the family, but she didn't draw accurately. Or rather, she drew caricatures that were both eerily accurate and offensive. Mark's pencil managed to capture the majesty of the creature in real life. If only the poor snake were free in the wild.

If only she could do what she liked.

Jason was her dearest friend after Becca. She didn't have to pretend to be a proper lady with him or pretend to be someone she wasn't. Helen could just be her sour self and wander the woods, studying animals. But would that change when they were married? Would his church duties require him to behave differently? As a vicar's wife, would she have more freedom, or less? Hampford was her haven. She would hate it if it became her prison.

# *Chapter Eight*

Mark felt unsteady in Helen's presence. She made his blood hot and he had no idea what she would do or say next. He had a hard time focusing on the horrifying snake before him, let alone sketching it.

Oddly enough, he'd never held a baby before today, although young Arthur was certainly a large one. Something inside him changed when he held the boy. He was the younger son and his father had rarely even seen him. Mark was the spare after all. He couldn't imagine the late Earl holding him. Nor taking him with him anywhere. Pelford, however, seemed to revel in his son's company. He was the portrait of a doting father and not at all ashamed of it. He behaved as if nothing could be more enjoyable than a day spent with his toddler son.

Even Mark's mother was not the affectionate sort. When he returned from Waterloo missing a leg, she would not even look at him for months, let alone touch him or embrace him. She'd always preferred James, his elder brother. But even with him, she had not been physically affectionate. There had never been much warmth in his home or between the members of his family.

The only person who had loved him unconditionally was his brother James. He'd been Mark's mentor, friend

and the person he looked up to the most. James had taught him how to ride a horse, drive a team, flirt with girls and throw a wicked left hook. His elder brother hadn't looked away when Mark returned from the war without a leg. He hadn't treated him like a cripple or an incompetent fool.

How he missed him! Even more than Mark missed the whole person that he used to be.

Mark realised that one of the ways Helen showed affection was by touch. Like the animals she studied and talked about. That was why she had leaned her head against his leg that day in the garden and his shoulder today. Her touch was more eloquent than a thousand words. She had been comforting him both of those times. But when she took his arm and then his hand, she hadn't been seeking or giving comfort. Nor did she seem to pity him. She had touched him because she wanted to.

He could have laughed aloud. The one woman who was not repulsed by his scars and his wooden leg was already in love with another man. Not that he would have pursued her if she wasn't. Helen deserved a healthy man who could love her and that didn't have past demons. Still, he revelled in the simple pleasure of closeness to another human. A beautiful one at that. Glancing at Helen, he saw her light blue eyes were watching him. He continued to draw the Indian boa.

After several minutes, he held up his notebook. 'Does my sketch meet your approval?'

She smiled, nodding. 'You have a rare talent. Your drawings will look marvellous in the centre of my book. I only hope the person who creates the wooden block template will do them justice.'

Mark opened his mouth, but before he could speak a lion roared. He jumped in his chair.

Helen giggled at his reaction. 'She's ready to hunt, poor

thing. But cannot, because she is kept in a cage for people to walk by and gawk at.'

'The female lion?'

She scooted her chair closer to his, so that their knees were touching. Luckily, she was on his right side and it was his good knee. A jolt of desire flashed through his chest.

'The female lions are the hunters in the pride.'

'Fascinating.'

Holding her hand out, he saw that a spider was crawling in her palm. 'But not quite as fascinating as a spider. After the female mates with the male spider, she eats him.'

Mark laughed, both surprised and horrified at this tit-bit of knowledge.

'What are you two talking about?' Pelford asked from behind them. He was carrying Arthur in his arms, the baby's chubby hand still holding Mark's cane, his eyes half closed.

Helen beamed at her brother-in-law. 'The reproductive habits of arachnids.'

Pelford smiled, nonplussed. 'Sounds like titillating stuff. But Arthur needs to go home for his nap.'

Helen stood up first, yawning. 'I could use a nap myself, monkey. I don't like town hours. I don't like anything about London. I just want to go home to the country.'

She didn't offer to help him to his feet and Mark was glad of it. He hated feeling like an invalid. As though he was less than a man.

Once to his feet, he offered her his elbow. Helen grinned at him and placed her hand on his arm, squeezing it. She pressed the side of her body against his. Mark didn't think she was flirting with him. She simply seemed to enjoy his touch for whatever reason. Yet her very presence sent his heart racing and his blood pumping for the first time since he'd returned from war. She had no idea how beauti-

ful, how rare she was. Or how long it had been since he'd been with a woman.

Pelford hailed a hack and they took Mark home first. He tried to return Mark's cane, but young Master Arthur wailed when it was taken away.

Mark handed the cane back to the squealing boy. 'He can keep it.'

Arthur had the silver ball on the top of the cane back in his mouth and was sucking on it as if it were milk. Pelford thanked him.

Helen smiled and something inside his hollow chest shifted. 'We shall have to go again so that you can draw the rattlesnake and the anaconda.'

'Oh, goodie! I can hardly wait,' Pelford said ironically and everyone laughed, including little Arthur.

Turning around, Mark walked inside his house.

Alone.

As it had to be. He was too damaged for anything else.

# *Chapter Nine*

Mama and Frederica were waiting when they arrived home. Her elder sister was pounding on the keys of the piano as if it had offended her. She stopped playing when Samuel came into the room and rushed to her husband and son's side.

Frederica took Arthur from Samuel's arm and covered his face with kisses. 'Mama missed you so much. Yes, she did.'

Then Arthur was passed to his grandmother and covered in even more kisses. Helen thought that the little monkey had to be the most kissed baby in the world. He brought the ball of the cane back to his mouth.

Frederica turned to her husband. 'Where did he get the cane?'

Childishly, Samuel pointed at her.

Helen scowled at him. 'Mark gave it to Arthur.'

Mama raised her eyebrows and cleared her throat, a pleased look on her face. 'And who is Mark?'

Helen shrugged a shoulder. She didn't want her mother to get any matrimonial ideas about him. Mark was her friend. Her only friend in London. And she didn't want to marry him. He was an earl. He would have to live in the city to sit in Parliament and his wife would have to be a well-behaved political hostess. Everything that Helen hated.

'The man who lives in the town house behind us.'

Her mother swallowed as if trying to keep in all the things that she wanted to say. 'Does he have a last name?'

Helen shrugged.

Mama cast an imploring look at Samuel, who was studying his boots as if he'd never seen a pair of Hessians before. 'His name is Mark Wallace and he is the new Earl of Inverness. I believe his elder brother died last year.'

'An *earl*.'

Helen huffed. 'A *friend*.'

She half expected Frederica to say that Helen didn't have any friends. Besides Jason, who'd also been fascinated by her father's animals growing up. That's how he'd become like family to all of them. She loved Jason dearly as only a childhood companion could.

Unlike Frederica, Helen hadn't made any female friends at finishing school. She always felt as though she was a different animal than the rest of them. As if she were a striped zebra and they were dotted cheetahs. Too dissimilar to belong together. And the insufferable young ladies had teased Becca because of her reading and spelling difficulties—dukes' daughters were always held to a higher standard. Helen had spent the better part of three weeks walking around the school's estate and collecting enough snakes to put in the bed of every girl there. Frederica's reaction had been to cut off the hair of the main bully, while she was sleeping. All three sisters had been asked to leave the school. Which turned out to be a blessing, for Wick mistook Louisa to be their errant governess and they fell in love and were married.

'Tell me more about him,' Mama demanded.

Samuel exhaled slowly. 'Poor fellow lost a leg at Waterloo. He was a captain of the Highlanders. They were in

the thick of the battle and their casualties were some of the highest in the British army.'

Frederica dropped another kiss on her baby's head. 'Mark spent some time in your hospital in Brussels, Mama. I helped nurse him.'

Her mother nodded slowly. 'Perhaps we should have him over for dinner?'

Helen took a step back. 'I am not a cannibal, Mama. I don't eat earls.'

Samuel snorted with laughter, but quelled it when both Mama and Frederica gave him identical looks of disdain. The resemblance between them was sometimes uncanny.

'You know what I meant, Helen,' Mama said sternly. 'Lord Inverness is just the sort of fellow that I wanted you to meet.'

And just the sort of peer she planned to avoid. Helen stuck out her chin, defiantly. 'How do you know? You've never even met him, Mama.'

'I trust your judgement.'

'That would be a first,' Helen muttered underneath her breath.

Her mother held out a letter. 'Here is your letter from Becca and, judging by the thickness, no doubt enclosed within it is one from Jason.'

Helen turned the envelope over to check the seal. It was still intact. Unlike her daughters, Mama didn't open other people's post. 'Why do you say that?'

'Becca finds it difficult to write and never sends more than a page. There's at least four in there. Happily, your father franked the letter and it didn't cost us a fortune to receive it.'

Walking up the staircase, Helen was convinced that her mother truly was prescient. Nothing happened in their fam-

ily that she didn't know about. Helen opened the door to
her sitting room and perched in the window seat, leaning
her back against the pillows. Breaking the seal, she opened
Becca's letter.

> *Deer Helen,*
> *I am leerning very well. The tutor is VERY hansome.*

Handsome.

> *I think he likes me.*
> *Myself, Papa and all the animls miss you.*
> *I wish I culd be there with you.*
> *All my love, Becca*

Helen pressed the letter to her chest. Dearest Becca. She
really was improving. There were only a few misspelled
words and her mistakes were all close enough to be rec-
ognisable. Setting down Becca's letter, she picked up Ja-
son's. His handwriting was quite different from Becca's.
His strokes were longer and larger. He held his pen longer
to the paper and left more ink spots. Unfolding the letter,
a lock of light hair fell on to her lap. She picked it up and
held it between her fingers. He'd sent her a lock of hair.
How strange human courtship rituals were. She couldn't
imagine a horse holding on to a mare's old mane.

He'd also enclosed a small paper packet of seeds.

> *Dearest Helen,*
> *Spring is not spring without you here. The skies do*
> *nothing but rain and not even the tulips dare show their*
> *heads. I find the weather matches my own feelings.*

*The Ashbury parish is much as it always is. Mrs*
*Thatcher complains of her back aching. And Mrs Fos-*
*ter wants me to pray for her missing son. I think he*
*must have been pressed by the navy, for she hasn't*
*had a letter from him in over a year...*

She scanned through the next two pages that described
in detail his daily participation in the parish until she
reached the final paragraph. She couldn't help but wish
that he'd talked more about missing her, or shared in detail
his feelings about *her* instead of the members of the parish.
Helen reached the last paragraph.

*I hope that you do not think it is too forward of me.*
*But I have sent you a lock of my hair. I think of you*
*constantly and hope that you think of me. I know that*
*you do not like London, so I have enclosed a little bit*
*of home. May these seeds show you that flowers can*
*grow anywhere and under any conditions.*
*Sincerely,*
*Jason*

Opening the paper packet, she poured the little brown
seeds into her palm. From their shape and size, she could
not recognise the flower. The only way she would know
what the flower was would be to plant it and see if the
seed grew.

Mark shouldn't have been surprised to see Helen on
her knees in his back garden. Nor should he have appreci-
ated the curve of her backside and how it made his blood
pump. This time she wasn't weeding, but planting seeds.
She turned at the sound of his stuttered steps. She smiled

at him as if he were the only person in the world. He could get used to such smiles. But he reminded himself that they were reserved for a cheerful curate and not a melancholic earl. Black dots covered his eyes for a moment and he had to blink them away.

'How are you this morning, Mark?'

He liked that she always called him by his name.

'Well enough, *Helen*.'

Picking up her spade, she dug a few more holes and placed seeds inside each one. 'I didn't see you at the Richmonds' party last night. Frederica said that the Duchess of Richmond is your aunt.'

'She is. And I was there.'

Helen lifted her glove to block the sun from her eyes. 'But I didn't see you and I looked for you everywhere.'

Something tightened in his stomach at her words and his temperature rose. 'I was hiding in the card room.'

She sighed, shrugging her shoulders. 'Mama didn't let me wander there. She had my entire dance card mapped out. I even had to dance with your odious cousin Lord Watford.'

His lips twitched. Helen was certainly an honest young woman. Not that she was wrong. Watty was a pompous windbag.

'Your cousin called females *the weaker sex* and I was forced to set him right on the subject.'

Mark smiled widely, easily picturing the scene. 'Did your explanation include the reproductive habits of arachnids?'

She shook her head. 'No, but if he says something again, I shall set him straight on spiders. Or merely drop a jar of spiders in his carriage. That always worked on my former governesses.'

He couldn't hold in his laughter. He did not think she

was boasting idly. She would do what she said she would. 'What seeds are you planting?'

Helen set down her trowel and got to her feet, shaking the dirt off the bottom of her dress. 'I don't know. Jason sent them.'

'The cheery curate?'

She set a gloved hand on her hip. 'He can't help it if he is always in good humour. Nor that he smiles at everyone he sees. It is just his sunny nature.'

'Do you ever get tired of his constant sunshine?' Mark wouldn't have dared be so blunt with any other person.

Helen gave him a wry smile. 'Sometimes. But according to Chinese philosophy, darkness and light need each other for balance. The yin and the yang.'

'And are you the darkness?'

She shrugged her shoulders. 'Growing up, I was always the mischievous, sour one. I am the daughter with a sharp tongue and a bad disposition. Does that count as darkness?'

He shook his head. 'You know nothing of destruction, death and darkness.'

Helen walked up to him, so close that their chests were nearly touching. 'You are not the only one who has known death or despair.'

She smelled like a tree nymph and looked even more fragile up close. Willowier, as if a single gust of wind could blow her away. Her breath was sweet against his lips. It smelled sugary like fresh honey. An inch or two higher and her lips would be touching his own. His heart stilled. His breathing slowed. She took off her glove and cupped his face with her bare hand. Mark closed his eyes, savouring the feel of her skin against his own.

She lifted her face up and pressed her silken cheek against his scruffy one. 'You are not alone. Even though it

feels that way sometimes. And after the darkness there is always light. The sun rises again.'

Mark nodded, feeling his cheek move against her soft one. Then he held still, afraid that if he moved, she would let go. And he couldn't bear it if she did. Somehow, Helen knew that he needed her touch more than her words.

More than her flowers.

More than even her friendship.

Helen understood wounded animals like him.

'Who have you lost?' he whispered in her ear.

She rubbed her face into his neck and he swallowed a moan of pleasure. For all of her scientific knowledge, she didn't seem to recognise an overly heated male. Her lips rested for a moment against his skin in what might have been a kiss. They felt feather-light and drugging, like her presence.

'My sister Elizabeth and my brother Charles,' she said, burrowing her head into his shoulder. 'They died of scarlet fever when I was only five years old. For years, I waited for them to come back. I thought they had only gone away for a little while. Like Papa and Mama had when they went to Africa for the better part of a year to return animals back to their habitat. I knew that they had left, but that they would come back. But Charles and Elizabeth never came back. And Lizzy was my only sibling who seemed to understand my otherness.'

Mark's already battered heart ached for Helen's loss. He grieved his only brother, but she had experienced the death of two of her siblings at such a young and delicate age. One where she had not fully understood that they were truly gone. He allowed himself to stroke her arched back and to caress her flaxen hair. It was so fine and so silky.

He kept telling himself that he was only comforting her

as she had comforted him before. A touch could be healing, but based on his burning temperature, he was stoking his own flame. He wanted Helen more than was decent. More than anything in his life before. She had resurrected his heart and now it beat only for her. It thundered in his chest. She could probably feel it and hear it. Her head was tucked against his torso. He could sense her heartbeat. Her heat.

Unable to resist, he dropped a kiss into her hair and then nuzzled his nose into the sweet smell of her locks. 'From what I have seen, all of your family loves you.'

Helen nodded, not moving her head from his body. Mark was glad of it, even though he would feel guilty later. He wanted this stolen moment. He wanted to remember this forbidden embrace for the rest of his life, for it to keep him company in the darkness. The afternoon that he had caught a fairy queen and held her as if she were his own. As if he could keep and cherish such a wild, magical thing.

'I know they love me,' she said, her voice slightly muffled from her face being against his cravat. 'And I love them, but it doesn't stop me from feeling as if I don't belong anywhere. I don't like cities or people or rules. I will never fit into the mould that they want me to. I will never be a proper peer's wife.'

Mark's hand moved to her neck to press her head closer to him. He, a broken man, wished to protect her from all the eyes and mouths that would find fault with her unbroken spirit. With her wild heart. 'Your otherness, or whatever you call it, draws me to you. Helen, you are unlike any person that I have ever met before. You carry an energy, a light, that brings joy to all that are around you. Don't try to diminish your light by becoming something you're not. My brother, James, was like you. Full of light. Full of life.'

Helen moved her head so that her eyes could see his face.

Mark didn't feel ashamed as a tear slid down his cheek. Before it could reach his chin, she wiped it away with one of her slender, but callused, hands. He held his breath as her skin touched his in a slow caress. Despite his brokenness, he wanted to hold her for the rest of his life.

'Tell me about James.'

He shook his head, unsure where to start. How to reduce his brother's life into a few descriptive words. 'In some ways it feels as though he was everything that I am not. He was always the obedient son. He did well at school and university, unlike myself. I was always in a scrape and James had to pull me out of it.

'My father loved him more. Trained James to be everything that an earl should be. He would have followed in my father's footsteps. He would have attended Parliament in England. I cannot seem to make myself help rule the country. I feel like a counterfeit for the real heir. I could never take his place.'

'No,' she agreed, her hands now pressed against his chest, but she made no effort to move away from him. 'Nor can I take my sister Elizabeth's place. We are all unique and special. You cannot be James the Earl, but you can be the most amazing Mark the Earl.'

He let out a sigh against her blonde curls. 'What sort of landlord has only one leg and cannot ride a horse? Who is broken in mind and body?'

'Have you tried riding a horse since you lost your leg?' she asked, her breath warm against the bottom of his chin.

Mark wanted nothing more than to angle his head a little and press his lips against hers. But he could not and would not betray her. Helen held him close because she trusted him. Because she believed he was her friend. And of all

the mistakes Mark had to live with, losing her belief in him would be the worst.

'No. But I would be unbalanced on the horse.'

'Even with your wooden leg as a counterweight?'

He hadn't thought that his false limb could help balance him. 'I don't know.'

Turning in his arms, she put his hands around her neck. His body was burning in all the places that their bodies touched. She was book wise, but innocent of experience. She had no idea how much she was torturing him with her touch. How much he longed for her.

'You should try to, Mark. And if that doesn't work, I am sure that you could drive a curricle or phaeton. You are only limited by your imagination and ingenuity.'

'Then you have no limits at all.'

Helen leaned up on her tiptoes and pressed a sweet kiss against his cheek. 'If only, my dearest friend. Young women seemed to be limited in all that we do. Society says it is to keep us safe, but I think it is to keep us stuck in a pretty bird cage, unable to fly free. It is only at home that I feel unencumbered.'

She stepped back from him and he let her.

'I am sorry, Mark. I meant to comfort you. I should not have made this about me. You are right to mourn James. He would want you to, but he would also want you to live. To experience everything that he did not get to do in this life. The best way we can honour Elizabeth, Charles and James is to be happy. To be whole.'

Mark leaned on to his good leg. His amputated limb had started to shake under the effort of standing for so long. But it wasn't just his body. His mind had been affected by the war, too. 'I can never be whole again.'

'I know you will never be the same as you once were,'

she whispered. 'But it is not your lost leg that is keeping you from being whole. It is your heart. You have to let him go and you have to forgive yourself for living. For becoming someone new.'

He had known he was a shell of a man, but Helen's words cut into what was left of his heart. She took his hand and pressed a kiss into his palm before leaving him standing alone in the garden, with only the ghosts of his past to keep him company.

James.

His old friends. He had led most of the Highlander soldiers to their deaths. The charge from Bossu woods had been a slaughter. He'd seen them die one by one on French blades, while bagpipes bellowed behind them, playing a fighting song turned into a funeral dirge. Flinching, he remembered the bullet tearing through his leg and him falling to the ground. Then Pelford picked him up and called for the few remaining Highlander soldiers to retreat. If only Mark had done so sooner. Could he have saved Robert Mackenzie? William Black? Fergus Johnston?

Would he ever be able to let them go?

But without them, who would he be?

# Chapter Ten

Lifting the locket around her neck, she opened it up to see Jason's hair inside. Surely he would understand that she was comforting a friend today. A friend who was hurting deeply. Unbidden, the thought of him holding another young woman flashed into her mind. Helen wouldn't have liked that at all. She would have been as jealous as a lioness fighting for the attention of the male lion in her pride. But Jason was a man of the cloth. It was not only in his nature, but in his business to mourn with those who mourn and give comfort to those who stand in need of comfort.

She slid the golden snake cuff up her arm. If she had to go to Glastonbury's ball, she would at least go as Medusa. Her ballgown was white again—alas—but trimmed in gold fringe, which gave it a Mediterranean look. Now if only she could turn men to stone. Particularly those who wished to dance with the daughter of a duke and pay her false compliments on her beauty and wit. She wasn't witty. She was blunt to a fault.

Sighing, she got into the carriage with her mother, Frederica and Samuel. She smiled when she saw a spot of drool on Samuel's shoulder. His valet, Mr Dunford, would be horrified that his master went out looking like that. Samuel must have given Arthur one last hug before leaving

him with his nurse. Frederica entwined her fingers with her husband's and leaned her head against his shoulder. Helen would have liked to do the same with her mother, but Mama was not the cuddliest of persons. She was more like a hedgehog.

*Oh, how she missed Becca!*

Becca was the best cuddler in the entire family and they could communicate with each other without words. But she would need to learn how to get along without her little sister. Becca wanted to have suitors, get married and leave the nest. It was only a matter of time. Helen wished to stay near Hampford Castle and Ashbury for ever. Why did she, a snake, always love birds that flew away from her?

'Now, Helen, try not to look as if you are being tortured while you are dancing,' her mother reminded.

She groaned and made a face at her mother. 'Dancing in circles for hours is civilised torture.'

Frederica giggled, taking her husband's hand. 'Not with the right partner.'

Helen made a fake gagging noise. Frederica and Samuel only smiled at each other knowingly. Oh, they were so disgustingly *in* love. She both hated it and longed for such a relationship herself. She and Jason loved each other and maybe they would be the same way, once they were married. Or they could continue on as the dearest of friends.

This thought disturbed her peace for some reason.

Helen entered Glastonbury's town house. Even though he and Lady Dutton lived together openly, they did not perform the social solecism of having his mistress greet the guests. Mantheria—who did not live with her husband and hadn't for several years—stood beside his wheeled chair. She smiled and shook hands with the other guests. They

were such a mismatched couple. It was no wonder that they had not worked out.

Glastonbury was still handsome, but he was much too old for Mantheria, whose youth and beauty rivalled any young debutante in the *ton*. But despite his failed marriage with her sister, Glastonbury treated Helen like an affectionate uncle. He never acted bored when she talked to him about snakes for hours. Nor did he mind scouring all of Greece to help her find and study the different varieties that were indigenous there. He was a dear.

Her eldest sister grinned when she saw them. She lost all her dignity and threw her arms around Mama, then made her way through Frederica, Samuel and finally to Helen, whom she squeezed extra tightly. 'I am so glad that you're all here.'

Pointing to her snake cuff, Helen leaned down and hugged Glastonbury, too. 'I absolutely love it. I wear it everywhere.'

'You are dauntless, Helen of Troy. Those who do not know that must learn it to their own peril.'

Helen smirked down at him. 'My company is certainly perilous.'

He chuckled. 'Of course you are. Go and destroy entire cities and civilisations.'

Touching the turquoise serpent around her neck, Helen wandered away from her family, hoping to escape unwanted dance partners. But she'd forgotten about Lady Dutton, Glastonbury's mistress, who was like an aunt to her. Lady Dutton was fifty-five, with more grey in her hair than black. She had a short, curvaceous figure and smiling eyes. She tugged along with her a man who looked younger than Becca. He had thin legs like a stork and a long giraffe-like neck that he hadn't grown into yet.

'Ah, Lady Helen, please allow me to introduce my

nephew, Lord Dutton. He is most sincerely hoping to dance with you.'

Helen scowled at her older friend, as if to say, *Not you, too!*

Lord Dutton looked as though he had swallowed an ostrich egg. His Adam's apple bobbed uncontrollably. He hated this as much as she did.

Helen held out her gloved hand. 'It would be my honour.'

She danced the Roger de Coverley with him and then Mama found her. Alas. Her mother had lined up the next five dances with partners, including the supper dance with Lord Watford. Mark's cousin was the eldest son of the Earl of Glencannon and held his father's secondary title, Baron Watford. Helen couldn't quite understand why he kept dancing with her. She had made no effort to hide her dislike of him.

Happily, the supper dance had *not* been a waltz, but a country dance. After a half an hour of hopping and twirling, Helen was hungry and distempered. She took Lord Watford's arm and he led her into supper. Standing close to him, she couldn't help but breathe in his scent. It was entirely different than his cousin Mark's. She could detect the ethanol in his cologne, its sharp alcoholic smell. There was also a flower, possibly a hibiscus. And the final note was vetiver, giving him a more manly smell. Scents were important in her family. Her mother was a perfumier, after all.

They got their plates and sat down. Helen decided that if she was eating, she didn't have to make conversation with him.

'I was surprised to see your sister greeting the guests,' Lord Watford said. 'My mother said that she and the Duke have been separated for many years.'

Helen set down her fork with a clatter. 'Yes. But they have remained friends because of their son, Andrew.'

'If they are friends, perhaps they should still live in the same house.'

She sneered at him. 'I don't think Mantheria, nor Lady Dutton, would much like that. However, we have travelled with them several times and have found accommodations in the same hotels or adjacent houses.'

'A wife should be obedient to her husband. The Bible says so.'

Helen snorted, choking on her beef. Coughing, she hit her chest to clear her throat. 'And how many ladies wrote books in the Bible?'

'None, of course.'

'Well, if they had, I can assure you that they would not have written that a lady should be obedient to her husband. Perhaps they were only writing about the cultural and social norms of their own societies. Would you like to be obedient to your wife?'

He stiffened. 'That's preposterous. The male is the protector and provider. The female owes her husband her obedience in exchange for her home.'

Helen laughed out loud in his face. 'You do not know your natural history, then. In many species, it is the female who is both protector and provider. The she-wolf hunts beside the alpha male. The female lion leads her own pride and protects her territory and her cubs. The female spotted hyena is larger than the male and dominates the clan. She is also in the front line of every fight. African elephants have a female matriarch who leads them to water. And both ring-tailed and black-and-white-ruffed lemurs are female led. Shall I continue?'

'They are but animals.'

'Humans are animals, too, and often more barbaric than any other creature. We destroy with our voices, as well as with our limbs and teeth.'

Lord Watford laughed, but there was no mirth in it. 'You truly are an original, Lady Helen. I can only be glad that there are not more women like you.'

'There are. They just don't always bother correcting pompous males of the species like you.' Helen stood up and left the supper room.

Narrowly avoiding her mother, she slipped away to the library. She'd visited Glastonbury's house several times and knew where all the principal rooms were. Opening the door, she was surprised to find that it already had an occupant—Mark. He was sitting on a sofa, reading a book.

Mark glanced up at her. 'I did promise to come to the ball. I didn't promise where I would be.'

Helen smiled, taking a seat beside him, breathing his lovely scent of leather, ash and musk. He smelled like a male of the species should. Humans often underestimated the power of scent, but to most species it was essential not only to their survival but to their power structures within the clans and their mating.

'How are you liking the party?'

She yawned. 'It's tedious. I'm not a night owl or a nocturnal creature. I just want to go to sleep.'

'No one is stopping you.'

For a moment, she wished she were a cat and could curl up in his lap and go to sleep. Yawning again, Helen lifted her legs on to the sofa and laid her head in Mark's lap like she would have Becca's. She felt his legs stiffen, but he didn't ask her to move. Rubbing her face against the soft material of his trousers, she closed her eyes and promptly fell asleep.

\* \* \*

Mark knew that he could not hold his breath for much longer. Exhaling, he watched to see if Helen stirred. She didn't. He watched her back rise and fall at a steady pace with her breathing. Her delicate head was resting primarily on his one thigh, but the top of her head and her silken white curls were on his other leg. Helen's features were even more fairylike in sleep. She could have been Queen Mab or Titania. She made him feel poetic.

He hadn't expected her to lay on his lap when he told her to sleep. But he should have. Helen had slept on his leg before and it had set his body on fire as it did now. Mark was no longer the cold, unfeeling shell of his former self. Helen made his blood boil. She made him forget the pain. Forget that he was a cripple. Forget that his friends were gone and buried in a foreign land. Forget the nights he woke up screaming and strangling his blankets. Forget that his brother would never ruffle his hair, or call him a fortune-hunter again. Even though second sons *had* to pay attention to a lady's dowry before they could court her.

Mark no longer needed to marry a fortune. He'd inherited his elder brother's estate and the responsibility of providing an heir to the earldom.

A child.

When he'd first received the title his mother had spoken to him about the importance of marriage—particularly to his cousin Niamh—and begetting an heir as soon as possible. James had been thirty and unmarried when he died. Mama begged him to not let another year pass before finding a wife.

Mark was now seven and twenty. His thirtieth birthday was not too far off. Not that he planned to marry anyone. He could not trust that he wouldn't scare a wife out of her

wits during one of his night terrors. Or worse, injure her. And when he was awake, his melancholia made him feel like a perpetual rain cloud.

Mark had thought his body and heart were done with women after Waterloo. But the only woman who stirred his blood lay sleeping on his lap. Tentatively, he reached his hand out and picked up one of her errant curls. It felt as soft and silky as a spider's web. A comparison that Helen would have appreciated. Releasing the curl, he could not stop his hand from touching the rest of her hair. He stroked her hair softly. She let out a small moan, but did not open her eyes. He continued to run his fingers through her hair, revelling in the power of touch.

Mark didn't think Helen was pretending to be asleep. The steadiness of her breathing and the sweet little noises her mouth made when he stroked her hair were too natural.

The door to the library opened and Pelford checked at the entry. Mark felt as though his hand was caught in the biscuit tin. Helen's head was in his lap and his fingers in her hair.

'Thank heavens. She's here. I got distracted for only a moment and she escaped the dinner room.'

Mark felt his face suffuse with heat as he held both of his hands in the air as if being waylaid by a highwayman. 'It's not what you think. She's simply tired. I have not compromised her in anyway.'

'I do not blame you, Inverness,' Pelford said heavily, walking towards them. 'Helen's personality is a force of nature. One can only try to survive her storm mildly weathered. If anyone did the compromising, it would be her.'

Pelford touched Helen's shoulder. 'Wake up, my sweet snake. Your mother and sister are worried and about to call in the Bow Street Runners to find you.'

Helen blinked her eyes open, sitting up. She stretched

out her arms over her head, yawning. 'Oh, Samuel did you have to wake me up? I was having such a nice dream. I was flying and then you made me fall.'

'Terribly sorry, but you must come back to the ballroom at once. Your absence has been marked. You need to dance with eligible young men.'

Helen huffed. 'I don't want to dance with them—they're boring. They only want obedient wives and social hostesses.'

Pelford chuckled, holding out his hand to her. 'Which you will never be, Helen. If you want, I'll dance with you.'

She accepted his hand and got to her feet. 'That is very good of you to offer and you are by far the best dancer in the family, but you're my brother now. I'd much rather dance with Mark.'

His heart stopped.

Helen glanced over her shoulder at him. 'Will you dance with me?'

Mark clenched his teeth, shaking his head. The phantom itch returned. 'I cannot dance, Helen. I don't have two legs.' Or a whole heart.

She smiled at him. 'Then you will not have two left feet.'

He could only stare at her blankly. She had made a joke about his missing limb. No one had done that before. Everyone else had pitied him. A laugh escaped his throat. Mark shook his head.

'Is that a no?' Helen asked.

Mark put his hands down on to the sofa, to lift himself to standing. 'I don't think it can be a yes.'

Helen turned on her heel to look at her brother-in-law. 'Samuel, command him to dance with me. You were a colonel. Surely that ranks higher than a captain in the army?'

Pelford's lips twitched. 'Usually, it is the man's choice.

But very well, I know better than to try to argue with you. Inverness, I order you to waltz with my sister-in-law.'

Helen giggled and grinned at him.

Mark couldn't help but smile back. Pelford was right. Helen was a force to be reckoned with. He offered his hand to her. 'For you, I shall make a fool of myself.'

She placed her hand on his. 'You couldn't make a fool of yourself, for there is nothing foolish about you.'

Limping, he escorted her down the hall and back to the ballroom. A waltz was playing. Mark felt sweat trail down the back of his neck. He didn't want every member of the beau monde to see his infirmity. To know that he was crippled both inside and out.

Helen didn't stop until they were on the edge of the dance floor. She turned her hand, so it was no longer on top of his, but clasping it. Her other hand, she placed lightly on his shoulder. Mark slowly reached out and took her waist. It was soft and curved and completely feminine. Helen didn't move, didn't sway, but waited for him to lead, which was not at all what he expected. He was sure that she would take the lead in any dance.

The first step back with his wooden leg, he took slowly, careful not to fall and bring her down with him. She followed him forward, waltzing at a snail's pace. Yet somehow, they were able to perform the correct figure. He led her through another box step, this time his hand firm on her waist. It was wonderful to hold her there. To feel her core strength. Her lithe body near his. He almost felt alive again.

Squeezing his hand, she smiled at him. Her expression of happiness was effervescent and contagious. He couldn't help but smile back at her. Other couples waltzed around them, quickly and efficiently. There was nothing quick or

graceful about their dance, but he wouldn't have traded these moments holding Helen for his entire Scottish castle.

The music ended too quickly, like all fairy reveries do.

Mark offered her his hand again, leading her to where her mother stood near the Duchess of Pelford.

'Ah, Lord Inverness,' the Duchess of Hampford said with a polite nod of her regal head. 'I have learned that you are my neighbour. We should be delighted to have you over for a dinner party some time. Is there a night that you are free?'

He usually avoided such invitations, but this time he didn't want to.

Helen leaned her head and whispered in his ear, 'Beware, Mama is a cannibal. She eats eligible young men. Especially tasty young earls.'

Mark valiantly tried to hold in his laugh, but it was a battle he could not win. The Duchess did not give him a stern look, but did give one to her daughter.

He bowed his head. 'I am free any night next week, Duchess, and would be honoured to accept your invitation.'

The Duchess nodded majestically. 'I shall send you a card.'

## Chapter Eleven

Mama waited until the next day to give her lecture. Helen wore her favourite old dress and her hair braided down her back. She didn't like the weight of it on the top of her head. It felt as if it pressed her down to the earth like Newton's laws of gravity. Donning her straw hat, she was about to put on her work gloves and climb over to Mark's back garden. She'd already finished watering all the plants in the conservatory and trimming off the dead blooms.

Her mother stood between her and the door. 'We made a bargain, Helen.'

She tilted her chin up. 'I danced most of the night. You know I do not like to stay up late. And these infernal *ton* balls go on until the wee hours of the morning.'

'You cannot simply slip into someone's library and take a nap. What if someone had found you? What if a gentleman had taken advantage of you?'

Helen gulped.

Samuel hadn't told Mama that he'd found Mark with Helen. She felt a tinge of guilt for every rude thing she'd ever said to him and all the terrible things she helped Frederica do to him when they were children. The snake in his bed and the bear cub in his room. The salt in his tea. The list went on. And Helen had been a very willing participant in all the pranks.

'Technically he wouldn't have been a gentleman, then.'

Her mother stepped closer, her hands on her hips. 'You could have been compromised.'

'I can't be compromised, because I wouldn't allow external forces to decide how I feel internally. And I wouldn't mind being ostracised by the *ton*, which is what you actually mean. I am not like the rest of them, Mama. You know this. I am a different sort of creature entirely.'

Mama sighed. 'Lady Glencannon said that you insulted her son.'

'I simply pointed out that the Bible was written by men and that wives did *not* have to be obedient to their husbands. If he chose to take *offence* at my words, I hope it is a stone fence and that it crushes his bones to dust.'

Her mother didn't laugh at her very poor play on words. 'Helen, what am I to do with you?'

'You remember Henrietta?'

'How does one forget a caracal?'

Helen tugged at the end of her braid. 'She died, Mama. After only two years in England. It wasn't because she lacked food or love. We did our very best, but she still died because this wasn't her natural habitat. London parties and the *ton* are not mine. I was meant to be near Hampford Castle. Near the river and in the wide-open spaces. Among naturalists and scientists…thinkers. I don't belong in a ballroom any more than a wild boar.'

Mama took Helen's cheeks between her hands. 'You are my daughter. There is no place that you do not belong.'

Twisting away, Helen sighed. 'You don't even care that I hate it here.'

'Of course I care. But, Helen, you can't escape from who you are. You are not a bird or a snake. You are the daughter of a duke. And as much as it is delightful to imagine living

in nature, you would miss exquisitely cooked meals, your family, your soft, warm bed and hot baths.'

'Then why won't you let me marry Jason? Is it because you think he's a different creature entirely because he's a curate and not an aristocrat?'

Her mother folded her arms across her ample chest, the one that Helen *had not* inherited. 'I have great affection for Jason. He was my daughters' dearest friend growing up, but I like him for his own sake as well. I have never met a person with a cheerier disposition who is both discerning and intelligent.'

Helen stuck out her chin. 'Then what is your opposition to our marriage?'

'You are.'

'What?'

'You would make Jason a terrible wife.'

Rubbing her eyes, she took a few shaky breaths. 'Why... why would you say that? You're my mother.'

Mama stepped closer and put a tentative hand on Helen's arm. 'I am your mother and I love you more than you will probably ever know. And I want your happiness more than anything and that is why I have opposed the match.'

Helen snorted. 'Because he isn't wealthy or titled?'

'Because Jason has chosen the church for his profession,' her mother said, gently squeezing Helen's arm. 'There are expectations for his behaviour in the parish, as well as his wife's. What is charmingly eccentric and admissible behaviour in the daughter of a duke would be highly inappropriate for a vicar's wife.

'You would be expected to behave above circumspection. You could not go out on your own to explore nature. You would be expected to stay at home unless you were accompanied by a servant or another female. You would not

be able to say what you think. If you offended the wrong people, you would cost your husband his living. And publishing your own writing would be considered scandalous and outrageous. You would be blackballed from the local society. The vicar's wife is supposed to be a pattern card of obedience, virtue and submissiveness. I'm sure you would fail on all three counts.'

Helen tore away from her mother a second time, feeling as if the truth of her words had clawed her skin like a puma. What if the life she had imagined with Jason in the country was nothing more than a dream? 'You don't believe in me at all.'

Her mother held up her hands. 'I do believe in you and I love you exactly how you are. That is why I do not want you to have to change. But if you marry Jason, you will have to, or you will both be miserable. Not even his cheery disposition could overcome the censure and scorn you would receive as a couple. He would be held to blame for not keeping you in check and the last thing he would ever do is try to tame you. Not that he could.'

Helen couldn't bear to hear any more. She spun on her foot and ran up the stairs to her room. Flinging herself on her bed, she decided that Mama was right about one thing: even if Helen was a wild beast, she did like soft mattresses.

Mark had received a pile of invitations for dinner parties. He had declined every single one. Matchmaking mamas were truly the most terrifying creatures in existence. Most debutantes were only seventeen years old and they seemed like children to him. Awkward, coltish and not yet fully grown. And likely to be horrified by his missing limb. He felt decades older than them in life experiences and more

like a grandfather than a suitor. Not that he wished to be a suitor to any of them.

He told himself he'd accepted the Duchess of Hampford's invitation because she was a formidable woman and not used to receiving no for an answer, but that wasn't it. He couldn't fool himself. He was coming because of Helen. Because she made him laugh. Because she didn't make him feel like a cripple. Because he never knew what she was going to say next. Because she was already secretly engaged to someone else and she didn't want to marry him. Because she made him feel like a real man again.

He wore his 'Cossack' silk trousers lined with linen, even though he suspected that every other male of the party would be wearing knee breeches. He had no desire to show off his wooden leg. Mark missed wearing kilts. Still, his new dark blue double-breasted tailcoat with gilt brass buttons was stylish, with overlapping collar points called a 'lark's tongue.' The collar was also notched with the letter 'M' on both sides.

Content with his appearance, Mark went out to his carriage. Hampford House was a short distance and in the past he would have walked it. But he didn't want to arrive out of breath and sweaty.

Mark was ushered into a spacious room where the Duchess of Pelford was playing the piano and other guests were speaking. Helen smiled when she saw him and came bounding up to him at a speed he could no longer manage. He thought she might bowl him right over, but she stopped just short of him, the fabric of her dress covering his boots. Helen was not wearing her usual white, but an indigo-blue dress with little puffed sleeves that looked as though they were from a Tudor painting: ivory-coloured silks billowed

out of the four little openings on each sleeve. Below the puffs were long sleeves that went all the way to her narrow wrists, where there were double bands at the cuffs and more ivory silk frills and ribbon. Blue ribbons had been woven into her pale hair. Helen had never looked more like Edmund Spenser's *The Faerie Queen*.

She beamed up at him. 'You came.'

He couldn't help but smile back at her. 'As you can see.'

Helen put her arm through his without waiting for him to offer it, leading him to a sofa on the other side of the room. 'It's best to get some distance when Frederica is fighting the piano or I will not be able to hear you.'

Mark laughed. 'She is certainly playing it with great gusto—but she plays beautifully.'

'She's clearly winning the battle,' Helen agreed, her arm still through his, even though propriety stated that she ought to have let it go once they sat down. 'I can tell you from personal experience that she is a formidable foe.'

She pulled off her long white glove and pointed to several thin, small scars on her arm. 'These are all marks from her claws.'

Before he knew what he was doing, he ran his thumb over the little ridges of skin. 'Really?'

Helen's breath caught. 'Truly. However, it would be remiss of me not to mention that I have marked her in several places as well. There's no creature quite as vicious, or as loving, as a sister.'

'Then I am glad that I do not have any.'

She nudged him with her elbow. 'Oh, but you are deprived. Sisters are the best friends you could have in the world. I miss my little sister, Becca, cruelly.'

'Was she too young to come to London?'

Helen slumped in her seat, her lower lip coming out slightly in a seductive pout. 'No. I was too badly behaved.'

'I am sure that is not the case.'

Sighing, she shook her head. 'No. It really is. There's a secret passageway behind the family rooms, where Becca and I eavesdrop on my parents' conversations. Mama wouldn't let Becca come because she said that a pair of Bow Street Runners couldn't keep track of us together in London.'

Mark tried to hold it in, but he couldn't help himself. He laughed. After nearly two years of no humour, he found that he couldn't help but laugh in Helen's company. At her words. Her antics. Her beauty.

Helen sat up straight and released her hold on his arm.

Glancing over his shoulder, he saw that the Duchess of Hampford was coming. She was a tall, imposing woman in dark purple, wearing a king's ransom of diamonds around her neck, ears, wrists, and a tiara in her hair.

'Lord Inverness, I am delighted to welcome you to our house. It appears that Helen has already made you feel at home.'

Mark struggled for a moment to get to his feet, before bowing to her. He hated when he wobbled on his wooden leg. 'Thank you for the invitation.'

'You mean her summons?' Helen said, with her sharp wit and even sharper smile.

The Duchess of Hampford gave her daughter a glittering smile.

Mark felt an almost overwhelming curiosity to meet the young man who had caught Helen's heart. The only thing he knew was that the curate's temper was amiable, unlike his own mercurial disposition. And he was not still fighting a battle that was long over.

Sighing, Mark thought he had once been animated and

amiable in company. Sometimes he thought that he'd left more than his leg in Brussels—that he'd left behind part of his personality. But it was hard to constantly be jolly when one was in constant pain.

The Duchess waved her fan. 'Why don't you both come say hello to Lady Glencannon and her son, Lord Watford. She is your aunt, I believe?'

'My late father's sister.'

Mark offered his arm and suppressed a smile as he watched Helen roll her eyes. 'I hope that you don't have any spiders on your person. I should hate for them to accidentally end up on me, instead of my cousin.'

Helen briefly tightened her hand on his arm. 'Alas, no. But I have been collecting them since I've arrived in London. I have thirty-six of them saved in my glass jar.'

An involuntary shudder ran down his back. 'Please say that you don't like mice as well as snakes.'

'I don't. My little sister, Becca, is the one who loves rodents, but Theodosia makes sure that I don't have any in my room. Or even in the house. A snake is better than a cat at keeping down the mice.'

He chuckled. 'I'll take your word on that.'

'You can take more of my words than that,' Helen said, grinning at him. 'My publisher sent a note over that I can overlook the pages before he does his final printing of my book. I shall take your sketches with me for the wood blocker to etch. I am so thrilled, I could roar like a lion.'

'I would love more of your words.'

It was true. Mark couldn't help but grin back at her. He wanted to hear and keep all her words for himself.

His smile faltered as he bowed to his Aunt Glencannon. She was a Friday-faced woman with a long nose. Her dark hair was swept back from her head in a ruthless bun. Her

figure was all sharp angles. His cousin, Watty, appeared even more at a disadvantage at her side as her foil.

Mark bowed to his aunt.

'I don't know what your father would think of you,' Aunt Glencannon said—her voice had no trace of her Scottish accent or ancestry. 'You haven't taken your place in the Parliament, nor in society.'

He felt Helen's hand tighten like a claw on his arm. 'Yes, my father and grandfather both served in Parliament.'

His aunt gave him a hawklike stare and he realised how much she resembled one with the plumage in her hair. 'Your elder brother also was remiss in his government responsibilities. He didn't come to London once after your father died.'

Mark couldn't blame him. He'd be running to Scotland right now if his wooden leg could carry him. 'I shall do my best in future, Aunt Glencannon.'

'Good. Your King is in London.'

Helen cleared her throat, her talon-like hold on him tightening. 'Actually, he's not. Mad King George is at Windsor Castle with his daughters. The Prince Regent himself told me at my coming-out ball.'

Mark wanted to chuckle again when he saw the look of indignation on his aunt's sullen countenance.

'How dare you speak of your King with so little respect?'

Helen tipped her chin. 'I am the daughter of a duke. I can do, or say, whatever I dashed well please. Besides, there is no love lost between the Prince Regent and his parents. He has been my mother's dear friend for decades.'

Aunt Glencannon brought a hand to her mouth. 'Well, I say!'

'What do you say precisely?' Helen countered impertinently.

Mark needed to intervene before an argument could

erupt between the two ladies. 'Aunt Glencannon, forgive me. I should have introduced you to Lady Helen at the first. Lady Helen, allow me to introduce you to Lady Glencannon. Her son you already know—Lord Watford.'

Watty gave Helen an oily smile and took her proffered hand. He bowed over it and then kissed it. Helen tugged her hand back mid-kiss and his cousin's face turned a blotchy red.

Helen curtsied to his aunt.

She gave her only a cold nod in return. 'It is a good thing that you have a large dowry, girl, otherwise no man in his right mind would give you a second glance. You are too thin and bad tempered.'

Instinctively, Mark took Helen's elbow. He had no doubt that she could hold her own in a cat fight, but the parlour was hardly the time or place. He pulled her away from his aunt and cousin over to a man who had to be Helen's brother. He had the same lanky frame, fair hair and light blue eyes.

'Didn't fancy a brawl, Inverness? I was about to offer ten-to-one odds on our Helen here. I have seen her hold her own against opponents twice her size.'

Helen stomped on her brother's foot. 'Mark, this is my annoying brother Matthew.'

He gasped in pain and rubbed his sore foot. 'Dash it, Helen. How can you even make it hurt in only dancing slippers?'

Mark bowed his head. 'A pleasure to meet you, Lord Matthew.'

'I'm actually the Earl of Trentham,' Matthew said, a wry smile cast at his sister. 'It's all hush-hush. But my wife caught a French spy and his British government counterpart, so, of course, being a man, I took all of the credit and the title.'

Helen smirked. 'Nancy said you helped a little at the end. A *very* little.'

Her brother grinned. 'How generous of her. I did nothing but stand there and hope for the best.'

Helen looked around the room. 'Where is Nancy tonight?'

Matthew, Lord Trentham, looked at Mark. 'I am afraid that my wife wished to be here and add her familial pressure to the match that neither you nor Helen wish for. But, alas, she is indisposed.'

Mark wasn't as opposed to a match as he ought to have been.

'Is she still vomiting?' Helen asked.

Matthew nodded, his face a little green. 'She got dressed to come for the dinner, but after the third bowl was required, she thought it best to stay at home.'

Shaking her head, Helen sighed. 'Poor thing. She's expecting another baby and is having a terrible time of it.'

Mark had never before been interested in other people's children, but after seeing the Duke dote on his son, he was. 'Do you already have a son and heir, Lord Trentham?'

'Something much better. A daughter. My only real contribution to the world. And again, my wife did all the work and *I* get the credit.'

'I hope Nancy has another girl. We have quite enough boys in the family,' Helen said, then explained to Mark, 'You already know Arthur. My brother Wick and his wife Louisa have three sons already and will be welcoming a fourth child any day now. And Mantheria only has a boy.'

Mark watched Matthew to see what he thought of another girl, instead of the required male heir to continue the title.

Lord Trentham nodded his head slightly. 'I, too, have

been praying for a girl, but if the baby is a boy we will still endeavour to love him as well.'

Mark snorted in surprise. Such words were usually reserved for female babies with a 'good try, better luck next time'. But although they were jestingly said, Mark didn't doubt their sincerity. Matthew didn't care about providing an heir to his title or his name. Yet, having a son to continue the family line was ingrained in the British nobility and gentry. He remembered his father drilling it into his brother. And then his mother into him, after his brother's untimely death. But it seemed that the Stringhams loved their children for their own sakes and not for their place in the dynastic line.

'I see Wick and Louisa coming in,' Matthew said. 'They're always late, which means that Mama will be starting the promenade into the dining room. If I were a better man, Inverness, I would take Helen off your hands. But I'm not.'

Matthew strode away from them, before Helen's punch could land on his arm. He took his mother's elbow.

Helen huffed. 'My brothers are such pests.'

Mark's own sibling had been the same. Oh, how he missed him. Missed having a family. He escorted Helen into dinner and there was no other place he wished to be. Mark was lucky enough to sit between the Duchess of Pelford and Helen. And far enough away from his aunt on the opposite side of the table that he would not be expected to make conversation with her. Or his cousin Watty.

Mark couldn't help but glance as the Duchess took off her long gloves and put them in her lap. She also had small white scars all over her arms. The Duchess caught him looking and he felt the blood rush to his face. He'd flirted with her when she was single and he didn't wish for her

to think that he still admired her. Especially since he was more than half in love with her little sister Helen. Not that she wasn't a handsome and intimidating young woman.

She must have noticed him staring, for the Duchess held out her arm to him. 'Yes, Helen gave me these scars. I dare say she showed you the ones I gave to her. Although it's impossible to tell which scratches are from each other and which ones were from our kittens. Helen unfairly claims they are all from me.'

'*All* the scratches on my arms are from both of you,' the Duke interjected, making everyone laugh. 'I'll show you some time, Inverness. The Stringham girls were feral cats growing up. Even Becca scratched me once. She was the youngest kitten and the nicest of the bunch.'

Helen leaned forward to speak to Pelford past him. 'Becca didn't want to be left out in torturing you.'

Pelford smiled. 'I close my case. Feral cats.'

'Oh, stop whining, Samuel,' his wife said. 'I took a bullet for you and that scar is much worse than any of our scratches.'

Mark found himself leaning forward. 'You were shot, Duchess?'

'Yes. Samuel and I were scouting for information in France just before the Battle of Waterloo. We were attacked.' She touched the curve of her waist. 'I was hit here... Not that I didn't get off a shot myself. I used to love to shoot. Not even Samuel could beat me in marksmanship. But now I cannot endure the noise of the bullets or the smell. They bring back too many memories of the battles and the bodies. I suppose it is little enough to sacrifice, since I was able to come home alive with Samuel.'

Mark used to love hunting with his father and brother, but now he could not. He also woke up gasping in the night,

his nightshirt covered in sweat that felt like blood running down his head and back. But the worst part was that when he closed his eyes, he saw their faces. His Highlander men. The ones whom he had called friends who had died on the field. His leg cut off and piled on top of countless others to be burned. The smell of burning flesh was worse than gunpowder, but both were imprinted on his memory for ever.

'My wife giving up her gun makes one less thing for me to worry about,' Pelford said fondly. 'Now if she didn't make eyes at every fence she sees, my life would be just about perfect.'

Helen bumped her silverware. 'Unfair, Samuel. When you're just as bad and horse-mad as she is.'

The Duke held up his hands. 'You see what I grew up with? It's no wonder I have so many scars.'

He watched the Duchess elbow her husband. 'You're about to get another.'

Mark laughed with Pelford and Helen. He'd almost forgot that there were other people at the large dining room table. The Duchess of Hampford sat at the head, her son, Lord Trentham, at the bottom. On her right side sat the Marquess and Marchioness of Cheswick, Sir Edward Monson, the Duchess of Glastonbury, Watty and his Aunt Glencannon. On the left, the Pelfords, himself, Helen, William Fitzgerald de Ros and Lady Georgiana Lennox. Georgy was quite his favourite cousin. She was the daughter of the Duke and Duchess of Richmond and still single, despite being two and twenty.

'What, pray, is so amusing?' Aunt Glencannon asked in a voice loud enough for the entire table to hear.

Georgy cleared her throat, smiling. 'My dear friend Frederica is only teasing her husband, Aunt.'

His aunt gave a dismissive sniff. Clearly, happiness in

marriage was something to be frowned upon. His parents' marriage had certainly been unhappy, even though his father had defied his family's expectations and married the daughter of a wealthy Scottish mill owner. Whatever love they'd once shared had been long spent by the time Mark came along. All that was left of their relationship was his mother's fortune, which allowed his father to live the life of an aristocrat. He had seen that Mark and his brother were educated at Eton and then Oxford. But aside from that, he'd spent nearly half of every year in England, without his family, and had little to do with either of his Scottish sons.

'Both the Duchesses were in Brussels during the Battle of Waterloo, Aunt Glencannon,' he explained. 'It is because of their tender nursing ministrations and wonderful red soap that I am here today.'

Aunt Glencannon sniffed into her napkin, clearly unimpressed with their services. She had no idea how horrifying a hospital could be. Yet the two Duchesses had been as comfortable there as they were in a ballroom.

'You forgot about me, Mark. I was there,' Georgy said, smiling.

He lifted his wine glass to her. 'You were. Thank you for all that you did too, Georgy.'

'Were you there as well, Lady Helen?' Aunt Glencannon asked, her hawklike eyebrows raised. 'You are over one and twenty, are you not? Why is it that you were not presented until this year?'

Helen inhaled sharply, her nostrils flaring out. 'It took longer to tame me than it does most young ladies. My parents decided to postpone my debut.'

'It was my decision,' the Duchess of Hampford said, from the top of the table. 'I do not see why we in the beau monde are in such a rush to get rid of our daughters. We

do not expect our sons to marry at seventeen. My husband, as well, did not wish to be parted from our youngest children yet.'

Aunt Glencannon sniffed again. 'It is different for young women. If they do not marry young, they grow too independent and do not become obedient wives. Besides, valuable breeding years are lost.'

His aunt gave Helen and then Georgy a glare. They were both over twenty and he didn't think either of them were particularly mouldable. Nor did they want to be considered as brood mares.

'Men do not want obedient wives,' Mark said. 'They want good companions.'

'Only a crippled man would say such.'

Several of the ladies gasped at his aunt's words. The Duchess of Hampford signalled to the butler to have the footmen serve the next course.

Helen placed her hand, palm up, on his thigh underneath the table. He nearly jumped out of his seat and his heart thumped. At first, he thought that she was trying to give him comfort. But he realised when he saw the sad look in her eyes, she was seeking it. Covering her cold hand in his larger one, he held it tightly, eating the rest of the meal with only his left hand. If any of the Stringhams or his aunt noticed that he was only using one arm, they made no comment.

After dinner, they went to a beautiful blue drawing room where several card tables were laid out.

'Lady Glencannon, Lord Watford,' the Duchess of Hampford said with a smile that appeared to be forced. 'I insist that you make up a pair with myself and my son Matthew. I've heard that you are both excellent cardplayers.'

Matthew passed by Mark and Helen. 'I'll fleece her for you and take you to Gunter's with the spoils.'

Helen giggled, before whispering in Mark's ear, 'He will, too. Matthew can make money out of thin air.'

'Come over here,' the Duchess of Pelford called to them. 'You two can take us on in whist…and no cheating, Helen.'

They sat down at the table.

Helen picked up the deck of cards and shuffled it fast, turning the cards into a bridge. She handled them better than any professional gaming house worker he'd seen in action. 'I don't always cheat.'

Pelford barked a laugh. 'Yes, you do.'

Mark found himself laughing with the Pelfords at Helen's expense. The card table they'd chosen was about as far from his aunt Glencannon as you could be in the same room. A choice that he didn't think was a coincidence. He'd never been much of a cardplayer before, but he could tell that Helen loved the game. She played with great flare and ruthless precision.

Helen set down a card. 'I trump your ace.'

And she had trumped him.

*Completely.*

# Chapter Twelve

Helen had tossed and turned for what was left of the night. It had never occurred to her before that her parents' objection to her marriage with Jason was because of *her*. She'd always believed they were being haughty aristocrats who thought the mere son of a rector too low for their daughter. But it was the opposite. She was too wildly behaved for *him*.

Fingering his lock of hair, she pictured Jason's handsome face. His smile. Never once had he ever censured or corrected her. Although, she couldn't recall him censuring anyone. His God was a loving one. A forgiving one. Jason would no more condemn a person than he would commit a crime. It was not in his nature. Not that he was stupid. He was very clever and learned. He'd earned a first at Cambridge. He merely believed that the greatest changes came from love and kindness, not from sermons on hellfire and damnation.

Jason would make an incredible vicar of Ashbury. He could become a wonderfully loving bishop, but social station had never been his goal. He would probably be content with a curacy until his father's parish became available. Jason would live and die in the same ten miles he had been born in.

Helen had believed that all she wanted was to marry

Jason and live in the country near her home. Now she was not so sure. The ladies in the Ashbury parish would censure and despise her unconventional ways the same way Lady Glencannon had. She would no longer have the protection of her father's name. Or her station in life. According to the church, a woman was supposed to submit to her husband. And if she didn't, Jason would bear the blame.

It was insufferable.

Unfair.

Could she change?

Did she even want to?

Was living near Hampford Castle worth giving up her freedom?

Stumbling out of bed, she pulled on a dress that she could button herself. She wanted to get out of the house. Out of her own head. She needed fresh air. Exercise. The feel of the earth beneath her feet. Helen slid on a pair of slippers, but did not bother to fetch a shawl or hat.

She opened the front door. It was raining so hard, that she could only see a few feet in front of her. The weather matched her mood perfectly. Closing the door behind her, she walked out into a curtain of rain.

Glancing out through the window of his club, Mark saw that it was still raining in endless sheets. There was no chance that Helen was in his garden today in such weather. And there was no chance that he would be there either. He was starting to care for her too much and his cold heart could not endure another loss. She would leave at the end of her London Season and marry a cheery curate. One without scars, outside or inside.

The best thing he could do was avoid Helen, the way he'd

avoided his cousin Niamh. There was no future for them. They both deserved whole and happy husbands.

Picking up his book, he tried to focus on the territorial habits of finches. The sound of thunder caused him to sit straight up in his seat. His breathing was sharp and shallow. It sounded like cannon fire. He tried to close his eyes to calm himself, but the images were worse. Sean Fitzhugh bleeding out from his neck. Angus Brown with a hole in his middle, just above his tartan kilt. He would never play the bagpipes again. More faces. More wounds flashed in his mind. Sweat dripped down the back of his neck.

He felt a firm hand on his shoulder.

Opening his eyes, Mark saw Pelford standing there. He wore no hat and his suit was soaking wet, dripping on the floor.

'Inverness, have you seen Helen today?'

'No.'

Pelford raked his fingers through his wet hair. 'Do you have any idea where she might have gone?'

Mark could only shake his head.

'It's not uncommon for Helen to disappear for hours on end at Hampford Castle, but everyone within a thirty-mile radius knows the family. She's safe enough there, but this is London. She left the house in the pouring rain without a hat or a reticule with a coin in it.'

Mark leaned forward too quickly, pain shooting through his knee from his wooden leg. 'Have you checked my back garden?'

Pelford gritted his teeth. 'I looked there first. I even forced my way into your home, looking for her... I'm sure your butler will have quite a tale to tell you when you get home. But Helen hasn't made any other friends in London.

I don't know where else she'd go. I've already been to both of her brothers' houses.'

'Have you tried her publisher's?' Mark suggested. 'She told me that her book had been printed and she was supposed to approve the pages before they were bound. She wanted to take my sketches there.'

Raking his hand threw his wet hair, Pelford swallowed. 'I have not. I shall go there next. If you see her by chance, please take her home.'

'Of course.'

He watched Pelford all but run out of the room, he walked so quickly. The man was clearly worried about Helen's safety.

Putting a hand over his racing heart, Mark was terrified for Helen. What if someone had kidnapped her? Hurt her?

Had she come to his garden and he was not there? She had made it her own little piece of nature in a stone city.

Where would she go?

There were no woods in London.

The River Thames was large and polluted with sewage.

Where would she find nature in the middle of a bustling metropolis?

'Hyde Park!'

Several eyes in the room were on him. Mark had said it aloud, in a room meant for reading. He had no time to be embarrassed. Struggling to his feet, he hobbled from the room and called for his carriage. He put on his hat and coat while he waited for the black carriage with the Inverness arms engraved on the side to pull in front of the white building of his club.

A male servant held an umbrella over him on his way to the carriage and opened the door. Mark lifted himself in and called for his driver to take him to Hyde Park. Lean-

ing against the glass window, he desperately looked for a sign of her. Unsurprisingly with the weather, there was not another soul in the park. The rain was coming down even harder than before. His carriage splashed and jostled through the mud. He had never wanted to feel this way again: helpless. If Helen wasn't here, he didn't know where else to look. He was not a whole man. He could not be her hero and fight away her foes.

Mark's driver continued down the road through the park until they reached the Serpentine.

A body of water named after a snake.

Mark hit the roof of the carriage with his fist. His driver stopped the vehicle. Opening the door, Mark stepped out into the mud, his wooden leg sinking further than his human one.

'Is everything all right, my lord?' his driver asked.

After less than a minute, Mark was already soaked to his skin. 'I'm fine, Mr Stewart. Keep the carriage close. I believe my friend is near.'

His driver nodded, but he probably thought that Mark had finally gone mad.

Lifting his wooden leg out of the mud, Mark managed to limp towards the large lake in the middle of the park. He stood on the pebbled beach. The rain caused thousands of rings on top of the dark water. He nearly turned back, when he saw something white in the distance. Wiping the rain from his eyes, he peered more closely. Helen was knee-deep in the water with her face tilted towards the sky.

Exhaling in relief, he hobbled slowly towards her in the rain and muck. He touched her wet sleeve.

She grinned at him, her face wet. 'Isn't this the perfect day? I love the rain.'

Mark released her sleeve. 'Your entire family is searching all of London for you, half sick with worry.'

Helen wrapped her arms around herself. 'I am so sorry. I did not know. I did not mean to. I only wanted to return to nature for a little while.'

His body tensed and he gritted his teeth. 'Pelford just went to your publishers. We need to get you home immediately.'

Helen nodded. 'Of course. I am sorry that I put you out. I should have left a note for my family. I just didn't think of it. Silly of me.'

Swallowing, Mark wasn't angry at Helen. Or rather, he was frustrated and exhausted with how she made his dead soul experience a range of emotions in less than hour. Fear. Hope. Desire. Unsurety. Connection. Exasperation. And joy. His heartbeat thundered in his chest as loud as the falling rain.

Helen took his arm and, instead of him helping *her* to the carriage, she assisted Mark as he kept having to pull his wooden foot out of the mud and sand. It was beyond humiliating. When they reached the carriage, she climbed in first. Mark gave Mr Stewart directions to Hampford House and pulled himself through the door and on to the seat. His muscles shook from the exertion. He was a wreck of a man.

Helen took his clammy hand in her wet one. 'How did you know where to find me?'

Mark's teeth chattered. 'I know you.'

But in his heart, he had fallen in love with her. This beautiful, wild, unearthly woman. And that was why he needed to leave her.

# Chapter Thirteen

Mark understood her! Even better than Frederica or Samuel who had known her their whole lives. It was a heady thought. She had never had a friend like him before. Not that she had much experience with friends. Peculiar girls didn't.

She laid her head on his shoulder and his whole body shivered with cold. 'You are not cold-blooded like me. You're positively an icicle. What can I do to warm you?'

'N-nothing.'

Helen sat back up, glancing around the carriage for a blanket. But it was April, for goodness sake, and Mark did not have a winter blanket there. She felt him shiver again beside her, his face unnaturally pale, his lips almost blue in colour. She feared for his health and his life. He was wet and cold because of her folly.

How could she warm him without a blanket or a fire?

Animals were much better prepared for the elements than humans. They had no feathers to shake off the rain. No fur to keep them warm. Only thin, cold skin.

Taking his hand, she pulled off his sodden glove and rubbed his cold hand between her two warmer ones. She felt his hand get warmer and the colour improve with circulation. But his hand was merely a limb. She needed to warm

his core. Like his lost leg, a person could survive without arms or legs, but the heart needed to keep beating. In cold weather, animals snuggled together for warmth, sharing their own body heat.

Helen thought about sitting on Mark's lap, but she was afraid that it would be difficult for him to balance her there with his wooden leg. He was already swaying to one side. Hiking up her skirt, she straddled his lap with her knees and wrapped her arms around his neck, pressing her chest against his hard, wet one.

'What are you doing?'

She couldn't help kissing his brow, near the long white scar that his hair usually hid. Even after such a short time, Mark was so very dear to her. 'Warming you. Is it working?'

He nodded against her.

Helen continued to feather kisses against the side of his face, until she reached his lips. Leaning back, she remembered her first and only kiss with Jason. She had never thought to kiss another man. But this was not just any other man. This was Mark. Her friend. The person who made her feel safe. Who made her feel less different.

Taking a quick breath, she pressed her lips lightly against his. Mark's lips were not dry, like Jason's had been. But Jason had not walked in the rain to find her. They were cold, wetter than Jason's, but also softer. Helen brushed her lips across Mark's again. They felt warmer this time and his lips responded to hers with delicious pressure.

Helen couldn't help but smile as she kissed him again. His hands cupped her face. They were still wet from the rain, but they no longer felt cold. He licked her lips and she parted them in surprise, only to have him kiss her open-mouthed. Mark tasted of peppermint tea and sugar, sweet

and irresistible. Her blood felt like liquid fire pumping through her veins. She could feel this kiss in her fingertips. In her toes. Helen no longer wondered why Samuel and Frederica could not stop kissing each other. She never wanted to stop kissing Mark. This feeling was too wonderful.

Mark deepened the kiss and Helen found that thinking was no longer possible. His tongue stroked hers and Helen made a noise that she had never made before. Her response to him was instinctual. Primal. Her open mouth moved over his in a rhythm that, somehow, they both knew. His hands moved to her waist, pressing her closer to his chest. To his heart. To the very core of his being.

Helen ran her fingers through his hair, cradling his head in her hands. He was so precious to her. He broke the kiss, but Helen did not move. She rubbed her face against his. Her delicate skin against his rougher one. Mark made a noise. An animalic sound of contentment. It wasn't a word, but it didn't need to be. They were beyond language now. Beyond the slithery impossibility of trying to describe a feeling with words. His lips returned to hers with more ardour than before. They were bruising in their intensity. Helen felt a burning in her heart and deep within her belly.

A want.

No. A need.

Something that she had never before experienced. She realised that this was why animals mated. Why species continued to thrive despite difficult environments. Every living thing wished to experience this oneness. This pleasure. Helen wanted to touch all his skin. To rub her burning body up against his. She was on fire and she could have warmed him to the very core.

Helen pulled back an inch or two from Mark's face,

breathing hard. Again, she couldn't find the words to express what she was feeling. He was breathing hard, too. She could feel the air from his mouth on her lips. The taste of peppermint. Helen knew she should move, but her legs didn't seem to work. Like her mouth, they were stunned into stillness. Mark's beautiful blue eyes, as deep as the Atlantic Ocean, stared into hers. He did not move either. Maybe he could not. She was straddling his legs after all.

Maybe the kisses meant nothing to him.

Perhaps all open-mouthed kisses caused one's heart to sing and blood to become fire. It was unfair to compare Jason's chaste salute with the heat of Mark's kisses. Jason's kiss had been a brief caress and she had not wanted more than that. But she wanted more of Mark. Helen could not stop herself from diving back in and kissing him with all the need of a lifetime.

While her mouth mated with his, she pulled up his wet shirt and let her hands explore the planes of his chest. The core of his body and soul. She could feel his muscles and springy hair. Everywhere her hands touched Mark, his skin became as heated as her own. Helen could not have believed that either of them had ever felt cold. His hands roved her back and she moaned against his warm lips.

The carriage came to an abrupt stop, Mark's hands tightened on her waist so that she didn't fall. Their faces were less than an inch apart. Instinctively, Helen rubbed her nose against his. She loved how touching him made her feel. Mark closed his eyes and Helen pressed one last soft kiss to his lips.

'Thank you for finding me,' she whispered.

Reluctantly, Helen climbed off his lap, pushing down her sodden skirts. She couldn't be found like this by her family. This was against society's rules of appropriate behaviour.

Ones she knew that she shouldn't break. She was on the seat beside him just in time for Samuel to open the door to the carriage. His eyes focused on Helen's wet figure and then Mark's. His coat was unbuttoned and his shirt tails were hanging out of his trousers. Her dear friend looked thoroughly compromised.

Samuel pulled Helen out of the carriage by her wrist and into a bone-crunching hug in the rain. 'If you ever scare us again like that, I'm going to kill you.'

Helen laughed as he released her. 'That makes no sense.'

He turned back to Mark. 'Inverness, I owe you a great debt.'

'No, you don't,' Helen insisted. 'I do.'

Mark's face was expressionless. 'I was happy to be of assistance.'

Did their kisses mean nothing to him?

Samuel's sharp eyes went from Helen's hot face to Mark's cold one. 'I'd best get Helen inside and dry. And you'd best get dry yourself. Good day.'

He closed the carriage door and swept Helen into the house under his wing like a mother hen. Frederica and Mama were waiting at the door with a blanket and a towel. They did not wait to put either on her before squeezing her between them. They wrapped her like a newborn calf and ushered her into the parlour, where the rest of her family was waiting. Matthew and Nancy hugged her first, while their daughter, Susie, squeezed her leg. Mantheria and her son, Andrew, were next. Followed by Wick, Louisa and their three sons.

Wick pressed a kiss to her cheek. 'Let me guess…you just fancied a stroll in the April rain?'

Helen's face grew even hotter. 'I didn't know that it

would put you all into a stew if I slipped out for a couple of hours. I am terribly sorry for the worry I've caused.'

Her mother pulled her into her arms. Helen was only of medium height, but her mother was tall. She rested her head beneath her mother's chin. 'We are not angry. We were simply worried. We all love you so much.'

'Who brought you home?' Mantheria asked.

Helen's eyes found Samuel's. She fervently wished that she hadn't been so terrible to him as a child. If he told her family that Mark had brought her home, she would be teased until her dying day. She could have melted to the floor in a puddle of embarrassment.

'Only a hack,' Samuel said quickly. 'At least, Helen is wise enough to wade in the Serpentine with her coin purse.'

Her mother squeezed her tighter, dropping a rare kiss on her hair. Papa was the more affectionate of the two.

'I'll go adventuring with you next time,' Andrew said, her young nephew smiling at her.

Mantheria shook her head. 'You most certainly will not. It is not at all good for a young lady to walk around unescorted. Someone could have seen Helen walking alone and the gossip would have been terrible.'

But someone *had* seen her.

Mark.

Not simply in her wet clothes, but into her very soul.

# *Chapter Fourteen*

Mark closed his eyes, but all he could see was Helen's beautiful form standing in the rain. Welcoming it on her face.

He realised that he was in love with her.

But she would never be his.

Leaning back against his pillows, he shivered again. He knew he was burning up with fever, but he was so cold. So very cold. He hadn't been warm since Helen touched him. Held him. Kissed him.

He hadn't kissed a lass since before the battle. But he'd kissed many women before then. The embraces were fleeting and pleasant. Quickly forgotten.

Mark could not forget *her* kisses.

Her touches.

She was his fever.

He felt her cold hand on his face. A small smile formed on his lips. Helen's hands were always cold. He almost believed her that she was cold-blooded. But this had to be some sort of fever dream. Lady Helen most certainly was not in his room, sitting on the edge of his bed, placing cool clothes on his burning face.

This imaginary Helen wasn't all wet. Her dress didn't cling to her lewdly, like it had before when she had ravaged his mouth with her kisses. Mark could tell from the

embrace that she was inexperienced, but that hadn't stop her from arousing him to the point of pain. Or making him feel more alive than he ever had before.

Mark lifted his hand and touched the silk sleeve of her embroidered pelisse—this phantom felt real. She picked up his hot hand and rubbed it against her cool cheek.

'I am so sorry, my dearest friend. Ever so sorry that my foolishness has made you ill.'

'I almost believe that you are real.'

She gently placed his hand next to his leg on the bed and picked up another cold cloth to set against his burning face. 'I am real. You can pinch me if you like.'

Where he wanted to pinch her would not have been appropriate. But in his current condition, he wouldn't be pinching any lass. He was either burning or freezing. Sometimes both at the same time.

'Spoilsport,' she said, her face near his own. 'I shall have to pinch you.'

With her slender fingers she pinched his shoulder lightly. 'There. Do you now believe that I am real?'

Mark did and his harried mind understood enough to realise that it would be disastrous for her reputation to be found alone with him. In his room. In his house. It was compromising, even if he couldn't have seduced her in his current condition. Society never cared about the details, only the disgrace.

With all of his strength, he tried to push away her hand that was bathing his face. 'You have to leave.'

'I will when your fever breaks. I promise.'

Closing his eyes, he sighed. 'Did my servants let you in?'

He heard her soft laugh. 'No. I broke in through the window. It was terribly easy. You should really get better

locks for your own safety if you're going to sleep on the ground floor.'

Against his will, his lips formed a smile. Happiness with Helen was more infectious than a fever. 'What time is it?'

'Two o'clock in the morning, I'd guess,' she said, bringing the cold cloth back to his burning skin. 'I heard that you were ill and I knew it was my fault so I decided to come and check on you. I've been here for about an hour and I will be gone before your earliest scullery maid awakes to start the fires.'

'Then your family doesn't know where you are?'

'Of course not,' Helen said, he could hear the smile in her voice. He wanted to open his eyes and see it, but he was too tired to lift his eyelids. 'They rarely know where I am at Hampford Castle and that's how I like it. But that's enough talking, you should sleep. I will watch over you, like you watched over me at the lake, dearest friend.'

Mark resisted the pull into the darkness, but when her cold but gentle finger tips began to stroke his forehead, he knew he was lost. Somewhere in the distance or in his dreams, he heard her humming.

After a few days and several doses of laudanum, Mark's fever abated. He assured himself that it was a good thing that Helen hadn't repeated her nightly visit. He'd almost decided that the entire episode was a figment of his imagination, but then his valet had been surprised when he saw the cloths used to mop Mark's brow were embroidered with an S that looked like a snake. Helen *Stringham*, the snake charmer and fairy queen, had brought them for him.

The morning after he fell ill, both a doctor and an astounding number of potted plants had arrived. Even feverish, Mark remembered that Helen didn't like cutting off a

flower's life. She preferred to let it grow to its fullness or be replanted in a garden.

The following day, his servants had received a basket full of medicines and scented soaps. Then more potted plants. His poor servants did not know what to do with so many of them, so they'd spread them throughout his town house. It was like living in a greenhouse. Or an enchanted fairy garden. The sort of place he would imagine a sprite like herself living.

Mark had his valet prepare clothes for him to go to his club. He couldn't go to his back garden. She might be there. And he couldn't stay in his own house, because every flower and leaf reminded him of her.

He needed to cut Helen out of his life. Mark had let her roots grow into his heart and that would only mean pain for them both. Helen was engaged to someone else and wanted a different life than what he could offer her. And Mark wanted her in every way. He wished to teach her how to kiss. How to make love, which she would probably call mating. Mark half wondered if her love and light could fill in the missing pieces of his soul. But she would never be his. And he could never be hers. Helen deserved so much more than half of a man who had let his friends die and who was only half alive.

Taking his usual chair by the window at the club, Mark took out his sketchbook and began to finish the illustrations of the snakes for Helen. The pictures had been their original bargain. She would tend his garden in return for them. The only way to end things finally between them was to give her what she'd always wanted.

He was done with all but the last snake—a rattlesnake. The one that Helen said was her favourite. The one that

warned others to stay away by the sound it made. If Helen had made such a warning sound, would he have heeded it?

He shook his head.

Helen had careened into his life, leaving him little choice.

Mark's memory was not perfect, but it was very good. Especially when it came to images. His initial sketch was good enough to identify the snake. Now all he had to do was add the shading and sharpen the image. Pressing his finger on to the page, he purposely smeared the graphite. He took particular care to make sure that the rattle appeared correctly.

He didn't notice that Pelford had taken a chair beside him. Which was odd, because Pelford was not a small man. How long the Duke had sat reading his paper, Mark couldn't say.

'Ah, Inverness,' he said. 'I was hoping to see you here.'

'I trust Lady Helen has not gone missing again.'

Pelford guffawed, shaking his head. 'No. Although I dare say she is ready to run away from home. My in-laws have assigned each other days to watch over her. Needless to say, she does not like the idea of a nursemaid.'

Mark could easily imagine her indignation. Wild creatures did not like to be caged. 'I should think not.'

'I still feel in your debt, Inverness. If there is anything that you need, please do not hesitate to ask me.'

Mark tore out the six illustrations from the sketchbook and handed them to Inverness. 'Give these to Helen for me. That is all I ask.'

'You do not intend to give them to her yourself?'

Mark shook his head, standing up. 'I think that it is better this way. She is already engaged to someone else.'

'Jason? He is her best friend, aside from Becca, but I

don't think she loves him. At least, not how a woman should love the man that she marries.'

Warmth fluttered in his belly as his mind tangled with uncertainty. Without another word, he walked slowly down the hall and called for his carriage. It was raining again, but only a light mist. Nothing like the torrential downpour when Helen went walking in the park. Sitting in his carriage, he couldn't help but think of her. He wished for the thousandth time that things were different. That his brother was alive. That he still had a leg and was a saucy Scottish adventurer who liked to woo wealthy women. Helen was certainly wealthy. Would she have fancied him then?

His butler met his carriage with an umbrella and Mark descended cautiously. The last thing he needed was to fall in a puddle after his cold. When he entered his house, he took off his hat. The marble floors gleamed and there was not a worker in sight. Passing the new wallpaper, he opened the door to the parlour only to see a woman standing there.

'Mother.'

Behind his mother, his aunt and Cousin Niamh got to their feet, smiling at him.

Aunt Fiona held out her arms to him. 'Come and give your auntie a *smuirich*!'

# Chapter Fifteen

Helen sat next to her brother inside his new carriage. 'I thought Nancy was my nursemaid today.'

Matthew nudged her with his elbow. Two-year-old Susie was happily sitting on his knee. 'Alas, Susie and I had to fill in for her. She is feeling a little under the weather and, since I am the one who wrote your original contract with the publisher, Nancy thought that I would be a suitable replacement.'

Helen tweaked one of Susie's curls. 'I do not mind you coming, Susie.'

The little girl grinned at her. She had the same freckled nose, dark curly hair and brilliant blue eyes as her mother. 'I love you, Aunt Hellion.'

Matthew guffawed, bouncing his daughter up and down on his knee with his mirth.

Helen couldn't help but smile a little. 'Actually, darling, it is Aunt *Helen*.'

'I know that, Aunt Hellion.'

'Correct her, Matthew.'

Her brother shook his head. 'Never. That is the best wit any two-year-old has ever come up with. I knew I contributed more than just my good looks to my daughter.'

'She's the spitting image of Nancy.'

Susie chose that particular moment to show her aunt and father how well she could spit. She pointed to the floor two feet away. 'Look how far!'

'Marvellous, my darling,' her father assured her. 'Another skill you inherited from me.'

Helen couldn't help but giggle. 'Very impressive. Just remember it's Aunt *Helen*. Sounds like melon.'

The carriage pulled in front of a narrow wooden building that would have been all the better for a fresh coat of paint. Preferably in a bright colour. The sign hanging above the door read 'Gibbs and Thomas'. Matthew held Susie in one arm and opened the door with the other. Helen walked in and was met with the delicious smell of fresh paper. The second note her nose detected was leather. And the final note, a hint of ink. Now if this smell was a perfume, she would spend all her pin money on it.

She saw pages hanging on lines, like clothing. Machines with movable type. Tables where workers were painstakingly adding the letters in the correct order in a wooden frame to make the templates for the pages. There were *clicks*, *clacks* and the sound of metal pressing against paper. She could live in this habitat.

A clerk came to meet them. Doffing his hat, he bowed. 'May I 'elp you, sir?'

Helen huffed. Why did strangers always address the male in the party?

Matthew gave a thin-lipped smile that was more menacing than friendly. 'My lord, actually. I am Lord Trentham and I am here representing the interests of my client, Lady Helen Stringham, who sold a book to Mr Gibbs.'

The clerk bowed a second time, lower than before, his nose nearly to his knees. 'I shall fetch Mr Gibbs at once, my lord.'

'And ladies,' Matthew added.

Susie pointed her thumb at her chest. 'I am Lady Susan.'

Helen couldn't help but mimic her niece. She touched her own chest. 'And I am Lady Helen.'

'Aunt Hellion.'

The clerk bowed again. 'My ladies.'

He returned in less than a minute with an older man. Helen would have guessed he was in his fifties. Portly around the middle, hair receding on top, and a pair of rectangular spectacles perched on his nose. Like the clerk, he gave Matthew a brief nod. 'My lord.'

Susie huffed, pointing her thumb at herself again. 'I am Lady Susan.'

'That's right, darling,' Matthew said. 'Never let a man ignore you in a conversation. But perhaps Mr Gibbs was merely waiting for a proper introduction. Mr Gibbs, allow me to introduce you to my sister, Lady Helen Stringham, and my daughter, Lady Susan.'

Helen couldn't help but smile as Susie bowed her head, while still in her father's arms. Even at two, she knew exactly who she was and how she expected people to treat her. If only her diction was a bit better on pronouncing *Helen*.

Holding out her hand, Helen smiled. 'It is a pleasure to meet you in person, sir. I am most excited to see the printing of my book.'

Instead of shaking her hand, Mr Gibbs bowed over it. Happily, he didn't kiss it. Susie held out her hand as well and the publisher bowed over it just as formally. Her niece giggled and jumped, kicking her father.

Matthew groaned. 'The accuracy of your kicks is unparalleled, my darling.'

Helen snorted and couldn't help but smirk at him.

Mr Gibbs held out an arm. 'If you would follow me this

way, my lord and ladies. I shall show you the first set of proofs.'

He led them back to a windowless office, where Helen's book was in large broadsheets on the table. Each sheet held sixteen pages on it. The sheet of paper had not yet been cut into individual pages, but it was thrilling none the less. Helen walked towards the desk, pulling off her gloves. They might have fallen to the floor, but she didn't stop to see. She touched the paper, feeling the smooth, slight grain of the wood pressed into fresh pages. Leaning down, she inhaled the heady smell of fresh ink and wormwood. She would really have to talk to her mother about making a perfume with this intoxicating smell.

Turning to the publishers, Helen gave her most polite smile. 'Mr Gibbs, I was wondering if you would be able to add six pages in the middle. Six beautiful illustrations of snakes. I've already commissioned them to be drawn. They should be available any day now.'

'It'll cost extra to cut the wood blocks for the pictures.'

'I'll happily pay it.'

'And the additional expense of weaving extra pages into the centre of the book.'

'Every single farthing.'

A slow smile spread over Mr Gibb's face. 'In that case, my lady, it will be done.'

'Good.'

As she turned back to the desk, her eyes roved the pages. Her words. Her painstakingly written and researched words were in beautiful, neat paragraphs, chapters and pages. Running her fingers over the dried ink, she felt the slight indentation of the printing press type. It was incredible that only twenty-six letters arranged in numerous ways could produce such a thing.

Lifting the large sheet, she saw that a clerk had marked a few mistakes on the next set of sixteen pages. There was punctuation missing on one page and a misspelled word on the other. She peeked at the last page. It was actually the beginning of her book. The top of the pile was the last chapter. She found the title page: *A Guide to Snakes*. Not the most thrilling name ever, but it accurately explained what her book was about. Then she looked for her name. She quickly found *Stringham* on the page beside it, but it was all wrong. It read: *Mr H. Stringham*.

She stepped back from the table.

'It turned out rather well, Lady Helen,' Mr Gibbs said, looking at her over the rims of his spectacles. 'As you see, only a few mistakes need to be corrected before the final printing and binding of your book.'

Helen cleared her throat. 'Yes. I noticed one mistake myself. The name. You said that it was written by Mr H. Stringham... I am Helen Stringham. You are welcome to call me by my title, Lady Helen Stringham, or use my marital status, Miss Helen Stringham.'

Mr Gibbs shook his head. 'I am afraid that is not possible, my lady. If this were a work of fiction, adding your real name to the title page would help sales enormously among the titled ladies and commoners. But our readers are well-educated men. They would not purchase a book written by a young woman.'

'What about an old woman?' she asked pettishly.

The publisher shook his head again. 'There are not many women who have written published books and, forgive me, the few women who have been are rarely vulgar enough to use their own name.'

Matthew let out a low whistle. Her brother was no doubt waiting for Helen to lose her temper and give Mr Gibbs

a well-deserved set-down. If Helen had been a snake, she would have bitten the man, spreading poison slowly to his veins until it stopped his heart. But she was not a snake and she had no intention of making a scene. When she did, the event rarely went in her favour.

'Why is it when a man publishes under his own name, it is not considered vulgar? Are you not perpetuating a seventeenth-century standard? One that Ben Jonson himself broke by publishing his works underneath his own name. Claiming one's own work is not vulgar.'

Mr Gibbs blinked at her from behind his spectacles. Matthew smiled. He of all people would appreciate a reference to the o' rare Ben Jonson. Matthew was a wordsmith of no equal, but he did not use his gift for fiction, but for contracts. And really detailed Parliamentary speeches that Nancy had to edit down for time.

'Be that as it may, I am the publisher, Lady Helen. And I will not print your name on this book.'

'Matthew, what about the contract?' she asked, appealing to him. 'Is there anything that stipulates that Mr Gibbs has the power not to include my name?'

Her brother sighed. 'It's a bit murky. The contract is mostly focused on the financial aspects, how much of percentage you'll receive from each sale. The only verbiage on content was that you agreed to make editorial changes recommended by the publisher. All changes have already been made. Whether or not Mr Gibbs has the authority to exclude or change your name in print is not directly specified. We could sue him, of course, but it would probably take the Chancery Court years to come to a decision. You'll probably have written your fifth book by then.'

Matthew thought that she would write more books. And why shouldn't she? Helen had loved penning the first one.

Papa had read every page and given a little feedback, but most of the work, nay, all of the work had been her own. She didn't want the wrong name published. Or someone else's name. Or no name at all. It was just another way the males of the human race silenced the females. She would not stand for it.

Turning on her heel, she lifted her nose in the air. 'Mr Gibbs, I shall pay the entire cost for the printing of the book as long as it has my name. My full name.'

The publisher's already pasty face turned a paler shade. 'My partner would never agree to such terms, my lady. Publishing a woman's book would be the ruination of our company. We might as well sell the printing presses at once and declare bankruptcy.'

Helen sighed, her eyes focusing on Susie. How were humans ever to evolve to equal partnership between the sexes if brave women did not demand it? If they did not open themselves for ridicule and public scorn as they fought for change. For opportunity. For a voice. A female voice. For women who were free to speak, think and dream however they wished.

'Why don't I save you some time, Mr Gibbs?' Helen said, with a smirk. 'There is no need for you or your partner to declare bankruptcy. I shall purchase this building, the printing presses, all supplies, your employees, and your company. Name your price.'

'This is most irregular.'

Matthew grinned. 'You'll find that most Stringhams are irregular.'

Mr Gibbs grimaced, breathing hard. No doubt he was processing this very large decision. He was not a young man and if he asked enough for his company, he would never

have to work again. The publisher opened his mouth and said a number.

Helen turned to Matthew. 'Is that fair?'

He set down his daughter, shaking out his fingers. 'Let's write up a contract, shall we? Do you have a pen, Mr Gibbs?'

Once they were back in the carriage, Susie rolled the ink blotter over her father's buckskin breeches leaving trails of black ink. She'd acquired it during the two hours they'd waited for Matthew to write the contract. Her niece had also wangled twenty-six type letters from the clerk. She'd used one of Helen's discarded gloves to hold them.

Her niece picked out a metal letter. 'H for Hellion.'

Helen smiled. 'Now find S for Susie.'

'And a M for Money,' Matthew said. 'Whose money are you spending, by the by?'

She looked at her elder brother hopefully. 'Would you be willing to advance me the sum?'

He lifted his hands like the weights of a scale. 'I am not unwilling, but I do charge a rather high interest rate.'

She touched her chest. 'But I'm family. I should get a discount.'

'I know and I just wrote the *Hamlet* of contracts for you without charging you a fee. It is a piece of art. The seminal achievement of my pen.'

Helen yawned. 'Is that why it took you so long?'

'Fifty-seven separate clauses to protect you and your future company. Once Gibbs gets his partner to sign it. And you come up with the ready, of course.'

Leaning against her elbow, she sighed. 'Do you think Mama would lend me four thousand pounds?'

'No,' Matthew said flatly.

'What if I told her it was a part of my dowry?'

'Still no.'

'Papa?'

'He'd only ask Mama for permission.'

Helen nodded. Papa had long ago learned not to commit himself to anything without asking their mother first. 'And how much interest do you charge?'

'I don't give fixed rates of interest, even to family. It would range between five to ten per cent depending on the market. It could potentially be even higher.'

'Enough to eat up all the profits from my sales, no doubt.'

'No doubt,' he agreed with a smile. 'If I were you, which happily I am not, I would use my feminine charms to extort the money from quite a different relative.'

A smile spread on her lips. 'Grandfather Stubbs.'

'He'll probably make you a gift of the money and give you a lot of good advice on running your company. But you'd best not bring any snakes or rodents to the interview. You'll have to charm Grandmother Stubbs as well, which is slightly more difficult. She will expect you to be well behaved and a perfect young debutante.'

Helen elbowed her brother hard in the stomach.

Matthew gasped. 'Almost as good of an aim as Susie.'

His daughter looked up from her letters at the mention of her name. 'Ices?'

'Yes. I'd almost forgotten. I bribed her with ices to come with me today.'

'You bribed your two-year-old daughter?'

Her brother intertwined his fingers behind his head, leaning back against the seat. 'She's very nearly three. And it's never too early to teach her sound financial principles.'

'Such as bribery?'

'Precisely. Bribery is essential in business to grease the wheels of a deal. Every company does it.'

\* \* \*

Helen couldn't complain too much, because she enjoyed ices at Gunter's as much as her niece. Today, she picked a most interesting flavour: currant. Not her favourite, but she did enjoy it. Susie sat in the chair beside her and got as much ice on her face and dress as in her mouth.

Matthew handed his daughter a napkin. 'Perhaps if you take smaller bites, darling, less will end up in your lap.'

Susie spooned up a heaping amount of ice.

'Or not,' he said with a chuckle.

Helen set down her own spoon. 'Would you mind if we stopped at Covent Garden for some flowers?'

'More potted plants for Lord Inverness?'

Annoyingly, she felt the blood rush to her face. Her brother was much too perceptive for his own good. 'He's been ill.'

Matthew smiled. 'Which I am sure has nothing to do with your walk by the lake in the pouring rain, nor your hackney ride home.'

Helen stiffened in her seat and stuck out her chin. 'I don't know what you're talking about.'

He turned to his daughter and smiled. 'Susie, Papa is now going to teach you another business principle called leverage.'

'You mean blackmail!'

Her brother shook his head. 'Such an *ugly* word.'

'What do you want?'

'I shall happily purchase a dozen more potted plants for your Scottish Earl, in exchange for you holding Susie in the carriage on the way home.'

Helen looked at her adorable and very dirty niece. 'She's all sticky.'

'And you will be, too,' Matthew assured her.

'But you're already dirty. Your buckskins are covered in ink.'

He held up both hands. 'Ten potted plants and I don't mention my astute observations to Mama. My best and final offer.'

'Blackmail.'

'Leverage.'

'Fine,' Helen said between clenched teeth, holding out her arms to her niece. 'Come to Aunty Hellion, Susie. We are going with your papa to buy some potted plants. The most expensive ones we can find.'

# Chapter Sixteen

The next day, Mark wanted to escape back to his club, but his mother stood between him and the door.

'Mark, you can hardly leave when you have guests staying in the house. What have you planned for their entertainment? Dearest Niamh has never been to London and I am sure there are a dozen places she'd like to see.'

He desperately wanted to point out that he had not invited his cousin, aunt or mother to London, but it would not matter. 'I thought you would all wish for a day of rest after your long journey.'

'Nothing of the sort. We were cooped up in a carriage for days. There is nothing we would enjoy more than a tour of London. It has been more than thirty years since your father brought me here as his bride.'

His mother did not add that his father had not brought her back since. Or that his mother had not been accepted into the bosom of the beau monde. Her accent was too Scottish and her background was trade. Not even her beautiful coppery hair and winsome smile had enabled her to join the higher levels of society. His father had simply left her at home with his children and gone to London alone for the Season. James and Mark had travelled with him when they grew old enough to go to school at Eton. Father wanted his

sons to be English. He would correct them sharply if they ever used Scottish brogue or even words.

Mark did not feel English or Scottish.

He felt as if he belonged nowhere.

His mother placed a hand on his arm. Her figure was trim and her hair still the coppery gold of her youth. But she had deep lines on her face, James had called them 'scowl wrinkles'. It was hard to imagine that she'd ever been young. Or happy. 'Where are you going to take us, lad?'

Mark said the first place that popped into his mind thanks to Helen. 'The Tower of London.'

'A prison? We rode a carriage from Scotland and you're taking us to a bowfin and scabby prison?'

His mother's Scottish brogue grew rougher when she was angry.

He shook his head. 'Not any more, Mama. It holds the Crown Jewels and an animal menagerie. It's one of the most frequently visited buildings in all of Britain. I promise, it is not foul smelling or dirty there.'

Mama nodded at this. 'I should like to see the Crown Jewels and I am sure Niamh will be happy for your escort. She would make you the most excellent partner in life if only you would court her. Shall we say a half-hour from now?'

Mark was about to nod, when he heard a knock at the door. His heartbeat quickened. Was it Helen? She was brazen enough to come and see how he did. His butler passed him and opened the door. It was a carrier holding potted plants.

'Don't tell me you've ordered more flowers?' his mother said in dismay. 'You've got more plants in this house than a *monadh*!'

The carrier must have heard her, for he touched his hat.

'I've ten plants for a Lord Inverness, compliments of Lord Trentham and speedy wishes for his swift recovery.'

Mama rounded on Mark. 'Recovery from what?'

'A minor cold is all.'

'No wonder you looked all peely-wally. Now don't haver. Who is Lord Trentham? I have never heard that title before.'

Mark leaned against the wall, his leg stiffening from standing too long. 'An earl. He is the second son of the Duke of Hampford. Lord Trentham was given the title of Earl for performing a service to the Crown.'

Mama brushed passed him, standing by the butler. 'Och! I suppose you can put them in the drawing room for now. Heaven knows we dinnae need any more plants.'

The butler dutifully delivered the pots to the drawing room, placing them in a row before the window. As Mark sat down in his favourite chair, he realised how much he missed Helen's company. More than the plants, she had brought life to his sorry existence. And she'd made him want to live again. With her.

But he'd resolved not to think of Helen any more. Even though it was apparent to him that it was she and not Lord Trentham who had sent the flowers. He wondered if the Duke of Pelford had given her the illustrations yet. He'd hoped not to have a painful interview. He didn't wish to see her again. It was too hard. And if his mother, aunt, and cousin hadn't arrived, he would have gone home to Scotland like a dog with his tail between his legs.

Niamh was the first to enter the room. She had the same beautiful coppery hair of his mother and aunt. His cousin was small, curvy and vivacious. Brimming with life. She bounced into the room. Not walked. She made him tired by just watching her.

'Aunt says that you are to take us to the Tower.'

'Aye.'

She perched on the armrest of his chair. 'And to see the Crown Jewels.'

'I hope you'll like them.'

'I'm sure I shall. Although I was hoping to do more in the city than visit a bunch of old buildings.'

'There's exotic animals, too.'

Niamh wrinkled her nose. 'Whist. I meant dancing and parties. Not dull stuff.'

Thinking of Helen, Mark said, 'Poisonous snakes with rattles are hardly dull.'

His cousin huffed and she appeared more a child refused a dessert than a young woman ready to be married. 'No one likes snakes.'

He spoke without thinking. 'My friend, Lady Helen, does. She has a ball python as long as you are tall and she wears it around her neck like a scarf.'

Niamh's green eyes widened. Pushing his shoulder with her arm, she exclaimed, 'You're not having me on, are you?'

Mark held his right hand up. 'Word of a Scot. I can introduce you to her, if you like.'

Except he couldn't. Because he was in love with her and he was only half a man. Because she was in love with a curate, but kissed like a courtesan and he had no intention of seeing her ever again.

'She must be an eccentric lady. A regular old crabbit.'

He'd heard Helen called much worse among the young bucks, but his cousin's mild criticisms irked him. 'She is intelligent and educated.'

Niamh popped up, shaking her head. 'Oh, no. She's a bluestocking. Mama says that intelligent women don't find husbands.'

'Are you saying that there are no intelligent men?'

His cousin laughed, a high sound. 'Oh, it is perfectly normal for a man to be intelligent. But a woman is supposed to be pretty.'

Helen was both.

'Why can't a woman be pretty and learned?'

Niamh giggled. 'Silly *sassenach*. Only ugly women study, for they have no other hope to earn their keep. They become governesses and teachers.'

'I take it that you are too pretty for either of those fates.'

His cousin laughed again. The high-pitched sound grated on his nerves. 'Is that a compliment, Mark? You must not flirt with me too dreadfully. I am only just out.'

Placing both hands on the armrests, he pushed himself to standing. 'I can safely promise never to flirt with you.'

Her lower lip came out in a pout. 'Poor Cousin Mark. Your poor leg. How you must miss it! Is it terrible being a cripple? I never thought that I would marry a man that wasn't whole, but Mama says that titles are more important than having two legs. Don't you agree?'

His head ached and he missed Helen. She had become like the phantom itch in his missing limb that he could not scratch. 'I would trade my title, castle and estate for my leg back.' For my life back.

Mark tried to limp out of the room, but the door was blocked by two formidable Scottish women: his mother and Aunt Fiona. Unlike his mother, Aunt Fiona had grown stout with age. There was no getting through her.

His aunt hugged him. 'Mark, it's so good to see you, lad. You've got a bit more colour in your cheeks.'

Mama tutted. She was not the hugging type. 'Have you called for the carriage yet?'

'Yes, Mama.'

He tried to walk past her, but she held out an arm. 'You

should escort Niamh out. Eejit. Did I not teach you any manners?'

Grimacing, Mark turned and offered his arm to his young cousin. She skipped across the room and took it, grinning up at him. He tried to walk as stiffly as he could, not to show his limp. He handed Niamh into the carriage, then his mother and aunt. When he lifted himself in, he noticed that the only available seat was beside his cousin. His mother and aunt were nothing if not direct in their intentions. Mark sat down as close to the wall as he could and as far from Niamh.

Needless to say, the carriage ride to the Tower of London was a wee bit constrained. All three women in his family were watching him. He escorted them through the cells where Queen Elizabeth I had been incarcerated by her own sister, Queen Mary. To the green where poor Anne Boleyn lost her head. Through the rooms that held the Crown Jewels. Lastly, to the menagerie. His amputated leg was sore and shaking by the time they reached the reptiles. His eyes lingered on the rattlesnake. It was curled up in a ball, its rattle out. Warning anyone from coming too near.

But it was too late.

He'd already been bitten.

# *Chapter Seventeen*

When Helen arrived home, she'd wanted to climb the stone fence and check on Mark. Unfortunately, her mother met her at the door and ordered her to go straight to her dressing room for a bath.

Her hair was still slightly damp when her maid arranged it for dinner. Helen put on the dress her mother had chosen. They were going to the theatre after. Helen liked plays, but according to Frederica, going to the theatre was being put on display. Like a painting. The candles in their box would illuminate them for all the other guests to see and gawk at. She shivered at the thought. Her maid wrapped her shoulders with a shawl. Helen could only thank her. She didn't bother explaining that the full body shiver had nothing to do with her temperature and everything to do with the *ton*.

Opening the door to the parlour, she found Samuel and Frederica kissing. A year ago, she would have gone back out, blushing. But their kissing was so commonplace that she simply cleared her throat loudly. They broke apart, smiling at each other.

Helen huffed. 'I like it better when you're quarrelling.'

'Some day you'll discover that kissing is much more enjoyable than quarrelling,' Frederica said loftily.

Helen glared back at her sister, but couldn't help but

think of Mark's feverish kisses. They had certainly been more than enjoyable. She'd dreamed of them and woke up this morning feeling warm and disappointed that he wasn't there.

Samuel stepped away from his wife and picked up a thin box. He handed it to Helen without a word. Opening it up, she saw Mark's finished drawings of the snakes. They were no longer simple sketches, but intricately rendered images of the original creature. Lifting them one by one, she saw that they were beautiful. Mark had seen the beauty of the snake as well as its dangerous nature.

'Is he feeling better?'

Her brother-in-law did not look her in the eyes. 'I saw him at our club yesterday. I think he is fully recovered.'

'Yesterday? Why did you not give them to me then?'

Samuel glanced at Frederica. Stepping forward, she took his hand. Somehow it felt as if they were now two against Helen's one. They were teaming up for something. Something unpleasant. She could tell from previous experiences.

Frederica gave her a pitying smile. 'You see, Helen dearest, Samuel wanted to talk to me about it first.'

Helen shook her head, snorting. 'He needed your permission to deliver a package to me? And you call me the bossy one.'

Her sister gave a speaking glance to her husband.

Samuel nodded, clearing his throat. 'Inverness doesn't want to see you, Helen.'

'But we're friends.'

'Not any more.'

Something inside Helen fell into her stomach. Her heart? Her lungs? Her spleen? It sloshed down there uncomfortably, making her belly turn. 'Is it because of my wading in

the Serpentine? It was one little mistake. Everybody makes mistakes. I didn't mean to worry him, or to embarrass him.'

Or to have kissed him.

'When he brought you home, you were as pale as death,' Samuel said slowly. 'And I think Lord Inverness has seen too much death in his life.'

Poor Mark. There were no words in any human or animal language that could have expressed her anguish. And she had done this to *him*. Her dear friend who was chased by the ghosts of his past and his lost leg.

'Do you think he hates me now?'

Samuel shook his head. 'Worse.'

Helen rubbed her dry eyes. 'What is worse than hate?'

Frederica stepped forward, pulling Helen into a hug. 'We think he loves you, Helen. And that is why he wants to stay away from you.'

Helen burrowed her face into Frederica's taller shoulder. Clinging to her sister for comfort and strength. 'If he loves me, why would he stay away?'

'Because you're engaged to Jason, Helen,' Samuel said, from behind them. 'He is being an honourable man. And Inverness was greatly wounded during the war.'

'I don't want him to be honourable. I want him to be my friend.'

Frederica patted Helen's damp hair. 'Friendship between men and women is difficult. And often not possible once you're married.'

Helen shook her head, rubbing her nose on the lace trim of Frederica's dress. 'That is ridiculous. Males and females of all species can be friends. It is not always about mating.'

Samuel coughed. He must have recalled Mark's state of disarray in the carriage.

But Helen did not stop. 'Mama has been dear friends

with the Prince Regent for thirty years and there is nothing sensual between them.'

Her brother-in-law patted her shoulder and Frederica held her tighter. 'I am not saying that men and women cannot be friends, but surely you feel differently towards Jason than you do to Mark?'

'Of course. They are different people. How could I possibly feel the same way about both of them?'

She felt her sister swallow before speaking. 'The thing is… Not everyone feels the same way about each other. Sometimes one person loves another and that feeling is not returned. Because it cannot or should not be. Mark can no longer be your friend because he has developed feelings for you.'

Helen twisted away from her. Mark could ignore those feelings, just like she did. 'Mantheria is friends with her estranged husband *and* his mistress! She even travels with them.'

Frederica held out her hands, but Helen didn't take them. 'Mantheria and Glastonbury have a child together. They all do it for Andrew's sake. They want him to feel as though he has a normal, loving family.'

'And when you are the wife of the vicar,' Mama said, walking into the room like the Queen of England, 'you will not be allowed to have *any* male friends. Even the slightest hint of indiscretion will ruin you and your husband. The lower and middle classes are much more constrained than the beau monde. Although women are held to a higher standard than men in all the classes.'

Helen breathed in deeply, finding it difficult to get enough oxygen to her brain. 'Am I never to have any male friends again?'

'You'll have Jason,' Frederica said, with a too-bright smile.

But somehow that didn't feel like enough. As much as she enjoyed his company, it had never been enough for her. Nor did she burn for him like she did for Mark's kisses.

Helen could only be grateful that they were attending the theatre this evening. She could not have danced and given even the appearance of good manners and civility.

Samuel had secured them a box at the theatre in Convent Garden. The play was supposed to be a comedy, but Helen was in no mood to laugh. Samuel and Frederica sat in the front row of the box, holding hands. She and Mama sat behind them. Helen watched him caress Frederica's hand with his thumb.

Would she no longer be able to be Samuel's friend either?

Her brother-in-law annoyed her to no end, but she enjoyed spending time with him. His wit was as sharp as his sword and he played the most amusing pranks on members of the family. Herself included. And there was no dare too foolhardy that he wouldn't take it. That was something that hadn't changed about him since they'd all grown up.

Yawning, Helen laid her head on her mother's shoulder. Mama, not one for public displays of affection, surprisingly put her arm around Helen and allowed her to snuggle closer. Closing her eyes, Helen decided that even prickly hedgehogs could be good cuddlers. Yet she missed Becca. Her little sister would have been on her side. She would not have lectured or corrected Helen. She simply would have supported and loved her. But Becca wasn't there because Helen couldn't be trusted to behave properly. A fair, but unkind assessment of their mother's that Helen had no doubt reinforced by her dip in the Serpentine.

Her mother patted her back. 'Helen, it's the intermission, you need to wake up.'

Blinking, Helen realised that she had been sleeping on her mother's lap. Mama fussed with her hair and Frederica giggled.

Samuel laughed, too. 'I take it this is your favourite play.'

Shrugging, Helen smirked. 'You all know that I am not a night owl.'

The door to their box opened. Helen expected to see Wick or Matthew, but not the stork-like Lord Dutton, the gangly boy she'd danced with once because Lady Dutton had made him.

He bowed. 'I hope you do not mind my intrusion, but I have a friend from university who is eager to see you.'

Her eyes moved to the doorway where a young man stood wearing a fancy new suit of clothes. His teeth were flashing in a large smile. His light hair curled around his ears, which endearingly stuck out a little.

'Jason.'

# Chapter Eighteen

Helen held out her hands to Jason, remembering at the last moment that hugging him in a lit theatre box would lead to a scandal. The *ton* had altogether too many rules. He encompassed her hands into his larger, callused ones. They felt warm, familiar and safe. He was a part of her special world at Hampford Castle and Ashbury village. The one without rules and restrictions. He was entangled in every childhood memory. Running along with Becca and Frederica in the fields. Swimming in the river. And playing all the leading male parts in Frederica's home theatricals.

Jason released her hands to shake hands with Samuel.

'How are you, old friend?' Samuel asked.

Jason smiled. His mouth was made for smiles. 'Never better than I am now.'

He shook hands with Frederica, too, although bowing over her glove would have been more appropriate for a young gentleman. But in his defence, almost all his childhood punishments had resulted from following one of Frederica's diabolical plans.

Even Mama gave him a small smile. 'Jason, how well you look.'

He grinned back at her. 'I have never been to London before, Your Grace. It is more wonderful than I imagined.'

Her mother raised one eyebrow—she was really good at that. 'You prefer the city to the country?'

Jason continued grinning, unknowingly stepping directly into Mama's trap. 'I confess I do at this moment. The hustle and the bustle. The people and the places. One could live here for a hundred years and not have seen everything.'

'Have you thought of taking a parish in town?' her mother asked. 'I know the Bishop of London and I could put in a good word for you. He is always looking for bright young men to fill appointments here. But I am afraid that there is a great deal of poverty near the docks. Even more so than in a country village. You might find it disturbing, or disheartening.'

He grabbed her mother's hand and shook it vigorously. 'I should be ever so grateful if you did, Your Grace. And I have witnessed a small view of the suffering here, but isn't that what a vicar is supposed to do? *Lift up the hands that hang weary?* Spend his life serving the poor and the outcasts like our Saviour did?'

Helen didn't breathe again until Jason released her mother's hand. Unlike some men who picked the church as their profession, Jason truly meant what he said. He loved people. All people. He was as blind to their sins and flaws as Helen was to poisonous snakes. Jason would make a wonderful vicar in the city. He would willingly serve a streetsweeper as thoroughly as he would serve a duke. But Helen was marrying him to live near Hampford. She had no interest in residing with him in London.

She did not get another word with him before he left with Lord Dutton. They all took their seats for the remainder of the play. Helen did not lean on her mother's shoulder this time. She sat up, as straight as a giraffe's neck. She tried to keep her mind on the play, but she couldn't.

Leaning over, she whispered in her mother's ear, 'You did that on purpose, because I don't want to live in London.'

Mama didn't look at all chagrined. 'I have known Jason since he was in short coats. He has the sweetest temperament in the world and I believe he will do a great deal of good in his life. He's the sort of young man that gives one faith in the clergy.'

'He could do just as much good in a country parish.'

'Jason's father is still a young man. He would not be able to take his father's parish for many years and he deserves a better place than that of a curate, don't you think?'

Gritting her teeth, Helen exhaled. 'Of course he does... You and Papa could help him get a living anywhere in England, but you specifically chose a large city far away from Ashbury to spite me.'

'Or to suit him,' Mama said, patting Helen's hand.

She jerked her hand away from her mother and folded her arms. Keeping her eyes on the stage, she didn't look at her mother for the rest of the night. Not even on the carriage ride home. Climbing into her bed, she admitted to herself that Jason would probably prefer a city. The more people the better. The greater the poverty, the more he could help. The more sorrow, the more he could mourn with them. The more sin, the more he could try to save them. Failing that, he would love the sinner.

Covering her head with the bedspread, Helen knew that she couldn't live in London all year long even to be with Jason. The two months for the Season felt too long. She was not made for bricks and buildings, but for rocks and lakes. She would feel like one of Papa's animals that were too domesticated to be reintroduced to the wild, so they had to be kept in an enclosure. Caged in on all sides by rules and propriety.

\* \* \*

Mark sat up in bed when he heard scratching at his window. He was about to call his servants when he realised that it was most likely Helen. Only a fool of a thief would go into the master's rooms. Although most bedrooms were on the upper floors, not the ground floor. He heard two feet hit the wooden planking. Realising that he was not wearing his artificial leg, Mark pulled the coverlet higher over his chest. Not that any cover could hide the fact that there was only one leg bump on the bed. He dropped the blanket and fumbled to light a candle. Despite all his resolutions, he longed to see her beautiful face.

He held the candle up and saw her light blue eyes and long hair billowing over her shoulders. She was wearing a diaphanous nightgown with a robe over the top of it. Such thin garments left very little to the imagination and his mind needed no encouragement to think of her that way. Mark hadn't worn a nightshirt before losing his leg. He was profoundly grateful to be wearing one now or Helen's lesson in male anatomy would be complete.

'I'm so sorry to wake you up, Mark. I am so sorry for everything. I ruin whatever I touch. Including our friendship. I just didn't think before I went for that walk in the park. Can you please forgive me?'

Exhaling slowly, Mark nodded his head. 'I will forgive you, if you promise not to send any more potted plants. If you do, there will be no room to walk in my house.'

She smiled and touched the leaf of a plant that reached all the way to her shoulder. 'Isn't it nice to be surrounded by living things?'

'I am already surrounded by living things. My mother, aunt and cousin have arrived from Scotland.'

'How lovely. When are you going to introduce them to me?'

He gulped. As much as he was drawn to her, it would be better if they no longer met. 'I don't know if that is a good idea.'

He watched as she moved to the chair by his bed. She climbed on to the end of it and wrapped her arms around her knees.

His temperature rose to the same heat as his fever. Mark tried to calm his racing pulse and beating heart. Helen thought they were friends. She clearly didn't have many male friends or she would have known better than to sit near their beds. He supposed it was her innocence. She didn't know the terrible things that human beings could do to one another. The pain and terror of war. Blood and bodies. Smoke and sorrow. He prayed that she never would.

Helen's eyes swallowed him whole. She rocked back and forth in the chair, still holding her knees tight to her chest. He saw a twig caught in her hair, probably from climbing over the fence to his garden.

'I promise to behave myself—I really can, if I try hard. I know that I don't always behave like a proper lady, but I will be on my best behaviour. Both Samuel and Frederica said that you didn't want to see me again. I think they were trying to let me down gently—to explain that you hadn't gone into your back garden or met with me because you didn't wish to. But please, Mark, give me another chance to be your friend and meet your family. I won't muck it up. I promise. No snakes. No social solecisms. No pettish remarks. I will be a perfectly well-behaved young lady.'

Mark's lips twitched. He doubted Helen would or even could be a perfectly well-behaved debutante. She was right. There was an otherness, a feral sense about her. She was a wild thing that belonged in lakes and forests. Revelling in the forests. There was a wildness about the land of Scotland

that he thought she would love. But she would never come to his castle. She planned to marry her curate.

'My mother is very… Scottish,' he said slowly, trying to figure out how to politely say that his mother hated everything English. Especially the people. Her family had lost their home and lands for supporting the Jacobite cause against the English Crown.

'Excellent,' Helen said, smiling at him. 'My sister-in-law Nancy grew up in Scotland and speaks Gaelic. I could introduce them. I bet they would get along like jam and scones.'

Rubbing his eyes, Mark shook his head. 'My mother brought her niece. My cousin, Niamh, and my aunt. She is hoping to promote a match between us. Both my mother and my aunt would view our friendship as an impediment to the courtship.'

The smile fell from her face and, heaven help him, she scooted the chair closer to him. Mark couldn't decide if he was in paradise or purgatory. She was close enough to touch but impossible to hold on to.

'Are you courting your cousin?'

He couldn't resist leaning forward and pulling the twig from her hair. He watched as her eyes closed and she took a sharp inhale at his touch. 'I am not courting anyone. I don't plan to marry.'

'Good. Because my father says that cousins should never wed. It causes interbreeding and results in physical deformities in the children. Papa says that's why the royal family is such a disaster: because too many first cousins married each other and produced offspring.'

There was nothing humorous about the situation Mark found himself in, but he couldn't help but smile at her explanation of inheritance. Nor how quickly Helen had not liked the idea of him courting another woman.

'Friendship between a man and a woman is difficult,' he said, sighing. 'Society will always assume that there is more going on and I am sure that your curate would not like the fact that you kissed me.'

She took one of his hands in both of hers. 'But I was just making you warm the only way I could think of. The way an animal would. It was the logical thing to do.'

'We are not animals, Helen.'

Her fingers squeezed his hand tightly. 'I know. Or I might have eaten you after I kissed you.'

A laugh tore out of his throat. She would have made a very good female spider in another life.

She smiled at him. In the candlelight, he could see tears floating in her eyes. 'Were my kisses really that terrible? Is that why you've been avoiding me?'

'They were devastating.'

Helen sniffed.

His hand moved to her face and he gently wiped away a tear. 'I cannot be your friend, Helen.'

'Why not?'

Unable to stop himself, Mark leaned forward and brushed a kiss against her forehead. 'The problem is that I like you too much and I am too broken from the war. You should go, Helen.'

How much he wanted her to stay. Even if that meant being eaten after she had her way with him.

Nodding, she stood up and released his hand. Tears streaming down her face, she climbed back over the window sill and closed it behind her. Mark looked at the twig next to the lit candle. The flame still gave out light, but the room felt darker without Helen's presence in it. His life would feel the same way after she was gone.

# Chapter Nineteen

Sipping on her hot chocolate, Helen replayed the previous night in her mind. She knew that she had been breaking every rule of propriety going to Mark's house, but she had needed to speak with him. She'd missed him keenly and how she felt when she was with him. He made her feel as though she belonged with him and, if she was completely honest with herself, she missed touching him. A hand on his arm. A head on his shoulder. His mouth ravaging hers. His hands turning her skin into liquid flame. The need to be even closer to him.

Blushing, she shook away those thoughts.

Mark was her friend.

Who didn't want to be her friend because he liked her too much. Which seemed silly in the light of day. But then he had mentioned Jason and Helen felt a smidgeon of guilt. Jason was also her friend and she enjoyed being in his company, but she didn't have an overwhelming compulsion to touch him at every opportunity. Nor did she long to curl up in a ball on his chest like a snake and feel his warmth and the steady beat of his heart.

How could a person *like* someone too much?

Helen didn't like very many people at all. Aside from her own family, the list of people she actually liked wouldn't have taken all ten of her fingers.

Mark had called her kisses devastating. Could devastating be a good thing? Or was she missing some sort of social nuance that other people implicitly understood? Samuel and Frederica had talked to her about Mark as if she were a little child unable to comprehend the most basic of explanations.

*He doesn't want to be your friend any more.*

She needed to let him go. He liked her too much.

*Like*, Helen decided, was the most annoying word in the entire dictionary. She drained the rest of her hot chocolate and felt the warmth of the beverage spread throughout her body. Helen asked her lady's maid to bring out her blue day dress. It complimented her turquoise snake necklace—something too valuable to wear during the day, but she wanted to butter her grandfather up. She knew he *loved* her, but she wasn't entirely certain he would give her the money that she needed to purchase the publishing house.

Stepping down the stairs, she found Louisa and all three of her sons waiting for her. 'What are you doing here?'

'It's my day to enjoy time with you,' Louisa said, smiling as she patted her large stomach.

Helen was happy to see her sister-in-law, but she couldn't help a sigh. 'You're here to play nursemaid to me.'

Matt, the second son, pointed at Helen. 'You're in trouble.'

'You'll be in trouble if I catch you!'

She chased after him playfully and all her nephews shrieked and ran through the house. The first one she tagged was Grey, the eldest. At eight, he was still only to her shoulder. Turning around, she heard Miles's sweet little giggles from behind the velvet curtain. He was only two years old.

'Now, where could Miles be?'

The curtain shook with his laughter.

Helen opened the cabinet. 'Not in here.'

She slammed the door loudly and he shrieked with laughter. 'Not behind the sofa. Not underneath the table. Not inside the buffet. I suppose the only place left to look is behind the curtains.'

Miles's chortles were high and sweet.

Helen tore open the curtain. 'Found you!'

He tried to run around her, but she swooped him up in her arms and gave him a kiss on the forehead. He was still giggling when she set his little feet on the floor.

Picking up her skirts, she ran from room to room looking for Matt. He had flaming red hair like his mama, but his personality was just like the uncle he'd been named after. When she arrived at the kitchen, Helen was breathing heavily. She stood still for a moment to listen for noise. Unlike his little brother, Matt was not giggling loudly. But she could hear the sound of someone breathing. Walking as lightly as she could, she followed the steady breathing to the door of the pantry.

She opened both doors. 'Found you!'

Matt yelled and tried to duck and run around her. But Helen hadn't grown up with a bunch of wild animals and girls for nothing. She grabbed him around the middle and lifted his feet off the ground, growling. He was nearly six and quite unwieldy, but she spun him around anyway. His laugh was as loud and as high as his little brother before she set him down.

'Can we play hide and seek, Aunt Helen?' he asked, grinning up at her.

She raised her hands into claws and growled. 'One. Two. Three.'

He gave another shriek and ran from the kitchen. 'Helen's coming to find us. Hide!'

Helen counted loudly to thirty, before running back

through the house to find her three nephews. She'd grown up visiting their London house with her parents, so there wasn't a hiding place that she didn't know about. One by one, she found her nephews.

Matt pulled on her sleeve. 'Can we play again?'

Smiling down at him, she shook her head. 'I'm afraid not. We need to go to Great-Grandfather and Grandmother Stubbs's house.'

All three of her nephews grinned. Her grandparents spoiled their great-grandchildren rotten.

'And then we can play tag at the park,' she allowed, glancing at Louisa who was sitting in a chair beside them. 'That is if your mother approves.'

Louisa smiled. 'I think a little fresh air would be wonderful.'

Helen helped her nephews into their coats and hats, before they all bundled into the carriage and rode to Grandfather Stubbs's house.

It was in a less fashionable part of town, but the house was a great deal larger than Helen's home. They were met at the door, not by the butler, but by Grandmother Stubbs. She was a prim and proper woman. Not a white hair was out of place in her chignon and not a wrinkle could be found on her navy-blue dress. Her mouth was not smiling, but her eyes were.

She opened the door wide. 'I was wondering what to do with all our extra biscuits. I thought we'd have to feed them to the dogs.'

Matt raised his hand and jumped up and down. 'I'll eat them, Grandmother!'

'Me, too!' said Miles in his high, sweet voice.

Grey nodded.

'Come in! Come in!' Grandmother Stubbs said, almost

smiling. 'I might even have some chocolates and sweets that I need help with as well.'

All three boys pushed and shoved their way through the door and down the hall that led to the kitchen.

Louisa walked forward, taking Grandmother Stubbs's hands and kissed her cheek. 'It is always wonderful to see you, Grandmother.'

The older woman finally smiled. 'Then you should come more often. Perhaps we could help with the boys when the baby is born.'

'Wick and I would love that.'

Helen entered last. She tucked an errant curl behind her ear. She'd meant to be dressed properly and behave with perfect propriety. But she had forgotten about all of that while playing with her nephews. She didn't have a mirror, but she was certain that her hair was a mess and that the bottom of her dress was covered in dust from finding Grey in the attic. Or was it Matt in the cellar? Either way, Helen looked exactly like the heedless hoyden her grandmother didn't want her to be.

Stepping to the door, Helen bumped her face against her step-grandmother's cold cheek. 'Hello, Grandmama.'

There was no smile in her grandmother's eyes now. 'What is this I hear about you falling asleep during balls? And hiding in the library? Such behaviour will not do. You are a grown woman now.'

Helen nodded, not bothering to defend herself. She was here to beg for money. 'Where is Grandpapa?'

'He's in the library,' Grandmother Stubbs said and, if looks could turn people to stone, the stare she was giving to Helen would have turned her into granite. 'But perhaps you ought to freshen up before you see him.'

She gave her grandmother a stiff nod and went directly

to the retiring room. There was a mirror and she brushed out her hair and pinned it back up in a lose bun. Her maid's arrangement had long fallen out. Poor Cartwright! She did such an excellent job on Helen's hair and Helen always managed to destroy it. Helen also tried to wipe out the wrinkles in her skirt and a bit of the dirt. She wasn't successful.

Taking a deep breath, she left the room and headed to the library which was really an office for her grandfather. She knocked on the door.

'Come in!' he said from the other side of the wall.

Helen opened the door and ducked into the room. Grandfather was sitting behind his desk and she went around and kissed him on the head.

He laughed. 'Silly girl. I've heard you've been a handful.'

She plopped down on his desk, not bothering with a chair. 'Did Samuel come here, too, looking for me?'

'I think Samuel went to every single person who has ever spoken a word to you, trying to find you.'

Helen could only shrug her shoulders and sigh.

Grandfather shook his head. 'Disappearing like that was badly done, Helen.'

She slumped. 'I know. I wasn't thinking. I was so tired of the walls and balls and calls. I wanted a bit of fresh air.'

'You mean fresh rain? At least you could have chosen a sunny day.'

'You're right,' Helen said, a smile in her voice. 'One should always run away in excellent weather. No one would have been angry with me at all in that case.'

'But you didn't come to see me to talk about that,' he said. 'Why is it that you only visit when you want my money?'

'That is not true.'

Grandfather Stubbs gave her a look—it was warm and loving, and full of laughter. He might have had a point, she

admitted to herself reluctantly. The last few times she'd visited, he'd given her money for her part in the publishing of her book. He'd given her pin money, when she'd lost all of hers swimming in the river. And there was the little matter of bribing an animal keeper to release his employer's snakes into the wild.

Helen nodded slowly. 'You're right. I am a financial parasite.'

He smiled up at her and patted her hand. 'You are no more a parasite than you are a snake. Although you like to pretend that you are poisonous, I know that it is only a façade.'

'I have always been rotten to the core.'

Grandfather shook his head. 'You've always been misunderstood, like the slimy snakes that you love. People make judgements based on their appearance that have nothing to do with the creature's feelings… I read this manuscript by a rather brilliant naturalist. It was a guide to snakes and the author stated that snakes were not sly by nature, but shy.'

He was talking about her own writing. 'That must be a really good book.'

'I can't wait to see it in print, even though I've heard that it will cost me a pretty penny to do that.'

'Matthew told you already, didn't he?'

Grandfather nodded. 'Are you here to wheedle four thousand pounds out of me?'

'Yes.'

Hitting his knees with his palms, he laughed loudly. 'I've always adored your honesty, Helen.'

'So that's a yes, then?'

Her grandfather took a deep breath and exhaled. 'It's not a no.'

'You're being more confusing than Matthew with a pen and a stack of paper.'

'I am willing to invest four thousand pounds in a publishing company, on one condition.'

She leaned forward. 'And what's that?'

'Matthew told me that you were insistent that your name be on the book as the author. Your full, female name. Why is that?'

'Because I wrote it.'

He raised both eyebrows. 'No other reason?'

Helen chewed on her lower lip. 'Because humans silence their females far too often and it will never change unless brave women speak out. Write their names in books. Demand to be heard and treated as equals.'

'You think that women are equal to men?'

'Well, we are clearly their superior, but I don't wish to boast. Grandmother Stubbs would find it unseemly.'

Her grandfather laughed again, but sobered. 'So, I am to understand that the aim of the publishing company that you want to purchase is to give voices to other women?'

She swallowed. 'I—I hadn't thought that far.'

'You need to. Before I will invest a farthing in your company, I want you to write a statement of what your goal is as the owner. Then I want you to give me a detailed plan of how you intend to accomplish your statement. If it is a sound business plan, I will make you a gift of the money outright.'

'And if it's not?' Helen asked in a small voice.

Grandfather smiled at her fondly. 'My granddaughter will not fail.'

Helen slid off the desk, feeling decidedly less certain of success.

# Chapter Twenty

Mark was about to summon his carriage to go to his club. There was really no other place he could go to escape his family or their unrealistic expectations. He had tried shooting at Manton's with Pelford, but the sound of the gunshots brought back the trauma of the battle and the dead faces of friends. His wooden leg made both fencing and boxing too difficult. He would not be able to retain his balance or speed for attacking. He hadn't even ridden a horse since his leg was amputated. Helen had chided him for not even trying. She was fearless.

He called for his butler. 'Mr Greeley, can you see that one of the grooms hires me a riding hack? The calmer and older the horse, the better.'

'For your young cousin?'

Mark shook his head. 'No, for me.'

Mr Greeley bowed his way out of the room and Mark followed more slowly behind him. When he reached his room, he asked his valet to prepare his riding clothes.

His valet blinked, but showed no other sign of surprise. 'Very good, my lord.'

After changing, Mark made his way to the front of the house and rested until the groom arrived in front of his

house with a brown-and-white-spotted horse. His butler opened the door for him and handed Mark his hat. The hack was already saddled, but Mark could see the horse's age in its yellow eyes and slight sagging in his legs.

The groom holding the reins bowed to him. 'Would you like help into the saddle, my lord?'

Mark shook his head. 'No. Thank you.'

He limped purposefully towards the animal and first placed his wooden leg into the stirrup. Setting his hands on the horn of the pommel, he put weight on his severed limb and swung himself into the saddle. The horse stepped forward a little bit and Mark held tightly to the pommel to find his balance. Closing his eyes, he tried to find his core. It was harder with only half a leg and a wooden artificial appendage on one side. It threw off his equilibrium. But his thighs were still strong. He could grip the horse and stay in place with them. And his arms had grown stronger since he'd lost his leg. He had to use them to lift himself up and down and in and out of things.

Taking a breath, he accepted the reins from the groom. He dug one ankle into the horse's flesh, forgetting for the countless time that he was missing a second foot. Despite only feeling pressure on one side, the horse began to move forward. The groom had chosen well. Mark didn't think that this hack could have galloped without dying. But its slow pace and uneven shoulders were perfect for Mark's purpose.

As his body moved with the horse's, Mark realised how much he'd missed the freedom that could be found on the back of a horse. Carriages and buggies had to stick to roads, but a horse could go anywhere. Astride a horse, he didn't feel like less of a man. He felt almost whole.

Mark rode slowly through the city until he reached Hyde Park. It was nearly midday and the fashionable of the beau

monde would not be promenading for several hours yet. The serious riders would have gone earlier in the morning. Hyde Park was filled with children and nurses. He stayed on the paved path until he reached the turn before the Serpentine. There was no wading in its waters today.

No Helen.

He saw a young child run in front of his horse. Mark jerked on the reins to slow his animal and avoid the boy. Then a whirl of turquoise ran in front of him, scooping up the child and carrying him to safety. Her blonde hair hung unbound down her back, her usually pale skin flushed from her exertions. She wasn't wearing a habit or a spencer. Her boots were liberally covered in mud and in her arms was the little boy. He couldn't have been more than two or three years old. Helen looked beautifully maternal holding a child.

'Miles, you have to be more careful,' she chided. 'You can't run in front of horses.'

'Helen.' Her name was out of his lips before Mark could stop it.

She turned to look at him and her mouth opened like a rose.

'It's Aunt Helen,' the boy corrected.

'Forgive me. I mean, Aunt Helen,' Mark said gravely.

Helen set her nephew down and they both watched him run as fast as his little legs would take him to his mother, Lady Cheswick.

He sensed more than saw her, move closer to him. She touched his leg—right above where the artificial one met what was left of his flesh and bones. 'I think we both know that I am the one who should apologise. I shouldn't have come last night.'

Mark no longer felt embarrassed that she was touching

his wounded leg. He could only focus on the way her touch affected his heartbeat. His pulse. His temperature. He remembered her kisses in the carriage. How much his body wanted her. How much his mind missed her.

Had her embraces truly only been to warm him?

Or had she enjoyed the kisses as much as he did?

Had the memory of the embrace kept her up at night, like it had him? Was that why she had sneaked into his house to speak to him?

He covered her hand with his own, leaving only one hand on the reins. Something he couldn't have done even five minutes ago. But every moment he spent on a horse reminded his body how to ride. That he'd grown up with horses. His brother James had taught him.

Helen was not wearing gloves, but he could still feel the heat of her hand through his leather ones.

'Foolishly, I am glad that you did.'

She smiled at him and he felt hotter than ever. 'Then you'll be at Wick's party tonight? I know he sent you an invitation. Well, Louisa did because I asked her to.'

Mark vaguely remembered a card from the Cheswicks. 'I'm afraid that it would be bad manners to leave my family at home.'

'You should bring them with you. Wick won't mind. All London parties are squeezes after all. What's two or three more people among hundreds?'

Lady Cheswick came up to them and pulled Helen slightly away from Mark so that she was no longer holding his leg, severing the physical connection between them.

The very pregnant lady smiled at him. 'My sister-in-law is correct. My husband and I would only be too pleased if you came tonight with your family. We should all like to meet them.'

He tipped his hat. 'Then we shall be there, Lady Cheswick.'

Helen clapped. 'And you can meet Jason. He's come to town for a short visit.'

His heartbeat slowed. Mark didn't need to be reminded who Jason was. The cheery curate was the last person in the world that he wanted to meet, but he'd already verbally accepted Lady Cheswick's invitation. And he knew that Niamh would love to attend a glittering party of the *ton*. His mother and aunt as well. He would simply have to suffer through it.

Without glancing at Helen, he touched his hat once more. 'I look forward to seeing you all this evening.'

Lady Cheswick inclined her head. 'Tonight.'

Mark urged his horse to walk again. It was not a grand dramatic exit, but a slow plodding one.

# Chapter Twenty-One

'An invitation from the Marchioness of Cheswick!' his mother exclaimed. 'How very flattering.'

Niamh twirled around. 'I shall dance the entire night. Poor Mark. Too bad that you cannot dance any more.'

He had danced—once—after his amputation. With Helen. The world had even seemed to slow down for those precious moment she had been in his arms. She seemed to fit there. For once, he didn't feel the pain in his leg or the missing pieces of his soul.

But he was happy to have an excuse not to lead his cousin out for a set. 'Alas, I shall have to enjoy your talent from the side of the room.'

'Niamh could sit out a set with you,' his mother suggested.

Both he and his cousin said no at the same time.

Niamh laughed. 'Please don't take offence, but I do long to dance.'

He raised both arms into the air. 'None taken.'

Aunt Fiona beckoned her daughter with one hand. 'Come, Niamh! We must begin getting ready at once.'

Niamh skipped to her mother, taking her hand.

Mama smiled at the pair. 'I shall send your maids up at once. Perhaps we will receive more invitations after this evening.'

Mark hoped that there would be no more invitations to meet Helen's secret fiancé or to watch her dance with her two-legged suitor. A younger, whole, and happier man. It would be torture, like her night-time visits.

The hours had passed all too quickly.

Before he knew it, Mark was sitting in the carriage with his mother, aunt and cousin. They all wore new dresses and large feathers in their hair. The green plume in Niamh's hair kept tickling his cheek and nose. It made him want to sneeze.

When they entered the house, the only difference that he could see between his family and the other beau monde ladies were their expressions. The *ton* prided itself on not showing emotion or enthusiasm. The fashionable ladies all wore a bored expression the way they would a necklace.

Mark introduced his mother, aunt and cousin to Lord and Lady Cheswick. They smiled and welcomed them warmly.

Lady Cheswick gently touched Niamh's hair. 'Another redhead. We must stick together.'

Niamh beamed at her. 'Yes, my lady. I should like that above all things.'

'Perhaps I can introduce you to some eligible partners,' she said, smiling at his cousin and then his aunt. 'It is hard not to know many people at a party and you are far too pretty to be a wallflower.'

His cousin naively agreed with her.

Lord Cheswick's lips twitched, but he was all politeness. He nodded. 'Inverness.'

Mark had only two arms, so his mother insisted that he escort his aunt and cousin. The ballroom was already crowded and a few brave couples were dancing. Including Helen. She was paired with a tall, fair young man. He was as young as she, his face open and happy. He didn't

carry the wrinkles of experience or the scars of the dead. He was as light and bright as she. He was the sort of man Helen deserved.

Yet, watching *her* dance with *him* was like experiencing Waterloo all over again. The dead and empty feeling in his chest returned.

The music ended and he watched Helen lead her cheery curate over to where he was standing with his family.

Mark bowed and spoke before she could. 'Lady Helen, it is a pleasure to see you. May I introduce you to my family?'

A smile lit up her face. She wore a white gossamer dress and with the diamond tiara in her nearly white curls, she looked more like a fairy queen than ever. She curtsied. 'I should be delighted to make their acquaintance.'

'Mama, may I present Lady Helen Stringham, daughter of the Duke of Hampford? Lady Helen, my mother, Lady Inverness, my aunt, Mrs Campbell, and my cousin, Miss Campbell.'

Helen curtsied again. 'It's truly a privilege to meet your family and please allow me to introduce my friend, Mr Robertson.'

His mother gave Helen a cautious smile as if waiting for her snub.

The cheery curate grinned at his family and Niamh smiled right back. 'The privilege is all mine.'

The orchestra began to play a lively country tune. He watched Niamh tap her foot to the tune.

'Mr Robertson, do you know the Roger de Coverley?' Mark asked.

'Helen and Becca taught me,' he said, then blushed. 'I mean, uh, Lady Helen and, uh, Lady Rebecca taught me.'

'May I suggest my cousin as an excellent partner?'

The cheery curate smiled at Niamh. There was nothing

leering in it. Nothing but good humour and the joy of living. How he despised this young man!

Mr Robertson held out his palm. 'I should be most honoured if you'd accept my hand in this set, Miss Campbell.'

Niamh quickly placed hers inside it and bounced away with him. He was starting to believe that his cousin never walked. She bounced or skipped wherever she wished to go. It spoke to her youth and to her energy.

He felt Helen move to his side, her shoulder brushing his before she placed her arm on his. Mark didn't think she even realised that she had done it. Her eyes were on his mother. 'Did you have a pleasant journey from Scotland?'

'Pleasant enough,' his mother said tersely.

Helen turned her attention to his aunt. 'And you, Mrs Campbell?'

'Tolerable.'

Mark sincerely hoped that Helen would realise that his mother and aunt were not being unfriendly, they were simply overawed by who she was.

'And are you enjoying London?' Helen asked. 'Where has Mark taken you so far?'

His mother's mouth dropped open at her use of his given name. For once, he wished that Helen would have behaved more formally. Despite knowing that she would never be his, he wanted her to make a good impression on his mother. His family.

But his aunt smiled. 'Oh, so many places. We've been to St Paul's Cathedral. To see the Elgin Marbles. The National Gallery and the Crown Jewels at the Tower of London.'

'Oh, I love the animal menagerie,' Helen said, smiling. 'Did Mark take you to see the reptiles? The rattlesnake is my favourite.'

'He did indeed,' his mother said, her expression growing even colder.

Helen touched the turquoise snake necklace around her delicate throat. 'I love snakes. Mark was kind enough to do some illustrations for my book that will be published at the end of this month. The woodcutter is frantically recreating his sketches for the wood blocks, so that they may be printed in bulk.'

'You wrote a book, Lady Helen?' Aunt Fiona asked. 'Is it a work of fiction? Like those lovely Gothic tales by Mrs Radcliffe that you sent me, Mark. I quite enjoyed them all, but *The Romance of the Forest* was my favourite.'

'Mine as well,' he agreed.

She shook her head. He could feel her curls brushing his shoulder. 'No. My book is not fictional. It is a guide to snakes.'

His aunt gave a full body shudder and he couldn't blame her. 'I am afraid that I am not very fond of snakes. Most books that I read are romances.'

'Or mysteries,' Mark added.

'Really?' Helen said, appearing fascinated by his aunt's words. She squeezed his arm even tighter, pressing closer to him. 'What other books do you find of interest?'

Aunt Fiona blushed and her hands fidgeted against her dress. 'I suppose a fine young lady like yourself wouldn't have much use for cookbooks, but I like to read through them and give ideas to our chef. I've collected over three thousand recipes. I'm also fond of reading fashion magazines and seeing the latest fashion plates from Paris and London.'

Helen leaned her head against his shoulder, moving her upper body closer to his aunt. Setting his body on fire. 'What sort of recipes, if I may ask?'

Tittering, his aunt blushed as red as her daughter's hair. 'French recipes, my lady. A French chef is quite beyond our means, but that doesn't mean their delicacies must be.'

Mark smiled reassuringly at his flustered aunt. 'How clever of you.'

Helen nodded her head sharply. 'Truly, that is brilliant. I cannot thank you enough for your answers. You have been a great deal of help to me.'

His mother sniffed, her teeth clenched. 'I do not understand the turn of your questions, Lady Helen. Surely our reading habits are of no interest to a young lady like yourself.'

'Oh, but they are. For you see, I am about to purchase a publishing company and I want it to cater to women. I mean—I want to publish female voices. I want to give women the sort of reading material that they are craving. The market has been too long dominated by the male species.'

Mark couldn't help but grin at Helen's enthusiasm as his mother scowled. 'It seems most improper for a young lady, even the daughter of a duke, to be involved in trade.'

*Proper* wasn't the best word to describe Helen, but Mark tried to intervene. 'Understanding a species and natural science well enough to write a book about it is quite an impressive accomplishment. For a man or a woman.'

Helen squeezed his arm again. She held him tighter than an octopus with eight tentacles. 'Thank you, Mark. I worked very hard on it. But to your point, Lady Inverness, I am also the daughter of a duchess and my mother owns a very successful perfume company. With the help of my sister Frederica, who is also a duchess, they have expanded their offerings to scented soaps. Have you been to Duchess & Company on Bond Street? That's her main shop,

but she exports her bottles to all of Europe. She's hoping to expand her wares to the Americas. Would you like to meet my mother?'

'The Duchess?' Aunt Fiona repeated, awe in every syllable of her strong Scottish accent. 'We would. We would very much like to meet her.'

Helen could only smile at Mrs Campbell. She was a great deal more agreeable than Mark's mother. That woman was as cold as a castle. And the niece, Miss Campbell, didn't seem to be interested in Mark at all romantically. She'd rushed off to dance with the closest young man in her vicinity. It had been Jason, but Helen did not feel even a hint of jealousy. Something that rather surprised her, for she had a possessive nature.

Still holding Mark's arm, she led them around the edge of the room to where her mother stood talking to someone. She tapped on her shoulder. It wasn't difficult to recognise her mother from the backside. She was taller than most women and had the bearing of royalty.

Mama glanced over her shoulder. 'Helen?'

She gasped when she recognised *who* her mother was talking to. Letting go of Mark, she dipped into a deep curtsy. 'Your Royal Highness. Please forgive me for interrupting.'

Helen gulped and looked up.

The Prince Regent smiled at her. 'You could never be an interruption. You're my favourite goddaughter after all, Lady Frederica.'

She did not need the glare from her mother to know that she should not correct royalty. She was used to being called by her sister's name, although they did not look anything alike. Nor were their personalities similar, besides the fact that neither of them followed societies many rules.

Prinny's eyes went past her to Mark, then to his mother and his generously voluptuous aunt. The Prince Regent's smile widened and his watery eyes narrowed. 'Lady Frederica, do introduce me to your friends.'

Bowing her head, Helen said, 'Your Royal Highness, Mama, please allow me to introduce Lord Inverness, his mother, Lady Inverness, and his aunt, Mrs Campbell.'

They all curtsied and bowed to the ruling monarch. Mark's mother's face grew even whiter and colder. Mrs Campbell's merry pink cheeks turned an attractive red. She giggled and smiled at the Prince Regent.

Prinny's eyes never left Mrs Campbell's face and figure. He was nearly salivating at this point. He held out his hand. 'Mrs Campbell, I believe this is a waltz. Would you do the honour of dancing it with me?'

Mrs Campbell's hand practically slapped Prinny's, she placed it in his so quickly. Helen couldn't help but smile wryly. Mark's matronly aunt was precisely the Prince Regent's *type*.

Prinny gave them one last smile over his shoulder and a nod of his head. 'Selina, Lady Frederica.'

Mama returned the gesture regally. Then she placed on a polite smile as she looked at Lady Inverness. 'I can see why Helen was in such a hurry to introduce us. Your son has become an invaluable friend to her. To us all.'

Lady Inverness did not return the smile. 'So it would seem. But I am not sure it is wise for my son to befriend a young lady who owns a publishing company.'

Her mother could not hide her surprise this time. Her eyes nearly popped out of her head. 'You own a publishing company? When did this happen, Helen?'

Instinctively, she leaned against Mark for support. 'I don't actually own a publishing company. I mean not yet.

Grandfather is going to give me the money once I form a viable business plan. Matthew has already written the contract and one of the editing partners has signed it. Once the other partner signs and there has been a transfer of funds, I will then own a publishing company.'

Mama took a deep breath, her polite countenance back in place. 'We shall discuss this later. Lady Inverness, might I introduce you to a few select friends? I don't recall you coming to London before.'

'One time was enough.'

Her mother nodded, ignoring the sharp tone in Lady Inverness's voice. 'Yes. Well, I am sure you would enjoy Lady Jersey's company. Perhaps she could give you and your niece vouchers to Almack's Assembly?'

'It's a very select club,' Helen added, not entirely sure that the Scottish matron would know the significance of the voucher. 'Only the highest of the *ton* are included in its numbers. It's quite an honour to receive one.'

Lady Inverness nodded and followed her mother.

Helen turned to Mark who was strangely quiet during the exchange. He really had the most handsome profile. 'Well, are you going to ask me to dance, or shall we stand foolishly beside each other on the side?'

His jaw tightened. 'I don't wish to make a scene, Helen.'

'Then don't.'

She released his arm and held out her hand to him. 'Waltz with me again. We shall stick to our own little corner and not bother another couple.'

It seemed like a full five minutes before Mark took her hand. It was probably less. It had to be less. Surely they hadn't stood looking into each other's eyes for that long, with her hand outstretched between them?

Mark folded her into his arms and Helen's heart raced.

She loved the feel of his touch on her back. His tight grip on her hand. The way their bodies swayed together slowly to the music. They may have been waltzing at a snail's pace, but every step was correct. She didn't doubt that before he'd lost his leg, he'd been an accomplished dancer. Her heart ached for his loss, but she wouldn't have changed anything about him. She cared for him just the way he was.

Closing her eyes, she marvelled at being in his arms. Touching him today at the park had not been nearly enough. She had not been able to smell his scent of leather, tobacco and peppermint. Or feel his gentle breath on her cheeks. The connection between them was primal—animal. Something she did not quite understand but couldn't let go. Somehow, he made her feel both safe and excited at the same time. Being near him caused her pulse to double and her heart to beat twice as fast. She'd never experienced this feeling before. This compelling need to touch. To be near another. It was as unsettling as it was essential.

'Have you gone asleep on me again at a ball?' Mark asked, a tender note in his voice.

Helen shook her head, opening her eyes. 'Do you not find that all five senses are sometimes too much? That you have to remove one, to better understand and experience the others?'

'Were you dreaming of dancing with Jason?'

She shook her head, moving closer to his chest. She stood so near to him that a feather could barely have fit between them. 'Of course not. You fill my senses, Mark. I was wishing this waltz would never end.'

'All good things must end.'

Helen gripped his shoulder tighter. 'Why must they?'

He released her and stepped back. 'Because the music

stops and the world starts up again. And no matter how much you want something, you can't always have it.'

They stood looking at each other. Unmoving. Helen's feet could not walk away, nor could her eyes turn from Mark.

'Oh, there you are, Helen,' Jason said, taking her elbow. 'Did you forget that I was your partner for the supper dance?'

She shook her head and forced herself to smile at him. She loved Jason. She had always cared about him. Her friendship with Mark had nothing to do with that. They were completely separate things. Taking his hand, she allowed him to lead her to the centre of the dance floor, instead of a corner, and they danced a Scottish jig. Helen saw Niamh with Lord Dutton. They were both short, redhaired, and looking extremely pleased with their partners.

Jason placed his hand on her waist and led her through the promenade. His touch felt comfortable.

Familiar.

But it did not excite her senses like Mark's had.

# *Chapter Twenty-Two*

Walking into Tattersall's, Mark felt as if every eye in the famous horse club was on him. He didn't want to ride a hack, but his own horse. He was done with hiding from life. He was a one-legged man, but he was still a man. Helen had shown Mark that he wasn't any less a person because of his injuries. Besides, his brother had taught him how to be a fine horseman and a good driver of a team of horses.

'What can I help you with today, guvnor?' a groom asked.

Mark took off his hat. 'I should like to buy a horse for my personal use, a phaeton and a matched pair.'

The man smiled. 'You've come to the right place. Lord Brunswick is selling his phaeton and pair. There will be an auction in a couple of hours, but you could look the chestnuts over now and see if you're interested.'

'I am interested.'

Mark followed the young man through a maze of stalls until he reached where two fine, thoroughbred chestnuts were housed. They had deep chests and fine shoulders. Mark took a comb from the groom and gently brushed each horse's fur.

'Do you know why Lord Brunswick is selling his horses?'

The groom shrugged. 'Rumour is that he lost a race with

'em. But I think it weren't the horses' fault. His lordship is ham-handed with the reins, he is.'

'I haven't driven a curricle in pair in over two years,' Mark admitted. 'I might be ham-handed now too.'

'I doubt that, guvnor. I can tell by how youse touch them, that you'd be soft with their mouths.'

Mark nodded, moving to stand in front of the horses. He touched the first's jaw and it was perfectly fine, but the second horse's mouth was full of sores. The groom had been right. Lord Brunswick had ruined one of the horses' mouths. The matched pair was not worth what they might have been.

'You've seen it then, guvnor.'

'Is Lord Brunswick hoping to gull some fool into paying more than they should?'

'His lordship dropped nearly sixteen hundred pounds purchasing them last year.'

Mark let out a low whistle and petted the injured horse's mane, before limping out of the stall.

'I suppose you ain't interested now.'

He shrugged his shoulders. 'For the right price, I am. I don't believe that an injury should stop a glorious animal from running.'

'You're a poet, guvnor.'

'Or a fool.'

The groom shook his head, laughing. 'You're a downy one. I didn't spot it up front, but you are, guvnor.'

'Then show me the best horseflesh for my new mount.'

Helen did not have a subscription to the lending library, but Frederica did. Fortunately, it was Frederica's day to play nursemaid. She pulled her sister by the hand into the library. The familiar and lovely smell of leather and paper met her

nose—with a hint of dust. Tugging her sister to the desk, she found an older man standing behind it. His glasses were small and round and enlarged his brown eyes. His face was round, too, and he had a friendly smile.

The clerk bowed to Frederica. 'Your Grace.'

Helen huffed. It didn't matter that Frederica was a duchess now. She was still just her sister and often behaved insufferably.

'Mr Stafford, always a pleasure to visit your library. My sister, Lady Helen, was hoping to speak to you about the most popular books that you lend out.'

His hand covered his log book, as if to protect it from roving eyes. 'What people check out is their own business, Your Grace.'

'Oh, no,' Helen said, stepping forward. 'I don't care who selects the books. I am simply wondering what titles and sorts of books ladies typically choose. I don't need any names.'

'Let's start with me,' Frederica said, smiling at the smaller man. 'I borrow and return at least a dozen novels every fortnight. I love adventure and romance.'

The clerk nodded. 'Fiction is very popular, especially among younger ladies. Elderly ladies typically borrow books on household hints and medicinal herbs. Chaperons and governesses always take the decorum books and the peerages. Gentlemen often borrow the classics and scientific books.'

Helen sniffed. Ladies could also be interested in science and very good at it. 'Do you lend any books on fashion?'

He shook his head. 'Nay. It changes too frequently, my lady, to be printed in a book.'

The clerk *did* have a point.

Any lady of the *ton* had a new wardrobe for every Sea-

son. No matron or miss would be caught dead in last year's fashions. If Helen wanted to publish something on fashion, a monthly magazine or a quarterly journal would be a better choice. Something smaller and cheaper that she could create quickly and change often.

She thought of Mrs Campbell's fascination with cookbooks. 'Do you lend out many cookbooks?'

Mr Stafford shook his head again, his round glasses slipping to the end of his nose. 'My clientele is a select group... The sort that doesn't do their own cooking. They have servants for such things.'

'Of course. Thank you, Mr Stafford,' Helen said. 'Shall we go, Frederica?'

Her sister shook her head. 'Not before I find some new books to read. I didn't take you here merely to help. I am all out of reading material.'

Helen scanned the shelves and noticed that there were rarely two copies of any title. The lending library had gone for diversity more than quantity.

Frederica huffed. 'It is as I feared. Not one of Mrs Radcliffe's books are in. They seem to always be out when I come.'

'And she writes...?'

'Gothic romances. Innocent young maidens kept in dark, isolated castles by evil counts and a few ghosts and spectres.'

Helen rolled her eyes. What nonsense! But if her books were never on the lending library's shelves, then they must be very popular. She would have to develop a taste for such books.

'Why do you borrow books, instead of buying them?'

Frederica smiled. 'I'm not much of a re-reader. I am one and done, as I tell Samuel. Once I know how a story ends,

I don't care to read it again. I should infinitely prefer a great variety of books by borrowing them from the lending library for a specific fee instead of purchasing only a couple of books bound in leather for the same price.'

'So, cost is a deterrent for you?'

Her sister blushed, a rare sign of embarrassment. 'Money is still tight from Samuel's father's debts. We try to be as money conscious as we can be. That's why we decided to stay with Mama for the Season. It was much cheaper than letting a furnished house.'

Helen was glad that Frederica and Samuel and Arthur were staying with them. The London house would have been quite lonely with only her and Mama. But her mind had swivelled from the original topic—Frederica loved Gothic novels, but she couldn't afford to purchase them.

'A penny for your thoughts?' a voice said behind her. She didn't need to turn around to know that it was Mark.

'My thoughts are worth at least a shilling,' she said, spinning around, and without thinking, she threw herself into his arms and hugged him tightly. 'I didn't expect to see you today. At a lending library of all places.'

Mark stumbled back a few steps as if her embrace had thrown off his balance. Helen clung to him tightly, unable and unwilling to let go. He smelled wonderful. Of leather and starch and musk. She wanted to rub her face into his jacket and burrow into his shirt. His heartbeat was loud and strong. His arms tight around her. The feeling of belonging there was stronger than ever before.

'Release Lord Inverness, Helen,' Frederica said from behind her. 'England does not wish for another war with Scotland.'

Recalling herself, Helen let go of Mark. She felt the blood rush to her face. Frederica shook her head, frown-

ing. How could Helen have let her surprise at seeing him allow her to behave in so unseemly a manner? She knew very well that she shouldn't be embracing unmarried earls in the middle of a London lending library. It was not only scandalous, but ruinous. And she had promised Mark that she would no longer behave rashly. Yet despite Helen nearly knocking him over, he had not pushed her away. He had returned her embrace and even now his eyes were smiling at her.

Touching the back of her neck, Helen said, 'England formally apologises to Scotland for its exuberant welcome. Are you still interested in my thoughts? I am now willing to sell them for only a penny.'

Frederica harrumphed. 'You'd have to pay me more than a penny to listen to them. I shall go and look for new books, but please remember to behave yourself. I'll have one eye on you and both ears.'

Helen waited for her sister to walk down to a shelf on the other side of the aisle before she spoke to him. 'I came with Frederica to get ideas for my publishing company. My grandfather won't give me the money for it until I have a business plan.'

His lips upturned. 'And that is why you were asking my aunt about her reading preferences. You are hoping to create a business plan that markets books specifically to women.'

She shifted her feet from one foot to the other. 'Yes, I would like to give more women the opportunity to write and read books. But I am not sure that is a feasible business plan. Many women don't have sufficient means to purchase books. Frederica prefers to borrow them like yourself. I'm not sure it would be profitable enough.'

Mark nodded. 'It would be hard to predict.'

'May I ask why you go to a lending library?'

'I rarely read the same book twice,' he admitted, leaning towards her. 'I like the variety it offers for only a monthly fee.'

She felt herself moving closer to him, until she was close enough again to smell the starch on his collar. 'So you don't wish to own a book because you won't read it more than once.'

He swallowed. 'Except for your book on snakes. I have every intention of purchasing a copy and reading it multiple times.'

She gave him a playful swat on the shoulder. 'You're just saying that because I am the author of the book.'

Mark grinned at her and a warmth spread inside her from her chest outwards. Her belly fluttered and the need to be near him overwhelmed her. Why did he have this effect upon her? Yes, he was handsome, tall, melancholy and absolutely wonderful. But Jason was tall and handsome, too, even wonderful in his own way. Yet she did not feel the need to touch him whenever they met, or the desire to press herself against his body.

Helen contented herself by merely intertwining her arm with his. Not even Frederica could object to that. 'I am to understand that you don't want to spend a great deal of money on the purchase of a book that you will only read once.'

'Particularly Gothic stories,' he said, placing his opposite hand over hers, his thumb caressing her fingers through the glove. 'Once you know the ending the rest of the story is less exciting.'

She pondered this. 'If, perchance, you could purchase a ghost story that isn't leatherbound, would you buy one that is made of only paper and much shorter than a three-volume novel? A penny for *your* thoughts.'

'If the book were only a penny, I think that anyone could afford it.'

Helen knew that wasn't strictly true. But she couldn't help but realise that inexpensive paper and printing would make books available to the general masses. Few could spend the cost of a leatherbound book. Only the gentry and the aristocracy could afford to have private libraries. The price of publishing made reading truly a privilege granted primarily to the wealthy. Particularly, wealthy men. The publishing sector of London only served a fraction of the entire population.

If she could produce a less expensive product and increase its circulation dramatically, she would reach an entirely new audience. The middle classes. The lower classes. Women.

'Are you all right, Helen?' he asked. 'Your eyes glazed over.'

Helen met Mark's gaze as she whispered, 'Penny press.'

His head leaned closer to hers. 'What did you say?'

'A penny press,' she repeated. 'I could publish short stories and magazines that cost only one penny. Then women could afford them. Working-class men or even the middle classes would be able to purchase them.'

Mark eyes widened as he thought over her idea.

'You're brilliant, Helen. I am sure your grandfather will approve of your idea. You are going to change the publishing world.'

His words made her heart soar, but she felt as if she'd been bitten by a poisonous adder. She couldn't move. She couldn't think. She didn't want to leave his side. They stood together without speaking a word, his eyes holding hers as if she were hypnotised. She didn't even hear Frederica's steps towards them.

Her sister took Helen's free arm and pulled her away from Mark. 'We can go now. I have a whole stack of new books to read. Good day, Lord Inverness.'

'I must go home,' Helen said, her gaze falling to her fumbling hands.

One of Mark's gloved hands caressed her cheek. 'You must, for you have a business proposal to write for your grandfather.'

Frederica dragged her out of the lending library. Her cheek burned from where he had touched her. Helen realised that she, too, liked him too much. But she couldn't be a countess or a socicty hostess. She couldn't be the wife he needed.

# Chapter Twenty-Three

Mark had taken his cousin to Astley's Amphitheatre and then to Gunter's for ices the day before, after being bowled over by Helen in the lending library. He was looking forward to an afternoon playing cards at White's. Pelford had put his name up for membership earlier that week and he had been universally accepted. The young Duke had also introduced him to several of his friends, who seemed happy to include Mark in their circle. These men would never take the place of the Highlanders who died at Waterloo, but they had offered him friendship. A new start.

As he walked to the door, his mother stood in front of it, blocking his way. She seemed to have a sixth sense as to when he was trying to escape.

'Where are you going?'

Mark felt like a child of seven, rather than a man of seven and twenty. 'I am going to my club.'

His mother shook her head. 'You cannot. I have already promised Niamh that you will take her driving in the park.'

He grinded his teeth. 'Mama, I will take my cousin driving today. But in future, I will not allow you to make plans for me. I am a grown man.'

'Then act like one. Propose to your cousin. Provide an heir for the earldom. Then we can go back home and leave

these rotten *sassenachs*. We're Scottish. We don't belong among them.'

'But I do, Mama. Despite you and Father making me feel as if I don't belong anywhere. Papa wanted me to be English. You wanted me to be Scottish. And I am both. I enjoy London and Edinburgh. I am excited to go home at the end of the Season to Castle Inverness and get to know my land and my tenants better.'

'You will need a wife.'

The idea of marriage no longer terrified him. 'It will not be my cousin.'

His mother folded her arms and gave him a cold glare. 'You've become too fine for a bonnie, Scottish lass?'

'She's barely more than a child.'

'Niamh has many childbearing years in her. It would bring our family closer together.'

'I don't want a broodmare. When I marry, I want a wife to spend the rest of my life with. A companion and equal.'

His mother slapped him across the cheek. She'd never struck him before and he was surprised how much it stung. 'Will you and your English lady wife toss me out of the house once you're married? Because I am old and common and Scottish? Will you push me aside like your father did, after he spent all my dowry?'

Rubbing his cheek, he shook his head. 'I have no English lady wife and even if I did, I would never ask you to leave. You are my mother and I love you. But I am a grown man and you need to treat me as such.'

Her hands clung together as if she were in fervent prayer. 'I'm afraid of losing you entirely, like I lost Jamie. My boy Marky did not come back from the wars. It was as though you were a stranger with my son's handsome face. I could

barely look at you. You'd changed so much. I didn't know who you were any more. You weren't my boy.'

Mark set his hands gently on her shoulders. 'A man came back in his place, Mama. Scarred and broken, but still strong.'

She placed her hands on top of his. Tears began to run freely down her cheeks. 'I ken I don't belong in this world. Your world.'

'Maybe you could, if you gave it another chance. Aunt Fiona danced with the Prince Regent, for goodness sake. You mingled with duchesses. Did any of them treat you with disrespect? Did any of them snub you like Father's family does?'

His mother shook her head. 'I barely said a word. I dinnae want to disgrace you.'

'Papa was the disgrace. How he separated all of us was a disgrace. But he is gone now. We don't have to live like he wanted us to. I am not ashamed of you. I will never be ashamed of you. And I hope some day that you will no longer be ashamed that I have only one leg.'

She nodded, tears still streaming down her cheeks.

Niamh came skipping down the hall. 'What's the matter, Aunt Merida?'

His mother wiped at her eyes with her hands. Mark pulled out his handkerchief and gave it to her.

She sniffed into it. 'Mark is ready to drive you to the park.'

Niamh jumped up and down. 'I am so excited! Shall I fetch my bonnet?'

Mark forced himself to smile. 'Yes.'

His cousin bounced back down the hall.

His mother called after her, 'Don't forget a spencer and parasol! The English sun is a wee devil.'

'And the Scottish sun is different than the English one?'

She patted the same cheek that she had slapped. 'Of course, it is…and I love you, Son. Truly. I always have and I dinnae care about your leg, you eejit. I care about you.'

Mark laughed. Trust his crabbit mother to make *idiot* a term of endearment.

He helped Niamh into his new phaeton. She was looking very pretty and pleased with herself in a new yellow spencer with a matching chipped bonnet. 'Do you think we'll see many people out at the park?'

She meant suitors.

Mark smiled. 'Yes. This time of the day is called the promenade and we will see a great many bucks of the first stare.'

Giggling, Niamh blushed. 'It is not that I don't like you, Cousin Mark. It's just that—'

He was a scarred, one-legged man in love with another woman. 'We are cousins, Niamh. Please allow me to introduce you to some of my new English friends.'

'And do they have titles?'

'Some of them,' he assured her as he gently led his new team of chestnuts through the many streets to Hyde Park. Mark was very easy with the reins. He had to let his horses' mouths fully heal. He'd learned from his own recovery that if you tried to go back to normal too quickly, you would inevitably do more harm than good to your body. And despite living with chronic pain, he was a hale and hardy man. He might be changed, but he would be a better husband than his father ever was.

Mark pulled up his carriage near several acquaintances and introduced them to his cousin. But it was Niamh who first spotted Helen and waved merrily to her. She was dressed in a crimson pelisse with military-style buttons and braiding. Her matching bonnet and feather were similar

to a soldier's hat. The bright hue complimented her natural colouring. Helen was walking with her sister, the Duchess of Glastonbury, and a group of friends including the young Lord Dutton. Manoeuvring the horses, Mark brought his phaeton over to the party.

Once he was to a stop, Niamh jumped out of the phaeton and practically into the arms of Lord Dutton. Turning her head, she gave him her excuses. 'I hope you don't mind me walking for a little bit, Cousin Mark.'

'Not at all.'

'If you should like, Miss Campbell,' the Duchess of Glastonbury said with a friendly smile, 'I can chaperon you and see you safely home. There is nothing quite like exercise.'

Niamh was all smiles to be escorted by a duchess. She readily agreed, leaving Mark alone in the phaeton. His eyes fell to Helen, whose cheeks were now a bright shade of red that rivalled her pelisse. Maybe his love for her was not hopeless. She had not been indifferent to him at the lending library. Quite the reverse. And he would be a fool if he let her go to the curate so easily. He was a soldier and he would fight for what he wanted. And this was a battle he could not bear to lose, but his attacks had to be subtle.

'Lady Helen,' he said. 'You look a little tired. May I give you a lift home?'

A smile slowly built on her lips and his pulse quickened. He longed to kiss her mouth again. She didn't hesitate, but held out her hand for him to help her up into the carriage. 'Please, my lord. I should be most appreciative.'

It was not a strain upon him at all to pull her up beside him. Helen, in typical Helen fashion, sat right beside him, the side of her entire body meeting with his. Mark was certain that his own face would be the same cherry red if he

stayed there much longer. He touched his hat to the Duchess of Glastonbury and urged his horses forward. He felt Helen linking her arm with his, eager to be close to him. She was too innocent and untried to understand that it was attraction between them and not friendship. Or that it was friendship that had turned into an intense attraction.

'I told my mother that I was not going to court, Niamh,' Mark said, measuring his words carefully. 'There is a difference between loving someone, like a cousin or a close friend, and being *in love* with someone. You can have warm feelings and care for another person, but being *in love* includes those warm feelings and a physical desire to become one with them.'

Mark didn't think that Helen was *in love* with her curate. If she had been, she would not seek out his company, nor would she long to touch him. He tried not to remember her wild kisses in the carriage. Or think about how much he'd like to become one with her.

He glanced down as she bit her lower lip, making it red and desirable. He wished to suck on it.

Shaking her head, Helen said, 'I've never thought of it that way. How one loves a family member is different than how one loves a mate.'

'The English language unfortunately uses the same word for all kinds of love, but Latin has four different ones. *Storge*, which is a bond of empathy between people. The love between friends is called *philia*. *Agape* is the love of God. And lastly, *eros* refers to romantic love.'

Mark tipped his hat to an acquaintance and Helen sat beside him, unusually quiet. He hoped that she would realise that his words were not idle conversation, nor something he wished to share with her, but that he was trying to explain his own heart and possibly hers. Friendship was

not a bad foundation for marriage, but it could not take the place of desire.

She cleared her throat. 'Do you think it is possible to love someone in multiple ways? To feel empathy, friendship and romantic love?'

'Yes, I do. I think the most wonderful and enduring love between two people would have all three,' he said, gazing into her light blue eyes. 'I hope to know such a love in my lifetime.'

Dropping her eyes to her lap, Helen added quietly, 'I think we all do. Anything less would be disappointing— no, *devastating.*'

The same word he had used to describe his feelings for her. Mark longed to speak more plainly, but he thought that Helen might be as skittish as his new pair of horses. He could only gently lead her towards a new idea or she would rebel against him. Glancing down at her face, he saw that she was in deep contemplation.

He watched her wave to several acquaintances as they nearly completed their circuit of the park. A man on horseback rode up beside Helen. He had fair hair, a crooked nose and was dressed to the nines. The man couldn't have been much older than himself and smiled at Helen in a familiar way that irritated Mark to no end. His countenance wasn't precisely handsome, but there was something appealing about his easy manners.

'Helen, my snake charmer, what have you done with your keeper?'

Mark gritted his teeth. The man called her by her given name.

She let out a gurgle of laughter. 'You mean my minder, Sunny. I should have known you didn't wish to speak to me, but to find Mantheria.' She pointed to a group on

the other side of the park and Mark could see his cousin Niamh's bright red hair. 'My sister's over there.'

The man called 'Sunny' laughed and tipped his hat to her. 'You are as sharp-tongued as ever, my dear snake. May I ask how you escaped?'

'Mark saved me,' Helen said with another laugh. 'But do let me introduce you. Mark, this is Sunny. Sunny, Mark.'

A bright smile formed underneath the man's crooked nose. 'Trust Helen to keep it simple, sir. I am called Sunny by my friends, but my title is Lord Sunderfield. And you are?'

This man was the Duke of Sunderfield. The largest catch in the matrimonial mart and he was on intimate terms with Helen and her family.

Mark touched his hat, bowing his head. 'Lord Inverness.'

'Good to meet you, Inverness,' Sunny said. 'I see you picked up Lord Brunswick's horses and that they are in much better hands.'

'Will you do me a favour, Sunny?' Helen asked from Mark's side.

'Possibly. I am not green enough to say yes until you tell me what it is that you want me to do.'

Apparently, Sunderfield knew Helen very well. This did not endear him to Mark. Or the fact that he made her laugh.

Helen giggled again. 'You will like this favour, I promise. Please keep Mantheria occupied for as long as possible.'

'And are you minding her well?'

She shook her head. 'Not at all.'

'I do love your bluntness,' Sunny said with a smile. 'I suppose that I could assist you for a little while. Good day, Snake, Inverness.'

They watched him ride away and Helen leaned her head on his arm. 'Sunny is in love with Mantheria. The *eros*

kind, but she cannot marry him because she is already married to Alexander, the Duke of Glastonbury. They are formally separated, but they share a son together and I think their relationship now is the *storge* kind. But you are right. Friendship and empathy are not enough. For either of them. Alexander lives with Cressida, Lady Dutton. And Mantheria has Sunny, but she doesn't live with him. She can't because she is still married to Glastonbury. What a sad and terrible coil to be in. To be married to one person, but in love with another.'

He lowered his voice and spoke from his own heart. It would be terrible for him to see Helen married to her curate. The final nail in his coffin. 'I can think of nothing sadder.'

She leaned her head against his coat. 'Sunny was quite right. They are lovely chestnuts.'

'They are sweet goers, but one of their mouths has sores in it, so I have to be gentle with them,' he explained.

'You're gentle with everyone.'

Mark wished that were true. But he had been a captain in the army. He had fought and killed other men. He had watched them die before his very eyes. 'I used to be a soldier, Helen.'

She nodded again, rubbing her face against his shoulder, causing his whole body temperature to increase. 'Yes. You were a captain and you flirted with Frederica. But I will forgive you, because my sister coquetted with every man between sixteen and sixty, until she fell hard for Samuel.'

He had danced with her sister and enjoyed a light flirtation with her before the Battle of Waterloo. It had been the sort of dalliance he liked best as a second son, one where he knew that there were no matrimonial expectations. She'd already been engaged to Pelford at the time, but making her fiancé dance to quite a merry tune of her own making.

But there was no need for Helen to feel jealousy. He'd been a different man then. A second son who teased that he was a fortune-hunter. There had been no expectations of him inheriting the earldom or the responsibilities that came with it. Such serious concerns were for his brother James. He'd been a silly boy, playing at war and discovering it wasn't at all what he had expected.

Taking a breath, he tried to make her understand. 'War is more than balls and fancy uniforms, Helen. I am no gentle man. I am a killer. And I watched every one of my friends die.'

She was silent by his side as they drove further away from her sister, but still in view of the other carriages in the park. 'It is the nature of all animals to protect themselves. To fight and even kill others that would harm them or the people that they love. Defending your country does not make you a murderer. It makes you a fierce protector.'

He shook his head. 'I don't feel that way. At least, not any more. Pelford tried to take me to Manton's and I couldn't bear the sound of the bullets. When I close my eyes, I see the faces of my dead friends. Their bodies on the battlefield. It is not a sight you would want to see. And sometimes I wake up screaming at night, dreaming that I am back in Waterloo.'

Helen rubbed his arm that she was holding. 'It does sound terrible, but if you do not show others what a battle truly looks like, then how can they know to avoid them in future? You are good with a pencil. Illustrate it for me. Show the world the devastation of war. The cost of their freedom that you paid. You and your men, who lost their lives to defend us from the French. The price you are still paying from your suffering.'

Stiffening in his seat, Mark didn't know if he could draw

such darkness. He had never tried to before. He wasn't sure that he could do his friends' bravery justice. He didn't know how such knowledge would affect how she felt for him and now that he'd decided to live, it had to be with her. 'It will change how you see me.'

'Maybe it will change how you see yourself,' Helen whispered, leaning her head against his shoulder again in the place that seemed made just for her.

Mark resisted the urge to lay his head on top of hers. Could he show her the innermost pieces of his soul? The brokenness? Could her delicate hands fix that part of him, too?

# Chapter Twenty-Four

Grandfather Stubbs read through Helen's business proposal. Twice. He did not make a sound. The only thing that she could hear in his office was her own heart beating. At last, he set down the papers.

'It is a good proposal, Helen. A brilliant idea, in fact, to make reading available to all men and women. My main concern is that it has not been tried before. You could bankrupt your publishing house within a year, if your penny novels are not a success. You also haven't found cheaper paper to produce such novels or proven that it could be a financially viable plan.'

Helen opened her mouth, then closed it. She shook her head. 'So, you're turning down my business proposal?'

'I am suggesting that you do more work, before you try to obtain the money from me,' Grandfather said.

Helen shuffled to her feet and grabbed the business proposal that she'd taken three days to write. She wanted to crumple it up and throw it in the fire. She walked to the door, turning the handle.

'Might I give you some advice, my dear?'

She gritted her teeth and turned on her heel to face him. 'What?'

Grandfather Stubbs laughed. 'You've never been any good at hiding your emotions. You're angry with me, but

I wouldn't ask more of you if I didn't think that you had it in you to give me.'

'I hope that's not the advice.'

He chuckled again. 'It is not… Helen, in business, it is rarely wise to put all of your eggs in one basket. A good business has several sources of income, so that if one does not work out, you can rely on another. Diversification in stocks and offerings is the best way to have a secure company.'

*Diversification.*

'If I had a basket of your eggs, I would feed them to Theodosia.'

Grandfather chortled. 'Your pet snake is welcome to any of my eggs.'

Helen shut the door rather louder than she meant to.

Grandmother Stubbs came towards her, unsmiling. Helen was the least favourite of the grandchildren. Her hair and clothes were never tidy. And her affinity to snakes did not help her prim grandmother like her.

'What news on your publishing company, Helen? Not that I approve of young ladies owning businesses, of course.'

Shaking her head, she tried to move past her grandmother. But she'd forgotten that in addition to a stony glare, her step-grandmother had an iron-like grip. She got her claws deep into Helen's arm. 'Tell me what your grandfather said.'

'I am sure he will tell you himself.'

Grandmother gave her the stare that turned lesser beings to stone. *'Helen.'*

'He said that my business plan was flawed, because it was based on one unproven idea. He said that I needed to diversify where my money comes from for my company to keep it successful.'

She nodded, slowly. 'Isn't diversification exactly what a publishing company needs? You read different books than your sisters. I read different books than your grandfather. How could one style or type of book meet all of our needs? It couldn't. You must take your one great idea and make it but a part of your larger plan. No doubt it would be wise to continue many of the things that the publishing house is currently doing.'

'That's not a bad plan.'

But her grandmother did not release her vice-like grip on Helen's arm. 'Change for women comes slowly, but it still comes. Do not lose heart. Never give up the fight for your voice to be heard.'

Helen could only gape at her grandmother. 'You don't approve of Mama's business. I thought you wouldn't want me to own a publishing company.'

'My stepdaughter has proved that a woman is more than equal to the task. She has gone to her shop and her factory. She has worked among her employees and knows every piece of the process in the manufacturing of her perfume bottles. What do you know of the publishing house?'

'I've only been there once.'

Her grandmother finally released her arm. 'Then go back and find out all that you don't know and make another business plan. And don't forget to include the best parts from your first one.'

Impulsively, Helen hugged her grandmother. 'Thank you.'

Grandmother Stubbs released her, the stern look back on her face. 'Now what is this I heard about you staring at a young earl on the dance floor and monopolising him? It will not do. No, it will not do at all. You must behave like

a proper young lady… Make sure that someone escorts you to the publishing house.'

'I couldn't go by myself if I tried,' Helen said with a groan. 'I've got a scheduled nursemaid for every day of the week. Matthew is today's minder.'

Her grandmother nodded in approval. 'Your mother is nothing if not well organised.'

Helen groaned again.

Matthew met them in the hall. 'Ready to go yet? I need to pop into Parliament today. There is a vote I must be a part of.'

Nodding, she said, 'Yes. Thank you for the advice, Grandmother.'

She followed Matthew out the front door and into his carriage. Helen wished that he would have brought his daughter, Susan, with him today. She was by far the more entertaining of the two of them.

'Will you take me to the publishing house?' Helen asked.

Her elder brother shook his head. 'I can't today. Perhaps Wick can take you tomorrow. I'm going to have to drop you off at Hampford House.'

She opened her mouth to protest, but then closed it. Her nursemaid was going to leave her home and unattended.

When they arrived at the London house, Matthew got out of the carriage and escorted her inside.

'Harper, my good man,' he said to the butler. 'I know that I am asking the impossible, but for the sake of both of our heads, could you keep an eye on the front door and stop this termagant from escaping, should she get into her mind to go for a dip in a lake or on a nature walk?'

Grunting, Helen gave her brother a playful shove to the door. 'I don't need another keeper.'

Since she couldn't escape, she went to the conservatory

at the back of the house. She loved all the greenery and even the animals.

'Pegleg. Small treasure chest. Pegleg. Small treasure chest,' Mademoiselle Jaune kept repeating as she flew around her head.

Helen sighed. 'I miss him, too.'

But she could hardly climb over to his garden with his aunt, mother and cousin staying there. One of them might see her and it would cause just the sort of scandal that would make her mother furious.

Helen kneeled and cut off the dead flowers from the tulips. They were a glorious little flower, but their lives were all too short.

Mademoiselle Jaune flapped over her head, before resting on her shoulder. 'Captain Jason. Captain Jason. Captain Jason.'

'Aye, aye, Mademoiselle Jaune. I am here and reporting for duty,' Jason said. His voice as familiar as any member of her family.

Helen stood up and turned.

He was smiling. But he was always smiling. Harper must have let him in.

Jason came towards her and surprised her with a brief kiss on her cheek. 'I have a living now, Helen. I have my own parish! We can marry as soon as the banns are read.'

A shiver of discomfort ran down her spine and she blinked. 'That's…that's wonderful news. Did the Bishop of London give you one?'

'Your mother took me to see him herself and he was the most amiable man, Helen. He told me about the struggles and the poverty in the docks and rookeries. But he thinks that I would make a great difference in so many lives.'

She smiled, sadly. 'I know you will, but, Jason, I don't

want to live in London permanently like Matthew and Nancy. One of the reasons why I agreed to marry you was so that I could live in Ashbury near Hampford Castle.'

Jason's smile dimmed slightly. 'I know. I know, Helen. But the Bishop of London promised me a parish in the country after I have served five years in the slums. He said that he never asks a vicar to stay longer than that, because they begin to despair. That the poverty and violence become too much for even the most zealous of churchmen... I know that it will be hard. Probably the hardest thing that I have ever been called to do. But Our Lord and Saviour Jesus Christ dined with publicans and prostitutes. He was not above anyone.'

'I have no doubt that you'll be an incredible light to all in your parish, even those who do not attend your meetings. But I could not live in London all year long. My soul would shrivel up and die.'

He took her hands. 'Then we must wait five years for marriage, sweetest Helen. I can promise you a healthy country parish nearer to Hampford Castle. One where I can continue to do good and you can commune with nature to your heart's content.'

Helen didn't know what to say. Five years was a long time. The *ton* would even consider her youth spent at six and twenty years old. Even then, she would be a vicar's wife. The people of his parish would be just as exacting of her behaviour as the beau monde. Everything she said and did would be judged and scrutinised. She was not a perfect lady. She did not want to be.

She moved her hands to the collar of his coat. 'Kiss me again, Jason. Once more.'

He puckered his lips and pressed them chastely to hers.

It was nice, but Helen felt nothing special.

Opening her own mouth, she tried to coax his rigid lips into the softer, deeper kisses that she'd shared with Mark. The kisses that had turned her blood to liquid fire. But Jason's mouth stayed firmly closed. It wasn't enjoyable at all. Only awkward.

She leaned back. 'Kissing is better if you open your mouth a little. Relax your lips and gently return the pressure of mine.'

Jason turned as red as a sinner on the Sabbath. 'We can't kiss like that until we're married. It wouldn't be proper.'

'Is being proper very important to you?'

'I love you, Helen. I have always loved you. Since we were children. But we cannot behave like animals. We should not engage in carnal embraces until after we are married.'

Helen stepped back. 'In five years.'

He held out his hands to her, but she did not take them. 'It is hard to wait. But it will not be too long and we'll be able to see each other when you come to London for the Season. You might visit oftener now that you've purchased a publishing house. Your mother told me all about it.'

Wrapping her arms around herself, she said, 'Then you won't mind having a wife who works in business?'

Jason's hands fell to his sides. 'Not if it gives you purpose and meaning until we are married. I am sure once we have children, you'll want to focus your energies at home, with them.'

Her eyebrows raised. 'My mother continued to work through childbirth and rearing.'

'But your mother is not warm like you. Surely you would not wish to ignore your children for your own vanity?'

She shook her head. 'I never felt ignored. And Mama's company is not about her vanity, it's about her passion.

Her talents. Scents and mixtures are what makes her who she is. If she had abandoned it when she bore Wick, she would have only been living half a life. Denying an essential part of herself.'

He no longer smiled. Not even the corners of his lips turned up. 'I could never deny you anything that you asked for. I love you, Helen. If you wish to continue publishing after we are married, I will not forbid it.'

A tear fell down her cheek. 'And I love you, Jason. I always have. But I have realised that I am not *in love* with you and that we would not suit each other in marriage. My parents were right. You want a wife who will be dedicated to her husband and children. A wife who will set an example in your parish to other women. One of obedience and piety... I could never be that wife. I am a wild creature and I have no wish to be tamed and domesticated. To be changed into another animal entirely.'

Jason's jaw clenched. 'I wouldn't try to tame you. I promise.'

'But you would be disappointed in me. You would be embarrassed by me. Our love for each other would sour. It is the love of children. The Latin word *philia*. It is pure and sweet. But we are grown now. I could never be an obedient wife of a churchman and you could not ask it of me... It is better that we part now. You will make an incredible vicar. I know that you will do a great deal of good and I will always consider you one of my dearest friends.'

He gritted his teeth. 'I should not have looked so high above me. Perhaps God is punishing me for my pride.'

Unclasping the locket, she held it out to him and placed it in his hands. 'It has our pictures and your lock of hair. Do not give up on your faith or on God. He is not punishing you. For you have shown me that He is the God of love,

instead of damnation. Of forgiveness, instead of condemnation. Your love and His will lift hearts wherever you go. But I have always wished to stay at home.'

Jason's hands clenched over the locket, but he didn't speak. He only nodded, as if words were too difficult to form.

'Goodbye,' Helen said.

He gave Helen one last imploring look, before turning on his heel and leaving the conservatory.

Helen sat down on a bench. She couldn't work on the plants. Her throat felt thick and her mind jumped from memory to memory with Jason. They had played together. Swam together. Been pirates together. Danced together. Grown up together.

Several minutes later, the door to the conservatory opened and her mother walked into the room.

Mama sat down next to Helen on the bench. 'I saw Jason before he left.'

'Then you know.'

Her mother nodded. 'I am so sorry, darling.'

Helen leaned her head on her mother's shoulder. 'You were right. We are not suited for each other as adults and I would make a terrible vicar's wife. Whether we lived in Ashbury or another parish.'

Mama kissed Helen's forehead. 'That doesn't mean that I am not sorry for your loss. I know that you loved him.'

She burrowed her head further into her mother's shoulder, nodding. 'I did love him as a dear friend. But I wasn't *in love* with him. I've learned there is a difference.'

Mark had explained it to her. But she didn't want him to feel *philia* towards her either. Or not simply friendship. She also realised, after Jason's lacklustre embrace, that she felt physical desire for Mark. *Eros.* Touching him was more

than about comfort, safety or friendship. It had become a need as real as eating.

But he was an earl.

Mark was everything that she didn't want in a husband. His home was far away from Hampford, all the way in Scotland. And if they married, he would expect her to be his hostess and a pattern card of perfection. Something that she couldn't even pretend to be.

Mama sighed. 'I hope you know that I was not trying to injure you by introducing Jason to the Bishop of London. I was looking at his best interests. I have always been very fond of him and I wanted to help him in his career.'

'He's thrilled to have his own parish. The poorer the better and he likes living in the city.'

Her mother softly stroked her hair. 'Jason has so much love to offer. It would have been a pity for him not to be able to find his own parish. His own people to help. A wife. Someone as dedicated to the work as he is. But your scientific calling is quite different than his religious one.'

Helen sat up, rubbing her eyes. 'Do you ever regret the time you've spent at Duchess & Company? The energy you've given your company instead of your family?'

Mama shook her head. 'Not at all. Without my company, I would be a cheetah without spots. It is a part of who I am. Never allow others to define who you are.'

'Not even the *ton*?'

'Especially not them.'

'I love you, Mama.'

'And I love you, Helen. More than you will probably ever know. A mother is only as happy as her saddest child.'

*Mantheria.*

But Helen didn't say her eldest sister's name.

# Chapter Twenty-Five

Mark tried to read the book about the South American and Antarctic birds called penguins, odd flightless birds that swam in the frozen ocean. It was sent to him by the secretary of the Earl of Trentham, but he knew that it had truly come from Helen. Penguins were certainly curious creatures, but his young cousin kept interrupting his reading, making it impossible for him to concentrate on the words in front of him. She kept asking him questions and then perching on the armrest of his chair.

'I don't know how you have the patience to read in London,' Niamh said, pushing his shoulder flirtatiously. 'There is so much fun to be had.'

She was trying *his* patience.

Aunt Fiona glanced up from her needlework, smiling broadly. 'Mark has certainly made our visit an enjoyable one. He has taken us somewhere exciting nearly every day.'

Niamh jumped back to her feet, hopping up and down on the balls of her shoe-covered feet. 'I have loved all the balls and parties. I wish there had been one tonight. Nothing is duller than staying home in the evening. My feet itch to dance.'

'Daughter,' his aunt said, giving Niamh a speaking look. 'Be thoughtful of your words, lass. You keep blethering

on about balls and poor Mark dinnae have two feet with which to dance.'

His mother cleared her throat and set down the hem of the dress she was sewing. Her lips even upturned, in an almost smile. 'My son does not need two feet to dance. He and Lady Helen were the most graceful couple on the ballroom floor at Lady Cheswick's party.'

Mark closed his book in surprise. His mother wasn't pitying him any longer. She finally understood that he was still an able man. She gave him a rare full smile and then returned to her stitching. Aunt Fiona looked at her daughter and then at Mark, before picking up her needlework and shaking her head.

His aunt must have communicated something in her gaze to Niamh, for she bounced back to his seat and perched again on his armrest.

'I hope you will waltz with me at our wedding,' she said in a voice barely above a whisper.

Mark could no longer dance around the subject. 'Cousin Niamh, I shall be frank with you. I am over ten years your senior. I am much too old to be your husband.'

Niamh bounced on the armrest. 'Mama says that doesn't matter. Women shouldn't be older than their husbands, but it is perfectly appropriate for a man to be much older than his wife.'

'Provided he's wealthy.'

'And titled,' she added, with a laugh that made the hairs on his nape stand up.

Aunt Fiona glanced up from her embroidery. 'What are you two laughing about?'

'Cousin Mark is flirting with me, Mama.'

His aunt flashed him an approving grin. 'Well, I don't

see what is to laugh about that. It's what we've all been praying for, lass.'

Mark swallowed, his throat dry. He wanted to bury his head in the dirt like a worm, but Helen would not have done that. She would have bluntly told his aunt the truth. Looking around the room, he saw the countless plants that she'd sent to him. Living, breathing creatures. She'd turned his dead garden into a blossoming one. His dark house into one of living plants and growing blossoms. Helen had brought him back to life like the flowers in his back garden.

He stood up, without a wobble on his wooden leg. 'Aunt Fiona, I am happy that you and Niamh have come to London, but as I just told Niamh, and I must reiterate, that I do not intend to flirt with her. Nor will I ever marry her. I am much too old for her.'

'Nonsense, lad. You're in your prime...aside from the missing leg.'

His mother gasped.

It seemed that neither his aunt nor his cousin could forget that he was missing a limb. Helen never seemed to notice it. Or if she did, she didn't care. 'You are forcing me to be blunt, but since we are living in the same house, it will not do for me to avoid the subject. I am not interested romantically in Niamh.'

Aunt Fiona frowned, as did Niamh. It was as if she finally realised that he was *not* flirting with her. The concept that he wasn't interested in *her* seemed entirely new. But he didn't think that Niamh was interested in *him*.

'Don't tell me you look down on her, like your auld father looked down on your mother?' Aunt Fiona said, dropping her needlework. She stood up, her chest heaving. 'My daughter is as good as any lady in England. Better even for she doesn't have their namby-pamby ways. She's a sturdy

Scottish lass. Just the sort of wife a man like you needs. And she has a fine dowry as well.'

Mark felt his hands curling into fists. 'Do you mean a cripple like me?'

'I really don't mind *that much* that you're a cripple,' Niamh added, smiling at him.

'Hush, Niamh!' his mother chided. 'Don't call your cousin a cripple.'

'But he is one.'

He'd been wrong. His young cousin still couldn't seem to understand that he had no interest in her. Nor her pity. 'Well, *I* mind that you mind.'

Aunt Fiona shook her head. 'Whisht. You're not making any sense, Mark.'

Inhaling, Mark held up his hands. 'I cannot say this any clearer. I will not offer for, nor marry, my cousin Niamh. I am not simply a cripple. I am a man. A decorated soldier. An earl. When I marry, it will be to a woman of my choosing. One that doesn't mind who I am now. And I am done with this subject.'

He limped out of the room. Glancing over his shoulder, he saw his mother smiling at him. Mark took the book to the back garden and sat in his chair. The grass had grown a little long because Helen had not come to visit. But the seeds she had planted had sprouted and a few were blooming into happy yellow flowers. Little drops of sunshine, like the happiness Helen had brought into his existence. New life.

Mark couldn't help but keep looking up at the fence and hoping that a fairy queen or a human changeling would appear there.

He had been outside for nearly an hour before he saw the top of her nearly white-blonde hair.

'Is it safe?' she called from the other side of the fence.

'From what?'

'Your mother,' Helen said, her gamine face peeking through the trees. 'She doesn't like me at all. I can tell. Most of my governesses didn't like me either.'

Setting down his book on his lap, Mark grinned back at her. 'There are no meddlesome mothers or mean governesses about.'

Something clattered behind him on the pebble path. It was a pair of red pruning shears. Above it, he saw Helen's backside climbing over the stone fence. Her hair was down and flying in the breeze. The dress she wore was yellow, like the flowers she had planted. She jumped the last couple of feet and landed heavily on the pebbles.

Turning, she looked at him. 'You were right about Jason.'

He swallowed, heavily. His heart felt as heavy as a stone. 'How so?'

Helen came even closer to him. So near that her dress brushed his pant leg. 'I do not feel romantic love for him. The affection in my heart is that of friendship and the empathy of shared childhood experiences. And I mostly accepted his proposal because I wished to stay close to my home.'

'Did you tell him?'

She nodded.

Of course she had told the curate to his face. Helen was blunt to a fault.

'I asked him to kiss me and I felt nothing,' she said, a pretty pink stealing into her cheeks. 'It was nothing at all like when I kissed you. I didn't want to devour him whole.'

Mark's pulse quickened. He had no idea what Helen was going to say or do next. She kept him in a constant state of terror and delight. 'I am glad to hear that.'

Her face turned from pink to red. 'I was wondering if I could kiss you again? But I don't want to be your countess.'.

'Why not?'

'Scotland is too far from Hampford and I would make a terrible hostess. I always say what I think and Mama says I have no tact.'

'Do countesses have to be hostesses?'

Helen nodded. 'Yes. And they have to move to where their husband lives and provide him heirs like a brood-mare. Not that I would mind the mating part. But will you kiss me or not?'

Warmth coated his belly and his own cheeks felt hot. Mark would take what he could get. 'Yes.'

Helen beamed at him. 'Can I sit on your lap? That was nice, too.'

Mark couldn't trust his voice to speak, so he only gave a sharp little nod. Helen carefully sat on his good leg and then her legs draped over his wooden one. She held very still as if allowing him to retain his balance—a wise thing, for since he'd lost a limb it was hard to find his equilibrium. Tentatively, he placed his arms around her waist, fearing that this was all a dream and that Helen would disappear. She placed her hands on his chest above his heart. Her lips twitched upwards as she felt his heartbeat as hard and as loudly as a cannon firing. After she pressed her hands against his waistcoat, they coasted upwards to his shoulders and then around his neck.

'I love the way you feel,' she whispered, her voice more a breath than words.

He could have happily let her touch his chest underneath his shirt like she had in the carriage, but they were sitting in his back garden. His mother, aunt or cousin could come outside at any time. He had to keep their kisses light and not

a full-on seduction. Helen was a physical creature and he doubted she would know how or when to stop. Nor did she want to marry him if they were caught and compromised. It would be a struggle to keep his own feelings in check.

She moved her head against his cheek. Her skin was soft and scented against his own scratchy whiskers. She rubbed the side of her face against his, causing him to moan with need and want. He could feel her smile as her lips brushed their way from his cheek to his mouth in a slow burn. In the carriage she had kissed him like a barracuda, ravishing his mouth with her own.

When she slanted her mouth towards his, it was with brief, teasing brushes of softness. Her hands moved from behind his neck to cup his face. She kissed him lightly again, but he felt her tongue lick the seam of his lips. He obligingly opened his mouth and let her tongue in and it found his own. He wished to domesticate this wild little creature.

Helen pulled back a little, their noses practically touching. 'Did you feel something?'

'I felt everything,' he said, before pressing his mouth hard against hers, his tongue entering between her kiss-swollen lips. His hands moved up from her waist to her shoulders in a slow burn. He loved her gentle curves. Helen made a purring noise against his mouth and he moved his hands back to the dip in her waist to pull her closer to him.

He sucked, tugging on her lower lip and then making a trail of kisses to her ear. Instinctively, he nuzzled the sensitive spot on her neck there. She purred again and shifted on his lap. It was a good thing that he was sitting down and holding her, because for a moment he lost his balance, but she held him in place. He was going to spontaneously combust.

Mark took a few ragged breaths before Helen pressed her lips against his again. She rubbed her chest against his and he deepened the kiss. Her hands running through his hair and neck. There wasn't a part of him that wasn't on fire for her. That didn't want to make her his countess in every way.

The sound of the door opening caused Helen to practically jump off his lap. Her hair had been down before and his amorous handling hadn't made it any tidier. Her lips were swollen and red, and her skin had the beautiful pink flush of a well-loved woman. It was obvious what they had been doing.

Helen dived to her knees and picked up her pruning shears, turning her back to the person who was coming outside. Mark could see her beautiful form through the light material of her dress and he now knew how wonderful she felt in his hands. He could never let her go. He would have to convince her to come with him and promise that he would not try to change her. But the sight of his mother walking towards him was enough to cool his ardour and stop him from begging Helen to reconsider a coronet.

He sat up in his chair. 'Mama…uh, you see…uh… Lady Helen has been helping me with the back garden in exchange for sketches for her snake book.'

Helen glanced over her shoulder, still keeping her face mostly hidden. 'Yes. We are only gardening, in the garden, with gardening tools.'

His mother put her hands on to her narrow hips. 'Is that right now, my lad? I thought you said that you'd already finished the sketches for the lady.'

Mark felt his colour rise from embarrassment. She was no eejit. His mother knew exactly what they had been doing in the garden.

Before he was forced to come up with a bad lie or a ter-

rible truth, Helen said, 'You are correct, my lady. But your son has promised me more drawings. Instead of snakes, he is going to share illustrations of his battle experiences at Waterloo.'

Mama shook her head. 'Whisht. 'Tis best forgotten.'

Helen snipped off the dead head of a flower. 'Sometimes we must remember before we can forget.'

Her words had a wisdom older than her age. Mark had tried so hard to forget the pain. The ugliness. The hopeless-ness of battle, but Helen was right. He couldn't forget it. The sound of a gunshot caused him to stop breathing. More often than not, he woke up in his own sweat after having nightmares of his men dying. Of his leg being sawed off by a surgeon. Lying in the hospital, watching soldier after soldier die. Their screams of pain. There was no way Mark could forget what he'd seen and experienced, but he could find a way through the horrors. And if anyone could help him do that, it was Helen. His otherworldly, fairy queen.

''Tis not a Scottish proverb,' his mother said with a sniff.

Helen turned to face his mother. Her lips were still cherry red and ripe from his kisses. 'The Scots don't have all the answers.'

'Neither do the English.'

Mark used his arms to lift himself up to standing. 'I don't think any humans do, Mama. Why don't you take my seat and I will help Helen with the weeding?'

His mother took the chair and Mark limped over to Helen's side and slowly sat down. His arms shook a little with the effort and he couldn't help but wish that Helen hadn't seen him like this. That she couldn't see his limita-tions. But if his wooden leg bothered her, she made no sign of it. She simply handed him the shears.

'Cut off the heads of the dead petals,' she said. 'I'll do

the weeding. I don't trust you not to pull out the flowers that haven't bloomed yet.'

'I am grateful that you trust me enough to prune,' Mark said cheekily. 'I hope to be able to work up to weeding duty one day.'

Helen leaned forward and spontaneously kissed his cheek, in front of his mother! 'Oh, you will in no time.'

Mark couldn't help but steal a glance at his mother. He expected to see her frowning, but the look on her face was positively benevolent. He hoped that she realised that despite Helen being a *sassenach*, she was the person who had brought him back to life.

'Mind you pick up the clippings, Marky,' his mother chided. 'Can't have those in our garden. Keep your pile nice and tidy, like Lady Helen's.'

Grinning ruefully, he picked up his clippings and spent one of the most memorable afternoons of his life gardening with his mother and Helen. Mark could envision them all living together in Scotland. If only he could convince Helen that more than one place could be home.

# Chapter Twenty-Six

Wick was complaining before they even reached the door of Hampford House. 'Couldn't you wait until it's Matthew's turn again to keep an eye on you? He's the businessman after all.'

'Come on,' Helen said as he grumbled all the way to the carriage. 'Matthew is busy in Parliament this week.'

Her eldest brother helped her inside and then climbed in after her. 'Wouldn't you rather go to my house and play with the boys? We could take them to the park? Or Astley's Amphitheatre?'

Shifting in her seat, Helen said, 'I think that is a great idea. You take the boys and I will go to my publisher's house.'

'You need an escort.'

'But that doesn't have to be you,' she said persuasively. 'Perhaps Lord Inverness could accompany me to the publisher.'

'Mama wouldn't like it.'

She shrugged her shoulders. 'Mama wouldn't have to know.'

He gave her a stern look. 'All right. But you must promise not to get into any trouble and not to tell my wife that I was derelict in my duties.'

'I won't say a word to Louisa.'

'It's a bargain, Snake,' Wick said, then he leaned his head out of the carriage window and gave his driver directions to Mark's house.

She gave her brother a playful push on the arm. Touching Wick was like touching Jason. It felt loving and familiar, but not a whit of excitement. 'Wick, can I ask you an awkward question?'

'No.'

Helen ignored him as always. 'When you kissed Louisa for the first time, and I suppose every time after, was it different from kissing other women?'

Wick chuckled, pulling at his high collar. 'What a question! Only you would ask such a thing.'

'I need to know.'

Her brother smiled reminiscently. 'No. It was not the same. The other kisses were nice, very nice. But Louisa's kiss set my body aflame and brightened my heart... I suppose the difference is that I wasn't in love with the other women I kissed.'

'So, being *in love* with the person makes all the difference?'

'Being in love changes everything.'

Helen nodded, processing his words. But a man didn't have to leave his home and everything that he loved when he married. It was the woman who lost her roots. Helen thought that she might be in love with Mark, but she still didn't want to leave Hampford Castle. And Scotland was so very far away that she would not see her family very often. Nor the publishing house that she was working so hard to purchase and make successful.

Wick made her wait inside the carriage for him, but after five minutes both Wick and Mark came out. Her eldest brother had a spring in his step and a smile on his

face. Mark limped behind him more slowly, a small grimace on his lips as if every step caused him pain. Helen almost wished that she had not asked for his company, but then she realised that Mark had chosen to come. Just as he had chosen to go to parties, dance and even garden with her. She hated when people assumed that, because she was a woman, she had limitations. She thought perhaps that Mark felt the same way. He was a capable man, who just happened to have a wooden leg. He was able to do almost anything another man could, even if it was twice as hard.

Wick must have realised that Mark didn't want help either, for he jumped into the carriage and let Mark pull himself up by his muscular arms.

'You might as well sit by her side,' Wick said, pointing to Helen. 'Once I leave the carriage, I am sure my sister will move.'

Mark carefully sat down beside her and Helen placed her hand on her knee, the palm upturned. She was always touching him and leaning against him. She wanted him to initiate the contact this time and she didn't have to wait long before Mark's gloved hand encompassed hers in his warmth. He moved their joined hands to his knee and Helen's whole body felt flushed with happiness.

But marrying Mark would mean that she lost everything. Her home, her family and even her name.

'I told my driver to pick me back up before Helen goes and speaks to our grandfather,' Wick said. 'And not that I don't trust you, Inverness. Frankly, it's Helen that I don't trust. But I told my footman to keep an eye on you. So be on your best behaviour.'

Helen stuck her tongue out at Wick. For some reason, her brother brought out her most childish responses. 'I'm always on my best behaviour.'

'We both know that's not true,' Wick said with a chuckle.

Mark's hand shook a little in hers, but he managed to keep his mirth inside. And if the corners of his lips did tend to tilt upwards, she couldn't entirely blame him, for he of all people knew just how naughty she could be. Especially with him.

When the carriage stopped in front of Wick's fashionable brick town house, he tapped his hat and climbed out. She heard him call the directions to his driver and the vehicle lurched forward. Mark swayed against her as if finding his balance. She wondered if it was too soon to ask him if he would kiss her again.

She knew that delicately brought up young ladies were not supposed to ask eligible men for kisses, but having grown up around animals she knew that creatures did exactly what they wanted, when they wanted. There were very few rules in courtship there. A peacock would dance and show off his feathers, letting the peahens know that he was ready for mating. Some animals put off a certain scent when they wanted an intimate companion.

But what did young ladies do?

Helen opened her mouth to ask that very question, but before words could come out, Mark's hand cupped her cheek and his lips covered hers. First with gentle pressure and then growing harder by degrees. She knocked off his hat as she gasped with need as their mouths opened, her hands stealing to his hands and then slowly up the muscles of his arms. He was a slender man, but that did not mean that he wasn't a muscular one. The feel of his muscles and the taste of his tongue caused a burning deep in her belly.

Mark pressed a gentle kiss to her nose. More sweet kisses to her eyelids, her cheeks, her chin in a worshipful embrace. Helen had never felt more loved in all of her life

and in that very moment she knew that she was *in love* with him. She'd cared for him from the start, her handsome unkept friend who looked like a pirate and made her feel as if she belonged. As if being *other* was not a bad thing after all.

Their carriage came to a halt and Helen couldn't help but murmur a protest when Mark's lips left hers.

Smiling, he caressed the side of her face with his gloved hand. 'Don't forget, we are on our very best behaviour.'

'I already was,' she said saucily and pressed a kiss to his cheek.

Mark laughed and slowly made his way out of the carriage before offering her a hand down. Helen didn't need the help, but she accepted it anyway. She didn't need to hold his arm either, but she quickly took it when he offered it to her. Smiling bemusedly, Helen decided that it was quite nice when Mark touched her first.

Wick's footman opened the door and she and Mark walked into the shop. The clerk who had helped her the first day she'd come was there.

He took off his hat and bowed to her. 'Lady Helen.'

She realised that she didn't know his name. 'Hello, and your name is, sir?'

'Mr Leech, my lady.'

Bowing her head, Helen said, 'It is a pleasure to see you again, Mr Leech. May I introduce my friend, Lord Inverness?'

Mr Leech doffed his hat to him. Mark bowed his head in return.

'Is Mr Gibbs or Mr Thomas in today?' she asked.

The clerk shook his head. 'Nay, my lady. But I have the signed contract here to give to you. All that is left to complete the sale is the transfer of funds.'

Helen nodded, unable to keep a smile off her swollen

lips. 'Excellent, we will take it with us when we leave. I am here to learn every position involved in a publishing house.'

'I've worked in one for twenty years, my lady. It can hardly be done in a couple of hours.'

She smiled. 'I don't need to be proficient at each position. I simply need to understand the general workings.'

'And I am only here to help,' Mark said. 'Lady Helen is in charge.'

Mr Leech bobbed his head. 'Very good, my lord and lady. If you'll come with me this way.'

The man took them first to the lowest position, the typesetter. It amazed her how there were so many little pieces of type and together they made beautiful words on well-ordered pages. She saw the carved wooden blocks where Mark's illustrations were duplicated. Helen loved watching the printer make copy after copy of the same wooden block, inking it every time. She saw where they hung the pages to dry, like one would hang a wet blanket.

Helen pointed at the beautiful snake drawing. 'Lord Inverness is the illustrator, Mr Leech.'

'You almost make me like snakes, my lord,' Mr Leech said, grinning. 'Almost.'

'Don't they look incredible, Mark?'

He picked one up off the line and held it in his hands, a slow smile forming on his face. Helen had experienced something similar when she'd first held her words in printed form. There was something truly magical about publishing.

'I shouldn't wish to boast of my own talents,' he said, hanging up one sheet of paper and picking up another identical one, 'but I do think they turned out rather well.'

The next place Mr Leech took them to was the cutter. He sliced the large, dry sheets into their individual pages and was careful to keep them in the correct order.

The last person they visited was the man who bound the books together, sewing stitches on the pages as neatly as Wick's wife, Louisa, did on cloth. The bound pages were then attached with glue and stitches to the leather covers. Helen picked up one of the finished books and saw that even the leather cover had an intricately pressed design on it. On the spine of the book, she saw the title in gold filigree surrounded by decorative swirls and leaves, made with the same gold.

*Each book is truly a work of art!*

'How many copies do you typically print on a first edition of the book?'

Mr Leech scratched his bearded chin. 'It depends, my lady. Typically, no more than a hundred copies. If the book is a success, the second printing is much larger.'

Helen blinked. 'How much does it cost us to produce each book?'

'Close to a pound for a book as fancy as this one with as many pages.'

It was no wonder that Mark and Frederica preferred to borrow their books from a lending library instead of buying them. The price of her book was more than most maids earned in a quarter. The cost was certainly too great for the average worker.

Mark picked up another volume and flipped through the crisp cream pages. 'It is certainly a beautifully made book, sir.'

Setting the book down, Helen did a little working out in her mind. 'So, when Mr Gibbs asked me to give him one hundred pounds to assist in paying for the printing of the book, in reality, I was paying all the fees for its printing?'

Mr Leech swallowed and tugged at his collar around his thick neck. 'Aye, my lady. In that case, you took all the

risk and Mr Gibbs made all the profit. You paid the costs of printing and only receive ten per cent in royalties. You would never have made your money back, but the publishing house would turn a decent profit.'

'Books on snakes don't sell?' Mark asked.

'Not well, my lord.'

Helen harrumphed. 'What does sell well, Mr Leech?'

'Gothic romances and memoirs. Anything scandalous to do with the monarchy or aristocracy. You toffs love to read books that rip each other apart.'

Helen wrote this down. 'What of cookbooks, Mr Leech? Has this house published one recently?'

He shook his head.

'Household Hints?'

Mr Leech scoffed. 'Nay, my lady.'

'What of fashion?'

The clerk did not even bother to speak, just shook his head vehemently.

'How about the Napoleonic wars?'

She felt Mark stiffen beside her. The Battle of Waterloo had made General Lord Wellington the most famous man in Europe, but the glory had come at the cost of many lives. Of Mark's friends.

'Aye, my lady. We published a book of the Duke of Wellington's correspondence. Several other publishers have immortalised his story as well.'

Helen took in a deep breath. 'But what of the average soldiers? Or captains? Has anyone told their story? Or the stories of the men who died?'

Mr Leech's eyes fell to his fidgeting hands. 'Folks like to read stories about heroes, my lady, not about failures or death. It was a great victory.'

'At a great cost,' she countered. 'I do believe that I am

not the only person who would be interested to hear an additional account of the famous battle, nor see illustrations that help me to understand what happened there.'

Mark shifted his weight to his good leg. She hoped that he would be willing to write his experience and to draw what he saw there. The brave Highlanders that he fought with deserved to be remembered. They had more than earned their place in the pages of history.

'You are in charge, my lady,' Mr Leech said and Helen liked hearing it rather too well.

'I am, aren't I,' she said with a little smile. 'But you do have a great deal more experience than I and I am eager to learn from you. How do we find authors?'

'Folks send their manuscripts to us and they end up in a pile. I go through them and, if they have any merit, I pass them on to Mr Gibbs. He's the one that gives the ultimate approval and contacts the author. Then he passes the project back to me for the editorial work.'

Helen scribbled everything down as fast as her pen could write. 'And what does Mr Thomas do?'

'Nuffink, my lady. He hasn't been in the office in a couple of years.'

Mark snorted and Helen was similarly unimpressed with the former publishing partner.

'What is your official title, Mr Leech?'

He shrugged one shoulder. 'I'm a man of many trades, my lady. I have no official title. I started off as a typesetter who couldn't read and worked my way up in the house.'

'Would you consider accepting the position of foreman, sir?'

Mr Leech swallowed and blinked several times. 'You're not having me on, my lady? I'm not formally educated.'

Helen shook her head. 'I am not having you on. It ap-

pears that nothing happens in this publishing house without you. I should like for you to continue your work, but with the title and authority of a foreman. I mean to be involved in the business, but I spend a great deal of time in the country. I need to know that the publishing house is being run effectively day by day. There will be a pay raise and your own office, as well.'

'There's nothing I should like more, my lady.'

'Like Mr Gibbs, I do wish to help select the manuscripts that we publish,' she said, looking to Mark for reassurance. He smiled at her. 'And I would like to actively seek out female authors to publish books specifically for women. Half of the reading world is relatively neglected by publishers.'

'Very good, my lady.'

'How many books do you publish per year?'

'Between ten to twelve, my lady.'

She wrote the numbers down on her paper. 'And how many have you already selected for this year?'

'We have the entire year already mapped out, my lady. You and I would be selecting books for the next year's publishing season.'

Her eyebrow quirked up. 'Did the other authors all put up their own publishing costs?'

'Yes, my lady. All but Mr Mayhew. We've published three of his books before and every one goes through multiple printings. Typically, we make most of our profits off two or three titles. The other twelve books are to fill in our time and make only a small contribution to profits.'

'I have read Mr Mayhew's books,' Mark said. 'He spins a very good tale.'

Helen touched the tip of her pen to her lips. 'Let me guess. He writes ghost stories.'

'Gothic adventures, my lady,' Mr Leech added.

'Dreadful. But I am going to need his address. I am going to ask him to write a story in instalments. Each serial no more than eight to sixteen pages, front and back. Only one printing sheet. With an illustration on the cover page, which will also be made of paper. The cheapest we can find.'

Mr Leech bowed his head and stared at her blankly. 'You wish to use the cheapest paper, my lady?'

'Yes. Our cost on these small books needs to be less than a farthing. Ideally, a tenth of a penny. Can it be done?'

The new foreman squashed his hat between his hands. 'Aye. We could buy wood pulp paper and one sheet printings would be fast. We could have a hundred copies done in less than a day.'

'But we are going to need closer to a thousand on our first printing. I mean to be the first publisher of penny stories.'

'Penny Dreadfuls,' Mark quipped, making her laugh.

Poor Mr Leech's eyes nearly popped out of his stern face. 'Penny stories, my lady?'

'Stories that are available to everyone. Publishing at the moment only caters to the wealthy. Our penny stories will bring in readers of all ages and incomes with their ghostlike, dreadful stories. Working men in particular, I believe, will be interested in them and take them home to their wives and sisters.'

Mr Leech gave her a half a smile. 'It's never been tried before, but plenty of common folk likes myself enjoy reading sensational stories from the newspapers. I think you may be on to something, my lady.'

Helen clapped her hands. 'I hope so, for my business plan, Mr Leech, is to continue to publish twelve titles a year, as you have previously done. I will actively search out fe-

male authors to write and produce two or three books per year, specifically on subjects that interest women. We will also begin a women's fashion magazine that will be published monthly, starting January 1818. Also next year we will try selling a weekly Penny Dreadful in the spring and see if it is a viable business idea. If it is, we will continue the story indefinitely every week with a new segment.'

She liked Mark's name for the penny stories. It was catchy.

'I think it will be, my lady. I have never owned my own book before, aside from the Bible. I would be pleased as punch to be able to bring a penny story home to my wife and children.'

'I would be inclined to spend such a small sum as well,' Mark said. 'For so little, I would not wish to have to wait my turn for the novel at the lending library.'

She couldn't help but smile at this. 'Now, for our last piece of business today. Mr Gibbs did not want me to publish under my own name, but he was missing a key opportunity for advertising. Many people are interested in what a daughter of a duke writes. I want the title page reprinted and rethreaded to include my full name: *Lady Helen Stringham*. And I would like you to start printing at once. But three hundred copies instead of one hundred and I should like to see finished books by next week. Ready for sale.'

The clerk's face looked doubtful, but he did not argue with her.

Helen held out her hand to Mr Leech. He hesitated a moment before taking it and squeezing it tightly.

'Thank you for all your help today, Mr Leech. As of this moment, you have the use of Mr Gibbs's old office. Now, if you'll give me the signed contract, I will see that your former employers receive payment in full.'

Helen held out her hand and Mr Leech hesitated for only a moment before taking it and shaking it firmly. Mark offered the man his hand to shake as well and thanked him for his time and explanations. Mr Leech walked them to the door of the publishing office and Mark signalled to the carriage driver who had been walking the horses up and down the street. Again, he assisted her inside the vehicle, but this time Helen possessed the contract of ownership for the publishing house. She moved it to her opposite hand so that Mark could hold her hand again.

When they arrived at Wick's house, he came out to meet them and clambered inside. He took the contract from Helen and glanced over it. 'One of Matthew's, isn't it?'

'Yes,' she said with a little laugh.

Her brother flipped through the multiple pages. 'I could tell. He never uses one word when he can write ten. Inverness, should my driver return you home, or would you like to meet our grandparents?'

Mark's eyes met Helen's and he shook his head. 'I look forward to meeting them, but I believe that Helen would like to conduct her business on her own. I should hate for my presence to overshadow her hard work.'

She squeezed his hand tighter. He understood her. Mark saw her like no one else before had and he didn't expect her to change. If only he had a house near Hampford!

He kissed her hand before getting out of the carriage at his house and waving them away.

'I like him better than the curate,' Wick said, waving back. 'He doesn't preach to me and he seems to enjoy rain and snakes. You really ought to keep him around. I doubt you could find another fellow like him.'

It was a good thing that her brother was on the opposite

seat of the carriage, or she would have given him a push. 'How do you know he likes rain?'

'Because you came back wet in *his* carriage,' he retorted. 'Not even Mama swallowed Pelford's story of your returning alone from your forbidden jaunt to the Serpentine. You hadn't brought your coin purse so you couldn't have hired a hackney. You can't pull the wool over a Stringham.'

She huffed, dropping her shoulders. She'd learned that particular lesson all too many times before. 'Why didn't she say anything then?'

Wick leaned back against the squabs, a teasing smile on his annoying lips. 'Because Mama favours the Earl's suit. Matchmaking is an art and you'll soon find that our mother is a master. I am sure she knows more of what goes on then you have any idea of.'

'Then it's a miracle you married without her assistance.'

He laughed. 'True. But all four of my sisters were determined to help, including you.'

Helen couldn't even manage a smile. 'I think I love him, Wick. No, I know that I do. But I don't want to leave Hampford and everything I hold dear to be with him. To be a stranger in a strange place.'

Her eldest brother shook his head. 'Oh, Helen, let me put this in the sort of words that you will understand: a bird cannot fly until it leaves the nest.'

She touched the column of her throat and felt her flurried pulse. 'Snakes don't fly.'

'And neither do baby birds who stay in their parents' nests eating regurgitated worms.'

Wick held the contract until they reached Grandfather Stubbs's house and Helen didn't mind. His words made her mind spin. Was she preventing herself from living and hav-

ing new experiences by wishing to stay close to her childhood home? Staying in London hadn't been as terrible as she'd thought it would be. Helen had met Mark and she'd purchased a publishing house. Both life-changing experiences that would not have happened in Hampford.

The carriage stopped. Wick followed Helen into their grandfather's office and pretended as though he'd helped her the whole time at the publishing office.

The rogue.

He even listened as Helen explained her new business plan and gave her grandfather specific numbers and costs— thanks to Mr Leech— and a general outline of her publishing plans for 1818. Including the penny stories and a monthly fashion magazine.

Grandfather read through her hastily scribbled notes, before smiling at her. 'Now, this is a successful business plan. I will authorise Matthew to send Mr Gibbs and Mr Thomas a bank draft at once. Helen, you now own a publishing company.'

She squealed, jumping from her seat. She hugged her grandfather roughly and then squeezed Wick until he yelped.

'But you said I didn't help at all.'

Helen laughed, hugging him tighter. 'You didn't, but you're here and you give rather good personal advice.'

The door to the office opened and her grandmother stood there as if she'd been listening to every word of their meeting.

Helen ran and hugged her, too. 'Thank you for the wonderful suggestions, Grandmama.'

Grandfather raised a bushy eyebrow. 'You gave business advice, my love?'

Grandmother released Helen and held her head up with

dignity. 'I have run a household efficiently for more than four decades. How difficult could a business be?'

Helen and Wick laughed, but Grandfather smiled. His eyes were on his wife and there was a sweetness in his expression. After all these years of marriage, they not only loved each other, but they were still *in love*. Perhaps love gave a person—or a snake—wings to fly.

It was a heady thought.

# *Chapter Twenty-Seven*

Sitting up, Mark took out his sketchbook. He flipped past the pictures of Helen to a blank page. He began to draw his men. His soldiers. Their uniform coats and their kilts. He drew their feathered hats, their tartans and their boots. Flipping the page again, he drew the soldier who played the bagpipes as they marched. He drew Mackenzie with his sabre over his head, preparing to strike. He drew Black with his buckshot, loading his gun. Then he drew the enemy. In houses and barns. On higher ground. Flipping more pages, he drew the wounded. The carnage. The truth about the Battle of Waterloo.

Mark didn't stop there. He kept turning pages. Kept scribbling down the images that haunted his days and nights. The piles of limbs. The rows of wounded soldiers in churches that were makeshift hospitals. He drew the lamentations of wives and sisters, hovering over their beloved dead.

He penned his nightmares.

Mark filled every page in the book.

After sketching most of the morning, he dozed in his chair, enjoying the spring air and his perfectly tended garden thanks to Helen. Her gardening skills were something that raised her in his mother's esteem.

'At least the *sassenach* is willing to get her hands dirty. You could do worse,' his mother had said. 'Not that a nice Scottish lass wouldn't be better. Because undoubtedly she would.'

It was faint praise, but from a fiercely Scottish woman it was probably the highest compliment that Helen would receive. After being initially rejected by London society, Mark also believed that his mother liked Helen's less than formal manners and welcoming ways. The Duchess of Stringham had taken both his mother and Aunt Fiona underneath her wing of approval. His mother received a stack of cards and invitations every morning with the post. She shook her head and pretended not to care, but Mark knew that she did.

Mark saw Helen's blonde hair peeking over the fence and then a boot. She easily swung herself on top of the fence and waved to him. 'You're not going to pretend to be asleep today, Pirate?'

Mark stood up with as much effort as it took her to scale a stone fence. 'Pirate?'

He watched Helen swing both legs over to his side of the fence and slowly lift herself down with her arms, dropping the last few inches on to her feet.

Turning to face him, Helen smiled. It was blindingly bright. Perhaps if he truly were a poetic Broody Byron, he would compare it to the shining sun. 'I thought you looked like a pirate the first time that I saw you,' she said, walking towards him until her dress brushed the top of his boots. 'Your face was scruffy and unshaven. And your hair a little too long. Your dark clothes rumpled. You were like a melancholy hero in one of the Gothic tales that you read.'

'I take it that I made an excellent impression.'

'You did. Didn't you know that every girl dreams about falling in love with a pirate and sailing away with him?'

He swallowed, heavily. His heart felt as heavy as a stone. 'I don't know if I could be a swashbuckler any more.'

Helen came even closer to him. So close that her chest brushed his lightly, as he swayed on his wooden leg. 'Nonsense. All the best pirates have a pegleg. Ask Mademoiselle Jaune.'

The wind blew a lock of her finely spun hair into her face. Mark lifted his hand and brushed it back behind her ear. 'And what shall we do as pirates?'

'Go on adventures, of course,' she said, her warm breath tickling his chin, her bright blue eyes gazing into his.

'What kind of adventures?'

Helen placed her hands on his shoulders. 'The daring and amorous kind... I thought that you should know that I love you. The *eros* kind. And you don't have to say it back.'

Mark was certain that his own stone heart had stopped beating. 'I don't want to be your bird with a broken wing.'

Helen shook her head, wrapping her arms around his neck, pulling herself tightly against him. 'Pity has no place in love. You are a bird that no longer flies, but has realised it can swim. Swimming is probably better for a pirate anyway. They are always on the water.'

Mark's arms could no longer stay at his sides. He put them around Helen's slender form. Folding himself against her. Touching the narrow curve of her spine and waist. 'I'm not a pirate. I am an earl.'

'If I kiss you, like they do in fairy tales, do you think you'll turn into a prince?'

'We'll never know unless you try.'

Helen smiled and softly rubbed her lips across his. Over and over. The contact as fleeting as a butterfly's wing

brushing against his mouth. Then she opened her lips and he lost himself in her touch. The texture of her tongue. The taste of her mouth. The pressure of her lips against his. The feeling of her hands running through his hair. Touching his cheeks, his scar, his neck.

He nipped at her lips.

Helen froze, leaning back in his arms in surprise. 'You just bit me. You are a pirate.'

'Did you like it?'

'I loved it.'

Mark lowered his head and nipped at her lower lip again. She purred like a cat. Her hands moved from his neck to explore the muscles of his back, causing *him* to purr against her lips. When her hands dipped slightly lower than his waist to his backside, he was the one to freeze in surprise.

Helen smiled against his mouth. 'You're not the only pirate.'

'Indeed? And what shall I call you?'

'Captain Serpentine, of course.'

Mark snaked his arms around her even tighter and they kissed and kissed until his lips were swollen and he was shaky standing on his wooden leg. He sat down in his chair and pulled Helen slowly on to his lap. He had to shift his weight to the side, to make accommodations for her size and shape.

Helen wrapped her arms around his neck and laid her head beneath his chin. 'I love touching you.'

He chuckled. Her silken hair brushing against his swollen lips. 'You touch me every time we meet.'

'I cannot seem to help myself. My fingers twitch and tingle with the need to touch you.'

'I'm not complaining.'

She murmured something not quite understandable and

ran her hands over his chest. Stopping when she touched his sketchbook in his upper coat pocket, she fished her hand into his jacket and pulled it out. Helen opened the first page and found the picture he'd drawn the first time that he'd seen her, when he'd thought she was a fairy queen.

'I look fierce.'

'Fiercely beautiful.'

Helen flipped the page and saw another sketch of herself. Mark could feel her smiling against his chest, even if he couldn't see her face.

She wouldn't be smiling much longer.

Turning the page, Helen gasped but did not speak. She did not say a word as she turned page after page of his memories of battle, of blood, of war. Ugly images. She closed the book and put it back in his pocket.

'The damage in me runs deeper than you realised. I should have warned you about the horrors you would see.'

Helen shook her head. 'I would never have looked away.'

They were silent for several minutes, Helen's head tucked under his chin.

'What are you thinking?' he asked.

'Not what you think I'm thinking.'

'A rather sphinx-like answer.'

Again, he felt her smile against his chest.

'I was thinking that your illustrations are going to make my publishing house a lot of money. Your memoir of the Highlanders' part in the Battle of Waterloo.'

'I am no hero, Helen. I was simply a soldier. One that got wounded and had to be carried off the field of battle. By your brother-in-law, no less.'

She lifted her head and gazed directly into his eyes. 'I thought that we'd already covered that part. You are not a hero. You're a pirate.'

'Pegleg. Pegleg.' He mimicked her macaw.

Helen smiled, lifting her hands, and brushing his long black hair away from his face. 'You shouldn't hide your scars, you know. Pirates are much more fearsome with them. I could cut your hair for you, if you like.'

'You don't like it long?'

She leaned forward and rubbed her nose against his. 'I like it long, but I love seeing your whole face even more. You really are disturbingly handsome.'

Mark touched her neck and pulled her face towards him for a kiss. Soft and sweet. 'The pirate and the fairy queen.'

Helen laughed merrily, rubbing her nose against his. 'I am not a fairy queen. It's the pirate and the publisher... I originally purchased the publishing house Gibbs and Thomas because they would not put my name on my book. But I've realised since how much having a voice means to me. And how much I want other women to be able to share their stories. Men, too. I am serious. I think your experiences and illustrations of the Battle of Waterloo will be very popular. Especially since they are written by the Earl of Inverness.'

'The horror of war.'

She brushed her lips against his. 'The indomitable spirit of humankind.'

Mark twirled a lock of her hair on his finger. 'Your mouth certainly has a way with words.'

She leaned her head closer to his. 'It's even better with kisses.'

He returned the embraces with great fervour, but he'd been too cowardly to say the words in his heart. He was not as brave or as bold as Helen, who showed her true self for all the world to see.

# Chapter Twenty-Eight

Helen felt as nervous as a goat in a lion's den. Her heart was palpitating out of her chest and her hands were as clammy as the skin of a snake. Theodosia hissed in her ear and Helen reluctantly laughed. Bringing her Ball Snake to a real ball was probably the most outrageous thing she had ever done. And she had done many outrageous things.

Technically, it wasn't a ball, but an assembly. An Almack's Assembly. The most exclusive club of the *ton*.

Helen walked into the room with Theodosia curled over her shoulders and arms like a shawl. It didn't take the other members of the beau monde long to realise that it was no ornament. Theodosia, naturally shy, pushed her head into the material of Helen's dress above her thigh. Helen hoped that her sweet snake wouldn't mind being put on display to help the sales of her book.

One of the lords dropped his quizzing glass. 'By Jove! It's a snake.'

She watched Lady Jersey angle her way through the crowd to the front. 'Good gracious, Lady Helen, what have you brought into my club?'

Smiling, Helen petted Theodosia's skin and gently urged her snake's head into her hand. 'This is my pet snake, Theodosia. Theodosia, may I present Lady Jersey?'

The lady laughed. Once she sobered, she held out a gloved hand towards the snake. She was a stout-hearted woman after all. One had to be to rule the *ton*. 'It isn't poisonous, is it?'

Helen shook her head, smiling. 'No. She is a sweet snake. Most snakes are shy creatures that are terribly misunderstood by humans. And I have written a book all about snakes. I am sure that you would find it most illuminating on the subject.'

Lady Jersey tentatively touched the top of Theodosia's head and her snake hissed. The lady jumped back, but laughed. 'I know that I should be furious with you, Lady Helen. But undoubtedly you have made this assembly the most talked-of night in the Season... Where would one purchase your snake book?'

Helen forced a smile. 'The publisher Gibbs and Thomas have printed only a few, select copies.'

'I shall send a footman first thing in the morning to ensure that I get one.'

'Thank you, Lady Jersey.'

Helen kept her head up and wandered through the room, making sure that every person there saw both her and Theodosia. She heard their loud whispers of 'She wrote a book' and 'About snakes' and 'How very eccentric.'

She wasn't being eccentric now. She would not have forced her shy snake to endure a night of stares for mere eccentricity. No. Helen was advertising her book in the best way she knew how. Instead of hiding who she was, Helen used her status and place in society as the best possible use of advertising. A simple paragraph in the newspaper would be forgotten.

Tonight never would.

After circling the ballroom, nodding and smiling, Helen

retired to the refreshments room. Her hands shook as she accepted a glass of punch. She sipped it quickly, hoping that the sugar would calm her frayed nerves. Setting down the empty glass, she accepted another from the footman and drained it.

'Better not drink too much,' Mark said, from behind her.

She turned over her shoulder to see him. His long black locks were shorn and styled around his face in the Brutus. The white scar that paralleled his hairline was easily seen. He wore a fitted black jacket that showed his strong upper body muscles to perfection. She wondered how in heavens his valet had got him in it and hoped that said valet would be able to get him back out of it again. He leaned gently on a new silver cane. He was impossibly handsome and entirely Mark.

'Cat got your tongue?'

Helen shook her head and Theodosia retorted by hissing in her ear, causing her to laugh. 'Oh, no. You're so handsome that you've left me speechless.'

He smiled and what was left of her sense evacuated her brain through her right ear. 'I suppose you want to touch me now.'

Mark held out his free hand and Helen eagerly placed hers inside it. 'I always want to touch you.'

'Shall we waltz?'

'With Theodosia?'

Her mother cleared her throat.

Trust Mama to be watching her like a vulture. 'I shall take the snake. I think Theodosia has more than accomplished her purpose tonight. I shall send her home with a footman.'

Mama was not a reptile person. Helen could not think of one time when her mother had ever touched one of her

snakes. Yet she was holding her arms out to Theodosia. Helen untwisted her snake from her neck and gently laid her into her mother's arms. Mama's arms sagged a little, for Theodosia was no lightweight, but she did not let go.

'Thank you, Mama.'

She only nodded.

Mark took her hand again and led her into the ballroom, where couples were already waltzing. He brought her to a corner and leaned his cane against the wall, before sweeping her into his arms. Helen couldn't resist moving closer to him.

She felt Mark laugh against her hair. 'Are you trying to compromise me?'

Helen lifted her head and shook it slightly. 'No. I am claiming you.'

Mark's smile made her insides melt. His touch alone was the only thing that was keeping her standing. 'Lady Helen, would you like to go riding in Hyde Park in the morning?'

They spun around together. 'Is that a non sequitur?'

He only laughed. 'You'll have to wait and see.'

It had to be a marriage proposal. Her heartbeat skittered at the thought, but then her brain reminded her that loving Mark meant leaving her home behind. Wings or no, she wasn't ready to fly away from the only place she'd ever belonged. 'But I can't be a proper countess, Mark. You know this.'

Nodding his head, he pulled her closer to him.

# Chapter Twenty-Nine

'Do you have the ring?' his mother asked him for the fourth time.

Mark nodded as he patted the ring that was currently on his little finger underneath his glove. 'Yes, Mama.'

She looked out of the window. It was raining lightly. 'Are you sure that you don't want to pick a better time? A rainy proposal isn't very romantic.'

He leaned forward and kissed his mother on the cheek. She blushed in surprise, but smiled as if she were pleased. 'Helen loves the rain and I promise I will make it very romantic.'

'Very well then. She'll certainly like Scotland, if she likes rain.'

Mark walked out his own front door and mounted his mare without any assistance. Riding around to the next street, he found a groom holding Helen's horse by its reins. Mark didn't have to get off his horse to lift the knocker. Helen burst out of the house wearing her crimson military-like riding habit and a matching hat.

The Duke of Pelford followed behind her with an umbrella over his head. 'Are you sure that you both wouldn't rather come inside and out of the rain?'

Mark looked around. 'And miss this beautiful weather—never!'

Pelford smiled wryly and helped Helen on to her horse. 'Enjoy the rain.'

'Oh, we will.'

Helen urged her horse until it was right next to his. Leaning over, she patted his mare's mane. 'What a beautiful creature. Is she new?'

Mark nodded and a bit of rain poured out of his hat. 'I hadn't realised how much I've missed the freedom of riding.'

'Then when we reach the park, we shall have a race.'

'Done!'

They rode together through the streets. There weren't many carriages out. It was raining and rather too early in the morning for fashionable people to be up and about yet. When they reached the gates of the park, Helen called out to race to a lone tree, a hundred yards ahead. Mark hadn't galloped yet, but his instincts kicked in and he held on for dear life. Helen and her horse led for the first half of the race, but Mark was not about to let her win. He urged his mare onwards and they won by a length.

Helen laughed and she pulled up on the reins. 'What is the forfeit?'

'Your heart.'

'It's already yours, but I still do not wish to leave my home. I know that it is silly and selfish. Wick compared me to a flightless baby bird that eats regurgitated worms.'

Mark looked over his shoulder at the dark waters of the Serpentine. The raindrops on the surface made hundreds of little circles that bumped into each other. He couldn't help but think that he and Helen were but two of those ripples. Destined to meet and come together.

'What do you love about Hampford Castle?'

She breathed in deeply. 'Walking in the woods, swim-

ming in the river and sitting in the sunshine. There is something mystical and renewing about being in nature. It is the one place that I feel as if I truly belong.'

'I bet you know the forest near your home like the back of your hand.'

Raindrops tickled her nose as Helen nodded.

'And I assume that you've already explored every den and glen.'

'Of course.'

'In Scotland, we have a great many forests, rivers and lochs. It would take you a lifetime to explore them all. The same nature that you love here is also there.'

Her hand tightened on the reins. 'But my family is not there.'

Mark wanted to be her family. Her everything. 'We could visit them often at Hampford Castle and invite them to swim in Loch Ness. You might even discover and write a new book about the sea monster that swims in its depths.'

Helen's eyes sparkled as her lips tilted upwards. 'I do love swimming and sea monsters and you most of all. And perhaps I will like Scotland, too. But I would make a terrible countess. You know that. I am blunt and badly behaved.'

Mark wiped the rain off his face. 'And I am a scarred, one-legged man who often acts like a Broody Byron. You've never tried to change me and trust that I will never try to change you. I love you exactly how you are and we *belong* together. The location doesn't matter. Whether it be in England or Scotland. The city or the countryside.'

He could see the indecision in her eyes. 'But what if I am miserable and I make you miserable, too?'

Angling his horse closer to her, Mark took her hand in his wet one. 'All I know is that I feel miserable when I am without you. And if being with you means that we have to

buy a house near Hampford Castle, then I will do it. You mean more to me than anything else in this world.'

Helen smiled more radiantly than ever and he knew that he'd finally convinced her. 'I do belong with you, Mark. And you with me. I think my body knew it from the first day that I climbed into your back garden. I couldn't stay away from you. I couldn't stop touching you. And I will try to like Scotland because it is your home and I love you.'

Helen would take a leap into the unknown for him. He needed to do the same for her. It was time to propose. 'I have it on good authority that rainy days are excellent for wading in lakes and swimming.'

Helen gurgled with laughter. 'They are.'

'Shall we?'

Together they rode to the pebble beach. Mark descended from his horse first and then helped Helen down. She kissed his chin in thank you. He laughed and shrugged himself out of his wet coat. Helen watched him wide-eyed as he unbuttoned his waistcoat and shirt. Her eyes dropped to the scar across his middle. Touching him lightly, she traced it with her finger. The rain was freezing, but he wasn't cold. He was liquid heat, even though all he had on were his trousers and one glove. He couldn't risk losing his family's heirloom engagement ring.

Sitting down, Mark took off his boot and stocking and detached his wooden leg. Something he wouldn't have dreamed of doing any place but his own chambers. And not even in front of his own valet. He'd always dismissed the man first. Yet they were relatively alone in the park. He didn't see any other riders who enjoyed the incessant drizzle of rain.

He wanted Helen to see all of him. Even the parts that were scarred and missing. And she didn't shrink away from

him. No, his Helen straddled his legs, touching his bare chest and dropping a kiss on to his wet shoulder. Her palms skimmed over the planes of his arms.

'I love your muscles,' she said, dropping another kiss on his opposite shoulder. 'Is that very naughty of me?'

Mark brought his hands up and cupped her face before slanting his mouth towards hers. Helen's lips were chilled from the rain, but they warmed up quickly in their hot embrace. Her hands roved his chest and then into his shorn locks. His tongue did battle with her own, but he nearly lost all control when she sucked on the end of his tongue.

He gently pulled back or there would be full on debauchery on this beach. 'Shall we swim?'

Helen pressed one more hard kiss to his mouth, before standing up. Mark watched her unbutton her red riding habit and take it off. She slipped off her boots and stockings. Watching her undress in the rain was erotic. She even stepped out of her dress, until all she wore was a light shift that skimmed the top of her knees. With the help of the rain, it left very little to his imagination. In her own way, Helen was showing all of herself to him, too.

She stood smiling, letting him look his fill before she said, 'Meet you in the middle!'

Helen ran into the water, causing a great splash. Once she was waist-deep into the lake, she dived.

Mark would have loved to get on to his feet and follow her in, but he was able to scoot himself down to the water with his hands and one leg. He dived deep underneath the water and stroked with both arms. His body soon forgot the cold. Kicking and splashing, he even forgot that he was missing a leg.

In the water, he was weightless.

In the water, he was fast.

But not fast enough—Helen beat him easily to the centre of the lake. She trod water, waiting for him to swim to her side. He stopped stroking just short of her, but close enough that the waves carried her hair on to his shoulders.

'Now what forfeit are you going to pay?' she asked with a smile.

Mark took off his glove. Treading with one leg was rather difficult, but he managed it. Using one arm to keep him afloat, he held the ring with his other. 'A ring.'

Helen held out her hand to him and slipped it on to her ring finger. It was a little large, but they were in freezing water after all. 'Do I get to keep the man and the ring?'

Mark smiled. 'A little greedy, aren't you?'

She shook her head, bobbing up and down in the water. 'It's survival of the fittest out here.'

His heart warmed despite being in the middle of a cold lake. 'Lady Helen Stringham, when I first saw you, I thought you were a fairy queen. You were too beautiful and ethereal to be real. But I discovered that you were not a figment of my imagination. That you are a brilliant naturalist, an avid gardener and a wonderful friend, who happens to know a great deal about the reproductive habits of spiders, swans, lions and snakes.'

Helen sunk a little in the water, before buoying herself back up. 'I am terrible at small talk and will make an awful countess. I don't like people or parties.'

'Then we won't have any,' he said, swimming closer to her. 'I am not looking for a hostess or someone to talk about the weather. I love speaking with you about any and everything that flits through that brilliant brain of yours. And one detail that you told me has stayed most in my mind—you said that swans mate for life. You said that humans were more fickle, but I don't think that's true.

'I mean to be true to you for all of my life and to love you, long after I have drawn my last breath. You taught me how to dance again. How to live every moment of my life to the fullest. Helen, I love you. I don't want a countess. I want a wife. Will you marry me?'

In typical Helen fashion, she threw her arms around his neck and caused them both to sink under the dark waters. Mark kissed her gently, before releasing her to swim back to the surface. Helen emerged laughing, throwing her wet hair back with a splash.

Mark caressed her cold cheek with one hand. 'I think I might have missed your answer?'

'Yes. A thousand, million, billon times, yes. But we must visit Hampford often.'

'I promise.'

They swam hand in hand, occasionally dunking each other as they kissed. Helen was a snake after all. When they reached the shore, they pulled on their wet clothes.

Helen's bonnet was full of water and she had to pour it out before she put it back on, laughing. 'I suppose Mama will insist on St George's for the wedding.'

Mark grimaced. He was getting more used to others' attention, but he didn't want to stand in front of a crowded cathedral with his cane. 'Are you sure we can't just elope?'

'Have you ever been to Gretna Green? The most famous town in Scotland after Edinburgh.'

He attached his artificial limb, shaking his head. 'No. But there is always a first time.'

Helen laughed and danced around with an ease that he knew he would never be able to match. 'There is no need for us to elope. I am already one and twenty. I don't need my parents' permission to marry whomever I wish.'

'Shall I get a special licence, then?' he asked, the words

half joking, half serious. 'We could slip away one morning and get married in private. Just the two of us.'

She reached out her hand and helped him to his feet. She pulled him in for a wet, rainy kiss. 'After, do we sail off into the Scottish sunset? To pillage and plunder?'

'Always.'

'Then yes.'

Mark lifted Helen into her saddle and mounted his own horse. He was too cold to notice the pain in his leg and too happy to care.

# *Chapter Thirty*

Helen dressed with great care that morning. It wasn't every day one got married after all. She wore her favourite day dress— a light green bombazine that flattered her tall, willowy figure. She picked a bonnet that had a bouquet of artificial flowers on it. But she wanted real ones to hold. Slipping down to the conservatory, Helen found her shears and cut herself the most beautiful bouquet of snapdragons, lilies of the valley and pink carnations. She was breaking her own rules about killing plants before they'd reached their full life cycle, but brides were allowed to be a little demanding on their special day. She tied the clipped flowers together with one of her hair ribbons. No doubt her lady's maid, Cartwright, would be quite furious when she discovered it missing.

*Mark loved her.*

He didn't want a proper wife or society hostess. Or even a gentlewoman who was adept at small talk. He wanted her. He loved her. Mark had said those beautiful words to her only yesterday and ever since she'd felt as though she was floating in the air. Her twisty, snake-like self could finally fly. Carrying her boots in one hand and her bouquet in the other, she tiptoed down to the kitchens. She would escape through the servants' entrance. Helen dashed across the

kitchen, only to find her mother standing in front of the door that led to the alley.

Helen gulped, clutching her boots to her chest. 'Mama, what are you doing here?'

*Awake at this hour. In the kitchen. Blocking my way out.*

Her mother sighed, placing her hands on her full hips. 'If you think that I am going to miss another one of my children's weddings, you are gravely mistaken.'

Wick had been right! Very little passed underneath Mama's nose that she didn't know about. Including elopements.

Helen felt the blood leave her face. 'What are you talking about?'

'Not only am I particular friends with the Bishop of London, I happen to be close to the Archbishop of Canterbury as well. He sent me a missive last evening, letting me know that he'd written my daughter's name on a special licence. He thought it might be of some interest to me and it was.'

She dropped her boots on the freshly scrubbed kitchen floor. 'Mark doesn't want to be the centre of attention. He is still sensitive about his leg. He'd prefer if we married in private.'

'Be that as it may, you are not getting married without your family,' her mother said, lifting her chin up. 'I've sent an express to your father. He and Becca should be here by dinner tonight at the latest. You may marry tomorrow morning with all of us in attendance.'

Helen opened her mouth, gaping. 'B-but what about Mark? He's waiting for me in the carriage outside.'

Her mother smiled, and there was a predatory gleam to her canine teeth. 'I will go and meet him.'

A chuckle escaped Helen's lips.

*Poor Mark.*

He would have to face the wrath of the Duchess alone. She laughed even harder as she trailed out of the kitchen and up the stairs.

The female figure who entered the carriage was not Helen, but her mother. The Duchess of Hampford sat on the seat across from his. His muscles clenched. His internal organs stopped functioning. The phantom itch in his lost leg was worse than ever. Touching his neck, he felt the veins standing out against his skin. He swayed in his seat underneath panic-induced vertigo.

*Had Helen changed her mind?*

He felt like a fly trapped in a spider's web, struggling uselessly to get free. Waiting to get eaten.

Helen's mother eyed him like a mouse in a cat's paw. 'I take it I am not the lady you were expecting.'

Mark dropped his hand from his neck and bowed his head. 'No, Duchess.'

The Duchess smiled. It was more terrifying than her frown. 'Helen has not changed her mind, but I have asked her to wait until tomorrow. Her father and youngest sister will be here and we will all go with you to the church and watch the ceremony.'

Mark swallowed. His throat was as dry as the Sahara Desert. 'I—we—we didn't mean to offend, Duchess. Helen and I only wanted a small, private wedding.'

'You do not have children yet, but if you did, you would realise how special tomorrow is, not only for yourselves, but for us. Invite your mother. Your aunts. Your cousins. Weddings are a day to feel not only the love of the person you marry, but your entrance into their family. Whether

you like it or not, tomorrow you will become a Stringham. Part of our pack. And we stick together, no matter what.'

The Duchess's words warmed his heart. He'd felt adrift since his friends' deaths at Waterloo. His brother's untimely death at Inverness. He'd felt like an island. All alone. But he would be alone no more. Helen would be at his side and she came with a large and loving family that seemed determined to make him one of their own.

'Very well, Duchess. Might I see Helen?'

'You may come to dinner tonight,' she said in a firm voice. 'And you can meet my husband and formally ask for his permission to wed our daughter.'

'I would be pleased to come.'

Lady Hampford didn't wait for a servant to open the door to the carriage. She jumped out on to the pavement like a woman half her age and strolled into her house with her head held high. Helen didn't resemble her mother in appearance, but he could see the similarities in their strength of personality.

And heaven help him. He was going to have to meet Helen's father.

# Chapter Thirty-One

Helen spent the afternoon watching out the front windows for her father and sister to arrive. It wasn't until nearly five o'clock that a chaise and four pulled to a stop in front of their London town house. Flinging open the door, Helen ran out to meet them. Becca came out of the carriage first and squeezed Helen tightly. Helen had missed her little sister dearly. She had missed their talks, hugs and even her sister's persistent snuggling. Becca was her better half. Then Papa embraced her so tightly, that he lifted her off the ground and twirled her around as though she was still his little girl.

When her feet were back on the pavement she kissed his scratchy cheek. He was wearing old buckskins and boots and looked like his usual rumpled self. She half expected him to pull a small creature out of his pocket.

'I am so glad that you came.'

Becca linked her arm with Helen's. 'I can't believe you thought of eloping without us. You should have invited me to come with you!'

Becca's words made Helen blush. She had thought of it, but as much as she loved her little sister, she wanted to be alone with Mark. She knew a great deal in theory about mating and she was eager to put it into practice. Besides, something about Becca had changed. Her looks were still as

beautiful as ever. Her shape the sort of curvy that Helen had always envied. Becca's blue eyes were dark like a lake and her brown hair shiny. But something was different. Helen couldn't quite put her finger on it. Perhaps it was the way her little sister held herself—taller and more assured than before. With a confidence that Helen could only be proud of.

Clearing his throat Papa, raised an eyebrow, 'You accompanying your sister on her wedding trip might prove a tad awkward, my darling. Perhaps, later, your mother will talk to you both about what to expect.'

Helen threw back her head and laughed. 'Oh, Papa. She gave us both *the talk* last year, after Becca asked during a dinner party if human babies were made the same way that animals reproduced.'

Their mother had snorted into her pudding, but quietly suggested that they speak of it later, alone. The next morning, she had sat down her daughters and explained how human babies were made, both like and unlike the reproduction habits of animals. Happily, Mama had not been embarrassed at all and let them ask as many questions as they liked. And they'd asked a lot. Helen had been quite surprised how many ways it could be done between humans. The animal breeds tended to mate in one specific way.

A smile on his lips, Papa shook his head. 'Where was I?'

Becca giggled, linking her arm with Helen's. She was at least six inches taller than her 'big' sister. 'The Vicar of Ashbury and his wife dined with us that evening, along with General Smith. Sadly, you developed a life-threatening illness that prevented your attendance. But it cleared up the next day.'

'Miraculously,' Helen added, with another laugh.

Papa patted the tops of their heads. 'The power of prayer, my children. Never underestimate it.'

They entered the house and the butler took their hats and coats. A string of footmen went to the carriage to bring in their trunks. Becca gave Helen one more hug, before dashing up the stairs to her room. She said that she needed a bath before the dinner party that night and wanted to look her best to meet the Earl.

Helen stood alone with her father in the main entry. She fidgeted with her hands and bit her lower lip.

Papa eyed her closely. 'I have a very important question for you.'

At least she knew that it wasn't about mating. 'All right, Papa.'

'Does this one's ears stick out? For it is a hereditary trait that will pass down to your children.'

Helen chuckled, shaking her head. 'Stop shaming poor Jason. There is nothing that he can do about his ears. And, yes, Mark's are perfectly flat against his head.'

Her father nodded. 'He sounds like a fine young man.'

'Based on his ears?'

'You can tell a lot about an elephant based on the length of their trunk or their tusks.'

Helen shook her head and Papa ruffled her hair. She was glad that her lady's maid had not arranged it yet. Poor Cartwright nearly had a heart attack when she learned that Helen planned to marry the next day and had not procured a proper wedding gown. Mrs May, the housekeeper, had to calm her down before she went into hysterics.

'I didn't want you to grow up, you know. I didn't want you to marry and move away from me,' Papa said, sighing. 'But I was wrong and entirely selfish. You were merely a duckling and now you are a swan. Majestic and awe-inspiring. And just as vicious as the one that bit Charles. Never be afraid to spread your wings…but visit us, often.

If you don't, we'll simply get a pack of hunting dogs and track you down all the way to Scotland and pitch a tent on your doorstep.'

A solitary tear fell down her face. 'I'll always come home, Papa.'

He kissed her cheek and enfolded her once again into his strong arms. 'And I will always be there.'

Mark felt as if he'd swallowed an elephant whole. He'd already survived several unpleasant interviews that day. The first with the Duchess of Hampford. The second with his mama who was shocked and very displeased that he'd meant to marry without her there. For a moment, he feared that all of the progress in their relationship had been lost. But he had apologised profusely for nearly an hour and she'd forgiven him after giving him a piece of her Scottish mind.

The third interview was with Aunt Fiona and Niamh. His cousin quickly congratulated him, but his aunt claimed that he had jilted her sweet daughter and cried loud, lusty tears. It took a quarter of an hour of soothing before she could be brought to understand that neither he, nor her daughter, were interested in the match.

The fourth, with his Aunt Glencannon and cousin, Lord Watford. His fraternal aunt spent the next hour telling him how much she disapproved of his choice. The bad blood in the Stringham family. The Duchess's connection to trade and how Lady Helen's overall manners were unacceptable. Mark listened patiently and ended their discussion by repeating his invitation to the wedding.

Happily, his final interview, with his Aunt Richmond and Cousin Georgy, lifted his spirits. They were both delighted by his choice and happy that he'd finally found love

and peace. They assured him that all of the Lennoxs would be there. That his side of the chapel would not be empty.

After a long afternoon, the last thing Mark wanted to do was go to the Stringhams for dinner. His cravat seemed too tight around his neck and the collar points too high near his chin, as the Hampford butler ushered him into the drawing room. His navy-blue striped waistcoat was also too tight, making it very difficult to breathe. The place was already full of Stringhams. They stood to greet him. Lord and Lady Cheswick. Lord and Lady Trentham. The Duke and Duchess of Pelford. The Duchess of Glastonbury and a young woman he'd not met before, but she was clearly a sister. Then the Duke and Duchess of Hampford.

Mark bowed stiffly to the Duke. The tall man had Helen's same bright blue eyes and his fair hair had probably once been the same shade as hers. It was more grey than blond now. He also had the same piercing stare as his daughter. But unlike Mark, he was not dressed in his finest suit. The Duke's brown coat was wrinkled and too loose to be fashionable. There was a carelessness in his appearance.

'I take it that you want a private interview with me, Inverness.'

He nearly said yes, but then remembered how much Helen wanted women's voices to be heard. 'I should like that, Duke. But I should like for the interview to be with both you and your wife. I hope to have both of Helen's parents' blessing on our marriage.'

'But not my permission?'

Mark swallowed, his throat dry. 'I have Helen's permission and that is all I need.'

The Duchess of Pelford clapped. 'Hear, hear. Another renegade is joining the family.'

'Anarchy,' Lord Trentham said, smiling slightly.

'Progress,' Helen said, from the door to the room.

Everyone turned to look at her and Mark's breath caught. Helen's blonde hair was a riot of curls with a blue ribbon threaded through them. She wore a snake necklace around her throat and another on her upper arm. She had donned a new white net dress that appeared as delicate as a cloud. On the hem there were three-dimensional blue flowers and gold and brown silk leaf motifs. She looked like a walking garden. Full of life and beauty.

'A lady doesn't ask a man's parents for their permission to marry him,' she continued, a little colour rising in her cheeks and making her appear even more enchanting.

'Which is probably a good thing,' Lord Cheswick said, with a snort. 'Lady Inverness would never have said yes to you.'

Helen stepped menacingly towards him and Lord Cheswick hid theatrically behind his very pregnant red-haired wife. 'Save me, Louisa.'

Lady Cheswick smiled and patted his hand. 'I will protect you, dearest.'

Turning on her heel, Helen huffed and shook her head. 'Ignore him, Mark.' She took his hand, intertwining her fingers with his. 'Come, you must meet my sister, Becca. She's quite the nicest of the bunch, unlike Wick.'

Mark squeezed her fingers and bowed to the new sister. She was different than Helen in every way. Her hair and eyes were darker. Her figure full and her countenance open. Even though he knew that she was two years younger than Helen, she looked older. Perhaps it was her air of confidence?

'Actually, it is my permission that you need to marry Helen,' Lady Becca said with a welcoming grin. 'And don't think that I shall give it easily.'

He fought to contain his own smile. 'Of course not.'

'Make him sweat,' Helen said, giggling and pressing her head against his arm. 'But don't take too long, Becca. The marriage is in the morning.'

Everyone in the room laughed, including him.

# Chapter Thirty-Two

Helen did not have to escape through the kitchens to go to her wedding after all. All five of her siblings were in her dressing room, waiting for her lady's maid to put the final touches on her appearance. Like most of her debut dresses, it was white muslin, but there was a cluster of large red flowers and creamy white leaf motifs embroidered on to the sleeves and skirt. The flowers trailed down the front of the gown in a scalloped hemline, giving it a tunic-like look. The low neckline had little red embroidered circles. She wore her mother's ruby necklace around her throat. Looking in the mirror, she thought for the first time that she might indeed have been a fairy queen.

'Have you made him sign a premarital contract?' Matthew asked from behind her. 'I could whip one up for you in less than an hour with enough clauses for you to keep your fortune and most of his.'

Mantheria pushed his arm. 'Stop it, Matthew. Weddings are more than written contracts.'

Helen's smile faltered. Her sister Mantheria's marriage was little more than a piece of paper now.

Mantheria swooped down, touching Helen's shoulders, and kissed her cheek. 'You look beautiful, my sweet snake.'

'You actually look a little green,' Wick said, with a teas-

ing grin. 'Shall I go ask Nancy if you can borrow her bowl? She's been carrying it around everywhere. I dare say she'll bring it to the church.'

Frederica and Becca both elbowed him in the stomach. Her eldest brother was lucky that Nancy wasn't there for his teasing. She was deadly with a dagger.

Wick held up his hands. 'What did I say?' He reached into his pocket and pulled out a pair of antique pearl earrings. 'Louisa picked them. The jeweller claimed that they were at least two hundred years old and charged me extra. I thought you'd like that.'

Helen laughed. 'I do! They are beautiful.'

Becca and Frederica carefully took the pearls and put them in Helen's ears. She was so glad that all of her siblings were there. In her dressing room. Riding in the carriages. Coming to her wedding.

Helen would take her family in her heart everywhere she went.

His mother had insisted that he wear her family tartan to the wedding—a kilt that showed his wooden leg. Mark understood how much it meant to his mother and the representation of their heritage. He agreed to it because he knew that Helen loved every part of him and it wouldn't have occurred to her to be ashamed of his missing leg. He'd finally realised that wholeness had little to do with limbs and everything to do with accepting yourself. For who you were. Who you are now. And the person you're becoming.

Pelford stood beside him as his best man. He was not wearing a kilt and he would never take the place of James or Mark's dead Highlander friends, but he was a part of his new life and new friendships. Leaning on his wooden leg, he saw that his side of the chapel was nearly full.

It was a small church, but Lord and Lady Glencannon were there with Watty. Aunt Fiona and Niamh sat in the back, wearing black. His mother had been alone in the first pew, until Georgy sat beside her and took her hand. Mama smiled. The rest of the Duke and Duchess of Richmond's large family filled in the other pews.

He watched the Stringhams come into the church. Unlike his family, they had brought their children. The Duchess of Pelford came in holding Arthur, who was sucking on his old cane. Lord and Lady Cheswick were trailed by three boys, each shorter than the next. Lord and Lady Trentham each held the hand of a pretty, curly-haired toddler. Mr and Mrs Stubbs followed them. The Duchess of Glastonbury and Lady Becca entered last and took their place at the front of the church.

Then Helen walked into the chapel. She was wearing a white gown, like she had the first time he'd seen her. A long veil covered her face and trailed down her back. Her parents were on each side of her. Helen linked arms with both of them. The Duke and Duchess of Hampford escorted her down the aisle. It was unique to have a father *and* a mother give away the bride, but it was all very Helen.

When she reached him, he lifted her veil and his breath caught. Helen was indescribably beautiful and she was going to be his wife. As they joined hands, Mark knew that everything he had experienced, every triumph, every sorrow, had led him here. To her.

He took her hands and their souls were intertwined. Mark barely comprehended the words that the reverend spoke, Helen filled all his senses. He loved her in every possible way. *Agape. Philia. Storge. Eros.*

Mark didn't recall breathing until she answered, 'I will', confirming that she would be his for the rest of his life.

The rest of the ceremony passed in a blur, punctuated by a burning kiss from his bride that set his skin on fire. She held on to his arm as they left St George's, her little nephews and niece tossing flower petals at them. His carriage had been decorated with flowers and ribbons. And they had tied old pots and pans to the back of it. The Stringham siblings must have got to it after he'd arrived at the church. Everyone who passed them would know that they had been recently married.

. He gave Helen a hand up into the carriage and she tossed her bridal bouquet into her little sister Becca's hands. Mark clambered in after her and closed the door. They waved to their families as their carriage drove away. Once around the corner, Helen leaned her head out of the window and told their driver to take them immediately to Grillon's Hotel. Then she tugged down the shades to cover the windows, making the inside of the carriage dark, but enough light peeked in through the cracks that he could see her glorious smile.

'What about our wedding breakfast?' he asked.

Helen placed both of her hands on his shoulder and straddled his lap as agilely as a cat. 'They will have to eat without us. I am not at all hungry.'

Taking off his hat and tossing it on the seat beside him, she licked his earlobe and then nibbled on the end of it, her twitching fingers stroking his hair and setting his body on fire like tinder. 'I want to lick every inch of you.'

He found himself quite amenable to this idea. Mark moved his hands to her waist, holding her body close to him, revelling in her small, but entirely feminine curves. 'After you lick me, are you going to eat me like a female spider?'

Helen kissed his neck and then sucked on it. 'Of course.'

She kissed his chin and made a trail to his lips, kissing him deeply. 'I dare say we won't be able to leave the bed for days. Possibly weeks. That's why we have to go to a hotel.'

If he wasn't already on fire, her words would have set him aflame. But he remembered that she was a virgin and for all her scientific knowledge and obvious enthusiasm, this would be her first time.

Mark rubbed his hands up and down her sides, making her moan sweetly. 'I promise to be gentle with you.'

Helen cupped his face with her hands, her mouth a hair's breadth from his. 'I am afraid that I can make no such similar guarantees.'

Then she ravished his lips.

\* \* \* \* \*